Praise for Talba Wallis and *Louisiana Bigshot*

"Smith has launched Talba Wallis on a welcome series of her own. Wallis is fine fun to get to know . . . a consistently interesting and likable woman of depth and complexity."
—*The Washington Post*

"Smith's new series is a whole other kettle of crayfish: wilder and funnier." —*Chicago Tribune*

"The fun, the excitement, the laughs, and the thrills that Janet Evanovich props up on the bestseller list every summer can be sampled just as richly through Julie Smith's new Talba Wallis series.

"[*Louisiana Bigshot*] is racial, it's sexual, it's political, and there's a big car tailing Talba and Eddie with trigger-happy goons inside.

"Join Edgar winner Julie Smith for a climax as harrowing as it is cunning." —*The Clarion Ledger,* Jackson, MS

"Highly evocative of the Big Easy, *Louisiana Bigshot* is an easy read filled with colorful, exciting people drawn with affection and intelligence. Talba seems to get smarter with each novel, and there's even a small cameo appearance by Skip Langdon, Ms. Smith's other New Orleans detective."
—*Dallas Morning News*

"Talba Wallis has to be one of the most distinctive female detectives in the business. . . . Her personality and her poetry are riveting reasons to read this book."
—*The Times-Picayune,* New Orleans

"The quirky pleasure of watching the Baroness strut her stuff is worth the price of admission." —*Houston Chronicle*

"Unusual subject matter set off by an appealing but streetwise heroine makes this a strongly recommended choice."
—*Library Journal*

P9-EDJ-480

Louisiana
Bigshot

Louisiana
Bigshot

———

JULIE SMITH

TOR®

A TOM DOHERTY ASSOCIATES BOOK
NEW YORK

This is a work of fiction. All the characters and events portrayed in this book are either products of the author's imagination or are used fictitiously.

LOUISIANA BIGSHOT

Copyright © 2002 by Julie Smith

All rights reserved, including the right to reproduce this book, or portions thereof, in any form.

A Tor Book
Published by Tom Doherty Associates, LLC
175 Fifth Avenue
New York, NY 10010

www.tor.com

Tor® is a registered trademark of Tom Doherty Associates, LLC.

ISBN: 0-765-34380-0
Library of Congress Catalog Card Number: 2001058282

First edition: August 2002
First mass market edition: August 2003

Printed in the United States of America

0 9 8 7 6 5 4 3 2 1

To four good kids:

Stella Tripp, Grant Smith,
Paloma Tripp, and Will Smith

Acknowledgments

It takes at least a village to write a book. My heartfelt thanks to my fellow villagers: Police Captain Linda Buczek, Doctors Ken White, James Robinson, and Mary Frances Gardner; attorneys Mary Howell and Jim Petersen; office mavens Kathy Perry and Randy Weaver; independent experts Betsy Petersen and Kit Wohl; and PI Fay Faron.

Extra thanks to another PI—Lasson Legros, *mon professeur.* If Eddie is becoming increasingly Lasson-like, it may be no accident. If Talba is, she's catching on.

Special thanks to the real-life "Sergeant Rouselle" for unwittingly supplying chapter one.

And eternal thanks to my beloved husband, Lee Pryor, who's always ready to go exploring.

Chapter One

Under normal circumstances, getting a Louisiana PI license is so routine as to be boring—you take a course, you pass a test, and you pay your money. Usually, there's only one slight catch—you can't be issued a license unless you're already hired. But Talba Wallis seemed to have found another one.

She *was* already hired, and she'd made ninety-seven on the test. For nearly five months she'd worked as an apprentice for Mr. Eddie Valentino of E. V. Anthony Investigations.

And still, she almost didn't get her license.

You have to submit a few little things with your application—a copy of your driver's license, five-by-seven-inch photo, and fingerprints. For the last, the State Board of Private Investigator Examiners provides official FBI cards. All you have to do is take them to any law enforcement agency that offers a fingerprinting service and plunk down a few small bucks.

"Piece o' cake," Eddie said. "Take ya ten minutes, max." So one gorgeous September day on her lunch hour, Talba drove out to 715 South Broad Street, headquarters of the New Orleans Police Department.

A good thing it's close, she thought. She had a client coming in at one, and at three, she had to resume her surveillance of a suspected errant wife. The woman was a college professor whose last class was over then, and Talba was in a hurry to wrap up the case. Eddie's jokes about "extracurricular activities" were getting tedious.

Nonetheless, she was in a great mood. She sailed in feeling buoyant and powerful. Finally, finally, she was getting the damned license. She liked the job a lot. A whole lot. And a funny thing, it was a great way to make friends. It wasn't something anyone ever thought about on career day at school, but once you said the words *private investigator*, it was amazing how many people blurted, "I'd love to do that!"

They wouldn't, of course. For one thing, there was the tedium—of records searches, surveillance, online research, court appearances, intake interviews, half a dozen other things. For another, most people thought divorce cases were sleazy, and these were a good chunk of the work. Actually, Talba liked them—she liked catching scumbags (of either sex) and, though originally hired for her computer skills, she'd turned out to be good at it.

It wasn't a job for everybody, but, despite the fact that she was such a computer wiz she impressed even herself, a sensitive and talented poet (in her opinion), and a baroness (she'd decided), it suited her.

So she was in an excellent mood as she entered the building. A female functionary sporting two-inch purple nails with a tiny picture on each of them pointed to a door on the right. No stairs, no elevator. Couldn't be more convenient.

Talba stepped through to a nearly dark, closet-sized anteroom opening onto a large, light, comfortable-looking room, which was populated by two people—an enormous seated woman in a black dress and a smallish, wiry-looking man in uniform. Both were African-American, as was Talba herself. The well-padded woman had a motherly look to her. Pencil in hand, she was poring over something in which she seemed to have a deep and abiding interest.

She may or not have heard Talba enter, but either way, she didn't look up. The man was talking on the phone. Talba stood politely for a few minutes, curious as to what was so important the woman couldn't take time out to serve a customer. And finally, she got tired of it. "Excuse me," she said.

The woman looked at her over nondescript glasses that couldn't hide a pair of bulging eyes. *A thyroid thing*, Talba thought, figuring it was causing the weight problem.

"I'm here to get fingerprinted."

"Whatcha need prints for?"

"I'm applying for my PI license."

"That'll cost ya thirty dollars. You can get it done for fifteen dollars at the Jefferson Parish Sheriff's Office."

"Here's fine. I don't mind the charge."

The woman raised an eyebrow, as if she disapproved of spendthrifts. "Ya filled out ya cards?"

"No, do I need to?"

"Use black ink and be sure ya print."

In the anteroom, there was an end table she could probably write on, but not enough light to see. "May I come in to fill them out?" There were at least five empty desks.

"This room's part of the police department." The woman went back to her paperwork, leaving Talba rummaging for a pen and hoping if she found one, it would be black.

She ended up going outside to fill out the card.

When she returned, the large woman seemed almost cordial. "Come on in," she said, with a near-smile, and Talba opened the dutch door separating the spaces.

The other woman came forward to sit at the front desk. "Let me have the cards and ya driver's license." The instructions on the application had been explicit—the fingerprinter must see the applicant's license. The woman studied the documents for almost five minutes before she finally raised her head, face outraged, suddenly a different person.

"You got different names on these things!"

It was true.

Talba's birth name was an embarrassment to all concerned—to herself, to Miz Clara, and to the human race in
general. A white obstetrics resident who thought he was funny
had named her. However, the state required the same name
on your driver's license that appeared on your birth certificate.

"Talba" was her own name, the name she'd given herself
and always used except when performing her poems, at which
times she used its ceremonial form, "the Baroness de Pontalba."

She pointed out where she'd written her official name on
the FBI card, in the space asking for aliases and AKAs. "I'd
prefer to use 'Talba' on my license," she said.

"You can't do that. Ya name's Urethra." It took all Talba's
strength not to wince.

Damn! Something was severely off here. The license was
issued by a state board—what right did a city functionary
have even to express an opinion on the subject?

But the fat lady wasn't the sort you argued with. Talba
said, "The board might agree, I don't know. Can't know till
I apply."

The woman wasn't listening. She'd begun paging through
a copy of the Yellow Pages, holding Talba's license and FBI
cards tightly in the hand that also held the book. "There's no
Eddie Valentino in here."

The card had asked for her employer's name and address.
"I work for E. V. Anthony Investigations. Eddie's the 'E. V.'
part." She pointed out the agency ad.

"I'm gon' call the state board." The woman got up and
waddled to a glass cubicle in the back of the room. Talba
heard her dial and say, "This is Sergeant Rouselle."

This woman was a cop? That was a shocker. She wasn't
in uniform and she wore no badge. Besides that, she seemed
not to have either the personality or the build for it. *Minor
bureaucrat* was the way Talba'd pegged her. The sort who
got off on ruining people's days.

Cop or no, she suddenly realized, she was about to become
snarled in a bureaucratic snafu that was going to make her
miss her one o'clock.

She walked back to the cubicle and held out her hand. "Sgt. Rouselle, I think I'll go over to Jefferson Parish, after all. May I have my license, please?"

The sergeant turned on her, shouting, bulging eyes blazing behind dirty lenses. "You're going to jail if you snatch this out my hand!"

Talba backed away, "I wasn't going to—"

The other officer got off the phone quick and strode over to the cubicle, patting air as if to calm a child. "Now, ma'am, just calm down. Just take it easy now."

"But I didn't . . . look, all I want to do is go. I'm on my lunch hour."

"I get the feeling you're worried you're going to get your boss in trouble. This is nothing to do with you and nothing to do with him."

What language was he speaking?

Who cared?

"Look, Officer, I'm on a schedule."

"Just take it easy and nobody's going to get in any trouble."

It suddenly got through to Talba exactly what the situation was: He was telling her the sergeant really could throw her in jail if she wanted to. All she'd have to do was *say* Talba assaulted her to get her license; or had pot breath; or anything she wanted to. In a word, she was trapped.

She sat and steamed. After about twenty minutes, Officer Rouselle waddled on out. "All right. You want to get finger-printed?"

Talba looked at her watch, considering. There was still time to make her one o'clock—barely—if the show could just get on the road. "Can we do it now?"

"*Now?*" the sergeant shouted. "Can we do it *now*? You don't respect my title or my position, do you? I need a little more respect out of you, missy. Hear me: you must use the same name on these cards as is on your driver's license. . . ."

Talba was desperate to scream at the woman: *It's not up to you, Fat Stuff! It's up to the state board.* But that was definitely going to get her arrested.

It developed the sergeant could read her mind. She just

stared, heaving a huge sigh. And then, still clutching Talba's license, she picked up the phone.

"Captain Regilio, please. Well, then, the lieutenant." Talba's heart thumped in a way it hadn't since she'd gotten in a shootout the previous spring. *It's the adrenaline*, she realized. *Damn! This petty bureaucrat has me scared to death.*

That pissed her off almost more than the rest of it.

Then there was the problem of how the hell she was going to explain to Eddie (or her mother or even her boyfriend) that she was innocent—whatever the charge. The fact was, she did have a mouth on her. The irony was, for once she was keeping it shut.

Eventually, two uniformed male officers and one white woman in shorts arrived to receive another ten minutes of Sgt. Rouselle's rants. "I called y'all in because this woman's trying to provoke me."

Take it, Talba told herself. *Keep your mouth shut or you're going to jail.*

Her teeth hurt from gritting them. Finally one of the other officers gently pried the license from Sgt. Rouselle's grasp and handed it back to Talba, who once again held out her hand. "May I have my fingerprint cards?"

"I'm gon' confiscate those. They're not your property, they're the FBI's."

Oh, yeah? So now you're the FBI?

She looked beseechingly at the others, but they only stared back poker-faced.

Well, who cared? At least she was legal to drive back to the office. She never had to breathe a word. She'd just go tomorrow to Jefferson Parish and no one would be the wiser.

She arrived back at the office at five after one. Her client was sitting in the reception room, and Eileen Fisher, Eddie's office manager, looked way too nervous for comfort.

"That Ms. Wallis?" Eddie hollered. "Ms. Wallis, could you come in here a minute? I just had a phone call from the state board. What's this about you gettin' arrested?"

It was a hell of a way to begin a career.

But Eddie had been gentle with her. "I'm gon' let you off this time, Ms. Wallis. So long as you learned somethin' from this experience."

"If you mean I'm supposed to suck up to some power-hungry harpie out of Kafka's worst nightmares . . ."

"I don't mean that a'tall, Ms. Wallis. I mean I hope ya learned to never, ever, for any reason do anything in any New Orleans city office you can do somewhere else. I mean that, now. Save us both a lot of time, lot of headache."

She was about to say, Yes sir, she sure wouldn't, and leave clicking her heels together, when he held up a finger. "And one more thing if you don't mind—could ya make some kinda effort not to be more trouble than ya worth?"

That was a month ago. She had her license now—in the name of Talba Wallis, thank you very much. But the whole gig looked to be falling apart again.

She could barely hear the words through the fuzz in her brain: *"Miss, are you all right?"* The speaker was the other driver, a white man in his forties.

Hell, no, she wasn't all right. Four days of surveillance and she finally had the pond scum in the Cadillac with the paramour, feet away from her camera lens. Inches from delicious triumph.

But now nothing. Nothing but a hurting back, a totaled car, maybe a missed paycheck. Maybe even the ax—after that little episode with Sgt. Rouselle, Eddie's patience was pretty thin.

And her mama, Miz Clara, did so love having her baby daughter employed! Even as a PI. Time was when Miz Clara thought there were only three suitable jobs for a Wallis child—doctor of medicine, speaker of the house, and first African-American president. But that was before she caught onto the stage-mom potential of having a flamboyant daughter who happened to be not only a poet, performance artist, and computer genius but also a detective.

And now a little thing like a missed stop sign was about

to ruin it all. One minute Talba was barreling toward truth and justice; the next, a force from hell struck with a sound like a gunshot, leaving her humiliated and hurting. For a moment she thought maybe it *was* a gunshot; she wouldn't put it past the lying, low-down sack of manure she was following.

But, no, it was a Ford Explorer—a car about twice the size of Talba's Camry—which had been lawfully moving through the intersection. She hadn't seen the car or the stop sign. A crowd was beginning to gather. A siren wailed in the distance. And Talba's back was killing her.

In her current state she really couldn't go back to the office and deal with Eddie about this thing. He could be slightly more of a pain in the patootie than Miz Clara herself.

There was only one good thing about this—that it wasn't Eddie's car that got wrecked. And not just because his was really his wife Audrey's Cadillac. It was handsomely appointed with the Global Positioning System that Talba had bought half-price from some fly-by-night spy shop having a fire sale. She had a weakness for shopping at spy shops; her idea was, with the GPS Eddie could track her if she got in a tight spot. But after spending a week's salary on it, she realized he didn't even have a laptop for the tracking system. So, under great protest, she'd made him let her install it in his own car.

Under *very* great protest. Eddie claimed the twenty-first-century PI needed only six pieces of equipment, one of which was a child's toy and only two of which were electronic—cell phone, tape recorder, video camera, conventional camera, binoculars, and Tee-ball bat. The last was the closest thing to a weapon he ever carried. "It's well-balanced, with a good grip, and heavy enough to do some damage. *And* it's absolutely legal," he told Talba when he presented her with hers.

Groaning, she retrieved it now, along with her maps and the other five items. She put the entire PI kit in a Guatemalan bag she had in the trunk, thinking that where it really belonged was in a new car. But she sure couldn't shop for one bent over like she was.

So she called Babalu Maya for an appointment and got the

tow truck to drop her at Whole Foods on its way to Camry heaven. Babalu, bodyworker extraordinaire (whose real name was probably Barbara), lived within spitting distance of the only store in New Orleans where you could buy a head of lettuce for the cost of a new Camry. Talba could walk the block and a half if she didn't collapse first; she could hobble it, anyhow. Or so she thought. She found the effort made her nauseous.

"Girl!" Babalu's face said Talba's pain was her pain. "I swear to God you're pale."

Babalu was white; she said things like that. Talba was not merely African-American but black. *Good* and black, thank you very much. She knew she was nowhere near pale, but she couldn't be looking her best.

"Give me that bag and sit down. Just sit down, now." Talba still had stairs to climb. Babalu exerted pressure on her shoulders; Talba yielded. And before she knew it, Babalu had done something, she hadn't a clue what, that made it possible to straighten up.

"Can you make it upstairs?"

Talba nodded gratefully and hobbled up ahead of Babalu, who evidently thought she might have to catch her if things didn't go well. Talba knew the drill so well she didn't even pause, just went into the first room off the hallway, removed her shoes and earrings, and slid gingerly onto the massage table.

Babalu said, "Tell me about it."

"Well, I didn't see the stop sign. This tank or something hit me on the shotgun side—caved in my whole front end."

"You are one lucky female." Babalu's pretty face screwed itself up. She had short blond hair that she wore in a careless, shaggy bob, clear, satiny skin, and some kind of chain tattoo crawling up her arm—Celtic knots, she said, but it gave Talba the creeps. Like some kind of metaphorical half-handcuffs. Babalu had smiled the time she mentioned it—and not a nice smile, either; as if the effect was deliberate.

Talba said, "Lucky. How come I can't quite see it that way? I'm pretty sure my car's a total."

"Oh, I'm so sorry. Wish I had one to lend you." That was the way she was, Talba thought. A nurturer; a healer. She knew Talba only as a client, and yet she behaved like a friend.

Talba groaned again and changed the subject, hoping for distraction from the intermittent pain. "Okay, enough about me. What's new with you?" She arched her back against Babalu's fingers.

"You haven't been here in too long, or you'd know. Feel that? These muscles think they're bone. A little stress, I'd say."

Talba ignored the last part. "Or I'd know what?"

Babalu waved her left hand provocatively; its fourth finger glinted. "I'm getting married."

Talba tried to sit up, just to take in the news. Babalu leaned over her chest and pushed her down. Tough. But her cheeks were flushed and she was smiling. Talba gave up. "Hey, that's fantastic!"

"Yeah. I'm pretty happy." The blush deepened.

"Well, tell me everything." This was good. There was nothing so distracting as a little romance.

"He's . . . cute."

"Yes? And?"

"Well, he's from Mississippi, and his name is Jason. He's about six feet tall with dark, gorgeous hair. . . ."

"Umm hmm. Blue eyes, I bet."

"Yeah. How'd you know?"

"You like that. I remember." A bodyworker, she reflected, was like a hairdresser or an exercise partner. There you were for an hour, just the two of you—of course you were going to talk about who you were dating. "He's probably an actor."

Babalu nodded. "Pretty good, too."

"I knew it. You're such a stage-door Jenny."

"I like people with talent—the way I grew up was just so . . . I don't know . . ."

"Stuffy?"

"What makes you think that?"

"You've got that deb look. Except for the tattoo, of course. And the zany hair."

Babalu laughed. "Carefully cultivated. We were trailer-trash, actually."

"Back to the guy. Does he have a day gig?"

"He's . . . ummm . . . a stock trader."

"A *trader*? With the market in the toilet?"

Babalu shrugged. "He seems to do okay at it."

"That's a fair-sized rock he gave you, anyhow." She realized Babalu hadn't said one really personal thing about the man. "What about him really, though? What's your favorite thing about him?"

"My favorite thing?" The question seemed to catch her off guard, but she recovered quickly. "You think I'm going to talk about *that*?"

"Don't. Ow. It hurts to laugh. Also, you're mashing a tender spot."

Instantly, Babalu's fingers lightened up. Talba sought once more to distract herself. "Okay, what do you like least about him?"

"Least?"

"Yeah, least. I know you're crazy in love and all that, but search your conscience—there's got to be something."

Talba could have sworn Babalu's hands tightened on her back—even pinched a bit. She heard a sound like a sniff. Damn! She sure didn't want to get a cold.

But it wasn't that. The sniff was followed by a sound like *snurf*, a smothered sound, but there was no mistaking it; Babalu was crying.

"What is it?" Once again, she tried to rise, thinking to hug the healer, but Babalu held her down.

"No. Let's finish the session."

Talba didn't move, but she wasn't about to keep quiet. "Girlfriend, what is it?"

"I think he's cheating on me."

Oh, boy. Talba had heard plenty of this kind of thing lately. Louisiana might have no-fault divorce, but there was still the issue of spousal support, which was why she was surveilling a low-down scumbag cheater when the Explorer slammed her. Proof of catting around could pay off handsomely, but that was irrelevant in Babalu's case. What was relevant was, the marriage was off to a rocky start and it hadn't even happened yet.

"You can't marry an asshole who's cheating on you. Babalu, hear me—you do not deserve this. Give the man his ring back."

"You're scrunching up again."

"You're getting me upset."

"Well, I just said he may be. He's probably not. Maybe he's . . . I don't know—maybe it's something else."

"Talk to me. Tell me about it."

"I can't. You're scrunching up. You want to walk out of here or not?"

Talba tried to relax.

"You know what I need? I need a detective."

"No, you don't. You need out."

"Could you relax, please? Look, can I come to your office tomorrow? Talk to you about it?"

She sounded so pitiful Talba said okay, maybe they could trade services. But she never thought Babalu'd show up.

Chapter Two

Babalu was there at nine A.M. sharp, which was more than Talba could say for herself. Because of her mishap of the day before, she'd had to take the 82 Desire, and you never knew with buses. She didn't get there till 9:20 and she knew from experience that Babalu's first appointment was at ten. "You're serious about this."

"How's your back?"

"Much better. How're you?" Talba asked the question gingerly, not wanting it to sound like an accusation.

Babalu's honey-blond hair needed washing; it more or less stuck up in spikes. The circles under her eyes were so pronounced it occurred to Talba she was doing drugs. But Babalu was the cleanest liver she knew—drank green tea instead of coffee, and nobody in New Orleans did that. "He stood me up again. I've got to know, Talba. I can't sleep or anything."

"I can believe that. Sorry we don't have any green tea."

"Coffee's okay today."

"You're going to need it. By the way, do you have a ten o'clock?"

Babalu nodded.

"We won't be out of here by then. We have this instrument of torture Eddie invented to scare away customers, called the intake interview. If you can survive it, you might as well marry the guy, because that proves you can handle anything."

It was supposed to elicit a smile, but Babalu wasn't in the mood. She whipped out her cell phone, canceled the appointment, took off the vintage jacket so nicely complementing her jeans, and sat down. Talba got the feeling she wasn't in the best of tempers.

"Sure you want to go through with this? It gets pretty ugly."

"I've got to do it, Talba."

Talba felt for her, though if the man in question were her own sweetie, Darryl Boucree, she thought perhaps a hit man might be more to the point than a detective. She began the tedious procedure of invading every single corner of Babalu's and Jason's privacy.

The first part was just like girlfriend talk. "How did you two meet?"

"At a poetry reading."

They laughed. Babalu and Talba had met the same way. Both were poets, as a matter of fact, in their nonworking lives.

"Is he a poet?"

"Well, he thought he was. Before people started throwing things at him."

"Oh. How'd he take it?"

"He kind of laughed. He was just trying it on for size. As I said, his art really is acting. But he loves it that I'm a poet."

Babalu's poems were full of metaphors about the body—about muscles and bones and joints. They were quite beautiful, Talba thought. Her own were much earthier, more inclined to narrative.

"Have you met his family?"

"Oh, yes. They're from Canton, just outside of Jackson. His daddy's a high-powered lawyer or something." She giggled. "I had to wear long sleeves so they wouldn't see the tattoo."

Talba raised an eyebrow. "Your idea or his?"

"Oh, mine. He seems to be the black sheep. I mean, they kept asking him questions about when he was going to get a job."

As well they might, Talba thought. "What did he say to that?"

"He said he had a job—investing."

"I thought you said he traded."

She flushed in embarrassment. "I guess he didn't want to admit that."

Talba felt frustrated. "What's he investing? He's a young guy, no job . . ."

"Well, that came out at the time. His mom said he was 'gonna run through all granddaddy's money' before his first child was even born." She shrugged. "I guess he has some kind of inheritance."

"How'd that make you feel? Talking like that in front of you?"

"Actually, they were pretty nice. I think they liked me."

Again, Talba raised an eyebrow; this time she left it raised and gave Babalu a stare like a snake about to strike.

Babalu gave her back a smug-cat look. "I practically wore a circle pin. I was raised in a small town too, you know."

"Girlfriend, you got more problems than the tattoo and the hair. What on earth did they make of that name of yours?"

"You mean Bobbie Lou? We didn't even have to lie—they just heard it that way." Talba and Babalu got to share a laugh, a good thing, considering the grimness of the circumstances.

And then it was on to the boring stuff, followed by the nasty stuff.

Where did Jason live? What vehicles did he have? Ever married before? Any children? Who were his friends? What was his schedule? How about his physical description, phone numbers, hobbies, interests, habits? Did he smoke, drink or do drugs?

Well, what *did* he like? Was he left-handed or right-handed?

Had he ever been violent? Was he a fast driver? (This was to plan the surveillance.)

Then, there was Babalu. Who were *her* friends and relatives and what did they look like? There had been cases of husbands buying lingerie with gorgeous blondes who turned out to be the wife's best friend helping him shop for her birthday.

Talba personally knew of one—Eddie had carefully videotaped the whole thing and ruined the surprise party.

What was their sex life like? This was Talba's least favorite question, but she had to admit, it was usually productive. Babalu pulled at a chipped bit of black nail polish. "Well, that's one of the things that's got me worried. He's kind of . . . lost interest."

Now, that was unusual. Usually, if there was a paramour, frequency increased; sometimes the misbehaver even got more inventive.

But this was an engagement, not a marriage. Talba could think of cases in her own life in which the relationship simply cooled on one or both parts. She figured that was probably what was happening here. It was all she could do not to reiterate that Babalu absolutely must not, should not, could not marry this man—he was wrong, wrong, and wrong. But what the hell—pretty soon she was going to have pictures.

"Is that why you think he's cheating on you?"

Babalu grabbed hunks of her dirty hair and pulled on it. "He just doesn't seem interested anymore. I think he's trying to break up with me."

"Why not just ask him?"

She was quiet, thinking a long time before she spoke. "I don't know if I could handle the answer."

"What makes you think—"

Babalu held up a hand. "Stop. I know what you're thinking. I need to do it this way. I want to know everything. I want to know and have him not know I know. I need to buy myself time to think about what to do."

"What to do! I'll tell you what to do."

Babalu's eyes misted over. "Talba, please."

Talba eased up. The healer, the talented poet she held in such esteem, was really much more fragile than Talba liked to believe. She remembered something Babalu had once told her about her name—*Maya* meant peace or something, but *Babalu* was an Afro-Caribbean god or saint, always depicted with a crutch. "It's the archetype of the wounded healer," she said.

Talba hadn't pressed it, taking it at the time for some kind of general metaphor, something about everyone being wounded. But it occurred to her now that this woman, so strong on the outside, had internal wounds so severe she didn't even have the self-esteem to get rid of a scrofulous piece of shit (who was cheating on her). Well, fine. Talba could help with that. And not by nagging either. It would be her pleasure to shoot a home movie that would stand up in court. Not that that was needed—she just liked to do things right.

The second Babalu left, Talba sat down to do what she always did after an interview, and found she hadn't done the first thing right. Eddie had taught her two primary rules of doing business—first, cash the check; second, run a background check on the client. Babalu had paid her retainer in cash (not surprising—she liked her own clients to pay cash), so the first wasn't necessary. However, due to that oddity, Talba had no way of knowing what her client's legal name was; and it hadn't occurred to her to ask. In fact, the whole background routine had slipped her mind, and now that she thought about it, she found it creepy. Maybe you made an exception when you knew the client. Certainly her subconscious had.

But something nagged at her: Did she really know Babalu?

She knew Babalu wasn't a charlatan. Maybe that was enough.

She busied herself backgrounding Jason instead, an eminently boring task, since everything checked out, down to a very decent credit record. (This was something PI's weren't entitled to, but Talba knew how to get it, and on this occasion, since a friend was involved, she went for it.) Granddaddy must have done well by him, she thought. That part boded well for Babalu; it was something to cling to.

Next on the agenda was a recon of the surveillance area, and it was nearly time for lunch. She could get some fresh air and do the recon at the same time—right after she rented a car.

Jason lived in the area of town referred to as the Lower Garden District, not to be even slightly confused with the Garden District proper, which was very proper indeed. The lower version was hip, upwardly mobile, mixed in just about every way, and a little dicey—actually a by-the-numbers neighborhood for an unemployed actor. It offered good deals if you didn't mind watching your back.

Jason's building was a rambling old Victorian that had been chopped up into apartments; he had the second floor front, and Babalu had said he usually kept the curtains closed so he could see his screen. Brown velvet curtains, she said; very masculine. Okay, fine. Apartment identified. Now the vehicle. Talba looked, with envy, for a dark blue Camry, and indeed there it was, its plate number nicely matching the one her trusty computer had just told her had been issued to a Jason Wheelock at this very address. All systems go. The bird was in the nest.

The next issue was her own security. There was a reasonable amount of traffic, both vehicular and pedal, and there were plenty of black people in the general mix. She wasn't going to stick out too much. She just wished her rental car weren't white, which was all they had by the time she got there. She felt a little conspicuous in it.

Yet she knew she probably wasn't. Unless there was a neighborhood biddy who spent her days peering out the window, chances were good no one would notice her at all. The surveillance ought to be a piece of cake—anything would be, compared to the turn her afternoon was about to take. She hadn't yet told Eddie about the accident.

E ddie felt himself shaking his head, which made him feel
old. "Ms. Wallis, Ms. Wallis." He wished he could come
up with a better response, but his young associate had left
him more or less speechless, and it wasn't the first time. "Ya
ran a *stop* sign?"

She'd just told him that. He was trying to wrap his brain
around it.

"Well? Did ya hurt yaself?"

She looked uncomfortable. "I, uh . . . I think I'll be okay."
She was holding something back.

He had a pair of reading glasses he liked to wear at times
like this. He perched them on his nose and looked over them
at her. "Spit it out, Ms. Wallis."

"Actually, my back was killing me, but I went to a bodyworker to get the kinks out and now she's our client. That's
who I—"

"The babe with the tattoo?" He was annoyed. How had she
turned an idiotic mistake into an opportunity for bragging?
He changed the subject quickly. "Just how did ya happen to
run a stop sign? Ya got carried away, didn't ya?"

Her hand closed into a fist. "I had him, Eddie. With a
redhead about half his age."

He shook his head again. "Ya wasted three days' surveillance running a stop sign? Ya know what I oughta do? Swear
to God I oughta—"

"Look, I can get him next week. He picked her up at her
gym. She's got yoga on Tuesdays—the client says that's his
golf day. What do you bet they have a standing date? All I
have to do is show up at the gym right after her class and do
an instant replay."

"Without the demolition derby, ya mean."

"I won't even charge you for it—I mean, it was my fault
I didn't get it."

He considered. "Ya almost got yaself a deal, Ms. Wallis. I
like the part about not chargin' me. The only thing is, how'm
I gonna explain to the client we need another week?"

He thought he sounded pretty tough, but she had the brass
to look him right in the eye: "Lie, Eddie. How else?"

He'd taught her that. That and everything in the world she knew about lying. It was her worst subject, too. She was great on the computer, a lot better on electronic devices than a law-abiding citizen ought to be, perfectly good at interviewing, and a pretty fair little rainmaker. But she was a truly lousy liar. At least she had been when she first started working for him, and this was the most important element (even more important than the secret of the Tee-ball bat) in a PI's bag of tricks. She was just starting to get the hang of it.

And now she was flinging it back in his face. Damn Talba Wallis. She reminded him way too much of his daughter Angela—always getting the best of him.

"You handle it, Ms. Wallis. It's your mess, not mine."

"But, Eddie, how can I claim I'm in the hospital if I'm the one calling the client?"

"You're in the hospital?"

"An Explorer hit me; I'm at death's door."

"Oh, I wish. I just wish, Ms. Wallis." He clenched his teeth. "All right, I'll call Susie Q and tell her." He looked at his watch. "But this time next week, I want the redhead wrapped up, and I want a full client report on this desk right here. Ya hear me?" He tapped his in box for emphasis. "Three P.M. Wednesday."

"Yessir." She was looking smug. Damn. He should have done something tougher, but what? Fired her? No way in hell was he going back to computer-jockeying. The fact was, he needed Ms. Wallis. She was female, she was young, she was black—all of which he more or less disapproved of—and she was a pain in the butt. But for right now he needed her, dammit.

He made his voice as gruff as he could. "Okay, what about Tattoo Tammy?"

"Cheating boyfriend."

"Boyfriend! Why doesn't she just break up with him?"

Something funny happened to Ms. Wallis's face, something he'd never seen when she talked about a client, and they'd had plenty who had all her sympathy. She looked all fuzzy and mixed up, like a child whose mama's in the hospital. "I don't know. She's clinging to him like a lifeline. I get the feeling she's kind of stuck together with Band-Aids."

"And you don't mind being the bearer of bad news?"

All that sweet fuzzy-muzzy left her; all of a sudden she was the woman in the iron mask. "I just want to help her get the sumbitch out of her life."

"Ms. Wallis, Ms. Wallis." He was shaking his head again. He hated it when she swore. Just hated it. "Ya mind keepin' a civil tongue in ya head?"

"She's going away for the weekend—suggests we do the surveillance while she's gone."

"Well, if the paramour's married, that ain't gonna work."

"Yeah, I know. I'll start it tonight."

"Where's the guy live?"

"Lower Garden District."

"You're not doing that alone. No way."

She gave him a cockeyed smile. "I'm a big girl."

"Yeah, sure. When hell freezes over." At least he could tease her.

"Actually, I'm fine there. Nobody even notices me."

"I can't even trust ya not to run a stop sign."

"You've got three other divorce cases. Who's going to do the surveillance on George Richardson if you do this one? Not to mention Walter Carpenter and Gina Piccolo."

The hell of it was, she was right—he didn't have the time. "Goddammit! Nobody in the whole town's gettin' along these days."

She smiled at him, knowing she'd won. "Except you and Audrey, I trust."

Why didn't she stay the hell out of his personal business?

He waved her away and didn't give her or her tattooed buddy another thought until she phoned Friday night.

The thing about these cheating cases, Talba had noticed, was that the wronged party usually had a pretty good idea of what was going on. Sure enough, just as Babalu had predicted, no sooner was she out of town than Jason closed

his chocolate-brown curtains and walked down his front steps
so obviously freshly showered and spiffed up for a date that
Talba could almost smell his cologne.

He got in his dark-blue Camry and drove to a restaurant
on Magazine Street, where he met an extremely attractive
woman who seemed a few years older than he, and the lovely
couple had the good grace to sit right by the window. Talba
got as good a picture as she could, but a flash wouldn't have
been cool in the circumstances.

So far so good. So beautifully according to script she
thought of quitting right then and there. But there could be
lots of reasons for having dinner with a woman—maybe she
was directing a play he was in; or maybe she was his aunt.

She looked like she had money—nice haircut, good manicure, expensive casual clothes. Talba wished she'd gotten a
look at her shoes and bag—these told the tale best. She was
willing to bet they were expensive. This woman definitely
didn't seem a match for Jason, who, she had to admit, was
quite a looker. But a more or less unemployed actor. This
woman was too rich, too straight, maybe too old. She probably wouldn't even speak to a tattooed person.

Eddie had a saying for domestic cases: *The longer, the
later, the stronger.* So far as he was concerned, if the subject
left the paramour's house at one A.M., it was a lousy case.
Three A.M. was a lot better. All night, of course, was pretty
hard to refute. Talba had brought a Thermos of coffee with
her.

Maybe they'd hold hands at dinner. Or kiss in the parking
lot. That would be good enough for Babalu—she didn't need
something to take to court.

But, no, they didn't. In fact, they maintained such a re-
spectful distance Talba thought perhaps the thing was innocent. And after dinner they split up, Jason going to the
parking lot, the woman in a different direction.

Oh, well. The night was young. Maybe he'd go to a bar
and pick someone up. In fact, he swung out of the lot and
waited—until a white Lexus drew up alongside him. The
driver was his dinner companion.

Okay, here we go, Talba thought. *We're going to Sweet Thing's house*. That was what Eddie called all the female paramours: Sweet Thing. She hoped this one didn't live in some white folks' neighborhood where they'd shoot her on sight.

Her hopes were dashed when Sweet Thing drove straight to Old Metairie, a swish suburb nearly as snotty as Uptown. But whatever the social prejudices of the residents, just about none of them were black. There was no way she was going to pull off a night in front of a suburban mini-mansion without someone calling the cops. This was the bad part of surveillance—you never knew where you were going to end up.

She called Eddie on her cell phone. "Boss, I need your help. I'm in Old Metairie."

"Well, hell. Get out."

"The subject's in some lady's house. I can't leave now— I've just about got him."

She heard him sigh. "Miz Wallis. I'll get ya for this."

She breathed a sigh of relief and gave him the address.

Eddie sighed. "I'll take a taxi and get out a block away or something. All we need is two cars on this, things aren't bad enough."

Talba cordially hoped it wasn't going to be a long night. Not only was Eddie getting on in years, but he had the worst bags under his eyes of any human she'd ever seen—great tumorous bulges paved over with purple gator-skin. You could make a *fine* pair of shoes out of them, now that she thought of it. But on Eddie's face, they looked like something from the lost luggage department. She sure didn't want to see them get any worse.

He slipped silently into the car. "Why didn't ya call ya boyfriend to join ya? Be half as cheap for the client."

It wouldn't, though. She wasn't going to charge Babalu for her half of the double hours. "Two black people in Old Metairie? Only thing worse than one."

"Naah. You could always start making out if anyone came by—nobody'd bother ya."

"I'll remember that for next time." It was a typical Eddie

remark—maybe serious, maybe a joke, but at any rate not her idea of a fun date.

"You take the first shift. I'm rackin' out." He leaned back and started snoring almost immediately. She could smell the alcohol on his breath and regretted getting him out of his nice cozy house on a Friday night—but she knew he'd do it to her.

She let him sleep. As long as no one came along, she didn't need him.

It was after one when Sweet Thing's door opened. Out came Jason and, sure enough, the lady was right behind him, in a Japanese kimono. He turned to kiss her good-bye, but she stopped him, pointing with her chin toward the rented car, which, if it hadn't been white, would have blended a lot better. Jason wrenched his body around, and Talba scrunched down. "Eddie. Wake up," she hissed.

"Wha . . . ?" He woke as suddenly and thoroughly as if a shot had been fired and assessed the situation. Talba sneaked a glance. "Omigod. He's coming over here."

The two of them must have had quite a bit to drink. Jason was swaggering toward them, puffed up like John Wayne. Eddie said, "Put your head in my lap."

"Do what?"

"Just *do* it!" He pulled her down, and as she floundered, struggling for breath, she raised an outraged face in his direction. He had his head back against the seat, mouth open, eyes closed, and he was breathing heavily. Getting the hang of things, she started to move her head in a rocking rhythm.

"Excuse me!" Jason said loudly, almost shouting, whereupon Eddie raised his head, faked a beautiful deer-in-the-headlights, and then there was silence, as Jason realized what he'd interrupted—or thought he had. Talba heard nothing for a moment, and then laughing, as Jason apparently told Sweet Thing the coast was clear—there were neither casing burglars nor spying PIs out there, just a couple of crazies getting off.

"Can I come up?"

"Miz Wallis, I wish you would. This is playin' hell with my dignity."

She sat up, pouting. "It didn't do much for mine, either."

"It was a beautiful thing, though. Faked him right out. And look over there now." The other happy couple, secure in the knowledge that no one was watching, were openly necking.

Chapter Three

Monday morning bright and early Talba matched the Metairie address to a Dr. and Mrs. Peter St. Clair, wealthy patrons of the arts who frequently gave bundles to various small theater groups. Apparently, Dr. Pete traveled and Mrs. Pete (whose name was Valerie) did what she pleased.

It wasn't any fun writing the client report. But on the other hand, Babalu certainly knew what to expect; maybe she wouldn't be too upset.

"Trust me," Eddie said. "She will."

Talba didn't ask her to come to the office—just couldn't put her friend through it. If Babalu was going to cry, she could do it in the peace of her own home.

Babalu's face was drawn, her cheeks too bright. Talba said, "Are you okay?"

"I just . . ." Babalu seemed to be moving in little jerks. "I'm fine, really."

She seemed so birdlike, so unable to keep still, Talba wondered briefly if she could be on speed. But she quickly dismissed it—there was hardly a less likely candidate in the state of Louisiana.

She declined her hostess's offer of tea in favor of just getting it over with. "Babalu, I'm sorry. You were right about him."

Babalu's head went slack against the back of the sofa, revealing a tiny scar at her scalp. "You deserve much better," Talba continued. "This guy is . . ." She finally settled on a word that might make her client laugh. ". . . a slut."

It didn't work. "We're talking jerk city here. Mondo dickhead."

Babalu wasn't into female bonding. She seemed to want to be alone with her pain. But just to be sure, Talba kept still, waiting for a sign.

Finally Babalu said, "Do you know who the woman is?"

"Someone named Valerie St. Clair."

This produced a completely different reaction. "Oh, shit! Oh, fuck! How could she do that to me? Oh, my God, what a bitch!"

"Who is she?"

"She's a client, damn her eyes! Big patron of the arts. I introduced them." Big ironic sigh. "I thought she could help him."

"Mmm. That's rough. I feel for you." She would have, even if the client had been a stranger. But she knew Babalu. Knew how nurturing, how kind she was. How much she wanted to be loved. "Listen, let me make *you* some tea." And so she stayed awhile, trying to heal the healer, and thanking the stars for her own boyfriend, Darryl Boucree.

That night, thinking about Babalu's pallor, her herky-jerky movements, her near hysteria, Talba was so disturbed she couldn't watch TV with her mama, and, in the end, couldn't even enjoy a recreational session of surfing the net. She wanted nothing so much as to call Darryl, to be reassured by the kindness and decency of her own man. Darryl was a high school teacher, musician, and sometime bartender, a guy who worked three jobs to help support his out-of-wedlock daugh-

ter. But he had a gig that night, and anyway, she would see
him the next.

Images kept coming to her. In the end, the only thing to do
was write a poem. But even at that, she wasn't successful. The
images were of birds in an oil spill, soaked and miserable, so
much tinier than when their feathers were fluffed; doomed if
they tried to remove the taint. They were too disturbing to
work with.

As if he knew—as if he'd guessed—Darryl arrived the
next night with flowers. "I don't deserve you," she
blurted.

"You do. *You* are a baroness."

"True, so very true." Baroness de Pontalba was the *nom de*
plume she used, and when she said it, she always emphasized
the pronoun—as in, "*I* am a baroness." She had named herself
after the pioneering nineteenth-century white woman who developed and built the famous Pontalba apartments at Jackson
Square. Quite a figure in her day, she was hated by her father-
in-law, who eventually pumped her full of lead. But the in-
trepid baroness survived and, with two fingers missing and
two bullets in her chest, went on to earn a place in history,
which was more than you could say for the father-in-law. To
this day he's remembered only as the man who shot the baroness.

But none of that was the reason Talba chose the name. She
picked it for two reasons—the first was that she wanted to
steal something from a white person, or rather from white
culture—in fact, very specifically, she wanted to steal a name.
She had her reasons for this, and they had nothing at all to
do with hating white people, which she didn't at all, or else
she wouldn't have been able to abide Eddie Valentino.

The second was that she wanted to be a baroness.

"Does Your Grace plan to invite me in?"

Actually, Talba hadn't planned to. The fact was that, after
a string of losers, Talba had finally brought home a boyfriend
who delighted her mama so much Talba suspected her of

wanting him for her own. Miz Clara would offer him supper and try to keep him around as long as she could. And Talba desperately wanted to go out. Now.

Even now, Miz Clara was getting impatient to see him. Talba could hear real shoes clicking behind her instead of her mama's accustomed scruffy blue slippers. " 'Zat Darryl Boucree I hear?"

"Sure," Talba said to him. "Come on in."

Miz Clara was all over him. "Darryl, how ya keepin' yaself? How come you been such a stranger?"

He hadn't, of course. Talba met him away from her mother's cottage as much as she could. She liked living with her mother—had moved in just for a few months and stayed—but a person had to have some semblance of adult life.

"Miz Clara," he said, "you know I can't stay away from you for long."

"Hmm. From my food, ya mean. I been makin' smothered chicken. Y'all want some?"

"Ohhh. That sure sounds good." He'd stay and eat it if Talba'd let him.

"Nosiree, Mr. Boucree," she said. "You promised me Italian."

"Okay. Italian it is." He'd promised no such thing, but he was a quick study. She liked that about him.

"My car or yours?" he said when they'd made their escape.

"Yours, of course. I hate that damn white thing."

He opened her door. "Have you looked for a new one yet?"

"I checked out the ads on Sunday. But I can't really afford anything new—or half decent, even. The accident was my fault, you know. If the insurance pays for it, you know what that does to my rates."

"Maybe you should just bite the bullet—you really need a car. Venezia okay?"

"Always." This was a great hangout for cops and all manner of hard-bitten characters. Eddie had introduced her to it. She loved it, though not for the food, especially.

"Well, you can't keep renting a car. That's a quick way to the poorhouse."

"I would have the one job in the world that absolutely requires a car."

"Sure can't do surveillance in a New Breed cab."

"Oh, God. Surveillance."

"What?"

"Nothing. Or rather, something I don't want to think about. I had to tell a friend her boyfriend was cheating on her."

They arrived at the restaurant and went in. Curiously, Darryl didn't pursue the subject. She asked him about school—he taught English at Fortier High School—and about his gig the previous night, and about his daughter, Raisa.

He had amusing stories about the first two and worry about Raisa. Always a difficult child, she was acting out more than ever. He wanted to find her a therapist; his ex was opposed.

Talba's stomach churned when she thought about Raisa. If she married Darryl—and things were heading that way—this giant, seemingly insurmountable problem became hers. Motherhood itself seemed insurmountable, much less third parent to a young volcano. Come to think of it, she'd not only get Raisa, she'd get her mother, and that would be even worse.

Yet she hated herself for thinking that way. She knew Darryl wouldn't if the roles were reversed. She wanted Darryl and she was going to have to accept this one day. Perhaps, she thought, she wasn't mature enough yet.

In fact, there was no doubt of that. Maybe she'd met him too early. She still had things to do, unfinished business that really had to be addressed.

Suddenly, a great sadness came over her—sadness for Babalu, who thought she'd found her man and had been betrayed; and for herself, though why, she wasn't sure. Maybe because sooner or later she was going to have to give up something. But not Darryl. Uh-uh. She wasn't that stupid.

His voice grew soft and monotonous when he spoke of Raisa, and he tended to look away from Talba. His way of dealing with the pain. It made her nervous, seemed to underscore her inadequacy. She was glad when he changed the subject.

Wrapping himself around a meatball, he said suddenly, "How's your own little problem coming? You thought about that any more?"

She knew what he meant and it wasn't her feelings about Babalu or even Raisa, for that matter. It was something so repellent she didn't want to think about it—largely because it loomed so huge in her life it made her feel tired. Feel like tucking her head away like a turtle, a favorite pastime of hers in times of stress. Yet it nagged and gnawed at her. It was this: long after he left her mother, her father had been murdered. When she got her PI license, she made up her mind to solve the case. This was her unfinished business.

And she really didn't intend to give up on it. But she hadn't even started.

She just shook her head, smiling, willing him not to press it.

He said, "Come on. Let's go to my house."

"What about tomorrow?"

"I'll take you home—we'll get up early. But you know what you ought to do? You ought to leave some clothes at my house, so you can dress there and go straight to work when you need to."

"Woo. I thought you'd never ask." She snuggled up to him.

"I didn't think I needed to. For heaven's sake, Talba—you know I want you there."

But the simple fact was that he didn't often take her home with him on a school night. Once there, she stayed—he lived across the river, at Algiers Point, and it made no sense to drive back and forth over the bridge.

He had a wonderful house in a quiet neighborhood, a Victorian cottage that he'd fixed up in manly but comfortable fashion. Her favorite part was the living room seating area, consisting of two brick-colored sofas on which to recline and drink wine and talk into the night. When they were settled there, he brought up the subject again—her unfinished business with the universe.

It was strange, she thought. Why was he doing it?

"Tell you what," he said. "I've got Raisa Sunday, but I'll take you car shopping Saturday if you'll start working on it."

"Why?" she asked. "Why do you care?"

"Because you haven't written a poem about it. That's a really bad sign."

It was. It meant she was turtling out on it.

Well, she had the next day off. It was Wednesday, but since she'd worked the surveillance the weekend before, (and also finished the report on the redhead), Eddie'd given her a mental health day. She could start in about eight hours, if she had the nerve.

She woke up thinking about it, about what she could do to pursue it, and it came to her that it might be easy, that she knew someone who might even know the answer—who could certainly point her in the right direction.

He was the retired minister of First Bethlehem Baptist, the church Miz Clara still went to, that Talba had been taken to every Sunday of her life as a child. She'd become reacquainted with him recently (on another case), and something he'd said to her then, something she hadn't understood at the time, made her think of him.

He'd told her that he'd seen her father in church after he left the family. Had he come back with his woman? If so, the old man might know her name; Talba could track him through her.

The minister's name was the Reverend Clarence Scruggs, and he'd been a terror in his day, petrifying her and the other kids Sunday after Sunday with shouted threats of "eternal damnation in the blazing flames of hell." Sometimes she had to sleep with the light on after one of his sermons. He was probably the reason she didn't go to church today. But, thanks to him, nobody could say she wasn't God-fearing. If she ran into God in a dark alley, she'd probably pull out the pepper spray.

The Reverend Mr. Scruggs was now living in public housing and he'd changed. When she went to see him last year she found instead of the raving demagogue of her youth a gentle old man with a rather stilted way of speaking, utterly devoted to his sick wife.

"Had it not been for my wife I might have lost my way entirely," he had told Talba. "She is my dearest love and it is a privilege to care for her."

He spoke of his anger when their child was stricken with "a rare and painful disease," though he was, as he said, "the fiercest soldier in the army of the Lord," and of his wife's loving gentleness with the child, and of the way it had transformed him.

Listening to him was a bit on the surreal side—even in conversation, he spoke in the cadences of sermons—but Talba had been utterly moved by the sincerity of what he had to say and by his amazing metamorphosis into a sweet old gent. She really should have been back to see him.

Darryl drove her home early enough that the two of them had time to grab coffee before Darryl went to work. As soon as her eyes were fully open, she said, "I'm going to do what you said."

"What?" But he hadn't forgotten; she knew he just wanted her to say it.

"I'm going to work on my big case. Today, in fact. Get ready to find me a fabulous car for pennies."

"I feel a . . . a what . . ."—he squinched up his eyes—". . . a Subaru coming on."

"A what? Why a Subaru?"

"You really want to know?"

"Sure—are you psychic now?"

"I've got a buddy who knows somebody whose uncle wants to sell one. Or something like that. I'll bet we could see it Saturday."

"What? All that rigmarole just to get me to work on the case?"

"Naaah. Coincidence. Maybe it won't work out—I'll take you to see every car in the classifieds. We'll have a lot of fun."

"That I don't doubt." She'd heard Subarus were pretty good cars.

She needed to take the reverend a present. But what? She couldn't get Miz Clara to bake him a cake even if her mama were home—any mention of her father and Miz Clara sulked. She ran him off after he took up with another woman and that wasn't even his worst trait; drugs and abuse were two others Miz Clara had mentioned.

In the end Talba cooked for the reverend herself. She had to go shopping anyway—her brother Corey was coming to dinner that night. She bought chicken and greens for Miz Clara to fix later on, and the makings for mashed potatoes and peach pie, her own contributions to the meal. For Reverend Scruggs, something sturdy, she thought, and ended up with pot roast. She spent the morning making it, then packed it up and drove to his building, a high rise for seniors. She hadn't wanted to phone first—she'd dropped in unexpectedly the first time and she wanted to do it again.

What she saw when he opened the door made her smile. It was the same something she'd seen before—the Reverend Mr. Scruggs wearing only pants, an undershirt, and a very distressed look at being caught half-dressed. He'd lost weight, she thought. "Why, Sandra Wallis." He called her by her childhood name. "I'm happy to see you, child. Happy indeed. You come in and make yourself comfortable. I'll be right back; let me just go see to Ella." She knew he was going to put a shirt on.

He returned in a fresh white one, hair spruced up as well.

"How is she, Reverend Scruggs?"

His face, animated before, showed briefly a flash of trouble and sadness, then tucked itself into a mask of stoicism. "The end is very near, I fear. That is, I fear for me, for I will miss her most fervently. But I rejoice for her, as she will soon be with the God she loves so much."

Talba remembered how much she enjoyed his nineteenth-century phrasing; what she'd forgotten, more or less, was the frightening figure of her childhood. No one could have told him when he was forty, or even fifty, she thought, that he'd end up a meek old man in public housing, and proud of it— proud of learning what he called "the way" from his wife.

She touched his knee. "You're one of my heroes, Reverend."

He looked away. " 'Brother' is fine, Sandra. You know that."

"I'm sorry about Ella."

"Do not be. She is beloved of God."

"I wish I'd known her. She must have been extraordinary."

"She still is, Sandra. She still is. With only a strand of her memory left, with barely a spark of strength, she still is."

"I brought you some pot roast." She had put the whole thing, vegetables and all, in a disposiable aluminum pan. "Half an hour in the oven at three-fifty."

"Why, I thank you. I will surely enjoy it." *Surely*. It was a use of the word that had almost passed from the language. Somebody really should do an oral history with the guy, she thought. "Perhaps Ella will even be tempted." The sadness flicked onto his face again and lit there. He shook his head from side to side. "She will very rarely eat anymore."

Talba's eyes filled up, not so much at his sorrow but at the thought that this would happen to Miz Clara one day, and to her as well, and even to Darryl. *We should really have a better way of dealing with death*, she thought, and then went back to pretending it didn't exist.

"Reverend, I need to ask you a question."

"I thought you would one day. Is it about your father, by any chance?"

"How did you know that?"

"You need to tie up loose ends. I understand that."

"Can you help me?"

"Perhaps." He nodded several times. "Perhaps. But not the way you think. I know what you think you need to know because of the kind of work you do, and I beseech you, do not pursue that course."

Beseech, she thought. "Why, Reverend, I don't know that I've ever been beseeched before."

"Don't make fun of an old man." He spoke so sharply she caught a backward glimpse of the man he had been.

"I'm sorry. I didn't . . ."

"Never mind, daughter. I know my speech is strange and stilted. It comes of reading the Bible several hours a day and having few people to talk to." Indeed, there was no television on the premises.

"I love the way you talk."

He put his hand on hers. "Listen to me. This is the important thing. You've got a baby sister out there somewhere."

Talba felt as if someone had poked her in the solar plexus, not an unpleasant sensation, and one she'd had before. It happened when she heard something so true, so unexpected, it was like having the breath knocked out of her.

Chapter Four

She knew about the baby, of course. The one her father had had with the woman he lived with after the family broke up. Perhaps because Miz Clara had so deliberately distanced her children from her former spouse, it had simply never occurred to Talba that this child was her sibling.

"My God," she said, unable to stop herself. Reverend Scruggs would probably call this "taking the name of the Lord in vain." She glanced at him to see if he was offended, but saw only concern. And eagerness, perhaps. *He's ministering*, she realized. *This is making him happy.*

"Reverend Scruggs, you're right. That *is* the important thing. I mean, if I do have a sister. I never even knew if the baby was a boy or a girl."

"A girl. I remember that; it was a girl. I baptized her."

"What?"

"I didn't tell you everything when you were here before. I couldn't—you know that. But I baptized that girl, and if she is alive today, she is your sister."

"Why wouldn't she be alive?"

"There is sadness in the world, Sandra. You know that too."

"But do you *know* anything?"

"I do not."

"Well, then. All right. I thank you for setting me straight. I'm going to look for her and find her. What was her name? Do you recall?"

He shook his head sadly, and Talba saw that he had already searched his memory. "I am sorry to say that I do not."

The next question was the one she had come to ask. "The mother's, then—my father never married her, did he?"

"I don't believe he did, no. But I do not recall her name."

Talba exhaled, disappointed.

"All I can be sure of is that it was not Wallis—therefore the baby's probably was not, either."

"There must be baptismal records."

"Perhaps." He looked vague and a bit doubtful. "You must ask Miz Blanchard about that." Lura Blanchard, who'd been church secretary in his day.

She asked for Miz Blanchard's address.

When she left, she gave the reverend a tight hug that must have surprised him—she was sure it embarrassed him. She hadn't lied when she told him he was one of her heroes. She'd always been depressed by those who said people couldn't change. What was the point of living if you couldn't change? Nobody she'd ever met in her life had changed as thoroughly as Clarence Scruggs, who had metamorphosed from a fire-breathing demon into what he'd then believed he already was—a true spiritual being.

It made Talba love him. Though she'd seen him only three times in her adult life, she loved him. The sight of him just about made her cry. *He's good enough*, she thought. *So I got a shitty father. This can be his replacement*. She made a vow to bring him something to eat once a week from now on, and knew she wouldn't, which made her ashamed.

It was hard seeing old people; sick people. They made you feel bad about yourself. She wondered about people who worked as care-givers—how they did it, what they were really like. Whatever they were like, they were different from Talba, but if she had a baby sister, she could at least treat her like family—even if it harelipped Miz Clara. Which it was bound to.

She hated the thought of calling on Lura Blanchard, who was much older than the Reverend and probably just as saintly, and who'd probably also depress her with the vague sense that she ought to be doing more for people, with guilt about her own youth and vitality.

The minute she saw Miz Lura, though, she realized she'd forgotten something about her—that she was the sort of old lady who'd probably bury all her friends. That kind didn't need to be cooked for.

Indeed, she was outside watering her yard, trying to keep the few surviving flowers alive in the late September heat.

She was a shrunken old lady who managed a certain elegance, having hair straight enough to wear long, in a bob that came to her earlobes, and the energy to dress up every chance she got. At the moment, she looked as if she'd just come back from something—taking food to old people, probably. She was wearing a polka-dot voile dress that would probably sell in a vintage store for decent money but that maintained its original freshness.

Talba had plenty of vitality for a twenty-something, but Miz Lura probably had more.

She squinted at Talba. "Who're you, child? I know ya, but these cataracts gettin' to me."

"I'm Talba Wallis, ma'am. My mama calls me Sandra."

The old woman turned off her hose and stepped forward to the sidewalk. "Oh, law. Sandra Wallis. Ya ever find the Reverend Scruggs that time?"

Nothing wrong with the woman's memory, either. Several months ago, she'd rifled the church records to find the former minister's address.

"I did. Have you seen him lately? His wife's about to die."

"Ella? I'm sorry to hear that. I always liked Ella. I better take 'em over some food."

"I'm sure they'd appreciate that," Talba said, wondering if

this meant she was off the hook and figuring it probably
didn't. "He sent me back to see you."

"Oh?" Miz Lura might have cataracts, but her eyes were
hawklike.

"He says he baptized my baby sister—the girl my daddy
had with—uh . . ." Her throat closed on the words; Miz Lura
didn't make her say them.

"I know who you mean, child. I know who you mean. You
come in, won't you? I'll pour us a nice glass of iced tea."

Miz Lura lived in a funny, countrified section of the Ninth
Ward, where the houses, unlike Miz Clara's, had little pockets
of dirt where you could grow flowers. They were as small as
hers, though, and this was a Victorian-era shotgun that dolls
could have lived in. It was painted plain white, rather out of
keeping with its gingerbread. Miz Lura probably had a no-
nonsense son or grandson who helped her keep it up. Talba
would have been shocked if it hadn't been neat as the lady
herself, and she wasn't disappointed.

There wasn't much furniture, and what there was looked
like items the son or grandson had passed on when his family
could afford something better. The plaid sofa just didn't seem
like the kind of thing Miz Lura would pick—particularly to
go with the fake Oriental rug and gold brocade chair she'd
probably inherited from own mother; or maybe from a lady
she'd worked for.

A nice picture of Dr. King hung over a table with a little
Virgin Mary statue on it, though to Talba's knowledge, Bap-
tists didn't go in much for Mary. Perhaps somebody'd given
it to her. There were votive candles on the table, too, set on
an embroidered white starched cloth—something you'd never
see in Miz Clara's house.

Miz Lura saw Talba looking at her altar. She said, "My
friend down the street's a Catholic—says when she asks the
blessed Virgin for something, she gets results. She give me
that when my grandson was sick last year—nearly died of
the sugar."

Diabetes.

Talba smiled. "Bet he got better, didn't he?" If he hadn't, she figured Mary'd have gotten the boot.

"He's as fine today as this fine weather. I promised Miz Mary I'd keep her in candles long as I lived if she'd do me that favor. I'm going to keep my promise, and I don't care if you tell ya mama."

Talba had to smile again. Miz Clara probably would be scandalized. "I wouldn't dream of it."

"How is Miz Clara?"

Talba said she was mean as ever and they went on like that for awhile, till finally Talba said, "Reverend Scruggs says I ought to go find out whatever happened to my baby sister."

Miz Lura squeezed some lemon in her tea and stirred it, trying to decide what to make of that. Finally, she said, "That sounds like a mighty Christian notion."

"Well, I don't know about that." Statements like that made Talba distinctly uncomfortable. "But he did make me curious."

"I should think so."

"He couldn't remember her name, though. Or her mama's."

"Don't tell me he thought I would!"

"Well, no ma'am, I don't think so. I think he thought you know where the baptismal records were."

Ms. Lura pursed her lips and sucked a little bit. "Let me see. Let me see—1983, was it?"

"Somewhere around there."

"Well, you know, we had that fire in 'eighty-nine."

"Fire?" Talba asked. Ever since her mama stopped making her go to Sunday school and church every week, she hadn't kept up with church history.

"Lightning struck our steeple—wasn't the first time, either."

Don't giggle, Talba said to herself. *Wrong audience for any of your jokes.*

But Miz Lura collapsed laughing herself, her body folding, her small brown hand slapping her skinny leg, which she simultaneously used to stomp the floor. (In ladylike fashion, of course.) "Kind of makes you wonder, doesn't it? Yes,

Lord, we must have had some sinners among us *that* year. Not much damage, but it did destroy the storeroom."

"Where the files were," Talba said. She'd already figured it out. "You wouldn't remember . . ."

Miz Lura was already shaking her head. "I never even knew that baby name. The mama, though. I remember *her* name."

"You do? How on earth can you remember something like that?"

Miz Lura nearly died laughing again. "I'm ninety-two years old, Sandra. Some folks say I'm losing my memory, but I can sho' tell you one thing—Miz Lura Blanchard know her own name. Yes, ma'aaaam. Sho' do."

"Miz Lura, you were not my daddy's paramour—I know that for a fact."

"No, ma'am. I shore wasn't. But that don't mean I don't know my own name." She fell to cackling again, really enjoying this, whatever it was. "That woman name was Lura. Just as sho' as you're born. Mmmm-hmmm. Lura. You can take that to the bank."

"Really? Lura like you?"

"Yes, ma'am. Lura like me. *Mmmm-hmmmm.*" She fanned herself with a round cardboard fan attached to a tongue depressor and sporting a picture of Jesus as a white man.

"And what was her last name?"

"Well, now, that I don't know. Never did, probably. But one thing I can tell you—she was a Methodist. Went to that church over by Claiborne. You know the one?"

A Methodist. What a thing to remember after all those years.

She left Miz Lura with promises to come again, thinking that if the woman had gone to the trouble of living ninety-two years, she at least deserved a visitor now and then.

That afternoon she phoned Darryl and reported her progress, feeling more peaceful and in tune with him than she had for a long time. Then she went in the kitchen and started cooking again, for Corey and his wife Michelle.

Corey had fulfilled the Wallis family destiny. He'd actually embraced one of Miz Clara's chosen careers for her children, though the lowliest of them. Corey was a mere doctor, but Miz Clara was happy to take what she could get. She was tickled pink in fact, and Talba resented him for making her look bad. But as Talba said in her own defense, in a democratic country, a baroness wasn't going to get elected president, or even to Congress, and Miz Clara would just have to live with it.

It was bad enough Corey was the favorite child—at any rate, the one most often bragged on—but Talba didn't like his wife, either. Why, she wasn't sure—a kind of reverse snobbery, perhaps. Michelle came from a prominent Creole family, Creole in the sense of light-skinned black. Michelle's skin was very light indeed, her hair very nearly straight. Was this what bugged Talba, the simple fact that she was so different? Sometimes she thought so. But it wasn't nearly so simple—it was more that she sensed a deep snobbery and disapproval coming out of Michelle, which in itself wasn't so bad. But the phoniness surrounding that made Talba plain tired—stuff like trying to compliment Talba on her taste when she clearly hated her showy baroness clothes.

Or maybe it was nothing deep and psychological at all. Maybe Michelle really was the narrow-minded little airhead Talba thought she was.

Miz Clara was frying the chicken and making cornbread to go with that and the greens. Talba was supposed to do the rest of the meal, and though she knew Michelle would prefer something like brown rice and a fruit salad, she took a perverse pleasure in mashing the potatoes with a ton of butter and milk and whipping up the peach pie. Well, the pie was for Corey—he dearly loved peach pie.

"Be sure and make plenty," Miz Clara said. "Remember, she eating for two."

Hope she gains a ton of weight, Talba thought. The one thing she could identify about Michelle that really did make her jealous was the woman's snaky body. Formerly snaky— she was about to have the first Wallis grandchild, a fact about which Talba felt deeply ambivalent. (Of course Michelle's family—the high-and-mighty Tircuits—were probably highly embarrassed about it, which was the irony of it all.) But to Talba, though the Wallises had neither name nor social position, their greater intelligence made them superior.

"There the doorbell now."

Talba was just pulling her pie out. "Go get on your shoes, Mama. I'll let them in."

Miz Clara already had her wig on, but she hated getting out of her blue slippers before she had to. She cleaned white people's houses for a living; she liked to give her feet a rest when she could.

Talba had to hug the damn woman; there was no way around it. Michelle's eyes flicked over her. Talba had on orange jeans and a lime-green T-shirt—not her performance clothes, which Michelle plain didn't get, but still chosen more or less to irritate her sister-in-law, who wore black slacks and a crisp white blouse.

Talba said, "You look nice," and watched Michelle struggle to think of a way to return the compliment.

"Big as a house," Corey said, but she wasn't. She looked like a snake that had recently eaten. "Nice pants, Little Bird."

"You mean that ironically, of course."

"Of course." He grinned.

For a long time, there'd been tension between them; lately, they were feeling easier with one another, and Talba felt she shouldn't blow it by being mean to his wife. She resolved to be good.

"Well, come on in and sit down. Mama went to get her shoes."

She got out some wine and Perrier (for Michelle), and they sat for awhile, talking of the Saints and the weather; when Miz Clara joined them, they got serious about baby names and due dates. They were well into dinner before Michelle asked Talba about her work.

"We seem to have a lot of domestic cases these days. You know—sitting in a car waiting for some guy to come out of a motel with his sweetie."

"How sordid! You mean you really do that?"

Talba picked up an entire breast and bit into it. (She'd have cut it if Michelle hadn't been there.) "Somebody's got to," she said. Michelle's delight in her own unworldliness rankled Talba, who tended to respond by baiting. "Anyway, I enjoy it. I love nailing the cheating bastards."

"Ah! Language." Miz Clara still acted as if Talba were a child. Everyone ignored her.

"It's a part of life I wouldn't care to know about," Michelle said.

"Well, I hope to God you never do. I caught the fiancé of a good friend the other night—it could happen to anybody."

Corey spoke up. "Talba, that's enough."

"Oh, well." She turned to Michelle with a raised eyebrow. "Anybody not married to my brother, I mean."

But the damage was done, and the evening never completely recovered from it. Nobody who was pregnant wanted to think about infidelity.

Why do I do stuff like that? Talba asked herself when they had gone. She started noodling at the keyboard.

The first thing that came out was a parody of an old song:

Who's the worst person I know?
Sister-in-law—
sister-in-law!

Damn, she thought, *Ernie K-Doe beat me to it.*

The next thing wasn't her usual style at all, which tended to be more narrative than didactic. It was a kind of admonitory rap:

Woman born of money
Woman born of pride
Woman born of Daddy King
And spawned of Mama Queen
Woman born of everything
Gets sold on the TV screen—
Woman, you no woman—
Woman, you a girl!

You think abortion shouldn't be
'Cause people ought to be smart
You think you too good to be taxed
'Cause the poor such lazy bums.
Well, let me ask you somethin' big—
What you do, 'cept for your nails?
What you do, whitey-pants?
What's smart about bein' so dumb?

You get a little piece of luck,
You think you queen of the sky
Anything bad ever happens—
You run to your daddy and cry.

Listen, woman born of money,
Woman born of pride
You ain't nobody special
'Cause you had a nice smooth ride.

Listen, woman born of money,
Listen, smooth life–rider,
You still a girl, but
You still be ridin'.
Your nails ain't done,
Your show ain't over—
What happens in the next two acts?
What if the fat lady sings off-key?
What if the curtain falls down on your ass?
You ready for any of that?

It wasn't a poem she could ever read in public—might not even be a poem at all, but it was a start. And for now it was good enough. It got to the heart of what bugged her about Michelle—and about certain white people, and anybody at all who thought they were better than anybody else. They weren't really complete people. Maybe that was okay if they weren't in your family; but when they were about to become your niece or nephew's mother, it tried your patience. Or so she told herself. Miz Clara would probably say she ought to go to church and leave the judgin' to God.

Chapter Five

Matter of fact, Miz Clara didn't say a word; just grumped around the next morning, making Talba feel duly reprimanded.

Sandra, ya just jealous, she might have said. She'd said it before. Or, *Why can't ya just accept ya brother's choice?* Which was more to the point.

This time Talba had an answer: *You never know, Mama. Maybe I will. The fat lady hasn't sung yet.*

Poetry was very clarifying, she found. She wished she'd written the poem before the dinner.

She went off to work as grumpy as Miz Clara, and when she got a call from Jason Wheelock, she was in no mood. She gave him her frosty baroness voice: "What can I do for you?" He paused a long time before he spoke. *Good*, she thought. *He's properly intimidated.* "I need to see you." His voice was low and serious. "It's about—"

She cut him off. "I know what it's about. I don't think we have anything to say to each other."

"Look, we really need to talk. Please . . ." He sounded as

if he were about to cry. When he paused to compose himself, she dived in.

"I really wouldn't be interested." She hung up with a momentary flash of satisfaction. *Let him suffer*, she thought. *I'm not going to put up with him coming over here and telling me there really was a perfectly plausible explanation. Uh-uh. Not in this life.*

She went back to the day's supply of background checks— Eddie loved giving her these, because he hated anything you did with a computer, and she quite enjoyed doing them. She'd hardly gotten her teeth into the first one when she heard the outer door open and close, then a man's voice talking to the receptionist, Eileen Fisher. In a moment, Eileen came in, her plain, round face strained and worried.

"Talba. Jason Wheelock to see you. He says it's urgent."

"Damn!"

"I could say you're in a meeting with a client."

But it was too late for that. Talba heard a man's footsteps coming down the short hall, and then Jason was looming behind Eileen. Talba had never seen him up close, but her impression was of a happy-go-lucky guy, someone who didn't really want the responsibilities of adulthood. The man she was looking at looked like he'd just lost his grandmother.

Did I do that? she thought.

She really enjoyed domestic cases. She liked catching the lying bastards and rubbing their noses in their own muck. If it broke up their romances, fine—they should damn well have thought of it before they cheated. She wasn't about to get sympathetic at this late date.

She said, "Jason, I really don't have time to see you today," and was in the act of rising to show him out when he said, "I'm sorry to be the one to tell you. Babalu passed away Tuesday night."

Passed away. It was such a mild phrase and told you so little, designed to buy time till you could handle the details. To Talba, it sounded like some kind of peaceful escape, as if the person had simply gone to bed and never awakened. But it was almost never that. There was always a story. And the story usually involved words that weren't nearly so soft.

The news was so shocking Talba paused, bent with her butt in the air, for way too long. Eileen looked like she was about to push the panic button. Her head kept swiveling toward Eddie's office. Talba really couldn't deal with her right now.

She straightened up. "What happened?"

"I'd like to come in and tell you." He spoke calmly, sounding like the adult she hadn't pegged him for.

"Of course. Eileen, it's all right." The receptionist fled.

"Sit down." They both sat, and Talba waited, searching her memory for any hint of poor health from Babalu.

Suicide! she thought, and the thought was like a blow. *What if she couldn't handle Jason's betrayal?*

"She died of an overdose," he said.

"Overdose? Of prescription drugs?" But Babalu never took drugs.

"Of heroin."

"Heroin! She's the last person . . ."

He nodded. "That's right. She was murdered."

Talba shook her head. "I don't know if I'm ready for all this. Why are you so sure?"

"Because she didn't use heroin."

"She did once, if that's what killed her."

Now he shook his head, "She didn't. She was a healer. I *knew* her. She. Didn't. Do. Heroin." Each word separate, jaw clenched, as if he'd been having an argument about it.

"What do the police think?"

"They think she committed suicide." His delivery was sullen, that of a child harangued by authorities. "They found your report."

"Suicide occurred to me, too."

His head was virtually flapping in the breeze again. "No way. She. Didn't. Do. Heroin. Therefore she couldn't have committed suicide."

"I know you want to believe that . . ."

"Look, don't you think I've been through hell in the last two days? I loved her. We were going to get married. I cheated on her and she's dead. I'd like to kill *myself* for what

I did." He wouldn't meet her eyes now, looking at his lap, speaking in that low, depressed, chastened voice.

Talba was at a loss. She wanted him out of her office, so she could think about all this, let the shock wear off.

"Well, I appreciate your letting me know."

"I didn't come here to let you know. I came here to hire you. I want you to find the murderer."

"Me? Of all people! Why me?"

"Because you knew her. You cared about her. She talked about you. She even read me some of your poetry. She admired you a lot."

"But you have reason to hate me."

"I don't hate you." He changed position, seeming uncomfortable. "The person I hate's myself."

I can see that, Talba thought, but didn't say. It looked as if a long, unpleasant morning was about to get a lot worse; she was going to have to humor him, at least for awhile. "Well, tell you what," she said. "Why don't we get some coffee and get comfortable. Would you like some coffee?"

She got up and went to get some, mind racing. At least he didn't seem dangerous, she thought. Who and what he was wasn't clear to her, except for one thing—he was a very depressed, very chastened young man. She could at least hear him out.

When she returned, he took the coffee without thanking her, hardly seeming to notice its existence. "I hate myself for what I did. But I'll tell you something—I did it out of . . . well, sadness. Babalu was distant. She was moody; she wouldn't tell me what was wrong. I felt she was trying to move out of the relationship. She wouldn't even . . ." He stopped, a kicked-puppy look descending onto his features as if blown there by the wind.

Remember, Talba said to herself, *he's an actor*. She said, "She wouldn't even do what?"

"She kept putting me off about the wedding date. She wouldn't set a date."

She shrugged. "She thought you were cheating on her."

"No. I mean, I wasn't then. This whole Valerie thing was a reaction—do you understand that?"

"I understand it makes you feel better to think that." He was making her impatient.

He sighed. "Listen, I *swear*—the whole thing started with her."

She heard Eileen start back down the hall and didn't bother to reply until the other woman arrived. "Everything all right?" Eileen asked.

"Fine." Talba nodded, reassuring Jason, she hoped.

He looked embarrassed. "I didn't mean to speak so loudly."

"I guess I was harsh. I'm sorry."

"No. You're right. I guess I sound like every asshole who ever cheated. But look here. Babalu's dead. I think something was going on with her, something she wouldn't tell me, and"—he swallowed—"I think she got killed for it."

Yeah. Something was going on. Like she was doing heroin. But that didn't ring true for Talba—she couldn't see Babalu doing heroin any more than Jason could. "What do you think it was?" she asked.

"I don't know."

"You must have some idea."

He was finally drinking his coffee, taking huge gulps purely for the caffeine. "No. I don't. Babalu was a very mysterious person."

Talba sighed. "You're not kidding. Anybody who calls themselves Babalu Maya's got *something* going on." Do you even know her real name?"

"Sure. Clayton Robineau."

"Well, there's two names that don't go together."

"Why?"

"Clayton sounds like she owns the town. Robineau probably pumps gas."

For the first time, Jason cracked a smile. "You're probably right. She's from a town named Clayton. Near Baton Rouge. Robineau's her married name."

"She was divorced?"

"Yeah." His face closed down with sadness and defeat.

"But I don't know much about the ex-husband. She wouldn't talk about him."

"Well, I'm intrigued about this town thing—her having the same name, I mean. What kind of family did she come from?"

He'd known that was coming. He all but winced. "She hadn't introduced me to them."

"You sure y'all were engaged?"

"You know we were. It was in your client report. I read it."

"You're not describing a person who acts like they intend to get married."

"That's what I'm trying to tell you. She was distant. And a lot more so lately."

"All right." Talba was taking notes now. Maybe he really was a potential client. "You must have known something about the family."

He nodded and crossed his legs, apparently grateful she'd asked him a question he could answer. "Her father was a banker. I guess that makes you a big deal in Clayton."

Talba's mind ran a movie: *"You've got that deb look . . . 'Carefully cultivated. We were trailer-trash, actually.' "*

"And her mother was some kind of beauty queen once upon a time."

Talba frowned. "That's a weird way to describe your mother."

"I don't think so. The way Babalu told it, that was the important thing about her. Look, there was a reason she didn't introduce me to her family. She didn't get along with them."

"She was estranged from them?"

"I guess so. Partially, anyway."

"Okay. What's their name—Babalu's maiden name?"

Jason was easy to read—or else he was such a practiced actor he made you believe what he wanted you to. He looked utterly amazed. "Patterson." He set down his coffee cup on her desk. "I swear to God, I didn't even know till after her death. I had to get her best friend to tell me."

She raised her eyebrows. This was getting ridiculous.

"Where were you planning to get married? The bride's home town?"

"She wouldn't discuss it." His voice was clipped, his eyes vacant.

Talba put down her pen. "Okay, she was mysterious. But when you get right down to it, who'd want to kill her? Any ideas?"

He shook his head.

"Well, I've got one," she said. How about your girlfriend?"

"Valerie? Are you kidding? She was just having a fling."

"Is that what you were doing?"

"Sure."

Talba pursed her lips. How like a man to assume that, because he had no investment in a relationship, the woman didn't either. "Well, how well do you know *her*? Maybe she's nuts."

He leaned back in his chair, putting his right foot on his left knee. "Okay, maybe I deserved that. I don't know, it wasn't that I didn't want to know Babalu, it was just that . . ."

That mostly you wanted to have sex with her. She said, "Mind if I ask what you two talked about? It doesn't seem to have been family history."

"Music," he said. "Poetry. Acting." He paused. "Religion. Babalu was a very spiritual person."

"What kind of religion?"

"All kinds. She had her own beliefs."

"Were they the same as yours?"

"No, I . . . I guess I'm not religious at all. And she liked everything—Hinduism, Buddhism; Santeria, even. She taught me what it was."

"Was she a devotee?"

"Oh, no. She wasn't part of any group—she went to a Catholic retreat last weekend and she wasn't even Catholic."

"What did you two have in common? It seems as if you hardly knew her. What did you see in her?"

He looked Talba in the eye and spoke with dignity. "She was a healer," he said. "I admired her so much. She was

gentle and wise. And fine. And she seemed so alone—I
wanted to take care of her."

For the first time, Talba understood what Babalu saw in
Jason, other than a pretty face. When he spoke like that, he
exhibited a gentleness and a fineness himself. Despite what
she knew about Valerie, Talba thought this was a man who
was capable of seeing Babalu for who she was and loving her
for it.

He's an actor, she reminded herself. Still, her instincts said
he was on the up-and-up.

"If I take the case," she said, "I'll need a retainer."

He nodded. "Of course. That's not a problem."

She recalled that he did have a decent credit rating.

"Look, is there any way we can get into her house? You
must have a key." It was probably illegal to use it, but she
figured now was no time to research the law.

"I do and I left some things there—you know, clothes and
stuff. I'm supposed to meet Mary Pat tonight to get them."

"Mary Pat?"

"Babalu's best friend. The family left her in charge until
they can clear the place out."

"Think Mary Pat would mind if I came along with you?"

"I think she'd be delighted. She's destroyed about this."

When he had gone, Talba called the coroner to confirm
Babalu's death. And then she went out and walked for awhile,
trying to get the thing to sink in.

Babalu dead.

Babalu and heroin.

That didn't compute at all—Jason was right about that. On
the other hand, it was an absurdly cumbersome way to kill
someone. For one thing, it would probably take two people.
For another, it would take heroin. If Babalu was murdered,
why choose such an offbeat method?

Well, anyway, now she had a good enough name for a
background check. But about all she learned was that Clayton
Robineau had lived at Babalu's address and owned Babalu's
car.

Chapter Six

When she arrived at Babalu's house that night, Jason was alone. "Mary Pat couldn't face it," he said.

So is this breaking and entering? she wondered. Had he really had an appointment with Mary Pat?

But, in truth, she didn't care that much as long as Jason wasn't dangerous, and since he'd hired her, she figured that she, at least, was in his good graces.

He opened the door to the stairway that had seemed such a hurdle on Talba's last visit. It seemed merely forlorn now. Talba realized there were details she still didn't have. "Who found the body?" she asked.

"I did. I usually came over after work. She didn't answer when I called, but I didn't think anything about it. The place was dark when I got here."

He flipped the switch as they reached the top of the stairs.

"I did this, and there she was." His eyes flicked to the narrow living room off to the right, to the sling chair right in their line of vision.

"In that chair?"

"She was half falling out of it, and she had foam on her mouth. I could see the hypodermic, still in her arm."

"What did you do?"

He had stopped at the top of the stairs, apparently unable to go any further. His hand half-covered his face. "I went over and held her. I knew she was dead. Have you ever seen a corpse?"

"Yes."

"Well. You know then. Her eyes were open, and when I touched her . . . Never mind. I can't go into that. But I did hold her. I had to hold her."

"What about the syringe?"

"The syringe?"

"Didn't that dislodge it?"

"Maybe. I don't even know. I just backed away and called nine-one-one and then everyone else I could think of. Mary Pat wasn't home—she was the one I really wanted to talk to. You know who I finally ended up with? You're going to laugh."

"Who?"

"My mother. I called my mother. She kept me talking till the cops got there."

"I thought the nine-one-one operator was supposed to do that."

"Is she? I hung up on her. I was bouncing off the walls."

The apartment was very stark. Talba had noticed that on previous visits. The walls were white and the furniture tended to the crisp rather than the cozy. There were books, though, in two tall cases.

"Mind if I walk through the place first, just to get the feel?"

"Of course not. Do whatever you need to do."

She walked down the hall, peeking briefly into the familiar appointment room. It was also a stark room, rather Japanese in flavor.

A small back bedroom was a little more cheerful. Painted yellow in contrast to the white of the rest of the place, it contained a bed with flowered duvet cover, Victorian dresser, and white rug.

The apartment was out of keeping with the New Orleans philosophy and lifestyle, which was something along the lines of too-much-is-not-nearly-enough. But, then, Babalu was no good-time Charlene. She probably had some spiritual reason for wanting things simple.

Still, Talba had always found the apartment, even in happier times, a bit on the depressing side. Even if Babalu were poor—and Talba imagined she made quite a decent living—there were small luxuries she might have permitted herself. Things like flowers, for instance. Inexpensive decorative items. Talba ought to know—she'd turned Miz Clara's cottage into something out of the Arabian Nights.

Should she go through the dresser? She didn't have the stomach for it—at least not now. She retraced her steps, and when she got to the living room, with its small dining area, stepped into the adjoining kitchen, which was spacious and old-fashioned. There was a desk here, and a file cabinet. Clearly, Babalu hadn't wanted the clutter in any of the other rooms.

Wincing, Talba noticed her client report on the desk. She grabbed the Rolodex next to it. "Okay if I take this?" There was a date book too—that was even better. "And this?"

Jason was hovering awkwardly in the background, drinking a beer—probably one he'd bought and stored in the fridge himself. Talba didn't see Babalu as a beer drinker.

"Sure. I mean, I don't think Mary Pat would mind. We've just spent two days calling every name in it—to let them know. I don't guess anyone needs it right now."

"The family didn't do the calling?"

"They haven't even been here yet—just had the body shipped back to Clayton."

"That seems cold."

She watched his Adam's apple as he took a good long sip. He seemed to be self-medicating. "She didn't get along with them worth a damn."

"Still, this seems extreme."

"Yeah." He put down the can. "Yeah, it does."

"You don't know what the problem was?"

He shrugged. "Maybe the tattoos. Listen, I'm weird by my parents' standards and I don't have a crazy name like Babalu, a profession that sounds like woo-woo to the average American, and some kind of weird chain going up my arm. And my parents probably aren't half as conservative as Babalu's. Her folks probably hate her for not being a little Hog-Calling Queen clone; or whatever it was her mama was." He turned away from Talba and opened the refrigerator door again. "I mean, hated her." He was obviously trying to get used to the past tense. He looked for another beer and finally gave it up. "You about finished here?"

"Sorry, I'm not. I need to look at her files."

"Oh." He was clearly going stir-crazy.

"Why don't you go down to Whole Foods and get a snack or something? I'll be fine by myself."

He hesitated, knowing he shouldn't go, but one more look around the sad little apartment clinched his decision. "Okay. Meet you there?"

Talba nodded but realized he probably didn't see her. She was already bent over the files, and he was on his way down the stairs.

Babalu hadn't kept a file on each patient, but she did have certain accounting records in the top drawer and a file marked "Important Stuff." Other than that, she seemed to have kept mostly magazine articles about breakthroughs in alternative healing. There were also plenty of catalogues offering vitamins, nonallergenic pillows, incense, feng shui equipment, and other New Age staples.

Talba pulled out "Important Stuff" and opened the second drawer. Here was poetry, files and files of it. So much of it that it would take weeks to go through. She thought, *I hope the family isn't so stupid they just throw it out.*

There were probably clues in here, if not to Babalu's death, at least to her life. There might be whistle-blowing poems—real reasons for her family to hate her. She couldn't take them now, there were too many. But maybe Mary Pat and Jason could pack them up for safekeeping—and possibly Talba's perusal—before the family found them and destroyed them.

For now, she closed the poetry drawer and opened the file marked "Important Stuff." Ha! There, along with a passport and other papers, were Babalu's marriage license and divorce decree. She'd been Clayton Patterson in her single life, and, according to her passport picture, a brunette. She had married a Robert Xavier Robineau.

There was one more item of interest in the file: a typed document on legal letterhead identifying itself as the last will and testament of Clayton Robineau. In it, she left all her professional equipment to Mary Pat Sutherland (also named her executor) and everything else to her sister, Hunter Patterson of Clayton, Louisiana. Odd, Talba thought, that so young a woman had thought to make a will—especially someone who lived as if she hadn't a penny. She compared the dates on the will and the divorce decree. Odder still that she was married at the time and hadn't named her husband her beneficiary. She plucked the will from the file for Mary Pat, someone she hoped to meet very soon.

Finding nothing else in the files, she made herself go back to the private areas of the house—go through the dresser drawers, the medicine cabinet, the closet. And still she found nothing—most notably no drugs, prescription or otherwise, except birth control pills.

She took a final spin around the living room, gazing idly at the bookcases, noting that Babalu sure didn't go in for cheap escapist reading. There were several shelves of poetry, and nearly everything else was some kind of Jungian tome or health-related paperback, many published by presses unknown to the general public. A whole shelf was devoted to religion—every kind you could name. How on earth, Talba wondered, did people live without fiction? She was about to pick up her things and leave when a book caught her eye that seemed very different from the others—much bigger, more important, and a little tattered. A Bible? she wondered. She pulled it from the shelf.

It wasn't a Bible. It was what alcoholics call the Big Book, and it was well read and well thumbed. If she had to guess, Talba would have said the reader and thumber was Babalu herself. That might to some extent explain her Spartan life-style, which gave new meaning to the term "clean and sober."

A last-minute look for frozen assets alongside the ice cream, and Talba was out of there. Not till she'd padded down the stairs and locked the door did she admit to herself how creepy the whole thing had been. She didn't blame Jason for deserting her.

She found him at one of the tables outside Whole Foods with a sandwich in front of him, only he seemed to find it as appetizing as a nice rodent stew. He was staring at the crowd in front of Lola's, across the street. Talba said, "I'll eat it if you don't want it." It was a vegetarian version of a muffaletta. She thought that he was probably a meat-eater who'd ordered the veggie muff for a reason—because Babalu would have—and now he was sorry. Watching him, she tried to memorize his face, and the way the sandwich looked, and the hopeless set of his body. The moment was a poem, and she tucked it away for safekeeping.

He pushed the sandwich over to her. "I guess I'm not hungry."

Talba nibbled at it, not sure she was either. "Tell me something, Jason. Why are the police so sure this was a suicide? They left her datebook and Rolodex—surely they wouldn't have if they'd had any other ideas."

"The police say there was a note on her desk. I didn't even see it. They found it."

"Did they show it to you?"

"Yes." His eyes looked far past her.

"What did it say?"

"It wasn't a note. It was a poem." He still didn't meet her eyes.

She was silent, and eventually it paid off.

"It was about betrayal. The title was 'To Jason.' "

She couldn't stop herself from gasping. Catching her breath, she said, "Jason, I don't know what to say."

He shrugged.

"I mean . . ." Should she say it? ". . . that sounds pretty convincing. I'm sorry. I'm so sorry." For him and for her role in it.

His eyes came back into focus and turned on her angrily, passionately. "Listen, there's a lot more to it. First of all, she must have written twenty poems called 'To Jason,' about everything you could name. Some were funny, some complained about me, some were love poems. It was one of the ways she communicated—one of the things I loved best about her. I know that poem. She read it to me the night before she died."

"She what?"

"Talba, I knew all about you and your report. She confronted me about it. And we didn't break up. She was angry, she felt betrayed, but we didn't break up. I told her what I told you and she agreed she hadn't been herself. She said she'd give me another chance. And she read me the poem and we both cried."

Talba realized she hadn't even asked when he saw her last. *Whoo, that's what I get for assuming. Eddie would kill me if he knew. I know what I'd have done with that information— dumped him on his butt. I guess I just thought anyone would.*

"You mean you were at her house the night before she died?"

"Not exactly. This happened on the phone."

"You must have told the police."

He nodded emphatically. "Told them and told them. They just keep saying there's nothing to point to murder. No forced entry, I guess they mean. And in their minds, there's a suicide note; ergo, it's suicide. They found the poem on the desk, right by the report."

"Well, where do they think she got the heroin?" Talba spoke more loudly than she meant to, causing passersby to stare.

In contrast, Jason's voice was almost a whisper. "I don't know."

She exhaled, ready to go on to another subject. "Well, look—did you know she'd made a will?"

"A will?" He looked utterly amazed.

"Several years ago." She handed it over. "Mary Pat's the executor. You know what that means? It means the family doesn't control her property quite yet—Mary Pat does. Do you realize there's a whole drawer of poems in there?" She hoped he'd take the hint. Legally, the poems probably belonged to the sister, Hunter Patterson, but Talba was afraid Hunter might not appreciate them.

When Jason said nothing, Talba continued, "Mary Pat could perform a rescue mission—I mean, keep them safe for Hunter. For a little while maybe."

She knew that what she was doing was unprofessional, but she couldn't help it. What if the estranged Patterson family simply tossed their hated daughter's life's work in the garbage? Talba had always thought certain things were more important than the law; it was one of her continuing arguments with Eddie.

"What's Mary Pat like?" she asked.

"Mary Pat? She's kind of wonderful. Curly red hair, dresses like a gypsy. Laughs a lot. She might be into Wicca or something—she sure wears a lot of jewelry."

"Does she like poetry?"

"I don't think I've ever talked to her about it. But she loves Babalu—they were college roommates. Loved," he said quickly.

Talba nodded. Good enough, she thought.

"Listen, Talba, I've been thinking—I wonder if you'd do me a favor?"

"Like get those poems out of there? Sure, I would."

He actually cracked a smile. "No, I'll get Mary Pat to take care of it. I was wondering if you'd go to the funeral with me."

She was taken aback. "Me? What for? I'd stick out like the proverbial thumb."

He looked sheepish. "Uh, yeah. That's why I'm asking you. See, they won't throw a black person out—they couldn't."

"And you think they'd throw you out? Come on—nobody throws anybody out of a funeral."

"Her dad told me if I come he'll personally whip my ass.

The cops told the family about the poem and the client report."

"Hold it here. Just wait a minute. You think my being there would stop him from whipping your ass? That's question one. Question two is, why would you want to go to this thing?" She didn't say it, but if she were the family, she wouldn't want him there either.

"She was afraid of them, Talba. I can't leave her alone with them."

She wondered if he knew how crazy he sounded. "Why was she afraid of them?"

"Because they were horrible to her."

"Abusive, you mean?"

"If extreme nastiness constitutes abuse, then yes, they were abusive, even in the last few months. As for childhood stuff, I don't know." He shook his head. "I just don't know. All I know is, she used to shudder when she mentioned them."

"Mentioned which one? Her mom or her dad?"

"All of them, though not by name, especially. Just 'my family.' The funeral's Saturday. It's really, really important to me to go. Say you'll come with me."

It would probably complicate matters, but she assented. For one thing, she wanted to say good-bye herself. For another, she wanted to meet these people her friend had been afraid of.

"One more thing." Talba indicated the date book. "Did you look at her schedule for the day she died?" She turned to it. "Only two clients all day—and both were in the morning. Did she die in the morning or afternoon?"

"They said she'd been dead no more than two hours. But Tuesday was her yoga day. She went at noon and usually came"—he looked around, as if surprised—"well, here, actually, for lunch afterward. Got home by two-thirty or three. She didn't have regulars Tuesday afternoons, but she'd take emergencies. She always liked to leave room in her schedule in case someone needed her."

"Don't I know it. Well, what I'm getting at here—" She focused on the week she'd had her own emergency. "What

I'm getting at is whether she had clients whose names she didn't write down. I see she did, because I came in the week before. My name's not here."

Jason only nodded sadly. She could tell he'd already been over this territory in his own mind.

In the end, neither one of them ate the veggie muff. Talba didn't even have the heart to take it home for later.

Once in her own space, when she could take the time, she went through Babalu's Rolodex and date book minutely, checking each name in the datebook against the Rolodex; identifying regular clients; trying to figure out if Babalu had anyone new in her life; seeing who she needed to talk to.

Only one name seemed out of context. There was no Rolodex entry for a Donny Troxell—someone Babalu had met for coffee recently—and no follow-up to the coffee date. Another name was conspicuously absent—that of her ex-husband, Rob Robineau.

Chapter Seven

Talba could kiss the kind of parents who gave their children middle names like "Xavier." Who could be easier to find than a Robert Xavier Robineau? She had him before she went to bed that night, and the next morning at seven-thirty, she was standing at his door.

This was another trick Eddie'd taught her. If ever there was a time when people were home, it was before their day got started. The hell of it was, it meant starting her own day about two hours before she was ready to get up. But it worked. She had to hand it to the old man—it nearly always worked.

Robineau lived in a scuzzy part of Metairie, out near Causeway. There were a lot of dirt-cheap apartments here—perfectly clean and decent, just no-frills—and Robineau had found himself one. Fortunately, it was the kind of apartment complex where you couldn't do any serious yelling without letting all the neighbors in on your business.

Talba knocked but got no answer. But she knew perfectly well he was home, because she'd first checked to see if his car was in its assigned garage slot. She knocked again, this time following up with a little speech, delivered with dignity, "Mr. Robineau, I have some bad news for you."

Still no answer. Very well then. Another knock, another speech, louder: "Mr. Robineau, I'm sorry to tell you your ex-wife has passed away. I'm Talba Wallis of E. V. Anthony Associates, and I need to talk to you about the will."

This time he answered. He was unshaven, wore only a pair of jeans pulled on over a pair of jockey shorts, the frayed waistband of which showed underneath. He was tall, thin, superficially a lot like Jason. But cruder. A whole lot cruder.

His hair was coarse and a little dirty. His features, despite his name, seemed more Irish than French. He did have the blue eyes Babalu was fond of, but this pair was small and mean. The most arresting thing about him was his tattoos—nasty black and green ones all over his chest, right shoulder, and arms. Talba had disliked Babalu's tattoo because of what it seemed to mean, but these she hated on aesthetic grounds. They were the carnival-art type—grotesque heads and skulls; swords and spiderwebs. She had no idea what would cause a person to want such things on his body, unless it made him feel tough. Likelier, it was just an outer reflection of the inner man. She wondered if the pictures were metaphors for what went on in this man's head, his own dark form of poetry. It was a chilling notion.

The man was looking at her sleepily, obviously having answered the door for no other reason than to keep her from entertaining his neighbors at further length. She didn't give him a chance to speak: "Robert Robineau?"

He said, "You say something about somebody dying?"

She nodded solemnly. "Clayton Robineau. I'm sorry."

"Clayton?" he asked.

"May I come in?"

She couldn't tell if he was really rattled or just pretending to be. He stepped aside for her.

The whole apartment smelled of smoke so stale it nearly made her gag. Ashtrays everywhere were filled to capacity. Empty beer cans were all over the floor and coffee table, along with plates of half-eaten food and a greasy pizza carton. The furniture looked like salvage.

"Maid's day off," he said. "Sit down."

"No thanks. This won't take long." It might, but she wasn't about to sit in this place.

"Clayton's my ex-wife," he said, reaching for a pack of cigarettes and shaking one out. "She get in an accident or something? Clayton's young. She wouldn't just die."

"Have you been in touch with her lately?"

He finished lighting the cigarette. "No, I—" Then he turned to her, shaking the match. "You tryin' to tell me somethin'? She was using again, right?"

Talba's eyes flicked to the man's arms. Sure. Track marks. He looked like a druggie, he smelled like a druggie, and he was one. She said, "Are you telling me Clayton was an addict?"

But she knew the answer before he spoke—it fit with the Big Book, it fit with this man, and it fit perfectly with the suicide theory. Her family would have told the police she was a former druggie—thus, the cops probably would conclude that heroin had been her death of choice; at the very least, that she knew how to score some. The thing made beautiful sense if you looked at it that way. But you could turn it around just as easily—it perfectly explained why Babalu's killer would choose such a cumbersome method.

Because if that was her history, it was just about the only kind of death you could name that would really look like suicide. Far from the ignorant protestations of Jason—and of Talba herself—it actually would be in character. Bablau owned neither prescription pills nor a gun and had no history with either. But Talba was willing to bet her license she did with heroin.

Robineau made a guttural noise that may have been what he used for a laugh. "Yeah, she was an addict. Big time. 'Zat how she died?"

"What kind of addict?"

"Heroin. What else?"

Talba said, "You, too, Mr. Robineau?" She looked point-edly at his track marks.

He didn't even take the bait. "We had a grand old time, the rich bitch and me. Hey, sit down, why don't you? I'm gonna get a beer. Want one?"

By now it was nearly eight A.M., about eleven hours too early for a beer, in Talba's estimation. Still, she might as well sit. Her legs felt a little weak. She found a plain wooden chair.

Returning with a Bud, Robineau plopped on the sofa. "You say something about the will?"

Talba dodged that one. "You don't seem very upset by your wife's death."

He made the unfunny guttural noise again. "Ex-wife, dar-lin'. Ex. Nah, I'm not upset. Why should I be? The bitch has been out of my life a long time."

"Why do you keep calling her a bitch?"

He thought about it a minute, finally shrugged from the waist up. "Figure of speech, I guess. Clayton and I had some good times. Parted on bad terms, though."

"Oh?"

"Yeah." He took a big slug of beer and passed a hand across his mouth. "We were into some pretty heavy shit. She—I don't know—found God or something, We used to fight all the time."

"You mean she got in a treatment program?"

"Yeah, I guess she did eventually. She cleaned up—came around and gave that speech they have to give, you know?"

"The ninth step."

"Huh?"

"That's what they call it in the twelve-step programs. Mak-ing amends. She apologized to you for any trouble between you—is that what you mean?"

"Yeah, that must have been what it was." He was quiet a moment and Talba could have almost sworn she saw a mo-mentary fleck of sadness in his eyes. "Man, that's some stupid shit!"

"What? Getting clean?"

"Nah. Nah, I respect her for that. Just that God-stuff amends crap."

"What do you do for a living, Mr. Robineau?"

"Construction, mostly. Painting; whatever."

"You're a carpenter?"

The guttural sound again. "Yeah, when I feel like it."

"How'd you meet Baba—I mean, Clayton?" Talba wasn't sure how long she was going to get away with this—asking seemingly idle questions—but she figured she might as well keep at it till he clammed up.

"What'd you call her?"

"She changed her name. Didn't you know that?"

"No. No, I didn't know it." He was suddenly subdued. "Why'd she do a thing like that?"

"I think it may have had to do with pursuing a spiritual path. Starting a new life, maybe. Why does that surprise you?"

He looked distinctly uncomfortable. "No reason."

"Did you see her after you separated?"

"Naah! I tried to." He gave Talba a kind of guilty half smile. "She got a restraining order."

Oho, Talba thought. She was beginning to get the hang of things. "Did you have a violent relationship?"

Robineau shrugged again, this time a small, almost involuntary gesture—it was funny, Talba thought, how vivid people's body language became when you could actually see their muscles work. "Towards the end, maybe. A little."

"How'd you two meet, anyway?"

"She used to hang out at the same bar I did. I liked her tattoo."

"So she drank then, too."

"Whoooeee, baby! There wasn't nothin' that broad didn't do. Bet your booty she drank. Drank, smoked, snorted, shot up . . ." He paused for effect. "Fucked." He looked at Talba sidewise to see if he was shocking her. "Oh, man, did she fuck."

"They have twelve-step programs for that too."

All of a sudden, he reared up, furious for some reason.

"Hey, who are you, anyway? Comin' in here first thing in the morning, askin' questions . . . you ain't a cop, are you?"

Completely nuts, she thought. *A raver. I need to get a purse big enough for my Tee-ball bat.* But she wasn't scared yet. She stood her ground. "I told you. I came about the will." She'd dressed in a business suit, hoping to pass for a lawyer.

"What about the will?"

"Tell me something, Mr. Robineau—do you think Clayton could have committed suicide? Did she have it in her?"

"Oh, man! Oh, man, if I had to guess, I'd say that's how it happened. Used to threaten it all the time. I used to believe her too. Once I even called her country club parents who wouldn't speak to either of us—man! I wouldn't ever do that again."

"Why not?"

"Oh, they sent her asshole brother down here, threatening to haul her ass off to the bin. Had to deck him to get rid of him."

Robineau'd probably decked Clayton too, quite a few times, which might explain why she'd made her will—she was afraid of dying and didn't want Mr. Wonderful to benefit. But if she was so suicidal, how had she summoned the courage to get out of the marriage?

"She was one sad sack of a woman." Robineau lit another cigarette, shook the match out, and gazed at the blue smoke as if it were inducing a trance, taking him back to a life he'd all but forgotten. His own face was sad as he spoke.

"She always said I didn't love her. Now why did she do that? Nobody could have loved her more than I did. I'd tell her that, ask her why she said it, and she'd say nobody could love her, that she wasn't loveable. You imagine anybody saying that? What the hell's a thing like that about?"

Talba was silent, wondering the same thing. Every family had an outcast, whether or not he lived at home—Talba's father was the one in her family. Babalu seemed to have been literally cast out.

Talba began to gather up her belongings in as officious a manner as she could muster. "Mr. Robineau, you've been very kind. I'm sorry to bring up such an unpleasant subject, but we were wondering if you know if Clayton made a will?"

He pulled back in an almost literal double-take. "Me? How would I know?"

She stood, afraid he was going to do the mad-bull turn again. "Well, it was a long shot. We haven't been able to find one, and we have to turn over every rock. I'm sure you understand."

Instead of getting violent, Robineau went childish on her. His mouth turned down, and his shoulders drooped. He removed the cigarette from his lips, as if the pleasure had gone out of smoking it. "I thought you came to tell me she'd left me something."

Talba gave him a professional shrug. "Well, I wouldn't rule it out at this point. We'll let you know as soon as we locate a will."

Liar, liar, pants on fire. Eddie'd taught her well.

There were times when Eddie thought maybe it was worth it to go back to computer-wrangling. Never, in all the years since he'd hung out his shingle, had he had a client die on him—certainly not the day after he turned in his report.

Though he could not, hard as he tried, make this Ms. Wallis's fault, it still griped him. He wondered, not for the first time, if she were more trouble than she was worth. But he had had the temerity to mention this at dinner the night before, when his daughter Angie happened to be over, only to be met with a double female chorus of ridicule, from Angie and Audrey both. He could see why Angie felt this way— she and Ms. Wallis were two peas in a pod, except that they were different colors—but why Audrey took up for Ms. Wallis was beyond him. What she said was that having competent help lowered his blood pressure, and what he said was, it damn sure might if he could just find any.

Usually, that was just banter, though, because he really did appreciate Ms. Wallis's computer skills. Not only that, he liked her voice. She might have the most beautiful voice of any woman he'd ever heard. It was so smooth and sugary and thick (yet tangy), it reminded him of butterscotch. If she'd ever write something pretty instead of that angry-black-girl stuff, she'd probably become an international star and leave on her own accord.

But for now, he was stuck with her—her and her dead client and the damn GPS she'd installed in his car. At least she had the good sense to consult him about what to do now. She was in his office, running it down for him—what the boyfriend (AKA "the new client") said, what the ex-husband said, what the cops thought. And now she was talking about going to some fancy-schmancy funeral in a town with the same name as the stiff. Who'd have guessed Tammy Tattoo was a runaway debutante?

He needed time to think. "Ms. Wallis, ya really think it's wise?"

"That's what I'm asking you, Eddie. I think it's a pretty bizarre request."

He shrugged. "Well, it's billable."

"This is about ethics, I thought. Is there some reason I shouldn't go? I mean, the family hates him—he's already said his reason for taking me is to keep them from throwing him out."

Suddenly it came clear to him. "Look at it this way, Ms. Wallis. Ya first loyalty is to ya client. It really don't make no never-mind what the family thinks. They're not ya client."

"On the other hand, if I've got to investigate this thing, I don't want to alienate them."

" 'Alienate' 'em. Can I ask ya something—you always gotta use a five-dollar word when a two-bit one'll do?"

"Always." She smiled at him, and he had the odd sensation she thought he was cute. Not cute like a hunk—cute like an amusing old geezer. It wasn't a cheering thought.

He flapped his arms. "Just go and be your own sweet self," he said. "Isn't that what Miz Clara would say?"

She looked him in the eye, the pretty smile gone, a perfect "11" over her nose. "Eddie, you think I'm wasting my time here? The police say it's suicide and the ex says it's suicide (although anybody'd be suicidal if they were married to him). Am I wasting this guy's money?"

"Well, what do you think?"

She covered the bottom half of her face with her hands and thought into the little pocket thus created. Finally, she said, "I don't think so. She was too hopeful a person, too positive to commit suicide. I just can't imagine anybody who'd want to kill her."

"Well, her family hated her, right? Then there was the boy-friend's girlfriend. Oh, yeah, and the ex who thought he was going to get something when she died. Hey, how about the sister who actually did? Maybe she plays the ponies or something."

"Eddie, are you making fun of me?"

He wasn't, actually. He was perfectly serious. "For Christ's sake, Ms. Wallis. Just round up the usual suspects."

"I bow," she said, "to your superior wisdom." And she actually did bow.

"For Christ's sake," he said again.

Chapter Eight

Her favorite thing about Eddie was the way he embarrassed so easily. Of course, it could be a pain when she wanted to exercise her usual vocabulary—as far as he was concerned public nakedness was preferable to profanity within the hearing of both sexes. But it was such sport to heap him with extravagant compliments and watch him squirm.

Besides, she really did respect him. He'd taught her a lot, despite being a royal pain. If he said go to the funeral Talba would go. Babalu was her friend, she might have gone anyway.

But one more thing to do first—it might help with the family to meet Mary Pat, get her on Talba's side. She could phone, but she was learning more and more that showing up on someone's doorstep was usually far the greater learning experience. If they tried to throw you out, they usually had something to hide, which was instructive in itself. If they didn't, you got a lot of bandwidth—appearance, expressions, body language, some sense of financial position and demographics, stuff you couldn't get on the phone. Eddie even claimed there were ways to tell if someone was lying—something to do with looking right, or maybe it was left. Not only couldn't she remember which direction it was, she couldn't even think to look and see if they did it.

But you learned stuff, anyhow—like in the case of Rob Robineau. A drunken, druggie, arrogant, violent, lowlife burnout. Would all that have come through on the phone?

What on earth had Babalu seen in him? Maybe, she thought, he reminded her of her daddy. It was so often the case.

Obviously, from the bequest, Mary Pat was also a bodyworker. She was much as Jason had described her, except that today she wasn't dressed like a gypsy, unless the gypsies had changed their national dress to overalls. "Cleaning," she said, waving a cloth. "It's what I do to relieve depression. Other people exercise, but that one's against my religion. I'm about to have a Diet Coke." Seeing Talba's expression, she said, "Listen, no one in the world's as pure as Babalu, certainly not little *moi*, and certainly not today. Want to split one with me?"

Talba couldn't help smiling. "Sure."

Mary Pat sat her down in a living room as cluttered as Babalu's was stark. "I'm glad to see you," she said. "I know Babalu thought the world of you—Clayton, I mean. We're going to have to get used to calling her Clayton if we're going to Clayton. You headed there? Want to go together?"

"I promised Jason I'd go with him. We could all go together if you like."

Mary Pat shook her head. "I can't. Sorry, but I'm too mad at him. I don't blame the family—I think he should stay away."

"You know about his hiring me, I presume?"

Mary Pat nodded, causing a pair of long, beaded earrings to swing as if caught in a high wind, but she didn't comment.

"Well? Do you think it's a bad idea?"

She shook her head as vigorously as she'd nodded, making the earrings change direction. "I'd love to believe Clayton didn't kill herself—but, face it, she had reason. I think he's just trying to assuage his guilt."

"You sound as if you don't like him."

"Under the circumstances, do you?"

Talba thought about it. "His pain is real. So far, I believe him when he says she was withdrawn the last few weeks—that she was the one who changed the relationship. But you'd know about that. Was it true?"

The redhead's face lost some of its defiance, its cocksureness. She stared at the street, through the window behind Talba. "I'm ashamed to say I don't know. You know how women grow apart when one gets in a relationship? You assume the other person doesn't have time for you; you don't call her as much."

Talba laughed. "It's usually true."

"Well, maybe it wasn't this time. Maybe I was the person who wasn't there for her. I'd forgotten how depressed she could get—I just assumed everything was going great between Jason and her. And all the time the bastard—"

"He says it wasn't like that—that he thought she was trying to dump him."

The woman's temper flared. "Why couldn't he be a man about it?"

Yes. Why couldn't he? It was the question women always asked when men behaved like boys—naughty boys, especially—and Talba had no answer for it.

She said, "I liked Babalu so much. But there was a lot I didn't know. I had no idea about the depression."

Mary Pat rocked her body back and forth. "Oh, yeah. She had it. Listen, Talba, she was capable of killing herself—if that's what you came here to ask, I hate to tell you, but she was. And her taste in men was horrible. It was one of the things that always got her down."

"I've met the husband."

Mary Pat shuddered. "At least Jason was better than Robbie Robineau."

"I found her will. Did Jason give it to you?"

"Yes, I remember when she made it. She feared for her life

at the time—darling Robbie was knocking her around. We finally had to get her to go to a women's shelter."

"Do you know about the drugs?"

Mary Pat looked down, avoiding the subject. "Yes." She raised her eyes. "We've been through a lot together, Clayton and me."

"How far back do you go?"

"College. She was an English major—all that poetry had to come from somewhere. I was into math, would you believe it?" And for the first time she laughed. Talba recalled that Jason had said she "laughed a lot." When she did, it made you feel good. "Various things got us both into the healing arts—most of them you don't want to know about."

It was the opening Talba was hoping for. "She said she took the name Babalu because of what she called 'the wounded healer' aspect."

Mary Pat gave a curt nod. "Oh, yes. She told everyone that—talk about wearing your heart on your sleeve."

"What was the wound, Mary Pat? What was she talking about?"

The woman snorted. "What wasn't she talking about? Heroin, abuse, divorce, you name it."

"Nothing else?"

"She hated her family, if that's what you mean."

"Why?"

Mary Pat only shrugged.

Sensing the end of the redhead's patience, Talba thanked her for her trouble and said her good-byes. She left feeling depressed, touched by Mary Pat's anger. Sure, Babalu had had it hard—yet she'd fought and come out the other end. To Talba, she seemed strong; to Mary Pat, apparently she didn't. Her best friend still saw her as having a broken wing, still in need of protection. Perhaps that's what their friendship had been about. No wonder the two grew apart when Babalu finally had a good relationship.

Semi-good, Talba reminded herself. *Only semi-good. He's not St. Jason yet.*

She was surprised, though. She hadn't liked Mary Pat as well as she expected to.

S he and Jason went to the funeral in separate cars. It had occurred to Talba that she might have work to do in Clayton afterward. She didn't need excess baggage.

It was a gorgeous day for a funeral. The little town of Clayton had a "historic district" and trees old enough to lend dignity. Under other circumstances, Talba would have enjoyed it. Today, it was as if she looked at it from a distance, as if it weren't really she who was there but a spy she'd sent to report back to her. She knew what this was about. It was part of the reaction she called turtling out—withdrawing into a shell when things got tough. Sometimes it took the form of going to bed and staring at the ceiling; today it was this feeling of distance. She wanted to fight it, but that might entail a loss of dignity she wasn't ready for. The last thing she wanted was to make a spectacle of herself.

Everyone was staring at her anyway, or at Jason and her together—the cheating boyfriend and the black PI who'd caught him out and then hooked up with the enemy. She questioned her good sense in coming.

The funeral was held in one of those smallish brick churches so common in small Southern towns. Though she'd been raised Baptist, Talba couldn't remember ever being in a white Baptist church. She'd been to one other funeral in her adult life, and it was that of a white person, but the church was Methodist, much larger and more urban. From the outside, she'd seen hundreds of little churches like this one and, now inside, she noted quickly that it held no surprises. As she'd expected, it was as plain and clean as a house in the suburbs. The pews were even made of the same light-colored oak you'd find in a new tract house.

So as to create as little stir as possible, she and Jason sat in the back. From their exile seats, they watched the family file in six strong, faces stern, jaws set. No tears that Talba saw. "The dad's named King and the mom's Deborah," Jason whispered. "Mary Pat filled me in. Then she had a sister, Hunter—weird name for a girl. . . ."

"No weirder than Clayton." If they'd been alone, she would have added, "What is it with white folks?" But this didn't seem the right place.

"The brother's King the Third."

"Don't tell me—they call him Trey."

"You got it. I don't know his wife's name."

"Looks like Hunter's divorced." She had a toddler with her but no man. The little girl was the only one in the family who wasn't decked out in black or navy. In her little pink dress, she looked like a Californian loose on the streets of New York. "What kind of person brings a baby to a funeral?"

The music started before Jason could answer the question, and by the third or fourth chord, Talba was sobbing. This had happened to her before, much to her dismay, at that other funeral—and she hadn't even known the deceased. It was just a phenomenon before, an oddity she couldn't explain, but this was true sadness, genuine feeling for Babalu and for other losses as well; she knew that. The music had the power to bring it all up. The feeling of being an observer was gone, as was everything, even the church, everything except the great waves of grief rolling out of her. So much for dignity.

She was sobbing so loud she would have been embarrassed if the music hadn't been louder still. When the hymn was over, she moved away from Jason slightly and worked on paring it down to a sniffle. The last thing she wanted was for him to put his arm around her. "Let us pray," she heard the minister say, and she took the opportunity to look over the crowd, which now stood blind and vulnerable, its collective eyes closed.

Once again, no surprises. Well-dressed, mostly white crowd, but there were a few people of color—more than Talba thought there'd be. The Patterson family maid was about all she'd expected. Mary Pat was near the front, wearing an olive dress with a double-tiered skirt and a lot of amber jewelry. There was always somebody who didn't own funeral clothes—if she'd thought about it, she'd have picked Mary Pat.

A couple of celebrities studded the crowd—United States Senator Susan Schultz and gubernatorial candidate Buddy Calhoun, whom Talba intended to vote for. In addition, she recognized John Earl Macquet, a New Orleans businessman whose wife had recently died of the classic pills-and-alcohol one-two punch. Friends of the family, probably.

She couldn't see the Pattersons all that well with everyone standing, but so far as she could tell, they were running true to stereotype. Deborah was one of those birdlike women with the perfect figures and the ever-so-smooth coiffeurs. King was a big man, blustery looking, with white hair. King Three was overweight, Hunter a little frazzled; there had to be more, but from a distance, that was it.

They sang another hymn and sat down.

"We've come to say good-bye to our daughter, and sister, and friend, Clayton Patterson," the minister said, and Talba thought crankily, *Tell me something I don't know*. But she hardly bargained for what came next.

"Clayton was a person who never had a moment's peace in her poor, sad young life. It was a life of attack and betrayal—a pattern repeated over and over. First by someone she loved and trusted; later by Clayton herself, and finally by others she loved and trusted."

His eyes traveled to the back of the church, and for a moment Talba thought he was looking at Jason. But surely not—no one would be that tacky.

"From the moment of that first horrible brutality—you in this congregation all know whereof I speak—from that moment on, our daughter Clayton lost her faith in human nature. And with that, she lost her way. And she never found it again." Here, his voice dropped and he bowed his head, as if he were talking about someone who'd become a triple murderer.

Talba whispered, "What's he talking about?"

Jason's forehead furrowed. "I have absolutely no idea."

"Our daughter was lost to us from that moment. She never

came back to our town; or to her loving family; or to God. All because of the destructive act of one violent human being, our daughter was lost—to drugs, to drink, to depravity—and later to false gods and golden idols."

Talba wanted to scream. She wanted to jump up and shout the man down. Jason was pale and his mouth was tight, moving slightly at the corners: he was fighting the same thing she was. Neither could say anything, and both knew it. *Mary Pat, please!* she thought. *Stop this unctuous asshole. Get up and say who she really was. Don't let these people get away with this crap.*

But there was never a place in the service where friends were invited to talk. Midway through the tooth-grinding banalities about how "our daughter" had suffered one disappointment after another, and then at last "one final betrayal" and was "driven to take her own life," Jason took Talba's hand and tried to break every bone in it. Talba didn't even ask him to let up. Focusing on the physical pain was better than giving way to the psychic pain.

She tried to tune it out—thought about how glad she was that she'd come. Jason could have reported this, but she'd never in a million years have pictured anything nearly so extreme, no matter what he said.

And then she thought about killing the minister. In the end, she made a vow—to right this wrong; the wrong done in the pulpit this Saturday morning. She still only half believed Babalu had been murdered, had yet to get outraged on that account. But this was beyond outrage. This was not salt but fire and acid in the wound. *It must be avenged*, she thought, much as the Reverend Scruggs might have.

Jason kept getting redder and squeezing her hand harder; Talba hoped he'd hang onto his temper. He made it, just. When the last note of the last hymn had been sung, he said, "Who the hell does that asshole think he is? He just crucified her."

As far as Talba was concerned, that was old news. "What

on earth do you think happened to her? Could she have gotten pregnant or something?"

"I have absolutely no idea. Come on, we're going to the cemetery."

"I don't think that's a good idea. Low-profile seems like the way to go—or as low as you can manage when you're an inkspot on a white sheet."

He didn't smile. "I'm going. They aren't getting away with this."

She shrugged. "Let's go together then."

Once they were in Jason's car, she started in. "Listen, you aren't planning to do anything, are you?"

"I'm going to punch 'em out. Methodically. One by one. Men, women, and children."

"Look, do you want me to work on this case? Do you really think a single one of them's going to talk to me if you make the slightest ripple? The best thing you could possibly do is impress them with what a gentleman you are." He didn't answer, which gave her more time to think about it. "Besides, Babalu would have wanted it that way."

He hit the steering wheel with a fist. "Yeah. I guess she would."

In the end Talba was glad they'd gone. Not that many people had. Just the immediate family, Mary Pat, a black woman—the maid, Talba thought—and six or eight other people, all of whose lives, from the looks of them, revolved around the local country club.

In the sun and the quiet, she was able to dissociate herself from the horror of the church and really say good-bye to her friend. She took pleasure in watching Jason introduce himself to each member of the family and tell them how much he'd loved their daughter. King Jr.—Big King, they probably called him—looked as if he'd been eating sour apples, but obviously he couldn't bring himself to whip Jason's ass right here in the cemetery.

Talba seized the moment to buttonhole Mary Pat. "What'd you think of the service?"

Mary Pat was crying. "Oh, Talba, she was right. These people are savages!" Talba liked her better all of a sudden. "They ought not to be allowed to live."

"What happened to her? What was the minister talking about?"

"I swear to God I haven't the least idea."

Chapter Nine

"**Y**ou're her best friend. She must have talked to you
about it."

The redhead shrugged. "Okay, I knew there was something.
I just figured her father molested her. That's the thing people
usually don't talk about. But I don't think that's what that
slimeball meant. This is something the whole town knew
about. Listen, she had a shrink—she was talking to somebody; I sure wasn't going to press her about it. You know,
half the time—I'm ashamed to say this, but half the time
people say they have some awful traumatic thing in their pasts
that's just too wounding to talk about, and once you find out
what it is, it seems almost trivial. You know what I mean?

"I mean, not trivial—but not anything that hasn't happened
to a lot of people—and something they really ought to just
get over. Do I sound harsh? It's terrible for them and all, but
you just want to shake them and say, 'Move on; enough already.' Well, Clayton was moving on, and she wasn't dram-
atizing, and frankly, I didn't even want to hear about it—
that's what shrinks are for." She gave her head a shake, which

made the beaded strands of her earrings click together.

"But you're the one who said you'd been through so much together—divorce, heroin . . ."

"But this other thing happened earlier. We didn't have to talk about it. There was too much bad stuff happening today to worry about yesterday."

In one way the minister'd been right, Talba thought—Babalu really had had her share of bad luck. It was just too bad he couldn't see how well she'd come out of it.

Whatever "it" was, though, she was determined to find out before the day was over. Glad she'd brought her rental car, she packed Jason off and headed for the parish library. To her immense relief, the librarian was a black woman. For a moment Talba considered asking her if she knew the story herself, but she was in her twenties—perhaps a bit young to have known Clayton.

After ascertaining that the librarian did, indeed, have microfilm of the *Clayton Weekly Courier*, she asked for the three years that Clayton Patterson would have been in high school. This was one of Talba's least favorite forms of research— why, oh, why, couldn't all these things be online? But she endured the tedium long enough to plough through Clayton's sophomore year and most of her junior year before she finally found what she was looking for—a banner headline shouting BANKER'S DAUGHTER SCALPED.

The first three paragraphs told the story:

> Clayton Patterson, daughter of Mr. and Mrs. King Patterson, remains in guarded condition today after being attacked by an intruder who broke into her bedroom and inflicted severe scalp wounds with a machete.
>
> Only hours after the attack, sheriff's deputies arrested Donny Troxell, 17, a classmate of Miss Patterson's at Clayton High School. The injured girl's father said the two had been dating, but his daughter had recently broken up with Troxell.

Talba's heart speeded up: she'd seen the name Donny Troxell before, and recently—in Clayton's datebook. Trying to ignore the pounding, she plowed on.

Sheriff Dickie Ransdell told the *Courier* he had "incontrovertible evidence" that Troxell was the assailant.

The evidence turned out to be a blood-stained, hair-bearing machete, which had been found in Troxell's car.

Talba pressed on, finding about fifteen more stories as Clayton recovered and Troxell was brought to trial. The girl's injuries were gruesomely detailed: she'd been attacked from the left, the machete shearing several inches of scalp cleanly away from her skull, yet, fortunately, leaving it attached by a thread. Eventually, after several surgeries, some of them performed by a New Orleans plastic surgeon, she'd made a complete recovery.

Throughout, from the first story to the sentencing, she claimed she never saw her attacker.

Talba thought back to the tiny scar she noticed the week before Clayton died—she'd known her for years and never seen it.

The paper even ran pictures of Clayton in various stages of her recovery—with head shaved and stitches showing; with an inch of hair and hideous scars; and so forth, until she was once more a beautiful high school girl.

Ye gods, Talba thought, *no wonder she couldn't stand to talk about it. This is worse than the injury.*

The young Clayton must have been hell-bent on revenge to permit it. That in itself was a measure of how much she'd changed before becoming the Babalu Talba knew.

At any rate, it worked—that and the "incontrovertible evidence." Troxell was convicted and sentenced to fifteen years at Angola.

Talba wondered if he'd served the whole sentence. Perhaps so—the timing was almost right. The crime took place sixteen years ago; his name had appeared in Babalu's appointment book a few weeks before she died.

Maybe he got out and came after her again, she thought. *How did the police miss this?*

But it was easy to see how they had—they didn't know about the scalping and no one bothered to tell them, since they reported a heroin overdose and a suicide note to the family. To anyone who didn't believe she was far too healthy in mind and body to go back to heroin, it looked open and shut. But, obviously, no one in Clayton fell into that category.

I wonder, Talba thought, *if I've just solved the case*. She couldn't wait to talk to Eddie about it.

But on the drive home, she found the person she needed most to talk to was Darryl. The newspaper's black-and-white images of Clayton, hurt and healing, pitiful, vulnerable, miserable, wouldn't leave her. She needed the warmth of his arms around her. She'd encountered violence in her own childhood—unlike Jason, Darryl knew about it. And he knew how to make her forget it.

Today, he chose to do it (quite unwittingly) by announcing that he'd all but sewed up the Subaru—only it was an Isuzu Trooper.

"Is that better or worse?" she said.

"Well, the main thing is, it's gray, which makes it almost invisible. Nobody'd notice it on surveillance."

"Ummm. A ghost car—I like it. Does it run?"

"It sure does. I took the liberty of having it checked out. We can go right over and see it now."

At that, her eyes filled with tears; she turned quickly away.

"What is it?"

She couldn't tell him what it was; it was gratitude, and not just for the car. She blurted: "Babalu had a boyfriend who scalped her."

"What?"

She knew he had heard her. It was just that the thing seemed so unlikely one had the need to have it repeated. On the way to see the car, she told him the story.

He said, "You think Troxell did it?"

"He's one hell of a grudge holder if he did."

"He'd have to be nuts."

"Well, isn't anybody who kills someone?"

"I don't know. Some people kill for gain."

"But don't they have a fundamental screw loose?"

They'd had this conversation before; Darryl took a slightly more cynical view of human nature than she did. "I don't know," he said. "What about drug dealers, polluters, insurance companies who don't provide the services they're supposed to—people die because of all of them. And they'd all tell you they're just trying to make a living."

"Well, anyway, this wouldn't be gain—I guess the motive would be revenge."

"For breaking up with him when he was a kid?"

"Like I said. Screw loose. Makes me think twice about trying to see him alone."

"A cop wouldn't do it without backup—why should you?" He looked at her sidewise but not with any real disapproval. He wasn't at all overprotective—in fact, hardly ever seemed to worry about her. She liked that; she was a worrier herself.

"Because I'd have to take Eddie, that's why. What kind of backup would that be?"

"You know, Baroness—"

"Your Grace will do."

"Did Your Grace ever think about getting a ladylike little firearm?"

Her tears came again. "You know I can't do that." She had an extremely unpleasant history with guns.

"Oops. Sorry."

"Oh, forget about it. Are we getting close?"

"Almost there." They were across the river, on what was always called the West Bank, though you had to go east to get there, in a neighborhood where a lot of the homes had bars on the windows.

"Bet the car's a wreck," she said.

"I told you—I've seen it. I think some mini-gangster bought it and then got a better car—hardly ever drove it. Too ashamed."

Actually, he exaggerated. It had a hundred thousand miles on it and was owned by a perfectly nice-seeming man who said he was a manager for the Burlington Coat Factory, but who knew? Maybe he dealt rock in a back room of his house. He did have a nice new Lincoln Navigator, destined to be vandalized soon, Talba thought, considering the neighborhood.

"Uh-uh," Darryl said later. "They're all afraid of him."

She had no idea if he was joking or not. But she did like the car. For one thing, she liked riding up high. For another, it was neither new enough nor shabby enough for anyone to take much notice of. And it was cheap, which was the deciding factor.

She wrote the nice man who might be a gangster a modest check and followed Darryl to his house, where she christened her new car by ceremoniously transferring to it her maps, tape recorder, two cameras, binoculars, and Teeball bat. Then the two of them returned the rental car and went shopping for groceries. "Tonight I'm cooking," she'd announced earlier. He cooked for her so much she felt guilty. "Miz Clara's famous fried chicken, coming right up."

"Awww. Can't we just have quiche or something?"

His little joke. She could fry chicken nearly as well as her mother, who was famous for it at Baptist church potlucks. When he had eaten plenty of it, and some rice and gravy she made as well, he talked a little about his daughter, and his worsening problems with her. While Darryl-the-pedagogue argued for therapy, Kim, his ex, had a different plan for solving the problem—she wanted Raisa to see less of Darryl. "Kimmie says I upset her," he explained. "Being away from home 'disturbs her schedule.' "

Much as Raisa terrified her, Talba was enraged. "What is that woman thinking? I'd say 'that bitch,' but I know she's your daughter's mother. . . ."

"Oh, Talba, come on. Anger never solved anything."

"The hell it didn't! Swear to God I could kill her for treating you like that."

He was getting upset. "Let's change the subject, shall we?"

"You always change the subject when I get upset."

"Well, who wants all that energy coming at them? Calm down, will you?"

"You sound like Miz Clara."

"You should listen to your mama." His voice was teasing; he was getting over it. "So listen, let's talk about *your* problem. The question of the unknown sister."

"Not only do you change the subject, you throw it back on me."

"This is what schoolteachers do."

"Okay, then, since you're so interested in my problem, maybe you'd like to go to church with me tomorrow."

"We're going to pray for resolution?"

She considered. "It's a thought. But not my first one. Lura was a Methodist, but no one knows anything else about her. So I'm going to see if anyone remembers her at her old church."

In the end, Darryl pleaded that the shock of seeing Talba in church might cause him to have a heart attack, and not only that, he had Raisa. So Talba went to church alone. She was pretty sure she knew the church Lura Blanchard meant when she said "that one by Claiborne." She had a perfect mental picture of it but no memory of ever having been inside. When she saw the sanctuary, however, it was as familiar to her as Miz Clara's church. She had undoubtedly been taken there, probably more than once, by her father and his woman.

What she needed was someone as old as Miz Clara, someone who'd been there then. Shouldn't be hard, she thought, looking around. The place was full of fossils. And so, after the service, she simply asked around.

"Hello, I'm Talba Wallis. I'm wondering if you remember a woman who used to be a member of this congregation? Lura, her name was. She had a baby daughter, but I don't know her last name." She might have added, "And a man friend named Denman LaRose Wallis," but she couldn't bring herself to say it.

Some of them thought they remembered Lura, but they really couldn't put a face to the name; most looked blank. And, finally, an old man in suspenders said, "You need to talk to Sister Eula. She know everybody ever set foot in this church."

All the bystanders said that was sure right, and the hunt for Sister Eula began, though she wasn't in the least hard to find. Sister Eula loomed large not only in their hearts but also in other ways—and so did her hat. It was the size and color of a lemon pie, exactly matching her form-fitting plus-size suit, which was smartly trimmed in black. Her skin color was light—the word *camel*, for some reason, came to mind. Her cheeks were round and heavily rouged; her voice was at least as imposing as her form. It seemed to come from her solar plexus rather than her larynx. Word got to her before Talba did. "I hear you are looking for Miss Lura Jones."

The woman was such a diva Talba almost forgot she was a baroness. "I . . . uh . . ." *If it's all right with you*, she thought. *If not, I'll just be going now.* "Yes," she finally managed.

"Speak up, child, I don't bite."

Ouch, you just did. "I'm looking for someone named Lura. I'm not sure about the last name."

"You are not a relative?"

"Not a blood relative, no."

"I am sorry to tell you that Miss Jones passed away some years ago."

"Oh. Well." Talba pretended to rethink the whole thing. "But there was a daughter," she said slowly, as if it were just dawning on her. "Wasn't there a daughter?"

Sister Eula drew up herself up another four or five inches—as if she could be more intimidating. She made

Miz Clara look like a pussycat. "I wouldn't know about that."

"Oh, there was. There was a baby, and I'm pretty sure it was a girl."

"You got good news for that girl? You a detective or something?"

Talba was taken aback. Did the woman know her? What the hell, why not go with that idea? She almost produced her license, but thought better of it even as her hand rummaged her purse for her wallet—the woman might recognize her last name. She finally opted for a friendly smile and a cocked eyebrow. "I didn't know it was so obvious."

"Who are you, girl?" Miss Eula was getting hostile, and Talba wasn't sure why.

"I'm trying to find her for a relative. My client believes she may be a cousin by marriage."

Talba suddenly found her heart was beating as hard as it had when the five-hundred-pound sergeant threatened to throw her in jail.

Sister Eula stared a hole through her. "Mmmm-hmmm," she said, and Talba had the sense that she knew exactly who she was. If her father Denman had come to this church with his woman, they'd remember. Or Sister Eula would. She looked at Talba as if she could penetrate every secret she had just by thinking hard enough. It was the look Miz Clara had used when she was a kid and she was lying.

Talba didn't know what to do but stare back at her, trying to keep her heart from breaking through her ribs and making a mess in this fine church.

Finally, Sister Eula said, "You all right, child. You all right."

Are you a doctor? Talba thought. *What's the deal here?*

"I recollect Miss Lura had a sister. Mozelle Winters, her name was. I b'lieve she moved to Memphis." And Sister Eula turned her back and flounced away, as if she were offended.

Chapter Ten

W*hat was that?* Talba thought. *A gypsy fortuneteller or a church lady? Sergeant Rouselle's mama, maybe?*

She couldn't wait to go home and get online. But in the end, what she found for Mozelle Winters was absolutely nothing.

And then an axiom of Eddie's came back to her: always call information first.

I'm an idiot, she thought, and dialed impatiently. But so far as BellSouth knew, there was no Mozelle Winters in Memphis.

She had heard Miz Clara come in from church. With the afternoon stretching before her—and a brand-new car—maybe she could persuade her mother to go for a ride. "Mama? you here?"

Miz Clara didn't answer. Having a nap, maybe. The Sunday paper was strewn all over the living room, as if she'd had a luxurious Sunday read. *Why not me?* Talba thought. She got herself a Diet Coke and settled down in a mountain of newsprint. In time, she even drifted off herself.

When the phone rang, she heard it but made no effort to answer. She had voice mail—hell with it. She took a deep breath, fell back into semiconsciousness, and couldn't have been further away when a banshee keening debouched from Miz Clara's room.

"Mama? Mama, what is it?" Talba flew into her mother's bedroom, screaming, wondering if something had happened to her Aunt Carrie, her mama's only sister.

Miz Clara shushed her, still listening, still keening. Talba heard her say, "I'm comin' right on over soon's as I can get a cab. No, honey, don't you worry about it. I'm sure I can get one."

Honey? She never called anyone "honey."

"Mama, I've got a car. I got it yesterday."

Miz Clara shushed her again, even seemed to be waving her off in impatience. After a century or so, she got off the phone.

"What is it, Mama?" Talba winced at the whine in her voice.

"Michelle's hemorrhaging."

Talba tried to process it. The baby wasn't due yet. "Did she go into early labor? Is she in the hospital?"

"Blood just start coming; they thought it was her water breaking, but, no, whole lot of blood come out."

The significance of it hit her. Her brother Corey was a doctor. If he thought it was serious, it was serious. And if he called his mama, it was really serious. He'd normally wait till it was all over to do something like that.

Talba pondered what it might mean. Only one thing, she decided. It had to mean he was scared to death.

"Where is she?"

"Baptist." She meant Memorial Medical Center, where Corey was on staff. Before it got gobbled up, it had been Baptist Hospital; to New Orleanians of a certain age, it still was.

"Let's go," Talba said.

"I gotta put on my wig." Miz Clara cleaned houses for a living. She liked to keep her hair in a near buzz cut.

"Mama. Let's go!" Talba was surprised at the urgency in her voice.

Miz Clara hated the car, of course—couldn't understand why Talba couldn't get a nice comfortable Cadillac or maybe an Oldsmobile or something. She griped about it all the way to the hospital, which got under Talba's skin so badly she nearly had a wreck on I-10.

Her hands were sweating. It occurred to her that she was actually worried about her sister-in-law.

Corey was in the maternity waiting room, pacing, his shaved head looking somehow dull, almost dusty. *I wonder if he shines it*, Talba thought.

He said, "I wish they let you smoke in these places."

He'd never smoked in his life.

Miz Clara's voice was uncharacteristically gentle. "How is she, baby?"

Talba would have given anything to have missed what followed. Her older brother the doctor, the successful one in the family, who had a big house in Eastover and the kind of car Miz Clara approved of, threw his arms around his mama and cried. "Oh, Mama, I'm gonna lose her."

Miz Clara's moment of gentleness was over. She gave him a shake. "Shush up, boy! You are not."

He looked at her as if she were speaking Russian.

"She's a healthy young woman and she's in good hands. Idn't she?"

Corey just stared.

"Well, idn't she?"

"Yes, ma'am. She's in good hands."

"And you know how to pray, don't you?"

He looked a little impatient at that, but once more he said, "Yes, ma'am."

"Well, start doin' it, son. Just as soon as you tell me what's going on in there." Her head jerked down the corridor.

"I don't know. They won't tell me."

Talba thought, *Ah, so that's what's gotten to him. He's out of control. He's a doctor and he can't do anything for his own wife.*

"Well, what'd they say? They musta' said something."

"They said she was bleeding."

Miz Clara said, "Hmmph."

"And shocky. Her blood pressure was dropping." He took in a breath and let it out. He spoke softly. "They said they thought they could save the baby."

"Well, then, they'll save it." Miz Clara's face was set, as if she could make the doctors mind her, like they were kids in a sandbox.

"I don't care about the baby." Corey balled his fist. "I just want Michelle."

" 'Course you want Michelle. And you gon' get Michelle. They didn't say they 'thought' they could save her, did they? That's 'cause they know they can."

Talba's palms were sweating; her heart was speeding again. She was catching Corey's fear. *What's Mama talking about?* she thought. *Does she really believe that?*

Corey looked a little calmer, though. He took off his smeared glasses and began to clean them. "Yeah. Maybe so. Maybe that's what they meant."

Miz Clara looked around. "Where are her people?"

Corey looked at the floor, avoiding her eyes like a child. "I didn't call them."

"What you mean you didn't call 'em, boy? They her people."

"I couldn't face them, Mama. I couldn't face them just yet."

Miz Clara crossed her arms and glared. Gentleness just wasn't her forte.

Corey spread his arms and this time looked her full in the face. His eyes were brimming. "Mama, I didn't want them. I wanted you and Talba."

Talba felt her own eyes fill up. Had he really included her too? And he'd called her Talba, not Sandra.

Miz Clara said, "Come here. Come here, son." She opened her arms to him.

Once again, Corey clung to his mama. She said, "I guess we don't have to call 'em just yet. Let's sit down. Let's sit down now." She led him to a chair.

Talba was feeling slightly like a voyeur, but on the other hand, he'd said he wanted her there. When they were children he'd been there for her, sometimes when she was so little she couldn't remember and had to be told once she grew up. Sometimes in ways she remembered—he babysat while Miz Clara worked her housecleaning jobs.

And then, because she felt he'd become a snob who'd forgotten the values—and the people—he was raised with, they'd grown apart. Part of that was just her own jealousy— she realized that now—and part was Michelle, but they were over that. They were close again.

Michelle.

Michelle who might be in there dying right now.

She wasn't, though—she couldn't be. Corey was just upset because she was his wife. His wife whom he loved so much he was crying on his mama's shoulder.

Talba glanced at the other two. They were holding hands now, heads bowed. They were praying.

She felt embarrassed. She shouldn't be watching this. And yet, she certainly wasn't watching with cool objectivity. She couldn't get her heart to slow down.

She tried deep breaths, thinking of Michelle lying on a table, her belly a mound rising out of her snaky body, her legs apart, blood gushing out. . . .

Worse, she saw Michelle's face, saw her pain. . . .

Oh, God, I see why Corey called us. The worst thing is to think about it.

What if they did save the baby and not Michelle? That was almost the worst case scenario. What was Corey going to do with a tiny baby?

She felt so sorry for him it was like an ache. This couldn't happen to her only brother. Just couldn't. He was so happy . . .

Happy?

She had never thought of Corey as happy with Michelle. But she thought back to the night they'd told her she was pregnant, a night she'd dropped in on them unexpectedly, very late, demanding information. An entirely untactful episode, in which she'd been focused largely on herself.

They'd stood in the kitchen holding hands, Michelle's belly barely beginning to curve, the light shining on Corey's bald head. And now that she thought of it, they were radiant. They were the image of a happy couple, a couple at the beginning of their lives together, looking forward to their baby. . . .

She isn't supposed to make me happy. She's supposed to make him happy.

Talba's eyes filled again. Who was she to judge Michelle? She could put up with her. Oh, yes. If she could just have her back, she could put up with her. At that moment, she realized, she wanted Michelle for a sister-in-law more than anything in the world.

She had to do something. She couldn't just sit here driving herself crazy. "Corey," she said. "You want me to call the Tircuits?"

He stared up at her. "You?" She knew what he meant and it shamed her. He was the older brother, accustomed to doing for her. She'd never made such an offer before.

"Give me the number. I'll be glad to."

He nodded and pulled out his address book.

The Tircuits couldn't have been more different from the Wallises if they'd been white. They were descended from Louisiana's Free People of Color, who had thrived in the nineteenth century, and they were virtually royalty in New Orleans. They were light-skinned, straight-haired blacks, called "Creoles" in this day and age, and they had money. They had an extremely successful business dating back to antebellum times.

They'd never given Talba the time of day.

But, then, she hadn't gone out of her way to befriend them, either.

Only when she had the number and had gone out to the corridor and turned on her cell phone did it occur to her she had no idea what to say. She was going to have to wing it.

A woman answered. "Mrs. Tircuit?"

"No, this the maid. Let me get her."

A maid. These were black people who had a maid.

"Hello? This is Ardis Tircuit."

"Mrs. Tircuit, this is Talba Wallis. Corey's sister?" She made the statement a question and hated herself for it.

"Yes?"

"Michelle's having her baby and—"

"Michelle isn't due yet." The woman spoke with authority, but Talba heard the fear in her voice.

"I think there may be complications." She swallowed hard. "Corey needs you." The lie slipped out cleanly.

"Corey? But what about Michelle?"

"She's in the delivery room."

"Already? How long has she been in labor? Why didn't somebody call?"

"Mrs. Tircuit, this happened very suddenly." Talba made her voice very calm. Somehow, that got the message across.

"Is she all right? Is my daughter all right?"

"We hope she's going to be."

The woman broke the connection, evidently panicked. Talba hoped she had someone to drive her to the hospital.

Talba was stuffing her cell phone back in her purse when it rang again. "This is Ardis Tircuit." Talba thought: *She must have caller I.D.* "What hospital did you say?"

"Baptist."

Reluctantly, Talba went back to join her mother and Corey. Miz Clara had her eyes closed. She looked like she was in pain, but Talba knew it was only a deep focus. She'd seen it before; her mother was rocking back and forth in prayer. Her brother was still holding hands with her. He looked like a trapped animal.

Talba simply didn't see how she could sit here with this kind of tension. She herself did not pray. What she did to tune the world out was read, and she was way too wound up to do that right now. Or to speak.

She ended up doing nothing, letting her mind wander, sweating and feeling miserable, until the first of the Tircuits got there. *Maybe I could talk to them for him*, she thought, but Miz Clara appointed herself family spokesman and when the elegant Mrs. Tircuit burst into tears, told her she had to be strong and trust in Jesus. *They're probably Episcopalians*, Talba thought.

Not that Episcopalians didn't trust in something or other, but Talba was pretty sure they didn't talk about it in polite company. Still, there wasn't an answer to what Miz Clara said; Ardis Tircuit could only nod and shut up.

Her husband arrived soon, in a business suit, and then a couple of sisters, the latter two wailing. It was turning into a deathwatch, everyone dressed up and praying or crying. *They certainly are pessimistic*, Talba thought. *It's as if they've already given up on her.*

And Talba realized that she hadn't, that she wasn't remotely ready to, that—like Corey—she couldn't imagine life without Michelle. "It's going to be all right," she said automatically, patting an arm here, a knee there, and actually, she felt that it was. Women gave birth every day, even if there were complications.

And yet—it oughtn't to take forever. What was happening? Talba imagined them doing a C-section, sewing her back up—what else? Transfusions?

Even as she was thinking it, the doctor came out, finger-combing hair just out from one of those surgical shower caps. She was frowning, intent on her hair, scanning the room for Corey.

When she found him, she smiled. "Everything's fine." She looked as if she was going to say more, but Corey's eyes closed and his knees buckled. One of the Tircuits caught him. Miz Clara said, "Lord, Lord!" Oddly enough, it was Talba who thought to ask about the baby.

The doctor smiled. "A beautiful girl."

"She's okay?"

"They're both fine. Mrs. Wallis had what we call an abruption. In simple terms, that's when the placenta starts tearing away." Everyone looked at each other fuzzily. "It can be life-threatening to the baby—and sometimes to the mother as well. In this case, the baby's heart rate started dropping so rapidly, it . . ." She looked a little squeamish and stopped, apparently realizing she shouldn't finish this sentence in front of the family. Talba filled in the blank for herself: . . . *it really scared us.* The doctor said instead, "We had no choice but to do a C-section." She smiled again, this time at Corey. "But you got her here in time, Dr. Wallis. They're both doing great. Congratulations on your daughter."

And then they were all hugging each other and crying, even Talba. She felt unbalanced, as if the ground had shifted.

Chapter Eleven

She slept the sleep of the dead and woke up Monday morning thinking of her newborn niece and her dead friend, Babalu Maya, AKA Clayton Patterson. A couplet came to her: "Life is a leaf / that hovers in the wind." She considered it, decided against. She had to get around to this one, though. Something important had happened to her—she just wasn't sure what it was.

She opened her closet and selected a white blouse and blue skirt—her unvarying choice for work. While the Baroness de Pontalba had almost as exotic a wardrobe as a drag queen, Talba Wallis the PI had once worked as an office temp; thus she had a closet full of white blouses and blue skirts. Why waste energy and money, she felt, on clothes she was never going to like anyway? The skirts and blouses were selected for blending in—always respectable, never noticeable. That was good for an office temp and even better for a PI. (She also had a good navy pantsuit for events like Babalu's funeral.)

She did some of her best thinking driving, and this morning

(having already contemplated the deeper issues), she thought about Babalu's name. No wonder she'd chosen it—this was a woman who'd been quite literally wounded.

Clearly, Talba needed to find out where Donny Troxell was. The source of so much of her friend's misery just had to be checked out. She thought about what it might be like to visit a machete-scalper; backup probably really was a great idea. Even if it was only Eddie.

Eileen Fisher was at her receptionist's post as usual, perusing the *Times-Picayune* for lack of anything better to do. "Morning, Talba."

"Hi, Eileen—Eddie in yet?"

"Uh-uh. He's in court this morning." She went back to her paper.

So much for backup. Oh, well, she probably wasn't going to find Troxell anyway. At least not before lunch.

Before she'd even put away her purse, she booted up her computer and performed the online verison of calling information. There weren't that many Troxells in Louisiana, and only two were Donalds. One of them lived in New Orleans. Just for fun, she did call information, and sure enough, Donald Troxell was listed. Good old Eddie—by using his antiquated methods, she could have had Donny in one minute instead of the ten it had taken.

But goddammit! Why hadn't she thought of this the night before? (Well, actually, there was a pretty good reason. She could give herself a break on that one.) Still, it was infuriating. Here it was, after nine o'clock—just about no chance of catching one Donald Troxell before he left for work. The frustration was well nigh unbearable.

Maybe he doesn't work, she thought. *Maybe he's a hopeless alcoholic, like Robert Robineau.*

He lived in the Bywater, which didn't tell her much—he could be a young professional fixing up a great old shotgun or someone in need of a cheap rental. Best to drive there, she decided—it wasn't that far from her own neighborhood. She was certainly going—and going right now, the hell with backup. He might be at work, but maybe he was married and had small children. If she was lucky, that would mean a wife with a big mouth at home.

The gorgeous old neighborhood was far from becoming gentrified. It had turned into a favorite of young white artists and others in the tattoo-and-piercings club. Good place for a poet, Talba thought, but surely Troxell didn't fall into that category.

His dwelling was about what she'd guessed—half a run-down shotgun double. If he was the right Troxell, he probably wasn't any poster boy for ex-cons-who-make-good. The place looked unoccupied, all closed up. But at least there were no newspapers piling up outside. Talba mounted the porch steps and rang the bell somewhat dispiritedly. To her surprise, she heard footsteps, even a dog barking.

The woman who answered the door was so far from what Talba expected, she figured Troxell had long since moved on. She wore jeans, sloppy T-shirt, and a bandana around her head. Her hands were dirty and her neck sweaty, but a tiny diamond pendant glistened in its folds, probably something she always wore. A gift from her husband, maybe. A raggedy old white Lab clung at her heels.

Something about her reminded Talba of the ladies of the Baptist church in Clayton. She had that blond softness they had, that small-town neatness, even in her work clothes. But she wasn't a country club type—more likely working class, Talba thought. She was about Deborah Patterson's age.

"Can I help you?" she asked.

"Yes. I'm looking for Donald Troxell."

"Oh." Distress crowded her face. "Are you a friend of his?"

"No, ma'am, I'm not. I just need to talk to him about something."

The woman cocked her head. "About what?"

"That's confidential, I'm afraid. Are you a relative of his?"

"Yes. I'm his mother. Come in, won't you?"

She ushered Talba into a house that was being dismantled. Sealed cardboard boxes were everywhere, and a stack of flat ones leaned against a wall, waiting to be made up. Other moving tools—magic markers and tape—were scattered around a dark, gloomy living room with an old sofa, chair, and television set still in it.

"Let's go to the back," the woman said. "I'm keeping the front closed up." She gave an involuntary shiver and glanced at the dog. Talba realized she was afraid of the neighborhood. "There's a cute little backyard where we can sit."

She led Talba through a deserted-looking bedroom, into a kitchen in the process of being torn apart, and finally outside, into a pleasant space furnished with a metal table, chairs, and a nice stand of banana trees.

"Can I offer you anything?"

Talba declined, wondering what was going on here.

"Sit down, will you?" She waited for Talba to obey, but didn't sit herself. "I'm sorry to tell you my son passed away earlier this week."

"Umph." Talba faked surprise, but in fact, she'd had a bad feeling ever since she entered the house. It had a forlorn look to it, like Babalu's. And a feeling; a very oppressive feeling.

"I'm so sorry," she said. *Who am I?* she was thinking. *Definitely not a PI working for the girl he scalped.*

The woman sniffed into a Kleenex. "Just as he was getting his life together."

It occurred to Talba that death was like pregnancy; in one, everyone patted your stomach; in the other, you also got your privacy invaded. "But what happened?" she blurted. "Donny was so . . . I mean, he was getting his life together. . . ."

Finally, the woman sat. "He was mugged coming home from work. They beat him, took his wallet, and shot him."

Talba gasped, and this time the shock was real. "Coming home from work? But what time . . . ?" She thought she was doing a poor job of fishing, but nothing solid had occurred to her yet; she sure wished she could get the lying thing down better.

"He still worked at the Wild Side—ironic under the circumstances, but it was so hard for him to find anything else. It happened about four A.M. just after his shift." She stopped in midsentence, looking quizzical.

"I know about the prison sentence, Mrs. Troxell."

She nodded knowingly. "Oh, yes, I suppose he shared about that."

And suddenly Talba had it; he "shared," he was getting his life together, and it was ironic that he worked at a bar. She took a chance that he was in AA. "I see you've figured out how I knew Donny."

For the first time his mother smiled. "These days, most of his friends are in the program. What was it you needed, by the way?"

"Oh, uh—Donny lent me a little money. I wanted to pay it back." Talba bit her lip hard enough to get tears to come to her eyes.

"Don't worry about that. Don't worry at all."

"Oh, no. Please." She produced a ten-dollar bill. "I just feel so bad."

"My son had the hardest life of anyone I know—and now this! It's just so unfair."

"It sure is. It sure is, Miz Troxell."

"It was like a second chance. The first time was like this too—just plain unfair."

"You mean—uh, that thing in his hometown?"

The woman nodded, the sadness in her face giving way to anger. "He was such a smart boy—and it was obvious from a very early age. His dad was just a plumber and I'm a waitress. We had four children and none of them had any more brains than we did—except one. We gave him everything, uh, Miss . . . ?"

"I'm Sandra," Talba said, "and I'm an alcoholic."

The other woman smiled. "Sandra," she said. "We didn't have much, but there was a really good guidance counselor at the high school, and she helped him get a scholarship to Vanderbilt. He was dating the daughter of the richest man in town. He had the world by the tail. And then one day she broke up with him . . . and they accused him of *scalping* her . . . and . . ." She started to cry again.

Talba touched her hand. "I know the story. But one thing I never understood—why did the girl break up with him?"

Troxell's face was stony. "He never knew. Poor thing never

even knew. He was so hurt . . . and then when he got arrested . . ."

Clearly Donny's mother thought he hadn't attacked Clayton. Best not to go down that road, Talba thought. She kept her mouth shut.

"He came out of prison a broken man. He never could hold a decent job or even hold his head up after that. His father was so disgusted with him he never spoke to Donny again." She sniffled and cried some more.

"I'm so sorry, Mrs. Troxell."

"And now I'm going to lose two of 'em in one week."

"I beg your pardon?"

"My husband's got diabetes. He's not expected to live out the week."

Again, Talba gasped, and again she didn't have to fake it.

"Already lost both his legs."

"Oh!"

"But I got the satisfaction of one thing. At least he and Donny made up. That's another thing that was going right for Donny. She cleared his name. Finally."

"Wait a minute; I'm not following."

"She came to see my husband and told him Donny didn't do it. And then Ralph asked to see Donny—for the first time in sixteen years."

"You mean the girl? The girl who got scalped?"

"Yes, ma'am. Ms. Clayton Patterson herself came to see my husband." Talba's mind was falling all over itself, putting pieces together. Donny Troxell had appeared once and only once in Clayton's datebook. What if he'd called her to beg? *Clayton, my dad's dying. Tell him I didn't do it. What can it hurt? Please. I've served my time. Just tell my daddy I didn't do it!*

All the newspaper articles about the trial had been clear on one thing: Clayton never accused Donny. She said she never saw her intruder. How likely was that? Talba wondered.

What if she did know who attacked her, and she told Ralph Troxell? The statute of limitations was probably up, anyway—or maybe her real attacker, if it wasn't Donny, had died in the intervening years. What if she'd broken a sixteen-year silence and started a chain of events that led to her death? And Donny's.

Mrs. Troxell said, "I went home for a bite to eat and some rest. When I came back, he told me she'd been there, and he'd called Donny."

Talba could barely contain herself. "You're sure she told him Donny didn't do it?"

"I sure am. That's exactly what she did tell him. And then the next afternoon he slipped into a coma."

"What a horrible story! I mean . . . wonderful, too. At least he and his son made up."

Troxell squeezed her wadded-up tissue and began to tear at it. She didn't say anything.

Finally, Talba said, "Was it all on the phone—or did Donny come over to see his dad?"

She raised her face, and it was almost radiant. "Oh, he came over. I thank God for that. They were actually able to see each other after all those years. Lord, I wish I could have been there! But I know Ralph. I knew I had to give him some privacy. So I stepped out of the room. And when he told me about it, he cried. Said he should have trusted in his son—said somebody was going to pay, and he was going to make 'em. That's why I thought he was going to live. He had something to live for."

"You think the girl—what's her name?"

"Clayton Patterson."

"Odd name. You think she told him what really happened?"

"I know she did."

"And your husband told you?"

"No. He didn't tell me. Later that night, he was in terrible pain. He couldn't really talk much. And then the next day he was as good as gone. Like that. Just like that." She fluttered her hand.

"Like a leaf that flutters in the wind," Talba said before she caught herself.

The woman looked at her oddly. "Beg pardon?"

"Uh . . . bad poetry. It's what someone said about life."

Troxell nodded vigorously. "Well, they could say it again. I've buried my boy, and before long I'll bury my husband too." Her jaw set hard.

"But he didn't go into the coma till the afternoon?"

Troxell shook her head, concerned with her own tragedy. Talba wasn't about to say what she thought.

Chapter Twelve

Eddie was glad he didn't have to hear the damn story on an empty stomach. By the time he got out of court it was time for lunch, and he'd snagged a couple of old cronies and headed for Venezia. He'd had a glass of wine with lunch, but, still, the thing was making him cranky.

"So what ya think," he said, "is that the old man was gonna blow the whistle on the scalper and the scalper killed two people to stop him, but neither one of the victims was the whistle blower. Doesn't make sense, Ms. Wallis. Make it make sense for me."

"He didn't *have* to kill the old man. Ralph was already in a coma." She spread her hands. "Look, for all I know, the guy induced the coma."

"Right. Right. Get it out ya system. Go on ahead."

"Ralph had one morning left. He could have called the guy and threatened him."

"But why would he? Why wouldn't he have just called the cops?"

"I don't know. He was dying. He must have known it—

maybe he just wanted the guy to know he knew."

At least she admitted there was something she didn't know.

"Okay, so maybe ya theory's right. Suppose he used his last morning to call the guy. And then that guy goes out and gets a friend and they give Clayton an overdose; then they go mug poor ol' Donny, who was just gettin' his life together. By the way, that AA thing was good. Your lyin's gettin' a little better."

She squirmed a little. "That's pretty high praise from The Man."

Eddie thought, *She's just a girl*. She was so damned uppity, sometimes he forgot that.

"But, no, it wasn't quite like that," she continued. "When I got back, I checked the *Times-Picayune*. There was a tiny little story about Donny's death—and it was the day before Clayton's.

"Who cares about that? The whole thing's just goddamn farfetched, excuse my French."

"Well, maybe there were two people in on the scalping."

Eddie raised an eyebrow, something he was pretty good at. She backed down. "Okay, okay, it's farfetched. But still. It's damned coincidental, right?"

That one he couldn't get around. Like most people who'd seen a few things in his life, he didn't really believe in coincidences. "Awright, let's look at it in practical terms. Ya client doesn't think his precious girlfriend who he loved so much he was humpin' somebody else, excuse my French, could of possibly O.D.'d, because she was too damn healthy and never touched the stuff. That about right?"

"About."

"Well, then you're doin' him some good. You're workin' on a facsimile of a murder motive here, and I'd be the first to say I wouldn't have thought you had a Chinaman's chance."

She shifted in her chair. Something had made her mad. "Thanks for the vote of confidence. And sure, I'll excuse your French. The racist comment's real nice too."

What the hell was she talking about?

He must have let his guard down for a minute. She gave him a superior smirk. "You don't even know what you said, do you? You think 'Chinaman's chance' is perfectly okay."

"Oh, for Christ's sake. It's just an expression." She didn't challenge him on that, just gave him another smug little look. (But later, when he told the story to his daughter Angie, he just about never heard the end of it.)

"Look, I just gave you a compliment. Why don't ya go ahead and ax the client if he wants to go on with it?" He spread his own hands in a great big, expansive anything's-possible.

"Eddie, come on. You know I've already done that." She was so impatient she was practically snapping at him.

That was about it for Eddie. "Why is it people your age know so damn much, huh? Lived half as long and know twice as much—how ya manage that, huh?"

Was that hurt on her face? It was. Kind of like the look Trudy, his wife's dachshund, got when he let the cat in the den.

"Eddie, I didn't mean anything. I just—"

"Look. Go for the defense lawyer, why don't ya'? If anybody knows what went on, it's got to be him."

"Exactly what I was thinking," she said.

"In a pig's eye," he answered, but he was joking now, over his fit of pique.

The truth was, this thing was giving him the shivers. He'd probably been far too negative with Ms. Wallis—he'd have to eat his words later. For even as she talked, his discomfort was growing. How did you explain not one but two fatal coincidences? The damn case was probably a lot more dangerous than it was lucrative, but he didn't dare say that to her. She'd only go after it all the harder.

Ms. Wallis, Ms. Wallis, he thought to himself, and shook his head the way he used to when his daughter Angie got too big for her britches.

———

Talba spent the rest of the day backgrounding the attorney who'd defended Donny Troxell in the scalping case. He was a native Claytonian (if they called themselves that) who'd gone to law school at Tulane, and who, if she read between the lines correctly, was probably a member of the same country club the Pattersons belonged to. His name was Lawrence Blue, for openers. Talba didn't know much about WASP names, but she figured that was one.

He had a wife named Kathleen and three children. He belonged to the Presbyterian church. And, as a small-town lawyer in Clayton, about the biggest thing that had ever happened to him was the Troxell case. That was at the beginning of his career.

He later moved to New Orleans, where he joined a well-known criminal defense firm and handled some pretty high-profile cases. Later still, he gave the whole thing up, moved back to Clayton, joined a distinguished firm that did insurance defense, ran for state senator, and won.

Back in Clayton, Talba had seen a picture of him as Donny Troxell's lawyer. He was an ordinary-looking man, with a tendency to plumpness. She wished she had a sheaf of pictures of him as his career advanced. As she imagined it, he'd put on more and more weight until, as a state senator, he was practically a caricature.

All in all, she figured she'd gleaned two useful facts—one being that Blue lived in Baton Rouge, where the legislature was now in session, the other that he was extremely active in the campaign of gubernatorial candidate Buddy Calhoun, whom she'd seen at Clayton's funeral.

Well, well, well, she thought, *perhaps we have common ground.*

As preparation for the interview, she popped by Calhoun's headquarters and got herself a campaign button, figuring she was going vote for him, so why not?

Calhoun was a decent enough guy, by all accounts, if a bit on the lackluster side. But the incumbent, Jack Haydel, was spectacular—in just about every unpleasant way you could mention. He was a sleazeball closely tied to gambling interests. In fact, he'd once been indicted for bribery, but he'd beaten the rap. Talba had no doubt he was guilty of that and much more. But Haydel had an even worse strike against him. A famous election a few years back had spawned a famous bumper strip: "Vote for the crook. It's important." In that one, the other candidate was a racist. Jack Haydel had the distinction of being both a crook *and* a racist.

So, sure, she'd wear a Calhoun button—and proudly.

The next morning she got up early to drive to Baton Rouge, her plan being to catch the senator on his way into the office. That way, if he couldn't see her then, she'd have the rest of the day to get him to work her in. (Also she had a reading that night—she wanted to get home early.)

She arrived in time to be there when the capitol building opened, made a beeline for Blue's suite, and simply loitered until she saw him get off the elevator. Truth to tell, he hadn't changed that much, hadn't turned into the literal fat cat of her imagination. He still had a bounce to his walk and most of his hair. He had a familiar look, as if they'd met.

She was wearing her blue business suit, so as not to look like a secretary, and she carried a briefcase, which contained a tape recorder she'd just turned on.

"Senator, may I have a moment?"

"Yes?" She thought his expression changed as she came into focus for him. "I'm sorry, I have an appointment."

"I have a . . . There's no easy way to say this. I have a death message for you."

"I beg your pardon?"

"A former client of yours has been murdered—his mother thought you'd like to know."

Blue drew back from her a bit, and instead of the shock he was supposed to register, she thought she saw fear. Wariness at the very least. He was practically checking the place for the nearest exit.

She waited a moment for him to calm down. He could hardly refuse news like this. Finally, he said, "What are you talking about?"

"I'm sorry to tell you . . . Donny Troxell was killed in a street robbery a week ago."

"Donny!" He went white.

"Senator, are you all right?"

"Donny Troxell?" he said.

"I'm sorry to be the one to tell you."

"I didn't even know he . . ." Blue stopped there, and Talba said, "Oh, yes, he's been out of prison several years."

"Donny never . . . *Damn*, that's a shame. Donny never had a chance."

Talba thought it about time to haul out her bona fides. "Senator, I'm an investigator looking into his death—"

"You're no cop!" He spoke with such vehemence it startled her.

"No sir, I'm not. I'm employed by the family." Never mind which family. She knew for a fact that Jason had family, and as long as he was part of it, she was employed by some family.

"This kind of thing is best left to the police."

"There may be a little more to it than a simple mugging, Senator. Did you realize Clayton Patterson also died a few days ago?"

"I did." He bit off the words, mad now, though Talba wasn't sure why. The blood had come back to his face, which was fast turning red. "What does that have to do with anything?"

"I don't know. Maybe nothing. I was hoping to ask you what you remember about Troxell's case."

"Young woman, do you think I don't know who you are? Just what the hell are you trying to pull here?"

He could have spoken to her in Chinese and she wouldn't have been more surprised. He knew her? What a ludicrous idea!

She said, "I think you must have me confused with someone else." But he said only, "I have nothing more to say to you," went into his office, and slammed his door.

What the hell was that? she thought, wondering how on earth she'd managed to blow it so fast, with so few words.

It came to her on the drive home. He must have seen her before, at Clayton's funeral. He was just another white face, while she was the all-too-obvious object of everyone's scorn. It explained why he'd looked so familiar to her, but there was a lot it didn't explain—like the way he turned white when she told him about Donny.

Only one explanation, she thought. He sold Donny out.

She wondered if she should try to get a transcript of the trial. But that would take a while and cost several hundred bucks. There were other people she could talk to—the judge, for instance. Also, everyone in the Patterson family.

She could try, anyway.

The day was shot by the time she got back to New Orleans. She didn't even bother going back to the office—just checked for messages on her cell phone and headed for Baptist Hospital.

Michelle was nursing the baby. It was the first time Talba'd actually seen her niece, and all she really saw now was the back of her head. But what a precious little back of the head!

"Hey," she said.

Michelle raised her adoring glance. "Hey, Talba. Look what I've got."

To her extreme amazement, Talba felt herself start to choke up. "Not bad," was all she said.

"Did Corey tell you what we're calling her?"

"Uh-uh." That had been the last thing on their minds the night before.

"Sophia." She pronounced it "Soe-fye-a." "Sophia Pontalba."

"What?" Talba nearly jumped out of her skin. Surely they weren't naming their baby for her—they didn't even accept her name.

Michelle shrugged. "Corey likes the name. I think it's a little pretentious . . ."

Of course you do, Talba thought.

". . . but he likes it." Michelle squeezed out a smile. "And we thought of you, of course."

"Well, that's really nice of you, Michelle. I don't quite know what to say."

Her sister-in-law looked gaunt after her ordeal. She wore no makeup, and for the first time since she'd known her, Talba felt as if she might be talking to a real woman, not a mannequin.

But that might be me, she thought. *Not her.*

"I'm real mad about one thing, though—I liked being the only baroness in the family."

The baby quit nursing, rubbing her head against Michelle's breast, as if to say, "Take me away, now."

Michelle turned her around and held her up to Talba, who said, "Hello, Baronessa," and held out her arms.

"Woooo. This is one sweet baby." Suddenly it really penetrated that she had a niece, and she was holding her.

And that she loved her.

Just like that, she'd fallen in love. She was absolutely nuts about the soft little bundle without a bit of personality, and she didn't even question it.

The rest of the visit passed in cooing over the baby and getting used to Michelle—to the idea that she was going to be around the rest of Talba's life, probably, and Talba actually preferred it that way. It was a little disconcerting, but it beat the alternative.

The baby shook something loose in her, something that might not be resolved for many years, maybe not for the rest of her life. She knew perfectly what it was—it was some kind of hormonal thing. It was something that came over women from time to time and never left some of them. She sighed, wondering where it would lead, and vowing to open up a little toward Raisa.

And out of the blue, as she was driving home, something else struck her. *I wonder*, she thought, *what my little sister's like.*

How the hell did you find someone with a name like Winters?

She went over what she'd done. Once she had the name, she'd started out by calling information in New Orleans (in accordance with Eddie's rule). Then she'd done the same in Memphis, then tapped into every online database she could think of, for both Louisiana and Tennessee. She could do a nationwide search for anyone named Mozelle Winters, and maybe she should. She could just call them all, one by one. Mozelle was an odd name—there probably weren't that many. But then again, Mozelle might be married, or married again.

She was in a kind of daze when she arrived home, completely focused on something that shouldn't have concerned a woman who had a performance to do that night. Actually, she was just reading at a restaurant and bar down on Carrollton Avenue, something she did at least once a month. But she thought of all her readings as performances. It befitted a baroness.

Without even taking off her jacket, she pulled out a phone book and looked up "Winters." She couldn't have said why; maybe just to verify that the words *Mozelle* and *Winters* didn't appear together in print. There was an M. Winters, but she already knew that from calling information, had already called that number. But there was no Mozelle.

However, she learned something from this simple act— something important. Common as it sounded, Winters was no competition for Johnson or Smith. There was only a column and a fourth of Winterses. Quickly, she counted them. About seventy-five.

Doable. Very doable. She could simply call them all and ask for Mozelle. The idea excited her—turning up a relative was really the best thing that could happen when you were looking for a woman, since you could never depend on women to keep the same name. This, she'd long since learned, was one of the most frustrating things about detective work.

She had worked her way from Alan through David before she realized she had to pull herself together—had to get a few minutes rest, forage something to eat, and find a fabulous outfit. Something orange, she thought. She had an orange T-shirt she could wear with a great African-print, sarong-type skirt she'd ordered from the Essence catalogue. What she really needed to go with that was a turban, but it was too late to make one. She started rummaging. Hmmm. A tie-dyed orange and yellow scarf. Very turban-like when properly tied. And a multi-strand brown bead necklace. That should do it.

Her outfit figured out, it was time for a ten-minute nap. Ever since she discovered those little bean bags for your eyes, she'd become a great cat-napper. She lay down with the bag on her eyes, but it wasn't thirty seconds before she was up and scribbling.

Three Sisters

What's a sister, anyhow?
Someone you raised with?
Somebody black?
Somebody African-American?
(Thank you, Brother,
I be BLACK if I want to.)
Maybe she got chains on her wrist and
She white as a Celt and
She touch me.
She touch my body like a mama touch a baby.
And I feel the pressure of her hands
And I feel the muscles of her hands
And I feel the muscles of her love
And I feel the muscles of her dread.
And I feel her dread.
And I feel her.
And I feel her dead.

She died my lifetime ago (though not hers)
'Cause we kill her, my mama and me.
We got our reasons; oh, yes . . .
We got 'em, child Corey.
Anybody kill—
they got reasons, don't they, honey?

Don't they, sweet baby?
Let me help you, precious.

But don't you say that "S" word.
Don't you do that now.
You say that word, child—
You utter those innocent syllables,
Mama feel her pressure rise in her vessels
Like a horse
Rarin' with that rider on it
(You know the one.)
Big brother drop his scalpel;

World

tilt on its axis.

Me

I got my private things to think.
I got a sound like thunder and a river like blood;
I got things that can make that child a orphan;
And don't you mention it, now.
Uh-uh, no. Not ever.

Not how
They ate her alive, my sister;
Not how they bit her and chewed her
Not how they spat her and shat her.
Not how her own kin
Devoured her,
(and not out of too much love, either.)
And certainly not
how they hunted her down.
And not . . .
How they did it again.

In her death
they did it again.
And my sister was born yesterday.

But my sisters are dead . . .
All three.

And I miss them.
All three.
And I love them.
All three.
(Or maybe I do)
And I hate at least two
And this poem is for Babalu.

The poem was purely impulse; the reading had been planned for months, ten poets lined up to perform. Six of the ten read poems for Babalu.

Chapter Thirteen

Into the belly of the beast, she thought as her alarm went off. Maybe she would talk to that judge today. One thing was sure—she was going to talk to somebody in Clayton. In fact, everyone she could pin down, even for a minute.

She made herself some oatmeal, thinking of her niece—her littlest "sister"—and of the poem and what it meant. She didn't know half of what it meant, and she might not find out for years. That happened a lot. What she did know was that writing it had made her calm again. For the past few days—ever since Babalu's funeral—she'd been in a strange state of heightened feeling, almost of desperation, and the poem had somehow snapped her back into harmony. She wondered if clarity came with that.

Whether it was false security or not, she felt strong and competent as she drove to Clayton, able to meet these white people on their own turf and make them sorry for what they'd done. That was what she wanted more than anything. To clear her friend's name among her own people. And yet why should she? she wondered. They were so unequivocally not worth it, she'd have laughed if anyone else had made the same confession.

Here was what she thought: if Donny Troxell hadn't attacked Clayton—and Clayton herself had told Donny's father he hadn't—then the people most likely to know anything (other than the defense lawyer) were the ones in the house at the time.

But what a lovely time she was going to have with *them*! Already they just adored her.

She put off talking to them by going to the library again, reading up on the Pattersons and their doings.

She'd sure been right about that country club thing. Well, the paper didn't actually say those words, but it had them going to parties and chairing events, even, in some cases, working for a living.

She already knew King was a banker; it developed that Trey was a lawyer, and Deborah, Mrs. Patterson, actually dirtied her own hands with honest labor—or something approaching it. She was a decorator. There were even quite a few clips on Hunter, the little sister—not that she worked for a living, but she did have an interest. She was an actress in local productions, and a pretty girl too. She'd once been married, though she might not be now. Her wedding picture, taken only four years ago, showed a baby version of Clayton.

The person who was most in the news was Deborah. She was not only on every board in town, she was a member of every multifaith organization as well. Which meant she was a church lady. And not the nice kind, Talba surmised, like Miz Lura. The scary kind, like Sister Eula.

The person least in the news was Trey's wife, who only appeared once, on her wedding day. Lonna, her name was. Talba kind of liked it. It wasn't pretentious, like Hunter or Clayton.

Or Pontalba.

Whom to approach? she wondered. The no-doubt racist dad? The good ol' boy son? Both of them had had their pictures in the paper with animals they shot and fish they caught. Talba didn't take this as a good sign.

The impeccably groomed, model-of-rectitude professional-woman church-lady mom? The notion was a bit on the terrifying side.

And the daughter-in-law hadn't been there.

That left pretty young Hunter. Because she was young and had an interest in the arts, Talba thought she might have some affinity with her. On the other hand, she was twenty-four, according to the local rag. That meant she'd have been only eight when her sister was assaulted.

Still, Talba thought. Still. She might have heard people talk. And if she remembered that night, she'd remember it well.

Talba had arrived with everyone's address in hand, already gleaned from online sources. She drove to Hunter's house but, for some reason, couldn't bring herself to go in. The mellowness of the early morning hadn't yet left her, and she had a need to absorb this young woman, to try to get some sense of her, before presenting herself.

The house itself was modest. The husband, if he was still around, probably wasn't much older than she was, just starting his career. There were curtains at the windows, but they seemed normal ones, not those balloon pouf things white ladies loved so much. The neighborhood was pleasant, which, in Talba's opinion, meant it had trees that had had time to grow a while.

Talba sat for about fifteen minutes, not sure whether she should make this a kind of surveillance or just go knock on the door, when it opened and out popped Hunter herself, in white capris and a tank top, bundling her baby into a stroller.

Well, that was a fine thing. Eddie had taught her how to follow a person in a car, but not the only person on foot in a white neighborhood. She'd have to wing it. She let mother and baby get a pretty good head start, then started the car and slowly passed them, cruising on down the street. After a few blocks she turned and parked on a side street, hoping Hunter kept walking in a straight line. When she passed, Talba did it again, but this time she spotted a small neighborhood park.

Bet she's going there, Talba thought, and went there first,

still remaining out of sight in her car. She'd gotten her first PI job because she had "the right demographics," and even Eddie deemed her race a plus, but here in Clayton, black wasn't a damn bit beautiful. That is, if you wanted to keep a low profile.

She waited to approach until the kid had found some more kids to play with, and more or less sneaked up as Hunter was watching them.

"Hunter?" Her first name; last names put people on the defensive, told them the speaker was a stranger.

The woman whirled, a pleasant, expectant expression on her face. "Yes?" Instantly, her eyes widened.

Fear, Talba thought. Not what she expected. "Busted," she said.

"What?"

"You sure recognized me fast."

"I recognize you, and I want you to leave." Cold anger now. That was more like it.

"Your sister and I were close, you know."

"I said leave me alone." Hunter turned her back.

This was going nowhere fast. *Eddie wouldn't have this problem*, she thought. *But what the hell would he do?*

He'd somehow get Hunter on a subject she was interested in, nothing to do with her sister. And Talba knew one, but it needed a good introduction. " 'Unbidden guests,' " she said, " 'are often welcomest when they are gone.' "

"What did you say?"

"I said don't send me away too fast—you might change your mind the minute I leave."

"Not even slightly likely." But there was a softening in her eyes.

"And I quoted Shakespeare because I know you're an actress. I've been wondering what it's like for a person in the arts, living in Clayton."

"Well, it's no picnic." Hunter looked almost startled, as if she'd surprised herself.

Talba was struggling wildly for rapport. Not sure whether

it was make-or-break, she blurted, "Tell me. Were you as upset as I was by your sister's funeral?"

The girl, watching the children, turned again toward Talba, and stared. "Oh, God. They hate her so much."

"Even you?"

"No. I didn't hate her. She was the only big sister I had." Her eyes brimmed. "That son of a bitch is the one I hate. Your client." Her face turned back toward her child.

"I did too, at first. Remember, I was the one who got the goods on him. It took a lot of courage for him to come to me."

"He might as well have shot her."

"Look here. Every story's got two sides. You know that. I can't tell you Jason's story—he's my client; but I can tell you, he loved your sister." Hunter turned angrily toward her again. "Oh, yeah, he cheated on her; and oh, yeah, it was ugly. But what I can tell you is that he was unsure of her. That he did it out of frustration."

"Now that I can almost believe."

"You can?"

"Oh, she could freeze you. She even did it to me sometimes. And I was the only one in the family she spoke to. She hated us worse than we hated her. She hated the whole town. And the whole damn town hated her."

Talba thought, *This is big. I can't lose it.* She paused for a moment, so as not to seem too eager. She spoke softly, almost whispering: "Why? Why did they hate her?"

"Omigod! Lily! Lily!" Hunter ran toward the children. One of the kids had smacked hers with a plastic shovel.

Talba looked on helplessly as Hunter soothed the kid and negotiated with the two other mothers, whose kids were also in tears by now. Hunter stuck around and talked to the moms after the kids had settled down. It was probably a good fifteen minutes before she came back to Talba.

"Where were we?" she said, perfectly cooperative. That meant she must have decided to talk, rather than just fallen into it. That was good. But the moment was gone.

Talba said, "You were telling me how much they hate her."

Hunter shrugged. "Oh, yeah. They do."

"But why?"

She shrugged again. "Because she's such a crybaby, I guess."

Talba noticed vaguely that they were still talking about Clayton in the present tense. She'd be doing it for months, she suspected. "You mean about the scalping thing?"

Once again, Hunter took her eyes off her offspring, and once again they were angry. "You know about that?"

Talba nodded.

"Sure you do. Everybody that knew her knew about it. It was the defining fucking moment of her whole fucking life. Look, I know it was a terrible thing and all that, but it turned her into Clayton-the-victim. That's all she was. Expected everything from everybody every second just because she got her precious self hurt."

"Like what? Give me an example."

Talba could have sworn a tiny flicker of surprise crossed Hunter's face, as if the question hadn't really occurred to her, but she just said, "You didn't know her. It's just the way she was."

She wanted to say, *I did know her. She wasn't that way.* But the last thing she wanted was an argument.

"May I tell you about my last experience with her?"

Grudgingly, Hunter nodded. "I hurt my back in an accident. I could barely walk, no kidding. I just got the tow truck to drop me there. She practically carried me up the stairs, Hunter. I arrived in a heap and I left walking. She could work miracles, almost. You could feel something very unusual in her fingers." Talba meant love, but she didn't quite have the courage to say it. "You could feel it, do you know what I'm talking about? Does that sound like someone who's a victim? Who only cared about herself? Wasn't she ever kind to you when no one else was?"

"Yes." Hunter's voice was choked. Tears rolled down her cheeks. "Lou Ann always took up for her. She talked about that too."

"Lou Ann?"

"Lou Ann Ferris. Her best friend in high school. She made me remember that. How sweet Clayton was when my marriage broke up; how she said I could come visit her anytime I wanted and stay as long as I wanted, and bring Lily. Mama and Daddy tried to make me stay with the bastard, even though he was cheating on me. And other times, when I was in high school, Clayton took up for me. When Mama got on me."

"She had a side to her no one in town saw. Why was that, do you think?"

"I don't know. I guess 'cause she was always so hateful to Mama and Daddy."

"Was she really? Or was that the family myth?"

Hunter wrinkled up her nose. "What?"

Talba dropped it; she could feel herself start to get argumentative.

"Tell me something. Do you think she was using drugs?"

"I sure didn't think so. But how else do you explain ... it?"

"Why didn't you think so?"

"Oh, you know. She was so pure. So holy."

"So completely the opposite of what the preacher said."

Hunter winced. "I was real upset about all that," she said softly.

"It must have been a hard night for a little eight-year-old," Talba said. "The night she got attacked."

Hunter's blue eyes got bigger and bigger as she saw where Talba was going, as if she just couldn't believe what was coming out of the black woman's mouth.

"Do you know? The weirdest thing. Nobody's ever asked me about it."

"Oh, come on. You never had a college gabfest, and everyone told secrets?"

The girl's eyes strayed back to the children. "I didn't go to college. I married a boy I grew up with. We went to school together, church together, swimming at the country club together, camp together. He probably knew more about me than I knew about myself.

"He knew me, but I sure didn't know him."

There was something so hurt about her, Talba ventured a guess. "Mean streak?"

"Mean, drunk streak. Oh, yeah. I could put up with it when it was me, but when it was that tiny innocent child . . ." Her eyes flooded again.

"I'm sorry." Talba paused long enough to give the words some weight. "So you never met anybody who didn't know your sister got scalped in her own bedroom with the whole family at home?"

Hunter tossed her head from side to side, as if trying to shake something off. Talba could see that the girl profoundly wanted her to shut up. She wasn't about to. "That kind of thing could stay with you forever. They didn't even take you for counseling or anything?"

"Well . . . no. I don't guess they thought about it."

"Do you ever dream about that night?"

"Oh, God! I used to. I used to all the time. And I started wetting the bed—at eight! Can you imagine? And Mama used to shame me for it."

Mama sounded like even more of a piece of work than Talba'd imagined. "I'm curious. Did you dream about what really happened or just some generic nightmare?"

Hunter just shook her head, her face a study in sadness.

"I'm asking because something real bad happened to me when I was a kid, and I dreamed about it. Even as an adult. Sort of waking dreams."

"What were the dreams like?"

"Blood," said Talba. "There was so much blood . . ."

"Oh, shit." Hunter collapsed in loud, rolling sobs. So loud Lily heard, burst into tears herself, and came running. Hunter picked her up and held her, and each, the child and the child-woman, tried to comfort the other.

Talba murmured that she was sorry and slunk away, disturbed that she'd upset an entire family unit, but thinking it a poor time to continue the interview.

She drove to the nearest gas station, found a phone book, and turned to "Ferris," amazed at her good fortune in unearthing a high school friend—apparently one who was still loyal to Clayton.

There were four Ferrises, and she started at the top.

"I'm calling Lou Ann Ferris. . . ."

"Sorry, you got the wrong number."

"Hello, I'm calling Lou Ann Ferris."

"Lou Ann Ferris, or Roxanne Ferris? My grandmama was Lou Ann Ferris, but she's been dead for eight and a half years. No, seven and a half. Harry, what year did Grandma die?"

Why did people love details like that? Talba wondered. She got lucky on the third phone call.

"Lou Ann Ferris? You must be an old friend."

"Yes, ma'am, Lou Ann and I . . ."

" 'Cause Lou Ann, she got married seven years ago. Married Dr. Fletcher Dumontier." Talba suddenly realized that the woman she was talking to must be the Ferris family's maid. "Yes, Lord. And two little girls, too."

"No! Well, I can't wait to catch up with her. I'm visiting from Baton Rouge, and I thought I'd call. You wouldn't have her phone number, would you?"

The woman did, and an address. Talba thanked her stars she hadn't gotten some more suspicious soul.

Dr. Fletcher Dumontier lived in a development on a hill outside of town, with plenty of land around it and a Lexus in the driveway. Lou Ann's, with any luck.

Talba mounted the steps of the mini-mansion, figuring there was probably a view of a golf course at the top; that was the kind of neighborhood it was. The woman who came to the door had short hair that fit her like a helmet. She was dressed in tennis clothes—plain sleeveless T-shirt and some sort of garment that appeared to be a skirt in front and shorts in the back. Her face was twisted up like she'd eaten something bitter. Talba wondered if it was a piece of her life.

Or maybe she was late for her tennis game.

"Hello, I'm Talba Wallis . . ."

"I know who you are." Ferris's face twisted tighter. "I remember you from the funeral."

Talba smiled, as if she didn't even realize she was being frozen out. "I just talked to Hunter Patterson. She sure is a nice girl, isn't she?"

This was a trick Eddie had taught her—never cut to the chase. Make them like you first. Say whatever you have to to get them on your side.

"All alone with that little bitty baby. I feel so sorry for her. . . ."

Ferris didn't change expression, didn't join in the conversation, and didn't ask what she could do for her visitor. Talba looked around, appreciating her surroundings. "This sure is a beautiful place you have here."

"If you don't leave by the time I count to five, I'm calling the sheriff."

Talba stepped back, acting out being shoved, and it wasn't that much of an act. In every way but physically, she had been.

"But . . . I thought you of all people. Being Clayton's best friend . . ."

Ferris reached over to a table, picked up a cell phone, and began punching in numbers. "One," she said. "Two . . ."

Goddammit, Talba thought. *I need some black people.*

Chapter Fourteen

Now where would you find black people in a town like Clayton?

They'd be working, she figured. Anywhere there was work getting done, they'd be doing it.

She tried the high school first, and sure enough, the principal was black; so was his secretary.

This was more like it.

Here, they politely directed her to the school library, where the librarian—who was white, but apparently not a Patterson crony—quite helpfully pulled out the yearbooks for the years in question. The late eighties, Talba figured. Anyone who'd been in school then probably knew Clayton.

There were five African-Americans—Ebony Frenette, April Mullett, Reginald Oliver, Marshannon Porter, and Calvin Richard.

Not that many, but at least three were boys, who probably wouldn't have changed their names. She handed back the yearbooks, asked for the phone book, and looked up all five.

Three of the names were there, among them, (glory be!)

Ebony Frenette. The others were Marshannon Porter and Calvin Richard.

Talba's stomach grumbled, prompting her to look at her watch. Nearly two, and she was starving. Not wanting to be seen around town any more than she had to, she drove to the outskirts and found a Wendy's, her unvarying choice when it came to fast food. At least there, she could get salads—not only were they good for you, there was so much to munch, such robust chewing to be done. And utterly without guilt. She didn't give the dressing a second thought.

As she worked her mandibles, she thought about things. She hadn't yet bearded the judge in the scalping case, but she wasn't up to it today. Today was a day for deep background, a good time to see if there were any loose tongues at all in this town. Because if there were, they'd almost certainly be attached to black bodies.

I *wonder*, she thought. I *just wonder*.

The person she was thinking of was the African-American woman she'd seen at the cemetery after the funeral. She was no spring chicken, though Talba couldn't begin to guess her age. Still, she was probably old enough to have worked for the Pattersons sixteen years ago.

Talba could feel her blood starting to race. If the woman had been there then, she was practically an eyewitness. White people talked about everything in front of the maid. Talba knew all about it from her own mama, who'd cleaned enough white women's houses to start her own fortune-telling business, as she was fond of saying. Miz Clara claimed they said everything there was to say about each other. She knew intimate secrets about women she'd never even met. And sometimes she knew what the future held too—if Elsie's husband was sleeping with Nina down the block, there was a divorce in somebody's stars.

"Law, the money I could make," Miz Clara liked to say, and laugh; there wasn't much about her job she laughed about.

If this woman, the current cleaner, had actually been there

when Clayton got scalped, there wasn't anything she wouldn't know about it.

Talba figured chances were good the woman would get off somewhere between three and six, and that was now. Perfect. It would take her awhile to find the house, and Talba could just sit in the car and wait till she came out, then maybe get her license number and run it to get her name. Or maybe talk to her right then. Some opportunity would present itself.

The Pattersons' house was enormous, located on a block with several of its sisters and brothers and a whole lot of poor relations, brick houses from the fifties. Evidently, the small ones were now classed as "teardowns." The others were all far too big for their lots.

The Pattersons' even had a circular driveway, though it hardly needed one so few feet from the curb. There was only a tiny patch of green at the front, planted with flowers of the season—mums, pansies, and a Calhoun-for-Governor placard.

Not a bad sign, Talba thought, wincing at the pun. *At least they aren't racist assholes.*

The house itself made all the sense in the world. The Pattersons had money and Deborah was a decorator. Even though all their chicks had flown from the nest, they'd have to have a state-of-the-art domicile. This thing had fan windows, antique-style lighting fixtures, and a fall wreath on the door that rang false in the still-steaming weather.

Talba was discouraged by the sheer size of it. Surely no cleaning lady could get out before six. She circled the block. She couldn't comfortably park on this block—it was way too white, way too quiet.

She circled again. She certainly wasn't going to call the sheriff and say not to bother her because she was a big city PI doing a job in Clayton. Somehow, she just didn't figure that was going to go down well.

No car was parked in the circular driveway. One of the others on the block might be the maid's, but Talba couldn't pick out a likely one. Her own Isuzu, though, was conspicuous. It could pass just fine in New Orleans, but it was too old, too shabby for this neighborhood.

She found that when she parked on a side street, she could just see the front of the Patterson house. The problem was, this street was as white and quiet as the other. She got out a book—never traveled without one, never knew when she might get bored—moved over to the passenger side, and held it up ostentatiously.

A few people came and went, some women with strollers, some men getting off work, some kids out looking for trouble. If anyone gave her so much as a second glance, she made a point of frowning and looking at her watch, as if getting really sick of waiting. It seemed to be working just fine, but after half an hour or so, she thought she was pressing her luck, and moved to the opposite side street. She'd been there about fifteen minutes when a man approached her.

"Excuse me, are you waiting for somebody?"

Talba nodded pleasantly. She had a nice little speech all rehearsed. "Umm-hmm. My boss. I'm with the Edible Complex catering service." She checked her watch again. "She's taking forever." Talba looked at the man and smiled her sweetest smile. "Giving an estimate."

"Where?" the man asked, "Which house?"

Talba shrugged. It was starting to get ugly, but it was too soon to panic. "To tell you the truth, I got so interested in my book, I didn't notice." She gestured at the book. "Have you read Susan Dodd's new book yet?" She figured he hadn't read much of anything, ever.

He was getting red in the face. "Let me tell you something, lady. You better figure the hell out where she is, and you better both be clean out of the town of Clayton within five minutes."

What to say to that one? *I have as much right as you to be here*? She thought not.

Instead, she looked at her watch again. "We really have been here quite awhile." She smiled at him again. "Sure, I can leave if I'm making you nervous. I'll call her on the cell phone and tell her to let me know when she wants to be picked up." All perfectly reasonable. But maybe just a tad too explanatory?

"You do that." The man crossed his arms and stood there till she had closed her book, slid back over to the driver's seat, and left.

So much for that idea, she thought, and headed crossly out of town, figuring to go straight for the judge next time she came to Clayton.

She was nearly back to the Wendy's where she'd eaten lunch when she saw the flashing light behind her—a sheriff's car, signaling her to pull over.

The man who got out was young and white, sunburned, with sun-bleached hair in a buzz cut, wearing a brown uniform.

"Can I see some I.D., please?"

God, how she hated to be asked for I.D.—she was going to have to get her name legally changed.

"N'Awlins'," he said, running the syllables all together. "Whatchew doin' in Clayton?"

"I have business here."

"What kinda business is that?"

She had no idea whether this was coincidence or the result of a phone call from the red-faced man. But something told her not to lie. She gave him the same smile she'd given the last one, all sweetness and innocence. "I'm a PI." She gestured at her purse, beside her on the seat, the same purse out of which she'd just dug her driver's license. "Would you like to see my license?

Suddenly the young man looked terrified. "You keep your hands right where they are."

Talba complied.

"Now put them outside the car." Once again she obeyed.

The man opened the door himself.

"Get out the car."

As soon as she was out, he spun her around and cuffed her. "Am I under arrest?"

He didn't answer, a favorite trick of cops, she'd noticed.

But she figured she must be, because he put her in the back of his car and took her back to his office, where he threw her in a cell.

No one asked her a single question; no one booked her or read her her rights or told her to have a nice day—just took her possessions and locked her up. *I could be here forever*, she thought. *No one even knows where I am.*

Sure, they had to give her a phone call, but the way they did things here in Clayton, she figured that could be next week or next month. She sat down and took stock.

As jails went, she figured it probably wasn't too bad, but it sure wasn't the Royal Orleans. The best part was, she was the only one in her cell, which was furnished with one bunk, one tired and stained mattress, one rough blanket, one steel washbasin, and one disgusting jail commode. The hell of it was, she was so nervous she was going to have to use it soon.

Nervous. Well, that was one way to put it.

They kept her there three hours before they let her use the phone, three hours during which no one spoke a word to her. Finally, a black deputy, a man she'd never seen before, flung open the door, blank-faced, and asked her if she wanted to make a phone call.

It was seven o'clock. Eddie'd be home already, and she didn't know his home number. It was written in her address book, but they'd confiscated that. Calling either Miz Clara or Corey was out. That left Darryl.

Please be home. Please, she prayed as she dumped her money in the phone.

"Hello?" Darryl's voice.

"Thank God. Darryl, I'm in jail."

"What? Why?"

"I don't know. Nobody'll say a word to me. I'm in the St. Sebastian Parish jail—I was in Clayton on the case. Call Eddie to come get me, will you?" And then she remembered something. "Oh, hell. His home number's unlisted. You'll have to go see him."

From Darryl's house, that would take almost an hour.

"Hang on, Your Grace. We'll get there as fast as our fat little legs will carry us."

But when Eddie arrived, he was alone, and Talba figured that was probably a good thing. It was almost midnight.

The bags under his eyes seemed to have tripled since the day before. They were the size of steamer trunks, the color of bricks crumbling from centuries of exposure.

E ddie had finished dinner (eggplant parmigiana), and, full of rich food and a cocktail or two, had repaired to his den and stretched out in his recliner for a little nap before bed. Angie was over for dinner; she was helping Audrey load the dishwasher and then she'd probably go home. Eddie couldn't understand why she'd never stay, watch a little television with the folks; but she always had "work to do." Or something.

Something shook him awake; an earthquake maybe.

"Oh, Gawd, you jumped like you got a guilty conscience. Come on; Darryl Boucree's here. About Talba."

"That's a reason to wake me up? Somethin' wrong? She get thrown in jail or somethin'?" He was joking.

Audrey's face was straight as a poker. "Yeah. She did."

He sat up too fast, causing the chair to fold with a thump and his head to swim a little. "Ms. Wallis?" He was getting accustomed to the idea; also to his sudden change of altitude. "Ms. Wallis got herself arrested? What'd she do?"

Angie was just walking into the room, waving a wet dish towel. She looked like she was going to a funeral. Even at her parents' house for a little home cooking, she was wearing her usual black—black jeans, black T-shirt, black sneakers. She'd look good in any color on God's earth and this was the way she dressed. Eddie didn't get it.

"DWB," she said.

"Huh?" Eddie was only vaguely aware of having heard the term.

"Driving while black. Look, I'll drive up and get her out. You stay here and rest." It pissed him off the way Angie always knew best. She was a lawyer, which he was proud of, but why the hell couldn't she have been a doctor? He'd never met a lawyer that didn't have more opinions than God, and Angie'd been like that before her first day of kindergarten.

"Angie, for God's sake." He struggled up out of the chair. "Where the hell is she? Excuse my French."

"Clayton. St. Sebastian Parish."

"Oh, Jesus." He stumbled to the living room, where Talba's boyfriend stood, looking worried, like an expectant dad or something. He was a tall black man with glasses, far too handsome for Eddie's tastes. (He'd once said that to Angie, whereupon she sniffed back, "You mean he looks too white.")

Eddie said, "Darryl, what's goin' on?"

"Talba doesn't seem to know. Says they picked her up, threw her in jail, and won't tell her why."

"Well, what the hell did she do?" Instantly, he regretted his mistake. "If you say DWB, I swear to God I won't even bail her out."

"DW—what? Oh, yeah. Well, she didn't mention that. And I don't know about bail. I could do that by myself. She wanted me to see if I could get you to come with me."

Now *that* Eddie understood. Deep in his heart he knew this was bound to be a black-white thing.

"I see what you're saying, Darryl. I'm gon' go get her, all right. But I think it'd be better if you didn't come along."

Darryl looked down at the floor, something Eddie would have guessed he didn't do very often. The man was a school-teacher, highly educated and used to respect. Here was a situation he couldn't control.

Finally, having thought it through, he raised his gaze and nodded. "Yeah. I expect you're right."

"Well, anyway, I'm white. This is just one of those things. I'm as sorry as I can be." Angie and Talba thought he was a racist—hell, Audrey probably did too—but he hated to see this kind of thing. It was embarrassing for everybody concerned and it put white people in a bad light. "You go on home now. We'll call ya once I get her out."

Angie was dying to go, of course—just perishing to get up on her lawyer high horse and give those back-country rednecks a lesson in law. Eddie was so damned pissed off he had half a mind to unleash her on them, but that wasn't going to help Ms. Wallis's case.

He drove all the way up to Clayton in the middle of the night, falling asleep once, waking up to find himself about to change lanes involuntarily and plow into somebody.

It was a damn shame he had to do this. It was a shame what they did to Ms. Wallis, first of all, but his having to get her out was even more of a shame, because it was going to blow his cover in Clayton. Ms. Wallis probably shouldn't even have come up there alone—these were just assholes abusing their power, and, like he'd told Darryl, it was just one of those things.

But if his cover was blown that was bad for the case. It sure would be nice if at least one of them could be anonymous here.

It looked to Eddie like there were only two people in the whole sheriff's office—a black deputy who looked permanently pissed off and a white kid who didn't look old enough to wear a badge. A really stupid-looking white kid. This was the one he was going to have to schmooze.

"Hey, there." He stuck out his hand. "Eddie Valentino out of New Orleans."

The kid didn't want to shake, but his name tag said "Greene." Why the hell couldn't it be a less common name?

"Deputy Greene, I presume? Say, you related to Lamar Greene? Former Jefferson Parish sheriff's deputy, back when I was on the job. Y'all a law enforcement family?" Eddie'd never met a Lamar Greene in his life, but he thought he detected a slight thawing in the deputy's stone-face.

The kid shook his head. "No, sir. Not unless it's some other branch of the family. Know quite a few Jefferson Parish deputies, though. You know anybody's still on the job?"

"Oh, sure. Almost everybody." And thus did the schmoozing begin. Fifteen minutes later and he and Deputy Greene were asshole buddies. Deputy Greene knew perfectly well what Eddie was there for, but somebody had to blink first, and Eddie was sleepy. When he figured the time was right, he said, "I understand you got one of my employees locked up." Like he had an office full of employees.

"Yeah. Yeah, we might. Got a little black gal says she's a

PI in there." He pointed toward a door that must lead to the jail.

They had her license. They knew damned well she was a PI, and they knew who she worked for—the name of the firm was right there on it.

"What kind of trouble she givin' y'all?"

He shrugged. "Guess she was tryin' to do surveillance without tellin' us she was there. Man called and complained about a suspicious person in a parked car. She gave him some crazy story, and he called us, axed us to pick her up."

"Ohgawd. I'm embarrassed. What's she say about it?"

He looked Eddie full in the face, lip curling so defiantly he knew the man was lying. "She didn't have no story. Wouldn't say a damn word to us."

"Well, what law'd she violate?"

"Trespassing, speeding, loitering, resisting arrest, battery." He shrugged. "You name it."

Time to pull rank, maybe. "Sheriff know you got her?"

"Sheriff's orders to hold her."

"Oh. Well. Who's the sheriff of St. Sebastian Parish these days?"

"Junior . . . uh, Dunbar Brashear."

"Oh my gawd. Is that little Junior Brashear? His daddy and I were up at LSU together. I remember that boy when he was just a little old thing. Get him on the phone, will you?"

The young man looked ill at ease for the first time. "He said to hold the nigger till morning."

Eddie fixed him with an old man's weary stare. "Son, I know Junior Brashear. He ain't never said the *n* word in his life. That ain't no way for you to be talking to me."

"Well, I don't happen to have his phone number, Mr. Valentino."

Damn! And things had been going so splendidly. He'd have Ms. Wallis out of jail by now if he hadn't lost his temper.

He ended up having to call Junior Brashear's daddy and going at it backasswards.

The elder Dunbar Brashear didn't even live in Clayton; he

was a retired gentleman up in Baton Rouge and damned unhappy to be waked up, but he knew enough to get his son to release a citizen he hadn't even arrested before he got his ass in a sling.

The whole thing ended with Junior Brashear coming down to the jail and doing the honors himself, looking a little like the Pillsbury doughboy with a three-day beard. Junior seemed like a man who liked his beer and drank barrels of it, waiting for his disposition to improve. The whole time he was there, he never spoke to Talba. His parting shot to Eddie was this: "I think you'll find you'd do well to keep your employees out of the partic'lar neighborhood we found Urethra in."

That made Eddie as mad as anything else that had happened that night, and he had a list as long as your arm.

Chapter Fifteen

It wasn't at all clear to Talba whether she'd been dragged off for being black in a white neighborhood or because somehow the Pattersons knew she was watching their house.

"Ms. Wallis," Eddie had said when she broached the question, "it just don't make no never-mind. If there's one thing to be learned from this, it's that you stick out too much in Clayton to work this case."

"Not where I'm going, I don't," she said huffily, and the next day, on about three hours sleep, she was back in her car, driving up I-10 to Clayton. She got Jason on her cell phone. "Look, everyone in Clayton's clammed up like they've got lockjaw. I need the transcript of Troxell's trial, but I'm afraid it might cost a few hundred bucks. Can you handle it?"

"Hell, yes," he said, his voice grim. "Get that if you don't do anything else. I need to know what happened there."

Okay, that was one good thing. Talba was humiliated at having had to call Eddie the night before. And all the more determined to make sense out of the case; well, frankly, to prove herself. She knew that was what it was, knew she didn't have to, and couldn't stop herself. She'd gotten up early, gotten online, and checked out Ebony Frenette, Marshannon Porter, and Calvin Richard. To no avail.

Okay, Eddie, okay, call information first, she said silently as she stood in a Clayton phone book, looking up their addresses in the phone book. She should have written them down yesterday.

She looked at her watch. It was still early enough to catch someone before work. Yes! Good planning might pay off, for once. She stopped at a gas station to ask directions, found Calvin Richard lived only a few blocks away, and decided to try him first.

She liked Richard's neighborhood. It was much more modest than any she'd yet been to in Clayton, neat as an English village, and, so far as she could see, black. Everyone on the street was black; even the dogs were black.

Let Deputy Dog find me here, she thought.

The Richard house was a wooden bungalow painted yellow with white trim; pansies bloomed in a neat bed out front. A gleaming new Cadillac sat in the driveway. Calvin must be doing well for himself.

She rang the doorbell and had to conceal her disappointment when the door was opened by a woman in her fifties. Nonetheless, she mustered a smile. "Good morning," she said. "I'm looking for Calvin Richard." Taking a chance, she pronounced it the Cajun French way—ReeSHARD—and apparently, she guessed right.

The woman nodded, brow furrowed. She was a full-figured woman without being oversized, dark with neat hair. She wore white pants, sandals, and a close-fitting T-shirt. She was probably somewhere around Miz Clara's age, but a whole lot sexier. It occurred to Talba that that was what a little money could do.

"Just a minute." The woman closed the door, which struck Talba as odd, but maybe her mama hadn't taught her any manners.

She had to wait quite a while, so long she wondered if the woman had simply brushed her off. But why say "just a minute" in that case? She tried to be patient, but it didn't come naturally. Finally, a man came to the door, a businessman about the same age as the woman, in tan slacks and a blue shirt. He had a tie hung around his neck, but not yet tied. *Yes*, she thought, *this is far and away the best time for an interview*.

"I'm Calvin Richard." ReeSHARD. That part was good. "You're looking for me?"

"No, sir. But I might be looking for your son. I'm looking for the Calvin Richard who graduated from Clayton High School in the late eighties."

"May I ax what you need him for?" The man's voice was gentle, a little too much so, she thought. For some reason, he was making her nervous.

"I'm a friend of a friend. Our mutual friend thought he might be able to help me with something I'm working on."

"Oh? And who would that be?"

Something was definitely amiss here. He wasn't supposed to be the one asking the questions. She tried redirecting the conversation. "Is he your boy? My friend says really nice things about him."

"Who would that be?" he said again.

"It's someone he went to school with." She decided to come clean. "I'm a private investigator working on a case—but don't worry. Calvin's not involved in any way. I just thought he might be able to help me with some information."

"Oh, I see. And what's your name, miss?"

"Talba Wallis. But it won't mean anything to him."

"No, it won't. Nothing will, I'm afraid." He heaved a deep, impossibly sad sigh. "I'm sorry, Ms. Wallis, our son is no longer with us."

Could she be hearing right? "I beg your pardon?"

"He was killed in an accident a few years ago. I'm very sorry I can't help you."

Even if it was the wrong Calvin Richard, Talba'd meant to ask lots of questions—how to find the other black students, for one thing; who the Pattersons' maid was, for another—but she was so shocked she could only stare open-mouthed.

Finally, she said. "I'm so sorry to have disturbed you."

"That's all right," the man said. "I know you didn't know."

What was the deal here? Everybody she went to see was already dead. At least Calvin had been for years—with luck, his death had nothing to do with the case.

It was starting to be too late to catch anyone at home, but she drove to Ebony Frenette's house anyhow, only to discover it was no house at all, but a large apartment complex. She had no apartment number for the woman.

She buzzed the manager, secured one, tried it, and got no answer.

Damn!

She sat down and tried to think what to do next. Maybe if she could just talk to somebody . . .

Slowly, she concocted a plan. She went out, bought a big bouquet of flowers, came back with them, and buzzed each of Ebony's neighbors till she found someone home.

"Yes?" A woman's voice.

"I'm sorry to disturb you. I have some flowers for your neighbor, but she's not home."

"What neighbor?"

"Ebony Frenette."

"Ebony? Ebony at work."

"Oh. Well, I wonder if you'd mind taking the flowers for her?"

There was a long silence, while the woman weighed the virtue of being a good neighbor against the lazy comfort of blowing it off.

Finally, virtue won out. "Awright. I got to get some clothes on."

Talba waited till the woman came downstairs, a much younger woman than she expected. She smiled as she handed over the flowers. "I knew an Ebony Frenette once. She was a nurse at the county hospital."

"Ain't this one. This one work for an insurance company."

"Oh, yeah. Which one?"

"I don't know. Just an insurance company's all I know." She pronounced it "insherntz."

"Well, thanks for taking the flowers."

Back to the phone book. How many insurance companies could there be in Clayton?

Quite a few, it developed. Talba called fourteen before she found Ebony. She decided to take a chance on a phone conversation. She had no qualms about saying who she was—she'd already planned it out. For once, she saw no reason to lie. So far as she knew, Ebony had nothing to hide, nothing to lose by talking to her. And how else to justify the kind of questions she wanted to ask? She asked to be transferred to Miss Frenette.

"Ebony? Hi, my name's Talba Wallis. I'm a private investigator and I think you might be able to help me with a case I'm working on."

"You got to be kidding! Me?"

"It wouldn't take more than five minutes or so. If you're going out for lunch, maybe I could meet you outside your building."

"Okay. Sure. Yeah. I'm wearing a tan suit, and my lunch hour's noon. Oh, and I'm African-American." The woman sounded flattered, as if a TV game show had called her.

"I figured that from your name."

"Oh, yeah. That's kind of a giveaway."

It was going on eleven now. Talba had plenty of time to go to the courthouse and order the Troxell transcript before meeting Frenette.

The woman who got off the elevator at noon was quite smart-looking, kind of in the Michelle vein. Despite her name, she was about as ebony as a paper bag.

"Ebony Frenette? Talba Wallis."

Frenette did a double-take. "You're a sister!"

Talba had to laugh. "You know what? I am."

"You're black and you're a woman—and young. You're young and you're cute too. They oughta do a TV show about you."

"Oh, yeah. I'm really interesting—you know it." Talba liked this woman. Well, maybe she was flattered by her, but there was something about her ingenuousness that was easy to take, and that might prove useful. This was a girl who blurted.

"You free for lunch by any chance?" she asked.

Frenette said, "You want to have lunch with me? Sure, I'll have lunch with you. You just tell me some stories."

"Maybe you've got one for me—did you ever think of that?"

They ended up going to a nearby sandwich place. Frenette was really quite pretty, seeming much younger than her thirty-two or so years. Though Talba herself was the younger, the woman was making her feel like some big-time city slicker. It was kind of fun.

Talba drew her out for a few minutes (as Eddie always advised), learning that she'd gone to college for two years, gotten pregnant, gotten married, loved her kid to death, but always regretted not finishing college, especially after the husband dumped her and she ended up being the breadwinner. She wanted to go back to night school, but little Tawana needed a babysitter, and Ebony hated to ask her mama, so maybe in a few years . . . and now she was dating a nice man who worked as a mechanic, but there was no financial future in it.

It was really a very ordinary life, Talba thought. No wonder she seemed exotic to Ebony. On impulse, she asked, "Do you ever get bored?"

Ebony seemed astonished. "Bored? No, ma'am, I don't get bored. I work way too hard to get bored." She bit into her white toast BLT so hard she almost broke a tooth.

Not for the first time, Talba wondered what it was like not to ever get bored. What did people think about when they painted houses or filed? Why did some minds have to twist themselves around poems, and others could stand at parade rest? Sometimes she envied ordinary people.

But what the hell, she thought. *I am a baroness.*

Ebony said, "You must have a pretty interesting life, huh?"

Talba described surveillance to her.

"Now I b'lieve that would bore me," Ebony said.

"Yeah, it probably would. It does me."

"So tell me—what you want to talk to me about? I've been

turning it over and over in my mind, trying to think, and I can't think of nothin'.'"

"This goes back a long, long way—you ever know a girl named Clayton Patterson?"

"Clayton! Yeah, I been knowin' Clayton. She died last week or something."

"Tell me about her."

"What for? What you working on?"

"Well, to tell you the truth, I can't. You know how it is when something's under investigation? You're not supposed to talk about it. But I'll tell you one thing—it's about something that happened back when y'all were in high school."

"Ya mean when Donny Troxell scalped her? Oweee, that was awful! I couldn't b'lieve Donny'd do a thing like that."

"Really?" Talba pretended deep interest in her salad.

"I gotta be honest. I never did like Clayton all that much. She just had . . . somethin' about her attitude. I just didn't like her. Now Donny Troxell—he treated me nice. I had a math class with him, and he even showed me how to do problems sometimes. Just as nice as pie. Wonder what Clayton did to make him mad enough to go after her like that?"

"I was hoping you knew."

They both laughed. "No, I don't know. Always did wonder. Let me see—Donny must be out of jail by now. I sure haven't thought about him in a long time. Wonder what ever happened to him?"

"Well . . ." Talba let time go by. "He died too, Ebony. About the same time Clayton Patterson did."

The woman came alert. "No! What happened to him?"

"He got killed in a mugging."

"I just can't believe it! It's a shame, you know that? I never thought he had a mean bone in his body."

"Well, I was just glad to find *you* alive. An awful lot of people from your class are gone already—you realize that?"

"Who?" Ebony looked wary, like she was about to get some bad news.

"Clayton, of course. Then Donny." She ticked them off on her fingers. "Calvin Richard. That's three."

Ebony's hand froze, her sandwich halfway to her lips. Her eyes turned to quarters. She was silent, perfectly still for a moment, and when she spoke, it came out in a whisper. "Calvin?"

Talba was starting to think she'd stepped into quicksand. "I'm sorry. I didn't realize you didn't know."

Ebony dropped the sandwich completely, lowered her head, and began fumbling in her purse. Tears were already starting to splash.

Talba handed her a handful of napkins.

"Calvin's dead?"

"I'm sorry, Ebony. I thought it was old news."

"I haven't seen him in years."

Ebony sobbed for awhile, Talba crossing and uncrossing her legs, hugely uncomfortable. Finally, Ebony closed her eyes, gathering up the cool to speak, and asked, "You know how he died?"

"His daddy told me he was killed in an accident. That's all I know." Talba was about to ask why Ebony was so upset when the other woman said, "I gotta run."

She picked up her purse and raced out the door, leaving Talba taken aback and stuck with the bill.

New Orleans was a small town in some ways—you couldn't go anywhere without tripping over your next door neighbor—but Clayton was a whole different animal. Extremely wearing on the nerves.

Nothing to do but push on. She decided to give Marshannon Porter a call—probably no one would be home, and there was no point paying a visit to an empty house.

But you just never knew. To her surprise, a woman answered. "Yeah?"

Talba thought fast. "Um. Mrs. Porter?"

"Yeah. This Miz Porter."

"This is Ms. Winters at Continental Bank. I have a credit application from your husband, but I see he forgot to fill in his employment. I'm calling to verify that he is employed."

Mrs. Porter was pissed. "Yes, he's employed. Of course he's employed!"

"The application seems quite complete other than that. May

I have the name and address of his employer, please? We'll
be happy to open an account for him."

"Sure." She was mollified. "It's the Gulf South Elevator
Company in Baton Rouge. I don't know the street address,
but he's got a cell phone—let me give you that number."

Dear sweet loyal spouse, Talba thought. *Marshannon's
sooo lucky to have you. It's just a good thing I'm not an
assassin.*

"What does he do for that company?" she asked. "I had an
uncle who was an elevator repairman."

"That's what he does. He's always having to rescue people."

"Ooh. Interesting job." It would keep him on the run too.
Probably that cell phone was going to be the best bet.

She tried the same thing she had with Ebony: investigator
working on a case; confidential; could she have five minutes?

"Lady," he said, "you sound downright interestin'. I'm
gon' take a break in about thirty minutes. You want to meet
me for a cup of coffee?"

She looked at her watch. "I'm in Clayton now. Can I make
it that fast?"

"Oh, yeah. Easy. I'll just wait for you if you're late."

They agreed to meet at a Burger King he knew, and as she
turned back onto the Interstate, a silver Lincoln Continental
followed and stayed with her all the way. She might have
thought nothing of it, except that she made it to the restaurant
with five minutes to spare, five minutes during which she
amused herself by looking out the window. The Lincoln
pulled into a Wendy's across the road. Even then she only
noticed in passing.

She hadn't thought about what Marshannon was going to
look like, but somehow, the minute he walked in the door,
she knew him. He was heavy-set and broad across the back,
with a fuzz of hair that he probably shaved off every few
weeks, unlike her natty brother, Corey, who kept his own pate
shiny as a button. He had a broad smile and he wore sloppy,
ill-fitting jeans with a shirt that had probably been clean that
morning but definitely wasn't now. She liked him on sight,
before he even said a word. There was something jolly and

benign about him. He seemed a simple person, at peace with himself, the kind you were supposed to meet in small towns; they seemed in short supply in Clayton.

He didn't give her time for her famous schmoozing, just blew in, shook hands, and said, "Whatcha got?" She wasn't all that sure how to answer.

Oh, well, she decided, answer a question with a question. "Back in high school," she said, "did you know a girl named Clayton Patterson? White girl?"

"Clayton Patterson." He smiled without showing his teeth and rocked himself a little. "Shame about Clayton. Well, sure I knew her. Everybody knew her. It wasn't all that big a school—and she did get herself scalped. What kind of case you workin' on?"

She hated that question. She made a mental note to start saying she was a reporter. "Can't say now, but I'll tell you one thing—you'll be hearing about it when it breaks. I can promise you that."

He nodded and gave her a grin. "Guess that's good enough."

"How well did you and Clayton know each other?"

He leaned over confidentially. Talba wondered if this was his way of flirting. "I'll flat tell you somethin', lady. You can believe it or not believe it, but I'm gon' tell you somethin'. Clayton had the hots for me."

"Well, who wouldn't, Marshannon? You're pretty cute." She figured that qualified as schmoozing.

He laughed, twisting his whole upper body toward the table to show his modesty. "No, I mean it. She did. Now I wouldn't date no white bitch, that never was my style, but man she could flirt!"

"I thought her boyfriend was Donny Troxell."

He nodded. "She led him around by the pecker. She sho' did that. But she ran after—don't take me wrong here—but what she liked was licorice sticks. You understand what I'm saying?"

Maybe, she thought, *I don't like him so well.* Yet he seemed eager not to give offense—it was just the way he talked.

"Look here, maybe I got a little braggy just now—my wife

says I'm always doing that. But I swear to God Clayton Patterson hit on me. And not just once, either. You think I kidded myself it was for my great charm and good looks? Hell, I wasn't the only one. I probably wasn't even in the top five."

There weren't five, Talba was thinking. *This guy's full of shit*.

But he pulled it out at the last second. "Well, really, there weren't but three—Reggie Oliver and Calvin Richard and me."

"I know," she said. "I looked at your yearbook. Where's Reginald Oliver now? I know Calvin Richard's dead, but maybe Reggie . . ."

Marshannon stared as if she'd switched to another language in midconversation. "What you talking about? Calvin ain't dead."

"I don't understand what's going on here. This is such a small town—how come no one knows Calvin's dead?"

"Calvin *ain't* dead, lady. Not unless he died over the weekend. I got a cousin still goes fishin' with him. He just brought me some fish they caught Saturday."

Talba said, "You sure?" and then realized how stupid she sounded.

"What makes you think Calvin's dead?"

Something told her to keep quiet on that issue. "I should have realized. I told Ebony Frenette he was dead and she bawled all over the restaurant. If it was true, she'd have already known."

"Ebony! She cried over Calvin?" He laughed. "Serve her right. Just serve her damn well right. Wooooeee! It nearly killed him the way she fooled around on him. They were high school sweethearts—'cept when she left him for somebody else. Which was often."

He laughed louder and larger. "Depended which day of the week it was. Could of been anybody. Usually was."

Sure, he was a big cute teddy bear, but his attitude was making Talba irritable. She spoke more brusquely than necessary. "You know where Calvin Richard is now?"

Her harsh tone seemed to sober him. " 'Course I do. He's in New Orleans. He's a cop."

Chapter Sixteen

Talba sucked in her breath, thoughts all a-jumble. Whatever answer she expected, it wasn't that one. This was so shocking it made her cordial again. "Is that so?"

"He's a sergeant." Marshannon spoke with pride: local boy had made good.

Why on earth would his parents say he was dead? She decided to risk a subtle inquiry. "Bet his parents are proud of him."

"Wooo. You know it." Okay, it was nothing to do with the job.

"Well, looks like I made an ass of myself about Calvin."

"You wouldn't be the first woman."

"The ladies like him?"

"I don't know what it is that guy's got." He guffawed again. " 'Ceptin' for good looks and brains. Few little things like that."

"Were he and Clayton Patterson an item?"

"Naw. Calvin had too much sense for that. Now she tried. You can bet on that. But Calvin wouldn't have none of that. Nooooo. Way too straight-arrow."

Talba smiled at him, ready to get out of there, chomping at the bit to get to Calvin. "Can I ask you one last thing? Who's the Pattersons' maid?"

He looked at her suspiciously. "Now, why'd you think I'd know a thing like that?"

" 'Cause Clayton's a small town—everybody knows everything."

"Tell me something. This thing you're doing—this investigation—it's got something to do with Clayton, don't it?"

"It might. She came from money. She had money to leave." A leaf from Eddie's book.

A slow smile came over him. "Oh, I get it. I'm startin' to get it. She left something to somebody. Awright, I'll h'ep ya. I can find that out for ya. I don't know who works for those people, but I got an aunt who will."

He pulled out his cell phone and spoke unceremoniously. "Who work for the Pattersons? You know, King and them. Yeah, I know her. Where she stay at? Okay." He put the phone away. No hello; no good-bye; no need to identify himself. It wasn't Talba's style, but she sure knew a lot of people who talked on the phone like that. He pocketed the phone. "Ontee say the lady name Betty Majors. She stay over on Pearl Street."

She thanked Marshannon and left with an embarrassment of riches. She'd sure been right about talking just to black people. If even a third of what he said was true, she'd learned more about Clayton Patterson from him than she had from the rest of the town put together.

Now what to do with it all? Make a run for Calvin, as had been her first instinct? Or try for Betty Majors?

She looked at her watch. Betty Majors ought to be getting off about now, and Pearl Street was close. Nothing made better sense than to go see her now. But something made Talba hesitate. Clayton was dead; Donny was dead. And Calvin's parents had told her Calvin was dead. The question was, why? The obvious answer was, to keep her from talking to him. They feared for him. Should Talba fear for him as well?

She did. And yet, how was she going to keep him alive by

going to see him first? His parents would have phoned to say she was coming, so he'd be warned. And he was a cop; he could take care of himself. She settled on Betty Majors.

She got back on the interstate and headed toward Clayton. She was three or four miles down the road when she noticed a silver Lincoln behind her. The one she'd seen before? Every other car on the road was silver these days.

She'd have to keep watching it. She changed lanes, made as if to get off at the next exit. Slowly, unobtrusively, so did the Lincoln. Did that settle it? Probably. She thought she should assume she was being tailed.

At first that was merely intellectually interesting, and then she noticed her palms were sweating. I'm turtling out, she thought, going into denial. It was an extremely dangerous defense mechanism. She couldn't afford to do it, she had to be alert.

She tried another lane change, noticed the other car did too.

Well, hell. He was practically insulting her intelligence, he was so bad at this. Who did he think he was, anyhow? Her palms were still sweating, but she was getting mad. That was good—it meant she was awake. She might as well make it work for her. What she needed was his license number. How to get that?

She pondered it almost all the way back to Clayton, keeping the car in sight, wondering if she'd been stupid with the lane changes, telegraphed that she'd spotted him.

Aha! She remembered Eddie's trick of tailing a car from in front—it was a neat reversal, and she could reverse the reversal. Get this car in front. She pulled off at a gas station.

And sure enough, it worked beautifully. The Lincoln sailed by, as if it had no interest whatsoever in a gray Isuzu Trooper. Talba shot out of the station after it, bearing down, but she had overestimated her steed. The Lincoln simply opened up, and no matter how hard she pushed the Trooper, it was no contest.

She was pissed off. There was an up side—not only had she lost him, he'd lost her. But it might not be over, she thought—in a town like Clayton, he could find her.

Once back in town, she tried the phone book again, and once again it delivered for her. There was a John Majors on Pearl Street, and she was willing to bet he was married to Betty.

It was Betty who answered the door, still in her white uniform—the woman Talba had picked out at the cemetery. "I know you. You the detective." She was more or less scowling, but her voice held no malice.

"Yeah, but I'm not really so bad." Talba gave her a winning smile. "I was Clayton's friend. Maybe you were too."

"I been workin' there a long time."

"Listen, Miz Majors, I heard what that preacher said, and that wasn't the Clayton I knew. Something's rotten in this town. Something wrong here. You know that, don't you?"

The older woman opened the door. "Come in, child," she said. "Come on in." She had a round sweet face, and only three or four gray hairs right around the part. She didn't really look old enough to have worked in one place for sixteen years.

"Would you like some iced tea?"

"Thank you. I b'lieve I would."

Talba used the few minutes it took Majors to get the tea to take in her surroundings. They certainly supported the cobbler's children cliché—the place was a mess. Dust was everywhere, and so were old newspapers, even a few dirty dishes.

Majors came back with one glass of tea only, held in her hand, not on a tray. She gave it to Talba and looked around herself.

"Lawd, lawd, I'm embarrassed. My girl Amber's s'posed to take care of this house. . . ."

"Oh, please," said Talba, unsure how to reassure her. "You're nice just to see me." She sipped the tea and nodded to show that it was good. "I saw you at the cemetery."

"Saw you too. Couldn't miss ya. You and the boyfriend everybody hate."

Talba risked a chuckle. "He's not half as bad as the husband was."

Betty made a noise like a squawk. "I heard that." She nodded and rocked her body. "I sure heard that."

Talba wondered if she'd established enough rapport by Eddie's standards to proceed. Betty had an expectant look, as if she were wondering when this show was going to get on the road. She was the one who broke the ice. "People are sayin' you don't think Miss Clayton killed herself."

Talba tried to hide her surprise. Her efforts at discretion were evidently laughable. "Do you?" she countered.

Majors answered without hesitation. "I know she had reason to." She let a beat go by. "They was mean to her, Ms. Wallis."

"Talba."

"I ain't never seen people be so mean to they own flesh and blood." She teared up and pulled a tissue from her uniform pocket. "I tried to he'p. I did the best I could, but ain't nothin' could he'p that child but another family."

"You tried to help recently? Or—"

The woman shook her head before she could finish.

"No'm. I ain't see Clayton for years, bless her heart. I tried to he'p then. When she was growing up. Somethin' bad happened to her, and I don't mean just that scalpin' thing. Mmmph, mmmph. Lot more to that than meets the eye."

Talba kept quiet, hoping for more. But Betty Majors only cried quietly into her tissue. Finally, Talba said, "What do you mean by that?"

"Wish I could tell ya, I surely do. I don't know exactly. But I sure do know there's somethin'."

Talba smiled. Time to play the maid card. "My mama does what you do."

"She somebody maid?"

"Lots of people's. She does day work. And she always knows everybody's business. Says people don't care what they say in front of the maid."

"Oh, she right about that. Most of the time they most certainly don't. I know when Mr. King got a new little chippy, I know how often he come home drunk, I know how many fish he catch over the weekend. Why, he don't even censor his nigger jokes in front of me. Now and then, when he tellin' one, he say, 'Now, Betty, you know I'm not a racist,' when I know good and well he is. He stupid enough to think I believe him, but most of the time he don't even bother. He just go ahead, tell his jokes, don't pay no attention to me.

"And I know all the same stuff about Little King—I ain' gon' call him Trey—and he drink nearly's much as his daddy and chase tail twice as much.

"I know when Deborah got her period and when she stop havin' her period once and for all. I know who she mad at and who she havin' a fight with, and usually it's two-three people at once. Ain't nothin' I don't know 'bout those people.

"And they give me a week off when somebody crawls in the window and try to kill my baby! Their oldest child scalped by an intruder, and they give me a week off! Clayton in the hospital, people comin' and goin', every kind of thing, and they give me the week off! Now what you think about that?"

"I think they didn't want you knowing their business."

Majors nodded with satisfaction. "Tha's what I think. And you know what else I think?"

Talba thought she did, but she asked politely, "What?"

"I think one of 'em done it." She nodded again, several times for emphasis. "Yep. Sho' as ya born. One of 'em done it. Scalped they own child."

"You think it was one of the parents?"

"Oh, could of been Little King. Yep. Sho' could of been him."

"Why do you think he would have done it?"

Majors shrugged almost absently, her tears dried now. She was clearly excited by the subject matter. "He might of done it out of pure D jealousy," she said.

"Of Clayton?" Talba couldn't believe what she was hearing. "I thought the rest of them hated her."

"No, ma'am. Uh-uh. Till that moment, till that night of reckonin', she was the apple of her daddy eye. All her young life, they love her just like all folks love they chirren. Then they give me the week off and when I come back they hate her." She snapped her fingers. "They never was nice to her another day in her life." She brought up another tissue from somewhere and wiped a few more tears. "Nobody oughta be treated the way they treat that child."

"What did they do, exactly?"

She turned her palms up. "Wasn't what they did so much as the way they talk to her. Mean. Just kinda mean. Like she know they secret and they hate her for it."

Talba squirmed. That was certainly the impression she was getting and it was ugly. She said, "I met the young one a day or two ago. Hunter."

For the first time in the interview, Majors smiled. "Sho' is a funny name, ain't it? Clayton. Hunter. King. Trey. Who those people think they is? Well, now, her I like. Young Miss Hunter, she my baby. She didn't have nothin' to do with that scalpin' and she never had no need to punish her sister for it. 'Course any time she nice to Clayton, the whole family mean to *her*."

Talba shivered, and not from the iced tea.

Chapter Seventeen

Talba ("the Baroness") Wallis could get so damn proud of herself. She'd just sashayed into Eddie's office, put her hands on her hips, and pronounced, "You are not going to believe what I got today."

Eddie rubbed his left temple, feeling a headache coming on. If her voice weren't so goddamn beautiful, she'd drive him crazy.

"That's what Audrey always says when she's been shopping."

"What?" Ms. Wallis looked taken aback.

He could see she didn't get the joke; he didn't know why he bothered. "Never mind, Ms. Wallis. Full speed ahead." That pretty much described her, he thought. If he were the poet instead of she, and if he were going to write a poem about her, that might be the title of it: "Full Speed Ahead."

"Somebody in Clayton's family attacked her. The maid says so—woman named Betty Majors. And if anybody'd know, she would."

"She heard 'em talking about it?"

"No. That's the interesting part. They gave her the week off."

"I don't see how you get a family scalpin' out of that one."

"They hated her after that—Clayton, I mean."

He wasn't getting it. "Uh-huh. What does that prove?"

Talba just looked disgusted on him—like she was some big college-educated character and she just kind of knew things by osmosis. He decided to try a new tactic. "You didn't tell me you were going back to Clayton—I thought I told you to stay out of that town."

"Uh-huh. That's why I didn't mention it."

"Don't you think you're getting a little too big for ya britches?"

Now she looked guilty.

"It's what ya mama says, idn't it? Sometimes I pity Miz Clara. I truly do."

She tapped his desk with her pencil, making some point or other. "Eddie, I'm a grown woman. You want to know what I did? I think it was pretty clever, actually—I didn't even go in the white neighborhoods. I just interviewed black people."

He shook his head. "Umph, umph. Ms. Wallis, Ms. Wallis."

"What's wrong with that?"

"Nothing's wrong with that. I was just thinking ya don't disappoint—I can always depend on ya to be resourceful."

"Why thank you, Eddie. I appreciate that."

She was childishly grateful for any crumb of praise. He wondered why that was—Miz Clara had to have been a good mother. Anybody who could fry chicken like that woman could was born to be a mama. He said, "What else ya got?"

"I don't know about this one." She spoke uneasily.

"Come on. Give it up."

"A man who was in her class said Clayton used to go after black guys. In high school."

Eddie whistled. "Ah. Now maybe we're getting somewhere. So Miss Clayton Debutante Patterson liked a little . . ." Suddenly he realized almost anything he could say would be offensive on some level.

"What the guy said was, she liked licorice sticks."

Eddie's cheeks went hot. "Language, Ms. Wallis!"

"What'd I say?" She wasn't doing a halfway decent job of looking innocent.

"You ambushed me!"

"Me? I ambushed *you*?"

"I'm gon' let it go this time, young lady, but in future ya keep a civil tongue in ya head, ya hear me?" He was uncomfortably aware that this was the way he used to speak to his daughter, Angie. "I will not tolerate foul language of any kind in this office."

"Sorry. Excuse my French." She was still giving him great big innocent eyes, but her lips were twitching.

"Goddammit, Ms. Wallis!"

"Oops. 'Scuse *your* French."

He sat there and fumed for a minute, trying to think of a way to recapture his dignity. Finally, he decided to trick her. "That gives Donny Troxell a hell of a motive." He left the bait dangling.

She took it without hesitation. "Yeah, but if she got into a relationship with another boy, that guy would have one too." Eddie had hoped she'd waffle about the possibility of a black kid as a suspect; he'd have enjoyed seeing her squirm.

He stuck the needle in a little deeper: "I kind of like that theory."

She pushed her hair behind her ears, a gesture that, in his experience, meant women were thinking. Maybe fiddling with their scalps stimulated their brains. "There's one other thing," she said. "There were five black students in that class, only three of whom were listed in the Clayton phonebook. One was Marshannon Porter, the man I spoke to. Another was Ebony Frenette, to whom I also spoke."

To whom I also spoke, he thought. He didn't even trust white people who talked like that, let alone black ones.

"The third is Calvin Richard. I went to see his parents, who reported him dead."

"Oh, shit! 'Scuse my French, Ms. Wallis. But it looks like half of Clayton Patterson's high school class has already kicked the bucket, and they've hardly been out long enough to have a reunion. Something fishy about that."

"Only he's not dead," she said, making Eddie feel like an idiot. "At least, Marshannon says he's not. And he says Calvin and Ebony were an item in high school."

"Well, if Clayton had something going with Calvin, maybe Ebony scalped her. Now that I do like. It's kind of a woman's crime, when you think about it. Women like to cut."

Talba nodded. "Yeah, ninety-nine percent of the machete attacks in America are perpetrated by women. I think I read it somewhere." It could have made him mad, but she smiled when she said it. "That's right, isn't it, Eddie?"

"Ms. Wallis, ya need to go shoppin'."

"Why?"

"Get yaself some bigger britches."

"Naaah. I'd just outgrow those too." Damn, she reminded him of Angie. "Listen, I got authorization from Jason to order the transcript in the scalping case."

Eddie raised an eyebrow. "Did ya now?" *Very good move*, he thought, but he wasn't ready to concede it aloud.

"Yeah, but it'll take a few days to get here."

"Always does."

"In the meantime, I need to go see the judge—"

Eddie stopped her cold. "No, ma'am, ya don't. You need to stay out of Clayton for awhile. Bad enough ya had to go get yaself arrested and make me blow my cover. I'll go talk to that judge myself. Matter of fact, I might even have a better idea. You just concentrate on this Calvin Richard."

"Did I mention Richard's a cop?" she asked. Dropping another bombshell. She must be having the time of her sassy young life.

"You think you're funny, don't ya? I haven't got time for this, Ms. Wallis. Ya got any more to report?"

"Uh . . . no."

She hesitated a bit too long. "Yes, ya do, Ms. Wallis. Come on now. Out with it."

"No, Eddie, I don't." She shrugged as if he were wasting her time. But he hadn't been a cop and a PI his whole life for nothing. She was holding something back. "I'm gonna tackle Calvin first thing tomorrow."

"I don't b'lieve I'd do that if I was you. He might not appreciate it."

"Why not?"

"It's Saturday, that's why. Let the man have the weekend in peace. Ya been working too hard on this anyway, what with that funeral last week and everything. Give it a rest, Ms. Wallis. Go home and go out with that young man with all the teeth."

"Eddie Valentino, is that a racist remark?" There was no fire in the words, but he supposed she felt she had to say them.

He sighed. "No, Ms. Wallis, it isn't. I s'pose it's jealousy."

Audrey and Angie had way too much to say about Darryl Boucree. All of it good.

In fact, Talba had forgotten it was the weekend. She did have a date with Darryl, though it was for the next night, and it wasn't a date so much as a forced march—Raisa would be along. She also had another date, if not with destiny, at least with herself, to work on her own case. But not till tomorrow.

She called Miz Clara, who answered gruffly, as usual.

"Mama, you sound like you're expecting the IRS."

"Ummph."

"You want to go see Michelle and the baby? I can come get you and take you over there to the hospital."

"They went home yesterday."

"Oh. Well, how about we go by Corey's?"

"All right. If it won't put you out." Miz Clara tried hard, but she couldn't keep the pleasure out of her voice. She was dying to see her grandchild.

Talba took her by, and they all got a basket of fried chicken to eat, and Talba felt downright kindly toward her brother's wife. Sophia Pontalba was just a tiny brown sweet thing . . . toffee, she thought, with amazement. *Toffee.* It was the way she'd described herself in her most famous poem, the one about being named Urethra. *I was right on the money that time. What a little brown sweet thing!*

On impulse, she said, "Mama, was I ever that sweet?" and everyone laughed.

"Lord, no! You was a mess from the minute you came into this world."

Somewhere, she thought, *I've got a little sister. Maybe she'll appreciate me.*

When she got home, it was still early enough to call strangers. She got out her list of Winterses and took up where she'd left off—at Dennis.

She hit paydirt on Kiana, who spoke almost as gruffly as Miz Clara. "This ain' Mozelle house."

Something about the way she said it telegraphed that she knew Mozelle. "Oh? You have her phone number?"

"No."

"Miss Winters, it's important. I'm a lawyer representing an estate—do you know what an estate is?"

"Yeah. I think I do." Talba was willing to bet she did—there was a definite softening in tone.

"I wonder if you could help me find her."

"Mozelle my mama sister. She don't have nothin' to do with us no more. She married to a doctor."

"Oh. I see. Do you happen to know his name?"

"I done forgot." It was like pulling teeth.

"Well, actually, we're trying to trace all the relatives of a Bartholomew Winters, who left quite a considerable estate— did your mother and Mozelle have the same father?"

"They sure did." Considerably more interest. Warmth, even.

After that, it was easy. Her mama's name was Leticia Hooks, and Leticia knew exactly what the doctor's name was—Matthew Simmons. She even supplied his phone number.

Talba didn't ask for his address—she was betting it was in the phone book, and she was half right. His office address was. Well, no problem, she had her trusty computer handy.

She certainly wasn't going to call—by now it was almost ten—but she was dying to know more. So she backgrounded him.

On paper he was exactly as advertised, a pediatrician who'd gone to LSU med school, owned two cars and a house in a good neighborhood, and had no liens or bankruptcies in his closet. She felt slightly let down, though she couldn't put her finger on why she was disappointed. Surely it meant her sister was being well cared for. The thought crossed her mind that he might know her brother, Corey—in fact, maybe it was inevitable, given the worldwide rule of six degrees of separation, which in New Orleans was more like two.

The girl would be Corey's sister too. What if they were friends, Matthew and Corey? What if Corey already knew his own sister and didn't know he knew her? What if Matthew ended up being Sophia's baby doc?

She thought, *Why couldn't I have been Corey? Scientific mind, plenty of money, no imagination—why do I have to put up with this instead?*

She was disappointed in the chase, that was what it was. She'd gotten so used to turning up dirt, it was like an addiction. So far as she could find, this man was so bland he'd probably never gotten his name in the paper, not even when he got married. Evidently, he didn't support political causes, go to charity balls, or otherwise hang with what Miz Clara called "the niggerati," a thought that set off another—if he'd been a different kind of man, her own sister might be about to become a debutante. Talba and Miz Clara would read about her making her bow, see her picture in the paper, and never even have a clue.

And that thought set off a third—Michelle being who she was, little Sophia Pontalba would undoubtedly be a debutante some day.

Talba's brain was spinning out of control.

She rubbed her temples as if that would stop it, and then, barely aware of the impulse before she acted on it, she backgrounded Calvin Richard, going through one of the services and finding nothing suprising. And then, as she nearly always did on a new case, she Googled him.

The search engine Google, she'd found, was great for turning up really personal things about people, like what sites they'd posted on. One man, for instance, a fellow from up around Shreveport, showed up on the Internet only twice. His name appeared with a photo of his wife's adorable toy poodle entwined with his own Rottweiler on a veterinary site; and also under an inflammatory letter he'd written to a white supremacist site. Since the man was a potential juror in a criminal case with a black defendant, the latter was hugely important information—enough to enable her client to get him dismissed for cause.

She had Googled Matthew Simmons to no avail, but Calvin Richard was something else altogether. Or his wife Tanitha was. There were lots of references to her, on sites about childhood developmental disorders. Checking one at random, Talba saw that a whole newspaper article had been scanned in about children so afflicted, one of whom was little Damian Richard. In it, Tanitha was quoted extensively.

Talba read it again. It was a *Times-Picayune* story that had been picked up by the wires and then had been scanned in to many of the sites—hence Tanitha's ubiquity. It covered the disorders themselves (the best known of which was autism), the particular ways in which children who had them suffered, what the lives were like of families in which they appeared, and the toll it took on them emotionally, in terms of effort, and financially.

Damian had been unlucky enough to be diagnosed with what the doctors called Pervasive Development Disorder Not Otherwise Specified (PDD-NOS), which, according to the article, some said was a euphemism for "We don't know what's wrong."

Damian seemed a perfectly normal little boy until he was about two and a half, when his parents noticed he still wasn't talking and, not only that, didn't even seem to hear well. He wouldn't look them in the eye and generally didn't seem to want to play with other children.

Then came an extensive—and no doubt very expensive—round of psychiatric and neurologic evaluations, which figured out very little except that Damian couldn't communicate like other kids and had severe problems with language—in other words, that he was going to need a lot of help. Indeed, he'd been enrolled in a special school which even had such arcane equipment as a "hug machine," and he was making progress.

Skipping through a few other articles on the subject, Talba learned that race wasn't a risk factor but that sex was, many more boys being afflicted than girls, that doctors had no idea what caused these disorders, and that education was considered crucial.

"The most important intervention," wrote one expert, "is early and intensive remedial education."

Tanitha, the original article said, had done exactly what Talba had done—researched PDD on the Internet, taken the doctor's advice to heart, and found a good school for her child, where she herself volunteered three days a week.

All well and good. But did Damian have a scholarship? How did a policeman's salary stretch that far? Talba just had to wonder.

Maybe the mom had money. Talba checked her out too. Nothing proved she did or she didn't. The thing bore looking into.

She went out to the kitchen to get herself some chilled white wine, maybe chat with Miz Clara a little. But her mother had gone to bed, and she couldn't call Darryl. Raisa was with him and she didn't want to take the chance of waking the child.

Oh, well, things could be worse. She happened to have a very good biography of that other baroness—the original one of Pontalba—which seemed particularly appropriate at the moment. She took her wine back to bed and snuggled in with the book.

But it was a long time before she slept and when she did, she dreamed—not nightmares exactly but disturbing movie dreams, stories in which things were oddly out-of-kilter. Anxiety, perhaps, she thought, given what she planned to do the next day.

She woke up feeling so much out of sorts that not even the smell of Miz Clara's coffee could cheer her up. Her mama was sitting at the old black-painted kitchen table, wearing ancient blue slippers, eating toast and bacon and reading the newspaper. She caught Talba's mood immediately.

"*You* a little ray o' sunshine."

"I haven't even said anything."

"You don't need to. You got a black cloud over ya head."

Talba said, "I need some coffee."

"You jealous, aren't ya?"

"What?" For a moment, it was hard for Talba to determine the context, but then she remembered—the last thing in Miz Clara's evening was the visit to Corey and Michelle's, whereas hers had included sojourns in the various worlds of Matthew and Mozelle Simmons; Tanitha, Calvin, and Damian Richard; and that other baroness. Catching on, she said, "Of whom? Corey?"

"Michelle. You want ya own baby."

"Well, I've got one. Little Sophia's enough for me right now."

"Umph umph. You ain't foolin' me. Don't fool me one bit."

Talba busied herself making toast.

"Why don't you just marry that man and get it over with?"

"So that's what this is about."

"I see the way you look at that baby."

"I love that little critter—any harm in that?"

"Sandra, go get ya own before it's too late."

"Well, well, well. Is this the same Miz Clara who used to lecture me on 'stayin' out of trouble?' Waiting to marry till I'd established a career? Becoming the first African-American female president? She was a pain in the butt, but at least I was used to her."

"You watch ya mouth, young lady."

That was the way the morning started. Talba looked at her watch. Ten o'clock on a Saturday morning—just about equivalent to seven or eight on a workday. She really couldn't put it off any longer.

The Simmonses lived in Kenner out in Jefferson Parish, on the far side of Metairie. Probably a good half hour away. Talba turned on the radio and sang along, anything not to think about what she had to do.

When she got there and saw the guardhouse, she almost turned around and bagged the whole errand. These people lived in a gated community. And no way, no way in hell, were they going to want to see her.

But the way out came to her so quickly it scared her, and she wouldn't even have to lie much. She could continue the routine she'd already started, only with a different twist.

Before approaching the guard, she called the number she had for the Simmonses. A woman answered.

"Mozelle Simmons?"

"Yes."

"Do you know what an heir-hunter is?"

"I think I do." As in the case of her young relative, she became a little more animated, decidedly more friendly.

"Are you the former Mozelle Winters?"

"Yes." Talba could almost feel her anticipation. There was no distrust, or even impatience in her voice—she evidently was content to let this one unfold as her benefactor wanted it to. Perhaps she feared that if she disturbed the protocol of the thing, her good fortune would go away.

"Do you have a sister named Lura?"

"Lura passed away a long time ago."

"And you're her next of kin?"

"Yes."

"Ms. Simmons, I think I can say at this time that I have some extremely important information for you—something that could enrich your life a great deal."

At this point, the woman's docility apparently ran its course. She sighed and for the first time, her voice was sharp. "I suppose there's some huge fee attached."

"There always is, Ms. Simmons. There always is. I'm outside your gate. Would you like me to come in and tell you about it?"

The other woman sighed again. "I suppose so."

Talba had seen plenty of houses like this one—her brother Corey had one. Corey lived in Eastover, home of politicians, musicians, and Saints (along with a number of white people, though perhaps none in those categories). This place was something like it, or at least the houses were—expensive, soulless, and utterly unattractive to Talba, who would have lived in a Moroccan palace if she could have. She might be a baroness, but she wasn't a European one.

The doorbell chimed some kind of ditty that was almost a whole song, but it too was soulless, and a little tacky. The woman who appeared at the door wore jeans that showed off a nice figure, and a crisp blouse. She was Miz Clara's age, and trim, her straight hair fashioned in a shoulder-length do that was actually quite glamorous. She looked exactly like a doctor's wife—and looked like she worked at it.

"Ms. Simmons?"

"Yes?"

"I have something very good to tell you, but it may surprise you a little."

She smiled and, up close like this, Talba could see just how much time and trouble had gone into her makeup, the shape of her eyebrows, her manicure. She thought that no matter how much money she made, she'd never get into that silliness.

"Yes?" Mozelle said again, her head cocked a bit condescendingly, as if she thought *she* were a baroness.

"My name is Sandra Wallis. You may have known my father. Denman—"

Before Talba could even get his whole name out, the woman fainted.

Chapter Eighteen

Talba could see it unfolding, in slow-mo and yet still so fast she couldn't stop it. The woman's eyes rolled back, she started to crumple at the shoulders, her legs gave way . . . Talba reached out and did break her fall, but that was the best she could do.

Mozelle came to almost immediately, and she woke up screaming, screaming what the hell was Talba doing and she had tricked her and for God's sake would someone throw Talba out. Since it was a Saturday, the whole neighborhood turned out, just about. But no one made a move to throw Talba out.

First, a man came out of the house, presumably Mozelle's husband, a pudgy man not nearly so attractive as she was.

Talba had managed to ease the woman to the ground and now stood slightly away from her, unnerved by all the screaming. She kept staring at the inside of the house, half expecting a girl to come out, a girl slightly younger than she—the sister who was probably going to hate her after this.

"What happened?" the man asked and knelt by his wife. "What you doing on the floor, baby?"

Mozelle eased up on an elbow. "This trash come around here, tryin' to trick me. . . ."

It wasn't the right accent for the neighborhood, and Talba wondered if it got any better when she wasn't upset. She doubted it. Mozelle's charms, for Dr. Simmons, were probably obvious before she even opened her mouth.

The man looked at Talba inquiringly, and there was something long-suffering in his glance, something that emboldened her.

She gave him a smile that was just the least bit ironic, though she spoke apologetically. "I guess I reminded her of somebody. She fainted dead away."

"Again?" he said to his wife. "You fainted again? Aren't you ever going to learn?" There was affection in his voice, and Talba thought she understood a little of their relationship. Drama on her part and reassurance on his seemed a couple of the key elements.

The woman turned on Talba, furious. "You come here just like your daddy, trying to get what you can from folks doing better than you." To her husband, she said, "Matthew, you make her leave. You just get that woman off my property. She Janessa daddy's girl, you know who I mean? You know?" She was still on the floor of the porch, her husband's arm around her shoulders, a queen giving orders.

This woman had reason to fear and hate Talba, given what her father had been to her sister, and, indeed, what she, Talba, had been to her. Talba suddenly felt ashamed that she'd forgotten how vivid yesterday's events could seem to people. "Mrs. Simmons, I'm really sorry I got you all upset. I can't remember a thing about your sister, or about you if I ever met you, or even about my daddy—I hope you understand that. I'm sorry for what went down a long time ago, and I understand why you feel the way you do. I just wanted to meet my sister—that's all in the world I wanted to do."

The man turned to his wife. "You're all right, baby. Come on up now." The woman stood.

She said, "Why you want to meet Janessa?" For the first time, her face was genuinely curious.

"I want to make amends to her. Truthfully, I want to know her. She's my sister, after all. Did you ever know the Reverend Clarence Scruggs? He told me to find her."

"I don't believe I did." The curiosity was gone, and Simmons had apparently recovered some of her anger. "But you're welcome to your precious Janessa." She put a lot of angry emphasis on the word. "If you can find her."

Talba had started to realize the girl probably didn't live with the lace-curtain Simmonses in their postmodern dream house. "You mean you don't know where she is?"

"Oh, I know where she's s'posed to be. But let me tell you something, Ms. Sandra Wallis—oh, yes, I remember you— she's bad to the core, just like you. Just like ya daddy. Just like all you Wallises. I never could do nothin' with that girl. Isn't that so, Matthew?"

The doctor looked miserable, but he nodded as bidden. "She never has been a walk in the park."

"Left home when she was fifteen," Mozelle continued. "Went to live with somebody else. I never could do *nothin'* with her. Uh-*uhhh*. Never could, not one day in her life. She could have had all these advantages." She swept her arm to show what she meant. "But nooo. That wasn't what she wanted. What she wanted was to be contentious and cantankarous. Well, see if I help her out when she come runnin' back."

Talba made a quick calculation. The girl would be nineteen now—apparently she hadn't come running back in four years. "Are you in touch with her at all?"

The two Simmonses shook their heads in unison. "No. We're not," the doctor said.

"Well, I wonder if you'd mind telling me how to find her? She is my sister, after all."

"She wouldn't want to see *you*," Mozelle sniffed.

But her husband said, "Now, Mozelle. You don't know what she'd want."

"Well, I know that about her. I raised that child from a baby. That poor little motherless child."

Talba just stood there, hoping the woman would become undone by her own rudeness.

She didn't budge. But the husband said, "Mozelle. This lady means well."

His wife flashed Talba a furious look and turned and went into the house.

Talba raised an eyebrow.

"You'll have to excuse her," her husband said. "She's touchy on some subjects."

Neither of them—none of the three of them—mentioned the horrors of the past, a past that had included Talba as well as her father. Mozelle was moved by it, that was plain, and Talba was sweating gallons. But none of them spoke of it.

"I understand where she's coming from," Talba said. "All I can do is try to do what I can now. I can't change anything that happened."

"Well, one thing. Least Janessa doesn't know."

"She doesn't?"

He smiled. "Mozelle gave her some story or other. Some things there's just no point in knowing."

"I thank you for that," Talba said.

"You seem like a nice lady. I'm gon' tell you how to find Janessa. She needs a positive force in her life."

"I promise I won't misuse it."

"I don't b'lieve you will. She went to live with her best friend's family. Coreen Brown's the girl's name."

Talba's heart sank, thinking of the investigative enormity of trying to locate a Brown. But he kept talking. "The family lives near the fairgrounds. On Mystery Street. They ought to be in the phone book, under Napoleon. Napoleon Brown." He glanced toward the door. "I'd look it up for you, but I don't think it's a good idea under the circumstances. You understand?"

Talba understood all too well.

She stopped at a gas station and looked up Napoleon Brown. He was there, on Mystery Street. She copied down both address and phone number, then drove there and parked in front. But she didn't go to the door.

The house was a 1940s raised bungalow, with a few steps leading to a small front porch. It was in decent repair, but the owners weren't house-proud. It looked closed up; deserted. But that probably meant either the occupants were away for the weekend or they simply liked to live with the front of the house closed off. A lot of people were like that. Still, she used it as an excuse not to go in.

Well, actually she didn't. She told herself she couldn't handle it today. She'd already had the guardian from hell, and tonight she was getting Raisa. She just couldn't sandwich in her brand-new, not-so-new sister.

She'd gotten only half a block when she started cursing herself for a coward. She started lecturing herself like she thought she was Miz Clara: *Get a grip, girl. You think putting it off's gonna make it any easier?*

She circled the block, and then did it again, first noticing how badly her palms were sweating, then counting down, breathing deep, anything to calm down. She parked, marched up to the door, and rang the bell. To her chagrin, she heard footsteps. Her palms started in again.

A woman Miz Clara's age answered the door, a slender, nice-looking woman with gorgeous silky dreads, wearing an Indonesian dress. She didn't look healthy, exactly; in fact, she was a little gaunt. It was a particular kind of thinness, though—Talba would have bet a pile she was a vegetarian, the sort who went in for supplements. She probably drank barley green for breakfast. This Talba liked; people like that were often intellectuals.

"Is this the Brown residence?" she asked.

"Yes. Can I help you?" The woman looked puzzled.

No help for it, Talba thought, and she blurted, "I'm looking for Janessa."

"Janessa?"

"Yes. A friend of Coreen's?"

The woman gave her head a little absentminded shake. "Sorry. You surprised me—I just didn't recognize you. Are you a friend of Janessa's?"

"I'm hoping to be. I got your address from her aunt."

"Oh." Now the woman was really puzzled; Talba was impatient and nervous, a nasty combination.

"I wonder if she's home," she said firmly, and apparently she'd finally spoken with enough authority to jar loose some information.

"I'm afraid she's at work."

"Can I call her there? Or go see her?"

"Can I ask why you need her?"

Talba made a quick decision. "I'm her sister," she said. "We've never met and I don't know if she even knows about me."

"Oh. Oh my God."

"Can you tell me where she works?"

"Uh . . . sure. Eve's Weaves. It has some other name, but I don't know what it is. Everybody calls it by its nickname."

"Beauty salon?"

"Yes. Janessa does the manicures."

"Do you know where it is?" This was like pulling teeth, but it was working; the woman was too surprised not to answer.

"I've been there, but I couldn't tell you exactly. It's in the phone book though."

"But not under Eve's Weaves?"

"It's Eve's *something*."

Talba figured that was good enough. "Thanks. I appreciate it."

And she left before the woman could ask her name.

Her heart was hammering and her hands wet, but she'd done it. After that, Raisa ought to be a piece of cake.

R aisa had to be one of the most beautiful children on the face of the earth. Her outstanding feature was crinkly, fine golden hair, not really blond, just gold. Talba had never seen anything like it on any child, black or white.

She was a child anyone would love if only she'd let them. Instead, she was single-mindedly dedicated to the proposition that whatever Raisa wanted, Raisa got. Spoiled, some might say, but Talba didn't think so. More the opposite. Deprived; though of what, Talba couldn't have said. Some material things, possibly. Her mother had very little money and Darryl couldn't contribute a lot. But Raisa had plenty of food and clothing, just maybe not all the television-hyped gizmos a child craved these days.

Bigger things were missing. First, there was her dad. Darryl and Kim had never married, indeed had barely dated when Kim became pregnant—and didn't really like each other. So Raisa was raised—for all intents and purposes—without a dad.

There was something else, though. Some withholding, some failure of love, perhaps merely a sense of promises broken that had shaped this child. When Kim had a boyfriend, she frequently dumped the kid on Darryl; when she didn't, she clung to her possessively. She had recently married, and Talba wondered where that would lead. So far, things had gotten worse.

The plan was for Talba to get to know her gradually. Tonight they were going to dinner and a movie—or rather, McDonald's and a movie; it was the kid's choice. Then Talba was going to drive chastely home.

Raisa met her at the door and burst into tears almost the moment she flung it open. "Daddy, it's that girl I hate! What's she doing here?"

Talba pushed past her. "Hello, darlin'. You'll get to like me. I promise." She pulled out a candy bar. "I have good things for little girls."

Raisa reached out and snatched it, and at that moment, Darryl walked into the room. "Raisa! Is that any way to behave?"

"She gave it to me."

"She did not."

Talba, trying to make peace, said, "Well, I was going to."

Darryl decided not to push it. He said, "Raisa, say thank you."

"No!" The kid stamped her foot and ran into her bedroom, a small chamber Darryl had furnished with bunks.

That was the way the evening began, and from there it progressed to Raisa's spilling a chocolate milkshake onto Talba's lap, apparently on purpose. Darryl, appalled, decided on depriving her of the movie as punishment, which produced a tantrum of approximately the size and duration of Hurricane Bob. By the time they left McDonald's, Talba's ears hurt so badly all she wanted to do was get away, but Darryl said no, that was what Raisa wanted—to drive her away. They could all three play Monopoly or something.

However, the tantrum showed no signs of abating when they got home, and when Raisa actually started throwing things, and Darryl went for her with a glint Talba'd never seen in his eye, Talba thought she was about to witness child abuse firsthand. Instead, he picked her up, put her in the shower fully clothed, and turned the cold water on. Talba wasn't sure it wasn't cruel, but anyway it worked. The kid came out docile as a bunny rabbit, got into warm jammies, and settled down to watch *101 Dalmatians* for the nineteenth time—thus getting a movie after all—while the adults tried to calm their nerves with a glass of wine.

Talba said, "I don't mean to be critical, but—"

"I know, she's getting worse."

"She is, Darryl. She needs to go see somebody."

And thus began yet another discussion that left them both in despair. Technically, Darryl really had no rights to Raisa; Kimmie only let him spend time with her because she needed money from him; any time he had a bright idea about child rearing she got furious and threatened to cut him off completely. Which upset him, because he really thought Kimmie was crazy—felt he was the only link to stability Raisa had.

While Talba had to respect that, it was a big fat thorn in their relationship.

Kimmie had called him one day when Raisa was two years old and told him he was a father. He'd accepted the news happily and without question and had come to love his daughter—however difficult. ("But you don't understand," he'd say to Talba, "she was the sweetest little baby.")

He could try to get official custody—or partial custody—

but he hadn't, and Talba understood that he was afraid—
afraid that DNA testing would show she wasn't really his and
afraid he'd lose. However much he did or didn't love the
child, Talba was sure of one thing—he'd never abandon her.
He'd just rather not face the thorny questions a court case
would produce. At least not yet.

Talba had two glasses of wine and left feeling worse instead of better.

Chapter Nineteen

Eddie's Saturday night was shaping up no better. He was truly pissed off about what had happened to Ms. Wallis in Clayton and had brooded about it till he hatched a plan. He figured his cover wasn't completely blown yet and he'd better take advantage of it while he could.

Angie came over that afternoon to get some of Audrey's red gravy. His wife made it by the gumbo pot and froze most of it in quart-size freezer bags, so she could take one out and thaw it every time she wanted to make pasta—which was about three times a week. Angie always got a couple of the bags, though judging from her skinny little body, she never ate any—at least not with spaghetti.

She was in an upbeat mood—for her. "Hey, Dad, how's Talba?"

"Mean as ever."

"That's Miz Clara you're talking about, isn't it? Talba's the nice one."

"Clara Wallis is the closest thing to a saint I've ever met in my life—and that's not just 'cause she has to put up with that hellion of a daughter. The woman fries chicken like a member of the highest order of angels."

Audrey sniffed, a little annoyed, because she was waging a one-woman fight to save Eddie from death-by-cholesterol.

"Hmph. Seraphim. I could make ya happy too if I wanted to kill ya."

"No, Mom, I think it's Cherubim."

"I know it's Seraphim."

Eddie sighed and left them to their argument. Angie trailed him into his den. "So how's the case comin'? I hear you had to get some old college buddy up in the middle of the night. I was kind of wondering about that—last I heard you didn't go to college."

"Well, yeah, I got a little tricky on that one. See, the deputy told me the kid was called Junior, and that told me his daddy's name, you understand? So I just said I knew him at LSU. Pretty safe bet he went there 'cause nearly everybody in the state did."

"Dad! What if he hadn't?"

"Well, the damn deputy wasn't gonna know—he didn't look like he could tell left from right. And Brashear senior wasn't gon' admit he didn't know me if I said he did. Not in the middle of the night when I was tryin' to help his son out. 'Course, I didn't mention where he didn't know me *from*."

She laughed. "Daddy, you got more nerve than me."

"Hell, dawlin', I wouldn't say that. 'Scuse my French. Nobody's got more nerve than you. But I got better social skills, I'll grant you that."

"I'd have gotten his precious son's fat ass fired."

"Angie, ya know how I hate it when ya talk like that."

"That asshole deserved it. I swear to God, I'd have—"

"Angie, ya don't know everything!" He spoke with a good deal more heat than he meant to. "Honey catches more flies than vinegar—or would you even know the meanin' of the term?"

Fury suffused her face. "You know why we don't get along? That's why, right there. Right there."

She whirled and left the house. Audrey came into the room.

"Why ya treat her like that, Eddie? No wonder she feels alienated."

He had no idea what either of them was talking about—but one thing, the whole exchange made a little drive to Clayton all the more attractive. He figured to just hang out in bars, and maybe he'd meet somebody who knew somebody.

The person he wanted to talk to was the kid, and that didn't mean a girl named Hunter. A boy named Trey was somebody he might have something to say to. Chances of getting him by himself on a Saturday night weren't too good, but, hell, it beat staying home and brooding about his daughter.

First, he went to the kid's house to see what the scene was. Nice house. Big. Money in it. It was still light, so no lights were on. There was a white Lexus in the driveway. He waited awhile, slightly worried about Junior Brashear's men, but only slightly—he wasn't nearly so conspicuous in Clayton as Talba would have been.

After awhile, a silver BMW drove up. A man got out and rushed up the steps. Damn! That would be Trey Patterson coming home from a quick one at some neighborhood bar. Classic suburban Saturday pattern—Eddie probably should have cruised the bars first. But then, he didn't know what the kid looked like at the time. Next, Trey would get dressed and go somewhere with the wife. Eddie'd bet fifty on it.

Sure enough, an hour later out came the handsome couple, or semi-handsome, anyway. The wife looked okay. Trey looked like he'd looked down the neck of a few too many empty beer bottles. She wore some kind of slinky pants outfit—black, like Angie liked—and he wore a sports coat. Probably a party, Eddie thought. With luck, it would be big enough to sneak into.

He eased out of his space and followed them across town to another house, a house he believed he'd heard about, one Ms. Wallis had described to him. He had a list of pertinent addresses with him, which he now consulted. Uh-huh. Trey's parents' home. They were probably going there for dinner.

It was dark now, and Eddie felt even more comfortable about doing his surveillance in peace, but, remembering the

Wallis escapade, he scrunched down as far as he could. He was almost comfortable here, and nothing was damn sure going to happen.

The next sound he heard was a car engine. Realizing he'd fallen asleep—something he almost never did—he consulted his watch. Nine-ten. The kid had been in there just enough time to get about half-bombed—certainly not long enough to have dinner—and yet, it was his BMW whose lights had just come on. What the hell was going on?

There was only one person in the car, and from the shape of the head, it was the kid. Maybe there was some kind of emergency.

This time he let him get a good head start before trying to follow. The neighborhood was so quiet, picking him up would be easy. In fact, there were so few cars out he'd be downright conspicuous.

In the end, he decided not to follow right away. If there was an emergency—like not enough ice cream for dessert—Trey would be back soon enough. But in twenty minutes he still wasn't back—and in thirty a cab arrived for the missus.

So much for emergencies. Eddie's guess was a fight, in which case the kid wouldn't be going home right away. He'd go to a bar. Just to be sure, Eddie cruised his house once, and exactly as he suspected, saw no BMW.

It was a small town. If the kid hung out any place at all besides the country club, Eddie was going to find him.

First, he cruised the main drag; the bar wouldn't be here, he knew. It would probably be in a mall, maybe a motel, something like that—a Mexican restaurant, maybe. Yuppies loved Mexican restaurants. But first, he had to find a bar where they could tell him where to go, and there was such a bar here.

He figured he could have bought a drink and slithered up to the subject, but it was getting late and he had a long way to go. So instead, he bellied up to the bar, looked around ostentatiously, slapped down a ten, and said to the bartender, "I've got a feeling I'm in the wrong place. This doesn't seem like a meet-and-greet kind of joint."

The bartender laughed. "You new in town?"

"I'm here for a week—got business in Baton Rouge. You telling me this is the liveliest place in town?"

"Buddy, we haven't got any lively places unless you count O'Leary's Irish pub. On Saturdays they sometimes have an Irish band, make you cry if ya drunk enough."

"That's it?

"Just about."

"No Mexican restaurant with a great big noisy bar and everybody in Hawaiian shirts?"

"Well, there's Earl's. Great big country dance hall kind of thing—doesn't seem like your scene, though."

"Now that's more like it. I want me some redneck women in jeans and tank tops."

The bartender shrugged. He was fast losing interest.

Eddie said, "I thank ya kindly, sir. Can I get directions?"

On the way out, he went to the phone and surreptitiously looked up the address of O'Leary's as well. Outside in the car, he flipped a coin—it came up for O'Leary's, but he went to Earl's anyway. His instinct told him Trey would want to talk to women—not necessarily pick them up, just talk to them. Also that the banker's son was less likely to be recognized at Earl's.

And, yes! The BMW was in the parking lot, conspicuous among the pickups.

Inside, the joint was a little too jumping for Eddie's taste. A live band made it almost impossible to hear. He wished he had Miz Wallis's young ears—though she probably wouldn't be caught dead in a honky dive like this one.

As he suspected, Trey wasn't dancing. He was just sitting at the bar talking to some guy—not even some woman. Eddie stood behind him, ordered a beer, and insinuated himself into the conversation, which was a piece of cake. Like a couple of walking cliches, the guys were talking about the Saints' prospects for the upcoming season. It would take awhile, but Eddie intended to hijack the conversation—the trick was to talk about something the other guy couldn't. And from the dim-bulb looks of him, that would be almost anything.

When he could get a word in, he said, "Where you boys from?"

"Right here," the stranger said.

The kid said nothing. Eddie said, "Me too. I'm thinking to move to New Orleans, though."

That brought his prey to life. "I envy you, brother; I really do. Sometimes I wish I could just get out of this place."

"I hear you."

The stranger said, "You ever been to a place called Michaul's? They got Cajun dancing there."

"No, I'm more of a jazz man myself." Just hoping the kid was a jazz fan.

Trey said, "My sister used to talk about a place called the Tin Roof."

His sister. It was a beautiful opening, but too soon to pick up on it.

Eddie said, "I know the Tin Roof. Jack Maheu's place."

"I don't know, I never got there."

"How come? It's sure not very far."

The kid got a faraway look. "In some ways, it might as well be on another planet."

The stranger said, "Hey, what's your problem, man? New Orleans ain't but a few miles down the road."

Eddie ignored him. "I know what ya mean, son. I know what ya mean. Philosophically speaking, it's kinda like the Emerald City."

The stranger said, "Huh?"

The kid said, "Exactly!"

"Ya ever feel like just gettin' in ya car and drivin'? Going out for a pack of cigarettes and not comin' back?"

"What do you mean? That's what I just did."

Eddie said, "Put 'er there, bro. That's how I got to this town. This very moment? I'm a missing person in Jersey." To the kid, he knew it would sound like this: "Dis very moment? I'm a missing poison in Joisey." He didn't even have to lay it on. That was just his native Ninth Ward accent.

The stranger said, "Get out of here!"

Eddie said, "Ten years ago. Couldn't handle it, had to go.

Outta there. Never looked back. Know what I mean?"

"Let me buy you a drink, brother. I been needin' to talk about the Emerald City." The kid pointedly excluded the other man, who now scanned the room and headed finally toward a forty-ish brunette with too-black hair. "You really do what you said you did?"

Eddie nodded. "Picked Louisiana 'cause I liked the music. You really do it too?"

He looked surprised. "Do what?"

"Thought you said you went out for cigarettes yourself."

Trey's face twisted into a bitter grin. "Naaah. Just had a fight with the wife. I don't guess I'll ever really have the guts."

"Ya still got ya wife, what could be so bad?"

The kid looked uncomfortable, like 'he had a rock in his shoe. "Hey, bartender. What's the hold up? Goddammit, I need that drink." He turned back to Eddie. "I've blown just about everything there is to blow and the whole town knows about it. And that's just for openers."

The drinks came. He drained off about half of his. Eddie sighed with satisfaction. He said, "So what's the down side?"

Trey put an arm around him and laughed. "I like you, my man. I don't meet many people like you."

"Hey, trust me, You wouldn't want to—name's Eddie, by the way."

The kid stuck out his hand. "Trey."

"Trey?" Eddie was deliberately needling him.

"Oh, hell, why not just call me Little King. Everybody else does. Behind my back."

Eddie lifted his glass. "You got it, Little K. Here's to ya." He drank and then said, "You a boxer or something?"

Trey laughed, and the sound was a sharp crack that disturbed the landscape, like a twig breaking. "Or somethin'," he said. "You got that right, Eddie. I'm somethin', all right."

"No, seriously. What's with the Little King routine?"

Trey turned toward the bar and stared into the depths of his glass. "Nothing. Not a damn thing. Except my dad's the king, see?"

"You're losin' me there, son."

"Yeah, you know, he is." Trey had now lit a cigarette and was starting to gesture with it like a teacher using a ruler—something Eddie had noticed people do when they're getting good and drunk. "I never thought of it like that before. It's like my dad's king of the whole damn town, and ya know what that makes me? Little King. Hell of a note, huh? How would ya like to be 'Little King.' "

"We gotta upgrade ya, son—could ya handle 'Crown Prince'?"

That caught the kid in mid swallow, and he thought it was so funny he almost spit on the bar—did, a little bit. "Funny! Hey, Eddie, you're a funny one, man. Crown Prince! Oh, yeah!" His voice turned bitter again. "Prince of nothing, man. Prince of nothing."

"Hey, it can't be that bad."

"You don't know the half of it."

"I don't know the eighth of it."

The kid turned toward the bar, laughing uncontrollably, in the manner of drunks, and Eddie hyena-ed right along with him. "Well, lemme tell you about eight things. My dad's king of the place, right? And me, I drink too much, cheat on my wife—who hates me, by the way." He stopped and nodded, as if Eddie had tried to contradict him. "Yeah, she does. She really hates me. And I pretty much hate her too—ain't that a hell of a note?"

Eddie sipped his beer and squeezed out a niggardly half-smile. "Hell of a note."

"And I hate practicing law too. Long as we're having true confessions. Therefore I don't do it to the best of my ability. In other words, I'm lousy at it."

"Man, I never saw anybody needed to go get a pack of cigarettes so bad."

"Huh? Wha?" And then he got the reference. He stuck an elbow in Eddie's rib cage. "Hey, you're all right, man."

"I mean it. That's some bad shit. Excuse my French."

"Well, it still ain't the half of it." He leaned confidentially close and whispered in Eddie's ear, his breath warm and fume-laden. "My sister was murdered last week."

Eddie turned a shocked face to him. "Did you say what I think you did? Ya sister was—"

Trey held a finger to his lips. "Shhhh. Quiet, man. We're not supposed to talk about it. They all say she committed suicide."

"But you think she was murdered."

"Hell, I know it."

"Hey, man, you're giving me goosebumps. Next, ya gonna tell me ya know who did it. And let me tell ya something, if you do, don't even stop for those cigarettes. Just get in ya car and start drivin'."

Trey pulled himself back and looked into Eddie's eyes, searching for truth. "What you talking about?"

Eddie shrugged. "Whole thing sounds dangerous, that's all."

"What you mean?"

"Well, ya did say she's dead, right? And now you're tellin' me there's some kind of cover-up?" He shook his head like there was no hope in the world and he knew it. "It don't sound good, man. What the hell happened, anyhow?"

"I don't know. I swear to God I just don't know."

"Thought you said—"

Trey put up a placating hand. "Yeah, yeah, I know what I said. Well, let me tell you somethin'. Anybody in this whole goddamn town could have killed her."

Eddie took a long pull on his beer, feigning disinterest.

"I'm not kidding, man. You know how many people wanted to kill her? My dad; my mom. Old Sheriff Ransdell. Just about everybody their age. I'm tellin' you, Eddie . . ." He hiccupped, and Eddie was terrified he was going to stop there, maybe just pass out cold. "I'm tellin' you . . . it's like a god-damn conspiracy."

"Come on, son. Why would they want to kill their own daughter? Don't make sense, what you're sayin'."

"Why? I'll tell you why. She knew too much, that's why." He polished off his own drink in one huge gulp. "Whole

damn town's in on it. With their goddamn high and mighty
goddamn Baptist goddamn . . ."

Eddie's heart was beating fast, and he was perspiring. He
felt like a poker player holding four aces and going light—
desperate to hold out just a little longer, keep them all con-
vinced of his harmlessness just long enough to . . .

He felt a hand on his shoulder. "Well, I'll be damned. If it
ain't Eddie Valentino, from N'Awlins."

It was a voice he knew. "Sheriff Brashear, as I live and
breathe." He turned around to face him. "Hey, Junior."

"What you doing, talkin' to this ol' boy here?"

"Ya mean my friend, Trey? Well, we were just—"

Eddie had his back to Trey at this point, didn't have any
idea how he was taking all this, but Junior Brashear interrupted him. "Hey, Trey. This guy mention he's a private eye
out of Noo Orleans?" Junior paused, reading Trey's face.
"Didn't think so."

"Goddamn it to hell." So that's how he was taking it.

Eddie felt the back of his head and neck go wet, as the
kid's drink hit it. An ice cube slid down his collar. Trey
passed him on his way out.

"Junior, you better stop him. He's too drunk to drive."

Junior swiveled his head, confused, and Eddie reached into
his pocket.

He caught up with Trey and pressed his card into his hand.
"Call me when you sober up."

Sure, the kid hated him now; tomorrow he might not even
remember him. But Eddie'd found out one thing—he had a
rudimentary conscience.

Chapter Twenty

Talba had a friend in the police department, and it was a high-up friend—Homicide Detective Skip Langdon. Actually, due to the departmental policy of decentralization, the homicide division had been dissolved and Langdon now worked out of the Third District. But she was still a homicide detective. And she carried a lot of weight. Talba phoned her first thing Monday morning.

"Hey, Skip, it's Talba."

"Baroness! How's the PI business?"

"Be great if Eddie weren't such a grouch. How's the police business?"

"Be great if people weren't so rotten to each other. What can I do for you?" She sounded distracted.

"You know a policeman named Calvin Richard?"

"Calvin Richard . . . hmmm. Calvin Richard . . . Is he a short white guy with—"

Talba interrupted. "Different Calvin. This one's black. And a sergeant."

"Well, I can figure out where he's detailed if you like."

"Actually, I was hoping you'd call him for me. I think he might have been warned about me and—"

"Warned! What did you do?"

"Asked a bunch of questions that were none of my business."

The detective laughed. "I'm all ears." The distracted air had disappeared.

"Well, there's this murder case I'm working—only y'all are calling it suicide."

"Oho." Langdon was one of the best investigators in the department. "You must mean Clayton Patterson."

"Now, how'd you know that?"

"I've had my doubts about that one myself. I even asked to see the autopsy report."

"And?"

"Let's say I still have my doubts."

"Any chance the case'll be reopened?"

"Negative. None."

"Skip, Clayton was a friend of mine. I can't tell you who my client is, but I've got a personal stake in this thing. You think you could get Calvin Richard to call me? Honest to God, I need a little help here."

"You've got my curiosity up."

Talba could see Langdon was angling for a quid pro quo. "All right, look. Clayton was the victim of a crime when she was sixteen; and Richard knew her in high school."

The cop waited. When it was plain that was all Talba had to say, she said, "So?"

Talba said, "Sounds pretty far afield, doesn't it? I think it could be related to this case. He probably won't call me unless you ask him to."

"Talba. I get the feeling there's a lot more to this."

"I thought you were going to scoff at it."

Langdon was silent, but Talba thought she heard something—maybe the hum of little wheels turning. The cop was trying to figure out how to get some more information. Finally, she just came out and said it: "Hey, look. If you get

anything interesting, give me a call, okay? I'll see what I can
do about getting it reopened."

"Now that's an offer. I sure will, Skip. Be glad to."

"I'll have him call you."

Talba hung up, wondering about something. Whatever was
going on here, whatever was being covered up, might not just
end at the Clayton town limit. Something about Skip's un-
accustomed interest suggested pressure had been applied in
New Orleans.

The problem with going through Langdon was that Talba
had to wait for Richard, and she hated waiting. Nonetheless,
it wasn't as if she had nothing to do—like half a dozen employee checks and a couple of fiancé frisks—her name for
prenuptial investigations. These tended to make her wince—
if people didn't know each other well enough not to need
them, they shouldn't be getting engaged in the first place.

Also, Eddie wanted to see her. She was about to go in and
see what he wanted when Eileen Fisher rang. "Jason Wheelock to see you."

Damn! The client. He slunk in with an uneasy look Talba
didn't like at all. *He's going to pull the plug*, she thought.

"Hey, Jason—things are really hopping. Did you get my
interim client report?" It was her second one, actually. "Interesting, hmm?"

"Yeah. More than interesting. Looks like Donny didn't do
it. So how close are you getting to finding out who did?"

She was afraid he'd ask that. When in doubt, lie; that was
Eddie's motto. She wasn't sure it applied to dealings with
clients, but nonetheless, she said, "Really, really close. Should
take another week; maybe less. That transcript ought to make
a big difference."

"God, Talba, speaking of that, I'm running out of money."

Damn! What about the rich parents? The trust fund or
whatever it was? The easy way he'd authorized the transcript?

"Jason, I'm going to solve it. I swear I am." She crossed
her fingers.

"I don't know, Talba. I'm really having second thoughts. I
wonder if I'm playing with myself here. Maybe we should

just wait till the transcript comes and then reassess."

She just stared, wondering where all this was coming from.

"I mean, I can't help her now. I started thinking: I'm not doing this for her; it's for me."

Talba spoke from the heart: "Jason, something really bad happened to Clayton—twice. At least two other people are dead—"

"What two other people?"

"Donny Troxell and his father. And the police aren't investigating any of the three cases. Something's going on here, Jason. Something pretty big."

Silence; silence eloquent as Shakespeare. "I've got to draw the line somewhere."

She was starting to panic. "Jason, listen . . ."

"Talba, I just can't justify any more money until we know what's in the transcript."

Something like grief came over her. She couldn't part with this case—not in the middle, like this. "I'm sorry," he said, "I know you say you're close, but neither of us really has any idea where this is going. Maybe it'll end next week, or maybe the week after . . . I can't just go on spending money like this."

She sat there for awhile, trying to absorb it. Finally, she said, "Let me go talk to Eddie." He looked at his watch. "Honest, I'll just be a minute." Eddie could sell snow to Eskimos—she wanted to get him in there and get his tongue going.

This morning the duffels under his eyes were brown with a slightly greenish tinge—the color varied according to atmospheric conditions. Or maybe Eddie's body chemistry. It was enough to make you believe in the medieval theory of humors.

Green must be a good sign, she thought. He was smiling, looking as close to happy as he ever got. She hated to ruin his day.

"Ms. Wallis, good morning. Sit down. Sit down." He was downright expansive. She was suspicious.

"How come you're in such a good mood?"

"Took a little drive up to Clayton Saturday night."

"And you didn't get arrested? Maybe we should drink a toast."

"Had a pretty interesting time, Ms. Wallis. Pretty damned interesting."

"Eddie, listen . . ."

"Had a man-to-man with Little King."

She gave it up for the moment, figuring she might as well hear him out. "Trey."

"A very drunk Trey. Thinks his sister was murdered. Says there's a cover-up and a conspiracy."

"All right! Now we're getting somewhere." She was so excited she put up her hand to high-five him, but he made a face at her.

"Get back, Ms. Wallis. You know I hate that black stuff."

"Oh, loosen up, Eddie. Come on—gimme five." Reluctantly, he slapped her hand. "See? It's kind of fun, huh?"

"Infantile," he said, but the corner of his mouth was twisted, like he was trying to hide a smile.

He liked high-fiving, he was just too damned uptight to do it. He was going to come around, though; she was going to see to that.

Talba sat down. A little seed of hope was taking root in her. She figured anything he had to say was going to help them keep the client. "So did Trey say who killed her?"

"Swore to God he didn't know. Said the whole town had a motive, though; or rather anybody in the whole town."

"Now, come on. Does that sound a little like an exaggeration?"

"Well, sure it does. But you gotta remember, for him the whole town probably means a handful of his father's best friends."

"Yeah! Listen to you, Eddie. You've got something there. Probably means five or six people, max."

Eddie sighed. "Well, ten or twenty, anyhow. You want to know the motive, or not?"

"Yeah. Yeah, I do." The question surprised her—she'd expected many motives.

"He said she knew too much."

"Knew too much? What could she have known? She was just a kid—how could she know about some adult crime or conspiracy or something? It doesn't make sense."

"Yeah, it does, Ms. Wallis. Yeah, it does. Use ya head." He made it sound like "hay-id."

She let her mind go blank, and, in time, something floated to the top. "Oh, my God! She lied. She did know who scalped her." She tapped her foot impatiently. "And it was somebody in the family. Just like Betty Majors said."

"Least it was somebody the 'whole town' was willing to cover up for. Let's backtrack here. Donny Troxell knows his father is dying, so he calls Clayton and talks her into telling him Donny didn't really do it, and King did."

"King?"

"Let's try him on for size." He shrugged. "Could be anybody whose name Papa Troxell recognizes. So Papa blows the whistle with his dying breath . . ."

"Maybe it wasn't his dying breath before he did it."

"Agreed. So King kills him (or *maybe* kills him), and then kills Donny and Clayton."

Put like that, it stopped Talba. "Kills his own daughter?"

Eddie drummed his fingers. "It's a sticking point, I'll grant you. Trey said his dad had a motive—along with everyone else in town—but I don't know." He stopped to think about it. "Naah. I can't buy it. If the whole town knows he did it, anyhow, then why kill his daughter—why even kill the Troxells—to cover it up?"

"Not King then."

"There's more to it, Ms. Wallis. There's just more to it than we got. And something else bothers me. Why kill Clayton now? She's always known who did it."

"Because she started talking. All of a sudden she was a threat."

Eddie shook his head. "I don't buy it, Ms. Wallis. The perp could just deny it. He could say it was the hallucination of a dying man, or that Donny and Clayton cooked it up to make Mr. T's passin' easier . . ."

"Hold it. Why should Clayton do a favor for Donny if he scalped her?"

"It doesn't have to make sense. It just has to make more sense than murder. And so far nothin' does."

"Well, there's something there. It's still tied up in a knot, is all."

Eddie picked up a pen and started pecking at some notes on his desk. "Go get 'em, Ms. Wallis."

"Eddie, listen. Jason's cooling his heels in my office. That's what I came in about—he wants to drop the case till we get the transcript."

Eddie looked up, baggy eyes boring into her. "Why the hell would he do a damfool thing like that? 'Scuse my French?"

"He says he's out of money."

"Well, shit, 'scuse my French. This one's just gettin' interesting."

"I thought maybe you could talk to him—tell him we've got some new information."

Eddie folded his arms across his chest, more or less hugging himself. He stared in her direction, but he was looking through her.

Oh, shit, she thought, he's furious. *Like I could help this.*

Finally, he said, "Tell ya what we're gonna do, Ms. Wallis. I've never done this in the history of E. V. Anthony Investigations. But we're gonna cut young Jason a deal. Tell him we're gonna go halvsies with him on this. We're gonna bill him for half our hours and eat the rest."

Talba was flabbergasted. "We can't afford to do that."

"I'm gonna pay you. Don't worry about that. Just go do it."

"But Eddie, why? Why the hell would you do a thing like that?"

"I feel real bad about that girl." He paused for so long Talba thought he was finished. "And real good about the future of this agency if we get out of this alive." She didn't have the least idea whether he was joking or not. It took some doing, but she talked Jason into the deal. Then she went back to waiting.

Calvin Richard called back just before noon. He sounded slightly sullen, like a kid who's been ordered to do the last thing he wants to. "Detective Langdon said to call you about the Patterson suicide."

"Yes, I have some information for the police on that."

"Is that right?" He spoke with that cop reticence, that poker-faced, tell-nothing blandness.

It irritated her so much she decided to mirror it. She kept silent until he spoke again. "How can I help you, Ms. Wallis?"

"I'm developing information that indicates Clayton Patterson was murdered."

"With all due respect, Ms. Wallis—I know you're a friend of Langdon's—but this is really a police matter. I presume you haven't seen the crime lab and autopsy reports?"

"I have not."

"Well, if you had, you might not be throwing around these allegations."

"So far I haven't accused anyone, Sergeant."

"How can I help you, Ms. Wallis?

"I'm calling you because you knew her."

"Oh?" He was doing it again.

"I've seen your picture, Sergeant, so I know you're African- American. I'm going to tell you I am too. There are things about this case I don't get, and I thought you might be able to explain them."

"What makes you think I knew her?" His voice was much weaker, almost shaky. She had a sudden vision of him wiping away sweat and wondered what she had said, exactly.

"You had to know her. You went to high school with her."

"Ms. Wallis, can I call you back on that?" He hung up, not so much as pausing for a good-bye.

Chapter Twenty-one

Eddie had two names he wanted to play with. The first was one Little King had given him: Sheriff Ransdell. Dickie Ransdell, he learned, upon further investigation. A man nearly seventy, and his friends still called him Dickie.

The other was the judge in the scalping case: Judge Gaylord Samuel. Eddie wondered what on earth his friends called him.

He spent the morning doing his own kind of investigation—Ms. Wallis would have gone online and looked up everything she could find about them. Eddie called around and got everything he could on them. It wasn't much, but bad action wasn't what he was looking for. Eddie was a great believer in connections. He was looking for cronies, names he could use to grease the introductions, little flattering anecdotes he could tell back to them, make them feel like he was their pal. He'd been damned lucky with Junior Brashear—he couldn't count on something like that happening again.

One thing his calls produced—bad news about the judge.

He was in the hospital recovering from a stroke. That didn't necessarily mean Eddie wasn't going to go see him, but he wouldn't try him first.

The sheriff was retired now and known to play golf. "Morning or afternoon?" Eddie asked, but his informant didn't know. If morning, he'd probably be home now, maybe having a postprandial nap and a little action with the wife. If afternoon, Eddie'd just have to wait till he finished playing.

He went to the house first, a fifties ranch-style in a deathly quiet subdivision. One car in the driveway, one in front; a good sign. He knocked.

No action. He knocked again.

Some kind of fluttering at the window.

He probably had interrupted a nap and hoped to hell it hadn't included an afternoon delight, or he was soon going to be facing one grumpy old man.

The man who opened the door was a shrunken, wiry grandpa with a sparse shock of brownish hair spread thinly across a shiny skull. He'd come to the door in his underwear; hard to make it clearer you didn't want to be disturbed. Eddie had a lot of back-pedaling to do.

"Dickie Ransdell? I sure am sorry to disturb you. Should have called first, but Jake Kellogg said, 'Just go by the house, he'll be glad to see you . . .' "

"You a friend of Jake's?"

"Jake and I go back thirty, thirty-five years. Listen, I really am sorry. Let me call you and—"

"No, no. Come on in. Let me put a pair of pants on."

He ushered Eddie into a living room equipped, in small-town America fashion, with television and two La-Z-Boys.

There were plenty of fake house plants, but that was the only sign Dickie lived with a woman—except that the place was immaculate. That certainly argued for a wife. Yet there were only the sounds of one person getting dressed.

Ex-sheriff Ransdell strode out again in polo shirt, polyester pants, white belt, and boots. His three or four strands of hair had had a comb run through them, and his face had been washed.

"You know Jake Kellogg, you must be from New Orleans. What brings you up our way?"

"Oh, Jake. I been knowing him so long I can't even remember not knowing him. He was telling me about the time you and him were after some ol' boy committed a robbery in Gonzalez, ended up over in Marrero in some titty bar—"

Ransdell finished for him. "And it turned out, he wasn't one of the patrons, he was a waitress—master of disguise, that one was. Broke a fingernail on the way to jail."

They guffawed a little and then Ransdell said, "Don't believe I caught your name, by the way."

"Well, where are my manners?" Eddie got up and extended his hand. "Anthony Edwards."

"What can I do you for, Mr. Edwards?"

"Jake tells me you were involved in a right interesting case a few years ago. Young girl cut with a machete . . ."

The sheriff's face scrunched into a scowl. "What the hell you doing comin' in my house like this? Claimin' to know my friends?" He moved fast, walking toward Eddie, trying to box him in.

Eddie raised a placating arm. "Now, take it easy, Dickie, take it easy."

All of a sudden, Eddie heard steps in the hall, light ones. A woman in a robe stepped into view, her gray-blond hair still disheveled from sleep. She had a rifle raised to her shoulder. "What's going on here?"

Eddie turned to her politely, nonthreatening as you please. "Well, ma'am, to tell you the truth I'm not sure."

The sheriff stepped back far enough to permit Eddie to pass by him. "You will leave our house now, and you will leave this town now."

"Yes sir, I sure will. Pleasure meeting you, Dickie. You too, ma'am." He hoped the irony wasn't lost on them.

He had taken the precaution of parking around the corner so that, in case of just such a crisis, his car couldn't be recognized. He returned to it and drove, at exactly the speed limit, to the county hospital, where he parked in a huge lot, his car becoming one of many just like it (or close enough).

Truth to tell, he was shaken by the freezing welcome. It wasn't every day he got thrown out of a former lawman's house at gunpoint. He needed to do what he had to as quickly as possible and get out of Clayton once and for all. The last thing he wanted to do was call Ms. Wallis to come bail him out.

He asked at the desk for Judge Samuel's room and was given a number, which he took as a sign that the judge was up to having visitors.

He was sleeping, his wife at his side, wearing a look of unutterable sadness. *I should go*, Eddie thought. *I shouldn't do this.*

But somehow, he couldn't stop himself. The man was very gray.

"Yes?" the wife said.

"Are you Mrs. Samuel?"

"Yes."

"Eddie Valentino, Mrs. Samuel. I wanted to ask your husband about an old case of his. Is he able to talk at all?"

She turned fearful eyes upon him, uncertain what to say. The man in the bed spoke in a whisper, eyes still closed. "What case is that?"

"Judge Samuel. How do you do, sir? I don't want to disturb you."

"You're not disturbin' me, son. I'm not going anywhere. Tell me what I can do for you." He sounded as if every word could be his last. The woman looked terrified. "Tell me what case you mean."

Eddie stepped forward uncertainly, so as to be able to hear. "It was the Donny Troxell case, sir."

The man's eyes opened, searing through space. "I'm not gon' talk about that!" Clearly the Judge couldn't turn his head to see Eddie. Just as clearly, he was furious. He started to cough. The coughs began slowly and built to a frightening crescendo. His wife called a nurse, who rushed in and began to reposition him. Eddie had no idea how serious the cough was, whether life-threatening or not, but if so, he couldn't help but notice that the judge garnered all his strength to hurl his possibly last words at Eddie: "You idiot!" Mrs. Samuel turned a face of pure hatred upon him.

Eddie got out of there fast. He felt small. Though he had no idea what he'd said that tortured this man, it was obvious his usual methods weren't working in Clayton. He felt bad for the judge and bad for his wife and very much as if he deserved the old man's parting epithet. He felt like an idiot.

He felt a deep need to gain back some of his self-respect, and he knew perfectly well there was a way around the stonewalling. But there was no talking cure here. If he and Talba were going to dig into the past, they were going to have to do it almost literally—with a mountain of paper and a pickax. There was nothing to do but wait for the damn transcript.

He was turning onto the Interstate when he noticed a silver car behind him, a Lincoln Continental, he thought. Actually, he'd seen the Lincoln for some time, but only now did it occur to him that it might be tailing him. He tried some tricks—changing lanes, even getting off the Interstate—and yes, he was definitely being followed. By someone who didn't care if he was made and yet, having been made, didn't simply go home, message delivered. Once on the frontage road, Eddie turned onto a nameless backroad, then stopped abruptly and let the car sail past, hoping to get its plate number, blissfully unaware that his young assistant had tried the same thing.

As soon as the driver realized he'd been had, he screeched into a one-eighty and barreled back toward Eddie, who was still parked, too startled even to take action. And then Eddie heard a sound like a backfire.

For a moment he clung to the reality of a split-second before: was it a backfire? In his heart, he knew it wasn't. It was a gunshot; he was unarmed and about to die.

The second shot hit the car, and Eddie hit the floor. Yet that was the last one he heard. Timidly rearing up after the longest minute of his life, he found himself alone on a deserted stretch of highway. He had to urinate so badly he didn't think he could get to a gas station.

What the hell, he could get out here and go. The guy wasn't coming back. His job was done.

He drove back to New Orleans in peace and entered his own office bellowing. "Ms. Wallis, get in here! I gotta talk to you now."

When a surprised Talba stumbled into his cubicle, he shouted, "Goddammit, 'scuse my French! Somebody just shot at me! Banged up Audrey's Cadillac too."

"Oh, shit, Eddie. What happened?"

"What happened? What happened, is we've wore out our welcome in Clayton, once and for good and all. Ya not going back there for any reason, and ya gonna give me ya word on that."

"Okay, Eddie. Sure." She looked scared to death. Good.

"And if ya do, ya fired. It's that simple. I am not having my employees getting shot at. Bad enough ya got thrown in jail. I mean it, Ms. Wallis, this is life-threatenin'."

Eileen Fisher crept into the room, nervous, her lightly pimpled brow now slightly damp. "Eddie, you okay? Somebody shot at ya?" She was his niece, though she avoided calling him "uncle" at the office.

"Hell, no, Eileen, nobody shot at me. I swear to God if one word of this gets to ya Aunt Audrey, I'm firin' you too. Swear to God, do ya hear?"

She nodded, face pink as a petunia. She just stood there a moment, the silence lengthening. Finally, she said, "I think I better get y'all some coffee."

Eddie waved her out of there. "Naah, we're fine. We're fine, okay? All in a day's work. You okay, honey?" Niece or not, he never called his employees pet names. However, if Eileen quit, there'd be hell to pay in the family. He had to calm her down. "There's no danger, Eileen. No danger at all. Ya okay with that?"

He finally got a smile out of her. "Yeah. Sure. Whatever ya say, Uncle Eddie." She was a good kid, just a little timid.

"Don't call me 'uncle' in the workplace."

She smiled at him over her shoulder.

Ms. Wallis, now. She wasn't timid. As soon as Eileen was

gone, she was full speed ahead again. "Eddie, who was it?
Brashear's goons?"

"Naah, hell. Brashear." He was starting to come down from
the adrenaline rush. "Brashear's lame as they come. It was
somebody else, Ms. Wallis. Private citizen." He could feel his
hands starting to shake. He put them in his lap so she
wouldn't notice. "They shot from a car. Followed me first—
then I pulled over and boom!"

Her face was full of emotion. She seemed so hard-bitten
half the time. But look at her now. "You could have been
killed," she said.

"Uh-uh, that wasn't the plan. The idea was to send a message loud and clear: 'Get the hell out of Clayton and stay
out.' Okay, fine, we get it. We been to Clayton. We didn't
actually conquer yet, but we came and we saw. And we ain't
going back."

He watched the little sunrise of surprise on her face at his
use of the Latin quote. "Hey, Ms. Wallis, wake up—I went
to Catholic school. Ya don't have to go to college to know
everything."

Her expression brushed his words away. She just loved
being superior, but she didn't like it worth a damn when he
caught her at it. She said, "What kind of car was it?"

"Silver Lincoln. Couldn't see the plate."

"He was on my tail, too."

"So that's what you were hidin'." He felt fury roar up his
spine; blood rush to his face. "Goddammit, Ms. Wallis! When
ya gonna figure out what's important and what's not?"

"Hey, Eddie, calm down. It could have been anybody. He
didn't shoot at me."

Eddie was so mad he couldn't even think of any words.
"Shit! Just shit! Get outta here, Ms. Wallis. Just get on outta
here."

"Eddie, I'm sorry." Three words he thought he'd never hear
from her. And then she left him to pull himself together, get
his heart to slow down, his hands to stop shaking.

———

Talba was genuinely sobered—not by Eddie's temper tantrum; she'd seen that before. Simply by the knowledge that somebody'd actually shot at him. It might be only a warning, but it was vicious.

She felt the need to escalate, to move in double time. And, anyway, she'd had it with waiting for Calvin Richard to develop a conscience. This time she didn't go through Skip. She called the department personnel office and let them ring him. And when she had him, she minced no words. "Sergeant Richard, this is Talba Wallis. Someone shot at my partner. It's time we talked."

To her surprise, he didn't resist. "Ms. Wallis, I'm real sorry about that. Listen, I'm sorry I hung up on you, too. I got some time now if you like—you want to come on by? I'll buy you a cup of coffee."

Just like that. Instant turnabout. She wondered why. He was attached to the First District, just outside the French Quarter. It was a prime location for coffeehouses, and she could have used a midmorning jolt. But evidently Richard meant the offer only as a figure of speech. "Let's go for a walk in St. Louis Number 1," he said. He was talking about the cemetery across the street. He wanted privacy.

Calvin Richard was a handsome man, his skin a good, rich mud color, his hair a buzz cut.

She said, "Your parents told me you were dead. Now why would that be?"

"Yeah. They told me they did that." He stared straight ahead, no expression at all on his handsome features.

"Why did they want me to think that?"

"I really couldn't say, Ms. Wallis." He was sweating lightly.

"Look, Calvin." She no longer bothered with "Sergeant." "Something very strange is going on in your hometown. I think Clayton was killed because Donny Troxell didn't attack her, and she was about to blow the whistle on the person who did. If I'm right, it's somebody mean enough to hire two goons to give her an overdose of heroin. I don't think it's you because it was somebody white. Somebody the other whites are covering up for. So tell me something—why are you helping them?"

He still wouldn't look at her. Still kept staring straight ahead. "You don't know what you're foolin' with."

"Don't give me that crap." She was angry now. Furious. "You knew that girl and you know who killed her." It was a shot in the dark, just something she blurted, but even as she said it, she knew it must be true. He knew and he wasn't saying. Though she had only a side view, she could see the rage and fear in his face. He walked away from her without a word, a good-bye, any recognition at all.

Her cell phone rang.

Chapter Twenty-two

Eddie said, "Ms. Wallis, ya busy? I got some real inter-estin' reading matter for ya."

The transcript of the trial had come in. It was a tome as thick as a dictionary, sitting on her desk in a pristine plastic cover. By the time she got back to the office, Eddie had gone to lunch.

Where to start? Jury selection looked long and boring. Okay, she could skip that.

She began with opening statements. The prosecutor, one Steven Ortenberg, said he would prove that Donny Troxell had been hurt and angry when his girlfriend, Clayton Patter-son, broke up with him, so angry that he went out and bought a machete with the intention of harming her; that he had re-moved the screen from her bedroom window, forced open the window, and attacked her with the machete, ripping the skin from the skull and causing horrible injuries; he had become frightened by her screams and left, once again through the open window, and later been caught with the bloody weapon in his car.

Pretty much the story as Talba understood it, from the way the paper had reported it.

The young defense attorney, Lawrence Blue, the man she'd talked to in Sacramento, who was now a state senator and had clammed up on her so completely, in those days was full of passion and idealism, if the words on paper were any indication.

He contended that Donny Troxell had not attacked Clayton Patterson, that he could not have attacked Clayton Patterson because he'd been with two friends that night, two friends who would testify, in this court of law, that he could not have done it. There was no evidence in the world that Donny Troxell had ever owned a machete, ever bought a machete, or indeed, ever even seen a machete before police showed him the bloody weapon they found in Donny's car the morning after Clayton Patterson was attacked, a car, in fact, that had sat in his driveway all night, unlocked.

There was not a shred of evidence to connect him with that machete, Lawrence Blue declaimed, not a fingerprint, not a witness, nothing at all except that it turned up in his car. And how did it get in his car?

"I submit," Lawrence Blue argued, "that it was placed there by someone seeking to incriminate Mr. Troxell. By the same someone who removed the screen from Clayton Patterson's window, but who, in his haste and confusion, also removed every single screen from the Patterson house and left each one on the ground underneath its respective window.

"Why was this done?" Lawrence Blue asked. "It was almost certainly done in some misguided attempt to prove that someone had entered the house from the outside, when no such thing occurred. I ask you, ladies and gentlemen of the jury, what crazed burglar removes each and every screen from the house into which he intends to break, especially, and this is important, ladies and gentlemen—especially in the case of a crime of passion, which my colleague, Mr. Ortenberg, would have us believe this was?

"Who would do this? A son, ordered by his father to make it seem as if someone had broken into the house, too young to make a rational decision, too terrified to think it through? A father, frightened and fearful, knowing only that he must protect his family, no longer able to think logically? You will find, ladies and gentlemen of the jury, that one of the screens was destroyed, and that that one was the one covering Clayton Patterson's bedroom window. It did not come off easily. Whoever tried to remove it failed, then removed the others, and finally, perhaps after having been ordered to do so, ripped it apart. In fact, the same person also broke the window of Clayton Patterson's bedroom, but, not from the outside, ladies and gentlemen. Not from the outside. The fragments of glass fell, not into the room, but onto the ground outside the window. No one broke in through that window. That window was broken from the inside in an attempt to make it look as if someone came in that way.

"Does it sound as if I am telling you Donny Troxell was set up? Was framed, as it were? Ladies and gentlemen, that is exactly what I'm telling you. Someone in that house, for whatever reason, attacked Clayton Patterson and then attempted not only to cover it up, but to fix the blame on Mr. Troxell.

"Later, Mr. Ortenberg will show you pictures of the injured Miss Patterson—pictures indicating a horrible crime—in an attempt to turn you against Mr. Troxell, yet these pictures themselves will show that Mr. Troxell did not commit the crime. They will show that Miss Patterson's wounds were caused by a diagonal cut to the left side of her face, a blow delivered by a person standing between Miss Patterson's bed and the door to her bedroom, not a person standing between the window and the bed. A person who was already in the house. Could Mr. Troxell have already been in the house? Anyone could have, ladies and gentlemen; anyone could have. But if Mr. Troxell was already in the house, why then does Mr. Ortenberg argue that he broke in?

"Finally, ladies and gentlemen, let's talk about timing. The attack, according to Miss Patterson and her family, took place around ten-fifteen P.M. Yet the first call to the sheriff's office came in at eleven-ten. Eleven-ten, ladies and gentlemen. At no time in that period was an ambulance or a doctor called. Fifty-five minutes between the attack and the call to the sheriff's office, and no call to a doctor or a hospital.

"Has any of you ever seen a scalp wound? Have you any idea how much a scalp wound bleeds? Picture your own child with a scalp wound. Imagine your horror.

"Wouldn't you call a doctor immediately? Or take your child to an emergency room? Certainly you would. Yet the family of one of the most prominent men in Clayton did not.

"I submit that the occupants of that house had a reason for that, ladies and gentlemen. A reason involving a cover-up and a frame-up. It is not our business here today to accuse anyone. Exactly who attacked Clayton Patterson may never be known. Miss Patterson says she was asleep and has no idea. But it was not Donny Troxell. It was someone who did not break into that house, someone who was visiting or who lived there. I can't tell you who it was—but it was someone that family wanted to protect."

Talba felt her palms sweating, the back of her neck sweating, sweat pouring off her waistband. Cover-up hardly began to describe this thing. If half the things Blue said were true, how the hell had Troxell been convicted? How, in fact, had the sheriff's office overlooked this stuff?

She read on. The prosecution's first witness was the first officer on the scene, Sheriff's Deputy Hubert J. Calhoun.

Deputy Calhoun said that he arrived at the scene to find Clayton Patterson crying, her head wrapped in bloody towels, and that the first thing he did was call an ambulance.

"Did you ask the Pattersons why they hadn't called an ambulance themselves?" Blue asked on cross-examination.

"No sir, I didn't," the deputy replied.

"Did you wonder?"

"No, sir, I didn't."

"Did you ask Clayton Patterson who attacked her?"

"Yessir, I did. She said she didn't know."

"Did you think that was strange?"

"No, sir. She said she was asleep at the time."

"Did you ask her who would have reason to attack her?"

"Yessir. She said she couldn't think of anyone."

"What led you to suspect Donny Troxell?"

"We developed that information based on statements of various witnesses."

"What witnesses were those?"

"Mr. and Mrs. Patterson."

"Did you examine the windows in her bedroom?"

"I did."

"And what did you find?"

"I found evidence of forced entry."

"Did you notice that the window had been broken from the inside?"

"No, sir, I didn't."

"Did you notice that all the screens on the house had been removed?"

"No, sir, I didn't."

"We went to school together, didn't we, Deputy?"

"Yes sir."

"And you were valedictorian, as I recall. Tell me something—how'd a smart fellow like you miss something as obvious as that?"

At this point Ortenberg objected, but Talba got the point. Apparently, Blue hoped the jury would too.

Talba read on. Though Mr. Ortenberg's case against Troxell was circumstantial, even she had to admit that Blue's didn't entirely live up to the promise of the opening statement. The biggest blow was that Troxell's alibi fell through. One of the witnesses simply wasn't called. The other hedged on the hours he'd been with Troxell, making it possible for Ortenberg to suggest that Troxell had enough time by himself to commit the crime. Clayton herself didn't testify, nor did either of her parents.

Still, Blue fought the good fight. In his closing statement, he seesawed back and forth, recapping the testimony of Ortenberg's witnesses and his own. "If you convict Donny Troxell, a most horrendous miscarriage of justice will occur. You have heard the testimony of the eminent forensics expert, Dr. Robin Taylor," (whom Blue had called) "that the window was not broken from the outside, and could not have been broken from the outside. And you have heard the testimony of Deputy Buddy Calhoun, valedictorian of his high school class, one of the most promising young men of our generation, that he didn't notice this extremely curious fact. . . ."

Talba stopped reading, feeling something like a cold wind on the back of her neck. She sucked in her breath, dropped the transcript like a hot coal, turned to her computer, and ran a search on Hubert J. Calhoun.

M s. Wallis came into his office late in the afternoon, waving that big huge tome and hollering so loud they could probably hear her in Shreveport. "Eddie. Goddammit, it's in here. What's going on in Clayton. *Exactly* what's going on."

"Ya mean ya solved the case, Ms. Wallis?"

"Goddammit, Eddie. This is ugly. Listen to this: what if I told you the arresting officer in that machete case was a young deputy named Hubert J. Calhoun who happened to be nicknamed Buddy? And then, what if I told you our only nonracist gubernatorial candidate, the hope of all decent people in the state, and certainly all black people in the state, was born in 1955 in Clayton, Louisiana?"

"Well, I wouldn't say that, Ms. Wallis. I was planning to vote for the other guy myself." He let her struggle with that one while he sought to regain composure. The hair on his arms was standing up.

"Eddie, for Christ's sake!"

He patted thin air. "Now, calm down, Ms. Wallis. Just calm down. Lay it out for me all neat and tidy. Dot your *i*s and cross your *t*s."

She sucked air and sat down. "Okay. Clayton's dad attacks her—or her mother or brother maybe, and the family's got big pull with the sheriff, so they cover it up. To do that, they need to get the arresting officer's cooperation. Which they get."

"You sayin' Buddy Calhoun was in on the cover-up? Why would he do a fool thing like that?"

"Plenty of reasons. Maybe he was just going along with the system—in other words, he was willing to be corrupted. Or he might have had a personal thing with the Pattersons. Friend of the family, say."

"Or maybe something we don't know yet."

"Could be." She was too impatient to dwell on it. "But he's really got something to lose if it comes out now."

"Yeah. The election."

She looked like she was in shock. "I feel so damn betrayed."

"*Never* put your faith in politicians, Ms. Wallis. Every one of 'em's scum. Never known it to fail."

"I thought this one was different."

"If you're right, this one is different—crazier and more dangerous. Reg'lar megalomaniac."

She sighed, deeply and cathartically, and went back to her storyline. "Maybe Calhoun's the one Donny Troxell's father called that last morning—because if Donny didn't do it, then his father'd know for damn sure Buddy Calhoun had helped frame him."

"Or maybe he just called his old buddy, Sheriff Ransdell. Way things work in Louisiana, that'd be good enough."

"So if Old Man Troxell was going to blow the whistle on the whole thing, Calhoun was going to get dirty, and it was sure as hell going to come out where the information came from. *That's* why Clayton was killed now, after all these years years. Because for the first time, she talked, and for the first time, it mattered. Donny Troxell, the same. Clayton met with him before she saw Ralph Troxell—she may have told Donny who did it, too. Or maybe Calhoun just assumed she did."

Eddie felt like going outside for some air. "Easy, Ms. Wallis. You just take it easy now."

But she was off in her own world. "So many things have just fallen into place—that's why Calhoun was at her funeral. And that sign in the Pattersons' yard! Some detective—I never even thought about it."

"You mind tellin' me what ya talking about?"

"The maid, Betty Majors, told me King Patterson was a

racist. I never put that together at all—why the hell would a racist be supporting Calhoun?"

Eddie couldn't even be bothered reprimanding her for swearing. He was getting too excited himself. "Probably his biggest contributor, under the circumstances."

"Well, I checked that out too."

He sighed. "I'm damn sure you did, Ms. Wallis. Damn sure."

"He has contributed the maximum allowable by law, but I'll bet anything if I kept at it, I could discover some ways he gave Calhoun more under different names. I just thought we'd better talk first."

"Yeah. Real good decision, Ms. Wallis. I don't mind tellin' ya certain things are startin' to make sense for me too. Like this: I see Sheriff Ransdell, I get chased, I get shot at. There's too much stuff happenin' here." He shook his head. "Just too much damn stuff. Tell you what. Why don't we just try something?" If what she thought was happening, they were as vulnerable as anyone else.

He got out a couple of ordinary-looking briefcases containing his most prized equipment—something so specialized he didn't even include it in the six items every PI needed. Most of them didn't need this—they could just hire Eddie. It was his sweep kit.

The first thing was to hook it up to the phone line system. That required leaving the office and took a few minutes, but the peace of mind was worth it. Talba followed, no doubt trying to figure out what he was doing—she could probably do it, too, just from looking over his shoulder. But he didn't have the heart to tell her to stay in the office. He found the large metal box where the phone bank was. "Uh-huh. Yep." Forget peace of mind. "We're tapped—every line in our office, including Eileen's. Let's just leave that on for now."

"Holy shit!" Talba's eyes were like a kid's. It would have been a pure delight to see her so unnerved if he hadn't been feeling real queasy right about then. All he said was, "Did ya forget you're a lady, Ms. Wallis?"

He led her back inside. He was about to do what he'd had

to do only once before in his own office. On the way back, he explained it to her. For Eileen Fisher, who'd seen it before, he wrote two words on a piece of paper and watched *her* eyes pop. The words were *Level Three*.

In his business, as Eileen well knew, Eddie recognized three levels of sweeps. Level One was for domestic cases—people who used Radio Shack stuff. Level Two was for small businesses. Level Three was performed when you were dealing with somebody with deep pockets, like the government or a large corporation. He had no idea who was on their tail, but he damn sure wasn't taking chances.

He wrote another note: "Everybody do their own office."

By now, Ms. Wallis knew what to do, and Eileen was already a pro at it. What was called for was a thorough physical search. You had to yank out all the drawers and turn all the furniture upside down. You had to pull the wall sockets out, unscrew the switchplates, look anywhere and everywhere your imagination led you. He had no doubt Ms. Wallis was going to be good at it. He figured she was no stranger to highly illegal electronic equipment. He knew perfectly well where she'd gotten the damn GPS—surfing the net for spy shops.

After a first round, they changed places and each searched someone else's office. Then they did it again. After two hours, nobody had found anything. Eddie resumed respiration. It could have been a lot worse.

"Okay, ladies, let's check the cell phones." These were more difficult to tap, but they could be checked. They registered negative, but he still wasn't satisfied. "We use these till we can get new ones. Eileen, go to a secure phone—pay phone if ya have to—and order some now. Let's have them by tomorrow."

He just hoped no damage had yet been done. They were in the reception room, Eileen Fisher's office, Eddie leaning against her desk. "Now think back real carefully, Ms. Wallis. What have you said on the phone? Who have you talked to and what have you said that might be dangerous to you or me or somebody else?"

"Shit! Just shit!" She was shouting. He thought she might kick something.

"Goddamn! I hate that kind of talk." And he hated the panic in her voice.

"Calvin Richard. I called him twice."

"And ya think he's in danger? Why?"

"He knows something—and you know what happens to—"

He didn't even let her finish. "Call him." He looked at his watch. "Try him at home—use ya cell phone."

She dialed, fingers fumbling, and he heard her say, "Calvin, it's Talba Wallis," then watched her lower the phone, staring at it, bemused.

"Eddie, he hung up."

"Do you know where he lives?"

She nodded, as he had known she would. Ms. Wallis always researched those things. "Let's go see him."

She didn't say a word, just followed, docile as a deer. That worried him a lot.

Chapter Twenty-three

For the first time in her life, Talba wished she smoked cigarettes. She didn't know Richard. In point of fact, he'd been horribly rude to her, but the fear that something could happen to him because of her was making her feel ill.

"Eddie, his little boy's got something wrong with him."

"What do you mean?"

"He's got what they call a development disorder."

"Okay, Ms. Wallis. Okay. I'm driving as fast as I can." He'd understood her—that this was a kid that needed his parents even more than most.

She kept talking, to relieve the tension. "He had to have all kinds of evaluations that must have cost a fortune, but now he's going to a special school that's helping a lot, apparently."

"Private school?"

"Yes—and you know how much those things can cost."

"You suggesting the Richards are getting a little help?"

"Well, suppose Calvin's not the slasher, but he knows who is—or at least he knows about the cover-up. And he's being paid off. They'd have damn good reason to trust him. Why would he drop a dime if it dried up the money?"

"They probably won't hurt him. But all the same we gotta warn him. By the way, who's 'they'?"

"The real slasher, maybe. Or could be Calhoun. Calvin told me I was messing with something I didn't understand."

Eddie said, "Understatement, hmm?" and they were silent for the rest of the drive.

A typical cop, Richard lived in the suburbs, not in the city in which he worked. Like Mozelle and Matthew Simmons, he lived in Kenner, but not in their gated community. It was strange, heading there again, and made Talba think of the sister she still hadn't met—whom she was putting off meeting.

The other houses on the block were new and relatively expensive. The Richards' probably was too, but that wasn't what you saw right away. What you noticed was that the place was surrounded by Jefferson Parish Sheriffs' cars.

"Oh, God, Eddie—what if we're too late?"

"He answered the phone, didn't he?"

"Yes." But somehow, that didn't make her feel any better. Eddie had once been a deputy sheriff in Jefferson Parish. She said, "This is your territory. Do you want to try to talk to them?"

He gestured at one of the several knots of civilians clustered on the street. "Let's try the neighbors." He smiled at her wryly. "I'll do it. Ya got the wrong demographics."

Actually, some of them were black, as were the Richards, but Eddie was a schmoozer, infinitely more suited to coaxing information than she was. She trailed him at a distance as they approached one of the groups.

"How y'all this evenin'?"

The group buzzed a little.

"Looks like there's trouble at the Richards'." He paused, and a few people nodded. "We teach over at their son's school—just on our way home when we saw the commotion. Anything we can do?"

A woman with short hair looked like she was about to pop,

a very thin woman with eyes that bulged almost as much as those of the infamous Sergeant Rouselle. Her hands fluttered, restless pink butterflies. "Somebody shot at Tanitha."

Talba made an *o* of horror. "Damian!"

The woman nodded. "He was with her."

"Omigod."

Eddie said, "Nobody hurt, though?"

"No, but we all heard it. It was a drive-by—can you imagine? In this neighborhood! Car just drove by and opened up."

"How many shots fired?"

A man said, "Two."

The short-haired woman shook her head. "Three. Three, swear to God. Calvin's a policeman, you know—it could have been somebody with a grudge."

"But the wife!" said another woman. "And poor little Damian."

A couple of the men grumbled in a way that said to Talba, *There goes the neighborhood.*

"Well, y'all tell 'em our hearts are with 'em," Eddie said. "We'll leave our cards in the mailbox."

Back in the car, they were silent, each trying to take in what they'd just seen, the magnitude of the thing building around them. After awhile, Talba noticed that Eddie wasn't driving back to the office.

"Where are we going?"

"We're driving around."

She didn't answer, thinking that was fine with her. There wasn't anywhere she especially wanted to be right now. "We're thinking," he continued.

Again she kept quiet. The last thing she wanted to do was think.

"We're thinking about how to keep that from happening on your street. And my street. And Angie and Darryl's streets."

"Oh, shit!"

"Now that ain't gon' help anything, Ms. Wallis."

She kept quiet again, a turtle safe in its shell.

Finally, he said, "What do we think is happening here?"

And she was stunned at the burble of words that poured of her mouth, as if she really had been thinking. "That was a warning. They didn't mean to hurt anybody, or they would have. Like when they shot at you. Also, they don't have to worry about the Richards—that's a family with plenty of reason not to wreck the gravy train. They just wanted to remind them of that."

"Agreed. Once again, who is 'they'?"

"Yeah. Who? I mean, Calhoun's got to be behind it, but . . ."

"Maybe not. With politicians you never know. It could be crazy supporters."

She shook her head, surprised at how clearly she could see it. "Uh-uh. This isn't dirty tricks, it's murder. Who'd care that much except Calhoun himself? Besides, how would they know about the cover-up? It's Calhoun."

"Ya mean it's somebody he hired. And I've got a real bad feeling about what that somebody's next assignment is."

"You mean us? You do, don't you? I was afraid you did." She was almost used to the idea. She was starting to look at it coldly—turtling out further still. But maybe that wasn't such a bad thing right now. She said, "It was more than one— it took two people to kill Clayton."

"They're real slick, Ms. Wallis. Real, real slick."

"How the hell do you deal with something like this?"

"Well, now, I was hopin' you were going to ask that. I been thinkin' about it. Ya really want to know?"

"Don't tell me to yell uncle."

She was surprised when he laughed. "Ms. Wallis, Ms. Wallis. Ya think I'm crazy? I'd never say a thing like that to you. 'Course, maybe we could just go to the police."

She thought about it. "It puts Calvin too much at risk. He could lose his job—or worse. And you know what I mean by worse. I just don't think we have the right." She let it lie for a minute. "Okay, I give up. What's your idea?"

"Ya famous demographics, Ms. Wallis. For this, ya got the perfect demographics; and also ya famous criminal abilities. We gotta go behind enemy lines; do a little spyin'."

"You mean computer spying? Illegal stuff?" Eddie was usually such a stickler.

"This is life or death, Ms. Wallis. Ya want 'em to get to Miz Clara? Or Calvin Richard's little boy? Ya gotta disappear right now and become someone else. Somebody with access to certain things."

She was amazed. She'd have thought he'd have gone all male and protective. Almost crossly, she asked, "What are you going to do?"

"I'm gon' run a little sting, Ms. Wallis. Got quite a little idea in the back of my head, but don't ax me any more yet. I got a lot of details to work out. I'm gon' have to bring in some outside help. Now, listen. I don't want you at home and I don't want you at Darryl's. Ya got any place ya can stay?"

She shrugged. "Hotel, I guess. Just tell me, will you—what the hell am I going to be doing?"

"Ya had a chance to background Calhoun yet?"

"Sure. He was born in Clayton, of fairly poor parents, and put himself through law school with that deputy sheriff's gig. After that, he came to New Orleans, where he worked for the DA's office, and now he's a bigtime lawyer who wants to be governor. Wife and kids, the whole thing."

"Uh-huh. So he's got two offices in New Orleans—a law office and campaign headquarters, most probably. Now campaign headquarters—that might be promising. How would ya feel about volunteering?"

"Ah." All of a sudden she saw the plan and thoroughly approved. "My name's Claudia Snipes."

"Huh?"

"That's the new person I'm waking up as."

"Where'd ya get that name?"

She shrugged. "I don't know. It just popped into my head." It was funny how clearly she was thinking. "But not campaign headquarters. How big is the law office?"

"Huge. But ya can't just volunteer to work in a law office."

"Uh-huh. You can if it's big enough—and you've got computer skills."

"Whatever ya say, Ms. Wallis. I don't know what ya talking about, but there ain't no news there."

The next morning, with the phone bugs still in place, she called the office and was greeted by Eileen Fisher's cheery, "E. V. Anthony Investigations."

"Eileen, it's Talba." She made her voice labored and slow.

"Talba, you okay? You don't sound right."

"I've got the worst cramps I've had since I was fifteen."

"Oh, Gawd, I feel for ya. I get 'em every month."

"Listen, can I talk to Eddie? I don't think I can come in today."

"Sure. You take care of yourself now."

Eddie answered particularly gruffly. "Yeah?"

"EdDEE. You know that prejudice you've got against female employees?"

"Miz Wallis? That you?"

"You know how you're afraid they'll get their periods and—"

"Miz Wallis, what the hell ya talkin' about? Ya sound like ya voice is comin' up from a tunnel."

"I'm sorry. I just feel crummy is all. I've got these horrible cramps and, you know, like, really, really heavy flow. I'm scared I'm hemorrhaging. I even think maybe—"

"Ya need the day off, Miz Wallis? Is that what ya sayin'? Could ya spare me the fuckin' details? Excuse my French."

He sounded so genuinely horrified she almost laughed. She'd picked this particular form of infirmity for the express purpose of getting a reaction so genuine whoever was listening couldn't mistake it. "Eddie, I wouldn't do this if I absolutely didn't have to."

"Just cut to the chase, okay? How about the Patterson case?"

"What about it?"

"It's our most important case of the moment. What kind of progress ya makin?"

"Eddie, I'm gonna be honest with you. I've got a real bad

feeling it's a dead end. Richard's not going to tell us anything. Talking to him's like talking to a dead fish."

"I don't care if he stinks like a fish. This guy Jason's got money and he's willing to spend it. You *will* pursue this case. Ya understand me?"

"Okay, okay. I swear to God I'll hit it with both barrels tomorrow. Just let me have a day off and—"

"Miz Wallis, you can have two days off if ya need 'em. Just get up a head of steam on this one. I can't work it for ya or I would. I gotta go out of town today."

"You do? What for?"

"Ya know the Fusco case? Billy Bob Bubba–type guy out in Plaquemines?"

"Oh, yeah. Divorce case. Made a lot of money in something or other, and the wife wants it. She's trying to prove he's having an affair."

"No, ya got it wrong, Ms. Wallis. He didn't actually make his money—took care of a fishing camp for some old boys from New Orleans; one of 'em took a shine to him and remembered him in his will. Well, anyway, Mrs. Billy Bob just wouldn't take no for an answer about Sweet Thing. But I did hours and hours and hours of surveillance and got nothing. Remember that?"

"I remember how pissed off you were." And because she was feeling kindly toward him, she said, "Excuse my French."

"Well, ya know what I did, Ms. Wallis?"

"I know I'm about to find out."

"I brought Muhammed to the mountain, that's what. That is, I invited him to the mountain. Sent him a prepaid coupon for two nights at the Beau Rivage. Champagne breakfast, the whole thing. Ya think he's taking his wife to that?"

"Let me guess. He told her he's got a business trip."

"To Mobile! He told her he's going to Mobile! I love it. I swear to God, I love it." Outwitting people was pretty much his favorite thing, and she was coming to see the appeal of it.

"So you're spending the day on the Gulf Coast with a video camera."

"Yeah. Last time I did something like this, they all but did it out by the swimming pool. Prettiest little movie I ever made in my life."

"Well, you just have a swell old time, Eddie. I'll see you when you get back."

"Take care of yaself, Ms. Wallis."

"Ohhhh, yeah." She executed a pseudo-moan. "I think I might go to the emergency room."

They hung up, she smiling happily to herself, hoping the listeners had enjoyed themselves. Eddie loved his little ruses so much, even she was half-convinced he was going off to do a surveillance.

So far so good. The next thing was to come up with a disguise for herself. Fortunately, her mother had a closet full of wigs, none of which were styled any way at all Talba would even consider wearing under normal circumstances. She chose a kind of church lady do that would look more or less professional paired with a plain white blouse, navy skirt, and rust-colored jacket. The jacket was essential for this kind of work, having deep pockets for carrying whatever she needed—in this case, disks. She put the whole outfit in a bag with a few other things and pulled on a pair of jeans.

She looked up her destination in the phone book, picked up her bag, got in her car, and headed for Eve's Full-Service Garden of Glamour (AKA Eve's Weaves). It was out in the Ninth Ward, and she decided to take St. Claude, a nice wide street with plenty of lanes. She drove very slowly, as if extremely relaxed, or else the possessor of a raging hangover. And pretty soon she saw a white Buick Le Sabre, a plain vanilla car, perfect for tailing, going about as slow as she was. She turned off onto a side street, and so did the car. *Uh-oh*, she thought, *It's going to be a long, ugly day*. She didn't want the guy to know she'd made him, which somewhat complicated things. She hadn't thought of an errand to fake to explain her detour. *What the hell*, she decided, *Somebody's about to get a surprise visit*.

She picked a house with no cars in front, parked, and rang

the bell. But while she stood on the porch, the Le Sabre didn't pass.

She slipped to the side, hoping there were no vicious dogs in the back. There were, only next door.

Amid a huge din that she hoped wouldn't draw a man with a gun, she crept to the back, hid, and waited till a car passed. The Le Sabre? She couldn't see. Well, who cared? If it hadn't passed by now, she'd probably lost it already.

She walked back to her own car, making sure to wave at the imaginary person at the back of the house. It was tempting to pretend to adjust the rearview mirror, but she didn't dare. Peeks would have to do. She slid back onto the street, and when she'd gone half a block, saw a white car doing the same. Damn!

Okay, then, Eve's Weaves anyhow. It was a weird way to meet her long-lost sister, but why not kill two birds with one stone? Well, three—she really needed a manicure.

She could sit across the table from Janessa, actually talking to her, getting to know her a little. Maybe she'd become a regular client, get to be buddies, then break the news.

Chapter Twenty-four

She parked and strolled in, expecting a sleepy neighborhood salon, and, except for being fairly busy, it pretty much met her expectations. There were two hairdressers, one of whom probably doubled as the receptionist, a manicurist to the right and out of sight unless she swiveled her head conspicuously, two clients in the chairs, and two clients waiting. Evidently, they welcomed walk-ins here, and so much the better. If she were here a long time, the tail might conclude she was malingering, and call it a day.

One of the hairdressers paused and looked her way. "May I help you?" The one who was also the receptionist. The woman in her chair also looked. "Talba Wallis!" the client sang out. "What brings a baroness to this neighborhood?"

It was one of the waitresses at Reggie and Chaz, the restaurant where she did her readings. "Hey, you're reading next week, right?"

"Hey, Marcelline. How're you doing? I just came in for a manicure." She broke out in a sweat. If Janessa'd been told about her visit, her well-laid plans had just gone terrible awry.

The hairdresser answered, "There's one ahead of you—it'll be about half an hour."

"I can wait." Oh, yes. Gladly. She'd now finished her Susan Dodd novel, but she'd brought a book of poetry. She could wait absolutely as long as she had to, and she hoped it was quite awhile.

She glanced at the manicurist and sucked in her breath in surprise. If she'd pictured a polished, spoiled Black American Princess, she couldn't have been further off the mark. This girl was as unlike her Aunt Mozelle as Talba was; and she was nothing like Talba, either. First of all, she was lighter, milk chocolate–colored; she was a whole lot heavier, and somewhat taller; and she was sloppy about her appearance. The worst case Talba'd expected was someone with a Queen-of-Sheba hairstyle and stiletto nails.

The way this girl looked really threw her. Her collar-length hair was unstyled, just brushed back from her face as if she didn't know what else to do with it. She wore a T-shirt and shorts that revealed heavy thighs, and she sat like a truck driver. To her surprise, Talba was as dismayed as Miz Clara might have been. She thought about why it bothered her so much.

It was because she associated this look—one she saw a thousand times every day—with a sense of hopelessness; a deep depression about everyday life, the unshakable feeling that it has to be like this. You have to be fat, for instance; and that's because food eases all the other things you can't make go away. Not a mere depression, but a lifelong condition, a sullen acceptance of your fate as bad, deserved, and unchangeable.

She associated it with something else as well—poverty and lack of education. Poor social standing and poor self-esteem. Miz Clara had scrubbed white ladies' toilets twelve hours a day to send her and Corey to college. Before that, she'd browbeaten them into doing their homework and doing well in school. She'd limited their television hours; she'd yelled at them and grounded them. She'd metaphorically gotten down on all fours and pushed their reluctant behinds into the middle

class. Talba forgot all that most of the time; took her educated
status for granted.

This girl, despite the fancy home from which she'd fled,
looked like trash. The thought shocked her. Talba didn't think
she was the kind of person who thought in those terms.

Depressed, she picked up her poetry anthology and wished
it were a novel. She needed something diverting, not chal-
lenging. After awhile, Marcelline the waitress stopped by to
chat on her way out. "Looking forward to your performance."

"Oh, you don't have to say that. You've seen my routine
a million times."

"Are you kidding? I bow to the Baroness." She executed
a sort of mock curtsy, causing Talba to giggle and other people to stare. Talba went back to her reading.

Despite everything, she managed to become sufficiently ab-
sorbed. She heard the summons, when it came, only as background noise, "Okay, I'm ready for ya."

The girl repeated it a moment later, louder. "I'm ready."

Talba looked up and caught the eye of the manicurist, who
nodded, eyes narrowed, as if she were summoning someone
to an execution rather than a feminine pampering experience.
Tucking away her book, Talba approached warily.

She smiled at the girl. "Hi. I'm Talba."

"I know who you are."

Talba sat down and held out her hands. "What's your name?"

Lowering her eyes, the girl spoke almost inaudibly. "Janessa."

"Glad to meet you." Not answering, the girl took Talba's
hands and began filing her nails.

This is weird, she thought. *We're holding hands.*

"How long have you worked here?"

Janessa flicked her eyes up, then down again. "Couple
months."

"You like your job?"

Once again, the girl's eyes flicked like a snake's. There
was no mistaking the hostility in them. "Why you care?"

"I was just making conversation."

For a long time, during which Janessa filed nails (none too

expertly), and snipped at cuticles, there was deep, pregnant silence. Finally, the girl looked up, glancing at Talba sideways. "Why you come to see me?"

"You know me?"

"I know about you."

"What do you know about me?"

"You the one that come here. You talk."

Talba was breaking out in flop sweat. This wasn't at all what she had in mind for a first conversation with her sister—in a public place with a murderer waiting outside; with the other taking the lead; without time to rehearse.

"I came here today just to see you, I guess. I thought we could talk another time."

"What do I look like?"

The question caught Talba offguard. In her view, Janessa looked awful; unacceptable. Badly in need of a big sister.

"You look fine," she said.

The girl lapsed once again into silence.

"Look, I don't care what you look like. Did they tell you why I came looking for you?"

Janessa nodded, not speaking.

"I'm your sister," Talba said, as much to inform herself as the other, to see how the words would sound.

For the first time, Janessa looked her full in the eye, her face ablaze with hostility.

Talba's stomach did a little flip. She pulled her hand from Janessa's grasp and looked at it. "Maybe I don't need polish today."

To her amazement, the girl burst out laughing.

"What's so funny?"

"You look like you think I'm gon' bite you."

"You look like you're going to."

Janessa reached for Talba's hand. "Come on. Let me polish ya nails."

"You sure?" Talba was no longer in the mood.

"Yeah, I'm sure. Let me pick the color." She turned around for a moment, surveying her rainbow. "This purple here." She looked closely at the label. "Professor Plum. Whatcha think that means?"

"Who knows?" Talba brushed aside the subject. "Why are you mad at me?"

Janessa began shaking the bottle. "I ain't mad at you."

"You're acting like it."

"I'm gon' polish ya nails, ain't I? Didn't I pick a special color and everything?" Her voice was furious.

She was still wondering what to say next when Janessa solved it for her. "You a singer or somethin'? What'd that lady mean?"

Talba smiled, not quite knowing how to break it to her. "I'm a poet."

"You a what?"

On impulse, she said, "*I* am a Baroness."

"You a what?" she girl repeated.

"That's my stage name. The Baroness de Pontalba. What I do is, I write poems and I perform them for audiences."

"Poems? Ya mean like, 'Roses are red, violets are blue?' "

Talba was starting to be amused. At least the girl was talking to her. "Well, something like that. Are you into rap at all?"

"Yeah, some. I mean, everybody is, I guess."

"Well, think of it like this. If the lyrics of rap songs weren't part of a song, they'd be poems."

Janessa paused in mid-operation, holding Talba's pinkie delicately in one hand, the polish brush with the other. "What you mean? The *whats* of rap songs?"

"The words. The lyrics are the words."

"Oh." The girl broke out in an unexpected smile. "You mean you write, like, words for songs."

"Only without the songs."

Janessa frowned in frustration.

"Look. I'm performing at a restaurant in a few days. Why don't you come hear me?"

Janessa looked away—not down this time, just anywhere but at Talba. "Ain't got no money to go to no restaurant."

It was funny. They were talking about everything but the fact that they were sisters. *But what did I expect?* Talba thought. *Were we going to compare nose shapes?* "Let me call you," she said on impulse. "We can work something out."

Clearly embarrassed, pushed into a corner, Janessa said nothing, just continued her clumsy purpling of Talba's nails.

Talba felt trapped. However unwittingly, the woman was holding her prisoner as surely as Sergeant Rouselle had. And by the same token, Janessa was her prisoner. *Already we're acting like family*, she thought. *We're stuck with each other.*

That thought amused her enough to get through the experience, and when the time came to go, she said, "Think about it." She left a generous tip.

The whole process had taken an hour, an hour of tension and boredom and disappointment and triumph, but not an hour in which she had a moment to worry about the man tailing her. He had all her attention now. She could think about Janessa later. That was way soon enough.

The Le Sabre was nowhere in sight, but she'd expect these guys to be halfway professional. Where next? She knew where she wanted to go, but, just in case, she thought she might go shopping first. There were plenty of stores at the Riverwalk to while away an hour or so.

She took St. Claude again, keeping a watchful eye in the mirror. She was pretty sure she saw the car again, but if it was following, the driver was being careful. Just to annoy them, if they were with her, she cut through the French Quarter, notorious for its traffic, and parked in a lot on North Peters.

Then she crossed the street and tucked herself out of sight at a coffeehouse, to see if a Le Sabre pulled into the same lot. She didn't see one, but the traffic was fierce, which was good. If she could lose them, they could lose her.

Next, she strolled to the Riverwalk, stopping to get a soft drink from a street vendor, hoping she looked like a happy young woman taking a mental health day. Once inside the mall, she decided on Victoria's Secret as an ideal place to make a spectacle of herself. First, the beauty treatment at Eve's, then some fancy lingerie—it would look as if she were getting ready for a hot date. She made a big show of looking at whatever could be seen through the window, holding nighties and bras up to her body, finally disappearing into a fitting room and waiting in line to make her purchase. If anyone was watching, he'd have no idea there was nothing in her enticing shopping bag except a pair of bikini panties.

She strolled back to her car, transferred the wig, clothes, and other items from their current bag to the Victoria's Secret bag, pretended to retrieve a straw hat from the back seat, which she put on, and then emerged once again onto North Peters. Next, she bought a Lucky Dog, which she ate by the river. Ostentatiously, she read the poetry book as she munched. If the tail was still with her, she must be boring the pants off him.

Finally, she went back to the street and walked in the opposite direction from the parking lot, toward Esplanade Avenue. There was a small women's clothing shop there, into which she ducked for a few minutes, and other stores further down the street—Tower Records, Bookstar, the French Connection. She could dilly-dally forever and never leave the block. Inside the clothing store, she took off the hat, just to make it slightly harder to recognize her, and walked toward the other stores, keeping a careful eye out for a taxi. If she didn't find one, she could keep wandering.

She didn't.

Okay, fine. She went into Tower Records, checked out some African musicians Darryl had been talking about, and popped back out into the sunlight, just as a taxi was drawing up to the curb to let someone out. She darted into it.

"Turn left as soon as you can," she said. "Then go to Dauphine and turn toward Canal."

The cabbie, a white guy with a steel-gray ponytail muttered, "Whatever ya want" in a seen-it-all voice. But she noticed he checked her out in the mirror, unsure what manner of screwball he had in his cab.

Going across the Quarter was going to be slow, so slow she might be able to see if they were being followed, though there'd be dozens of obstructions, mostly in the form of delivery trucks; if the Le Sabre was there, the obstructions might even work to her advantage, since at a distance, one cab looked much like another. She found this almost the worst part of the trip, feeling more trapped even than earlier, when her hand was being held by a hostile force who was also a relative.

By the time they turned onto Dauphine, she was sweating despite the AC, but there was no sign of the Le Sabre. At Canal, she said, "Let's go to the library."

"What library?"

"You know. The main library."

The guy didn't even bother with the mirror—he twisted to the back for an eyeful. "Lady, I ain't never had nobody want to go to the library before."

"Tulane and Loyola Avenue," she said.

She left the conspicuous straw hat in the cab, figuring she could always replace it. The library was actually the first real place on her agenda. By now, she was pretty sure she was free of her pursuers (if there was more than one), but she sure wished she had at least an inkling of what they might look like. White males, she figured. And there ought not to be many of those in the library during working hours. She kept an eye out as she prowled.

She had come to the library for its *Times-Picayune* files, invaluable for a certain kind of background check—the kind you couldn't yet get on the Internet. She knew what she wanted, though, and that ought to help.

She'd lost a big part of the day, and she was antsy, but she had to focus, at least for awhile. Before she got started, she made a phone call to a man she knew named L. J. Currie, telling him she'd meet him at his office at four o'clock. It was late in the day for him to get what she wanted, but too bad, this library thing was the most important thing she had to do today. If anything could help her, these old papers could.

She pored over them in peace and in silence, undisturbed by white men or, indeed, anybody, and in a few short hours she had what she needed—or at least a very good candidate. Feeling close to triumphant—but holding back, you never knew—she got a cab to her appointment.

L. J. Currie worked for a company called CompuTemps, an agency she knew that provided temporary technical workers. She'd discovered him when working for another PI, one who wasn't nearly so ethical as Eddie. Gene Allred had turned L. J. into his personal servant by the simple method of bribing him once, then forever holding the bribery over him. Talba had inherited this excellent contact. She'd found that, for the right price, L. J. could get you into any office you wanted, so long as it had computers in it.

He was tricky, though—he'd blown her off before; she couldn't afford to have it happen again.

But today he added a brand-new element to their arrangement. When they shook hands, he held her hand a little longer than necessary, something he hadn't done before. "Well, well, well. The Baroness herself. What have I done to deserve the honor?"

What the hell, she thought. *He must have finally accepted me.*

"It's what you're *going* to do, L. J. I need a job at O'Brien Calhoun Guste."

He was shaking his head before she got out the second syllable. "No can do."

"Here we go again. That's what you always say."

He shrugged. "What am I s'posed to do? They don't need anybody."

"Ah. So they are your client." Nearly everyone was.

"They've called me. Sure."

"I've got to get in there tomorrow."

"How you gon' do that, Your Grace? I haven't got a job for ya. Simple as that."

"Well, I've given that a little thought. How about if you call up and offer me for free?"

"What the hell ya talkin' about? The agency's not gon' put up with that."

"We don't go through the agency—only the law firm never knows that. Here's what you do: Call up whoever you deal with and say you've got a new candidate. Her credentials are way too good to be true—so good, in fact, you think she might be lying. So you want to try her out before you send her out on a job. If she's as good as she says she is, she can do anything in the office. If not, they can always use her for filing. In short, how would they like a top-quality geekette, absolutely free, for one day only?"

"No way. Who's going to take on somebody that might not be qualified?"

"Only everybody, if it's free. Who wouldn't do it, L. J.?"

"I got a reputation."

"So? This can only enhance it. I'm the best techie in the city—you know it and I know it."

"Bullshit. I got at least two guys as good as you are."

"Okay. One of the top three." She looked at her watch. "Come on. It's getting late."

"Baroness, I'm sorry. It just ain't worth the aggravation."

"It is, L. J. This time there's some real decent money attached." She usually paid him fifty dollars.

"Five hundred dollars."

"What?"

"That's what I'd consider decent money. Take it or leave it."

"L. J., it's four o'clock and I'm asking you to get me in at nine o'clock tomorrow—"

"They start at eight."

"Okay, eight. You think I'd ask you to do it for any less? You want five hundred dollars, you got it."

"Six hundred."

"Five hundred's what I've got."

"Uh-uh. That was too easy, Baroness. You got five, you gotta have six."

She sighed. "Dammit, L. J. Six." She hoped Eddie wouldn't kill her.

L. J. picked up the phone.

"And by the way, I'm Claudia Snipes."

He nodded, to show that he'd heard. "Hey, Leona. Got some good news for ya. I think I might be able to replace Philip after all." He gave Talba a sly grin.

She said, "You're gettin' too big for your britches, L. J.," and deeply regretted she couldn't stalk out before he got off the phone. But she had to stick around and find out who her supervisor was.

Chapter Twenty-five

E ddie's plan was to run a sting. He'd spent hours working it out, more hours pulling it together, and it was a thing of the most exquisite beauty. Truly one of his finest creations.

It was big, it was elaborate, it was a little preposterous, and it would have been expensive as hell except that he knew quite a few people willing to do him a favor.

He got up that morning, went to work as usual, took Ms. Wallis's revolting sick call, and then proceeded to take the mountain to Muhammed, exactly as he'd said he was going to.

First, he made the forty-five-minute drive to Plaquemines Parish, where he parked, and waited happily, feeling like a cat outside a mousehole. He'd picked up the tail on the way over, this time a light-colored Ford.

Shortly before noon, a Billy Bob Bubba–type guy—large gut, white shoes, real name Robert Fusco—came loping out looking like he hadn't a care in the world; in fact, looking a little smug and satisfied, exactly as if he were about to hole up on the Gulf Coast with his sweetie.

Billy Bob drove all the way back to New Orleans (Eddie following), parked, and went into a sandwich shop on Magazine Street, the kind where you have to stand in line to give your order. Eddie watched him get in line, then watched him watch a blond half his age, wearing shorts and near-bursting hot pink T-shirt, as she got up to get herself a packet of sugar.

As abruptly as he'd arrived, Billy Bob left, but Eddie waited. Sure enough, the blond—sometime-PI Eunice Kelton—followed at a distance. Eddie watched the blond watch Billy Bob get in his car, then watched Billy Bob wait as she got hers, then followed them both out to the Interstate, heading east to the Gulf Coast.

It was perfect, in his humble opinion. Someone would have to know Eunice and Robert not to think he was just a PI following a poor slob after young pussy and a golddigger after a score.

The tail was fairly discreet, staying well behind him. A helicopter, he thought, might have thought it an interesting caravan. He picked up his brand-new cell phone (Eileen had scored) and dialed the number of Catherine Mathison, another part-time PI. Catherine was someone he liked to work with when he needed someone to pose as his wife.

"Hey, gorgeous," he said.

"Whereyat, dawlin'?"

"When we gon' get married?"

"Whenever you want, baby. I've still got the ring from last time."

"You see anything you like out here?"

"Umm-hmm. Late-model Ford. That goldish color everything is these days?"

"Yeah. Shiny, kind of."

"No passengers. White male driving."

"Good. You get what you need?" Meaning the tag number.

Catherine said, "Sure did, dawlin'. This ain't the slickest deal I ever saw in my life."

"Okay. You know what to do."

Eddie hummed a Beatles song, waiting for her to pass him. He'd never really gotten over the Beatles.

There was a romantic place to eat in Bay St. Louis, with a deck overlooking the water. Eddie followed the two cars bearing Billy Bob and Eunice, watched them struggle for parking near the restaurant, and noted in the process that Catherine Mathison's blue Mazda was already parked in front. Then Eddie himself parked and followed the happy couple to the restaurant, as if he didn't know they were going there.

They were ushered onto the deck, where they sat in full view of God and everybody. You could see them perfectly from the street. Eddie watched them order, observed the waitress bring them a couple of beers, and when they had clicked bottles and kissed lightly, returned to his car, from the trunk of which he pulled a video camera, conventional camera with telephoto lens, and a brown bag containing a sandwich.

He also made a great show of stretching, even bending over and touching his toes a time or two. This was to put ideas into the tail's head.

The guy was going to need to stretch his legs. He was going to be hungry—they'd made sure this was a damned late lunch. At the very least, he was going to need to use the men's room. Eddie wanted him to feel extremely comfortable about the amount of time he had. He even went into the very restaurant where Robert and Eunice were yucking it up, got himself a soft drink to go with his sandwich, and used the facilities himself.

Then he returned to the street, found a good place to sit, ate his sandwich, drank his Coke, and idly watched a woman tourist wearing Bermuda shorts, plain blue T-shirt, sunglasses, and visor. Her graying hair was tied back, and she carried a large purse. She was meandering in and out of the various little shops along the shore, shopping happily.

When he'd finished his sandwich, he began slowly to attach the telephoto lens to his camera, working lazily, knowing he had all the time in the world.

He took a few pictures from the sidewalk; after that, he went back and photographed each car against the picturesque backdrop of Bay St. Louis. Finally, he returned to wait for the misbehavers to come out of the restaurant, which they did, hand-in-hand. He recorded that tender moment as well, and then they all three returned to their cars and headed for Biloxi.

It was almost a half-hour's trip. He phoned Catherine fifteen minutes into it.

"Any luck?"

She was laughing. "It was beautiful, baby."

"I saw you shopping. Nice gams, kid." She was the only woman in the world he ever flirted with, including Audrey. But he figured it was okay because she'd started it first, and she did it in front of Audrey, who was a cousin of hers. She'd been a radio reporter before her children were born, and she still liked the action.

"For an old broad, you mean. Listen, the guy's got a bladder problem. He was out of that car so fast . . ."

"Give him a break. It was a long drive."

"Well, at any rate, it didn't take no convincing. He went in a restaurant, he peed fast, then he came out, watched you for awhile, and went back in to get some food to go. He stood outside, eating and watching, just like you. I got some gorgeous pictures of him with his mouth full."

"Yeah? Any with it closed?"

"Whole roll. I'll have prints by the time you get back."

"Gorgeous, dawlin'. Just gorgeous." He could just imagine himself speaking that way to Ms. Wallis.

Several hours later, on his way back from Biloxi, he got her on the cell phone. "Ms. Wallis, whereyat?" It was a question, not a greeting.

"Never mind about that. Let's have another of those rolling meetings of ours."

She was being cryptic for some reason—maybe worried about her cell phone. What the hell was a rolling meeting?

"You know. Like when we did all that thinking?"

She must mean when they'd driven around. "Yeah, I gotcha."

"On the way to Darryl's."

The man lived on the West Bank; that was a start, but it still didn't explain how they were going to meet.

"Ya want me to come get ya?"

"No. I'll meet you on the way. Just try to keep dry, okay?"

It dawned on him that she was arranging a meeting on the Algiers Ferry. It should be perfect, really—the boat left frequently, there were always plenty of people around, and no one could hear them there. But it was pretty melodramatic.

"Ya think this is the movies?" he said.

"Eight-thirty, okay?"

He looked at his watch. "Should be fine."

After leaving Bay St. Louis, he had had to go on to Biloxi, watch Eunice and Billy Bob pretend to frolic by the pool, and film the whole thing for the benefit of the guy in the gold-colored Ford. All *is* had to be dotted, and this is what he and Talba had talked about on the office phone.

On the way out of Biloxi, he methodically but unobtrusively lost his tail, returning to New Orleans on I-10 instead of I-90.

He called Catherine Mathison. "Got pictures?"

"Gawgeous ones, gawgeous. I left 'em with Cutie-Pie."

That was Angie, his daughter. They'd set it up that way so Catherine wouldn't have to go to Eddie's office. If she were seen there she might be identified, the pictures might get lifted, anything could happen. This way he had a twenty-first-century woman, probably armed and assuredly dangerous, to guard them till Eddie got there. Angie'd said she'd be working late and Eddie didn't argue with her—she nearly always worked late.

She looked up when she came in, a gorgeous girl even in lawyer drag, her accustomed black. "Hey, Dad. I got your package." She handed over a manila envelope.

"Anybody strange been around?"

"Not unless you count Aunt Catherine."

"Let me call ya mama."

Angie nodded, going back to her work. He got hold of Audrey, told her he'd be home around ten and begged for something decent to eat when he got there. Already, he was starving.

Angie said, "Want to get a bite with me?"

She never asked him for a meal. He looked at his watch. Damn! Couldn't be done. "Rain check?" he said, and she smiled enigmatically. She'd probably never ask him again— only had then because she knew he didn't have time.

He took a look at the pictures. The guy was good, Eddie had to admit that. The man didn't know how to tail in a car, but if Eddie'd been followed on foot, he'd never made this guy. He was pretty ordinary-looking—medium height, sandy hair—except for one thing. He looked like a bodybuilder. This was one big, strong dude. Eddie didn't like that.

Catherine had also included the tag number of the gold-colored Ford. Eddie said, "Angie, can I use ya phone?" and dialed before she answered, phoning a friendly cop with the license number. It was registered to a George Goldman, who'd reported it stolen earlier that day.

He left to meet Ms. Wallis.

He was in line at the ferry dock when someone tapped on his window. He whirled, wishing his Tee-ball bat was on the front seat instead of the floor behind him. But it was a teen-ager—a black girl in a baseball cap and those stupid short overalls.

The girl was speaking to him. "Eddeee. Come on. Open up."

Quickly, he let her in. "Ms. Wallis. You're somethin' else. Ya gettin' ready for Mardi Gras or what?"

"Let's make a U-ie, Eddie. If we get on the ferry, and they do too, it won't be pretty."

Nimbly, he pulled out of the line and hung a U-ie onto the street, noticing no one else doing the same. "Does that mean ya think ya were followed?"

"Damned sure I wasn't. I was thinking about you."

"I think we're okay. They followed me to Biloxi in a gold-colored Ford—stolen, by the way. I don't see it anywhere."

"I had a white Le Sabre. See anything like that?"

Eddie checked. "No. The Lincoln, either. I think we're okay. If we were both followed, that means there are two of them, though."

He regretted it the minute he said it. She'd always maintained there were two.

For lack of a better idea, he got on the Mississippi River Bridge—why not? The entire Eastern half of the country was on the other side. They could get damned good and lost.

"Before I forget. Here's ya new cell phone. Eileen wrote the number on a business card." He handed the pictures over. "And here's what we got today."

Absently she tucked away the phone, but she plucked eagerly at the manila envelope he'd given her. "Oh, yeah," she said. "Come to mama. Oh, yeah."

"Ms. Wallis, what ya gettin' at?"

She reached into an envelope of her own. "Show and tell," she said, and handed him a photocopy of a police sketch. Actually, it was a copy of a newspaper reproduction of a police sketch. But it was plenty good enough. It was the man who followed Eddie.

Chapter Twenty-six

After leaving L. J. Currie, Talba had once again gone to the Riverwalk, where she'd bought a baseball cap, yellow T-shirt, short overalls, and running shoes, which created an effect that startled her. *Even a Baroness*, she thought, *can look ordinary if she tries hard enough. All I need now is bubble gum.*

Once again working on the convenience theory, she'd checked into the Hilton, just a few steps away, and ordered from room service. Plenty of time before she had to meet Eddie.

And she had one hell of a story to tell him. During her two hours in the library, she'd developed a really great candidate for Buddy Calhoun's hit man, the one problem being that there was nothing to tie him to the case.

That is, not till Eddie showed her Catherine Mathison's pictures. Her breath caught when she saw them; her heart did a spooky little jig. This was no fantasy game. This dude was tailing them, and he was nobody to mess with. Not only that, he had a pal, and they still didn't know who either of them was.

When she handed over the sketch, Eddie spoke nonchalantly. "Who we got here, Ms. Wallis?"

"I don't know."

"Whatcha mean ya don't know?"

"He goes by Stan. That's the best I can do for now."

"Ms. Wallis." Eddie was drawling softly, something he didn't often do. "Ya done good. Ya done real good. Now start talkin'."

"Oh, man. Where to start? Eddie, we got a tiger by the tail."

He looked grim as an executioner, but he kept his mouth shut; only nodded for her to get started.

"Okay, does the name Nora Dwyer mean anything to you?"

"Hell, yeah. Celebrated murder-for-hire case—long time ago. Real long time ago. Across the lake, if I remember right. Nora and her boyfriend hired somebody to kill her husband and dump him in the river."

"Almost right," Talba said. "It was *attempted* murder-for-hire. The husband got fished out before he was dead, full of whiskey and pills. So they pumped his stomach and he told some crazy story about two men who came to his house while his wife was out of town, tied him up, and force-fed him a bunch of pills. Guess he took care of the whiskey himself. Anyway, they squeezed Nora and she cracked. Said she had a boyfriend—car salesman named Carl Frobisher."

Eddie snorted. "Hmmph. No accounting for taste."

"You got that right. I mean, why bother?"

"If you were a man, I'd probably have an answer for ya."

"Well, anyhow, she strikes some kind of deal with the DA, says the boyfriend hired a hit man to do the job, and Carl ends up taking the fall. He admits to hiring a hit man, all right—guy he met in a bar named Stan."

"Oh crap, excuse my French. I think I see where this is going. I guess there's no point asking Stan's last name."

"You got it—no point in hell. Carl said he knew the guy only as Stan—gave him a thousand dollars up front and never saw him again, never did pay him the rest of his money."

"Which was? I'm just curious."

"A big two thousand dollars—three thousand to kill a husband."

"It's about what I figured." He picked up the police sketch. "So this is Stan?"

"Yeah. They never found him. Or his friend."

"Friend?"

"There were two of them, remember? Just like in Babalu's case. Almost the same kind of deal, too. Forced overdose."

"Well, that's all well and good, Ms. Wallis. All well and good. Stan's the man who followed me, and he's a hit man you can get for a pack of cigarettes. Real good news. So, what's the trick here? How'd you find him?"

"Easy. I figured if you were a prosecutor, you'd come across more lowlifes than the average guy. In fact, you'd be uniquely positioned to find yourself a hit man. All you'd have to do would be to take a walk down memory lane."

Eddie snapped to attention, eyebags jiggling. "Buddy Calhoun prosecuted Carl Frobisher? That what you're saying?"

Talba nodded, feeling slightly smug in spite of herself. "Yep. But I had to find out the old-fashioned way. No computers involved." She paused. "And there's a lot more."

Eddie pounded his hand on his chest. "I don't know if I can handle it."

"You know how New Orleans tends to forgive and forget. Remember that other woman tried to kill her husband a few years ago? That was murder-for-hire too. She's still loose, still has the same old friends, still gets her picture in the paper. So I decided to check out Mrs. Nora Dwyer. Now, Carl Frobisher wasn't much, but the husband seemed like a pretty respectable guy. Lawyer here in town—Gerard Dwyer. I figured Nora probably had some bucks, knew a few people; she might pick up the pieces and move on."

Eddie raised an eyebrow.

"I was right. I found her photograph on the society page no less than four times in recent years, once in a gorgeous evening dress at some gala, posing with John Earl Macquet in a tux. Incidentally, I saw John Earl at Clayton's funeral—along with Buddy Calhoun."

"Phew." Eddie leaned back against the seat of the car. "Mmm. Mmm. Mmm."

It was a lot to digest, and Talba knew it. She just let him be quiet for awhile, while he took it in.

She'd dropped a name to reckon with. John Earl Macquet was one of the biggest businessmen in New Orleans—a town not noted for big business. Macquet was in shipping; and shipping was one of the oldest, largest, most respected businesses in the city. He'd been at Clayton's funeral. He was a big supporter of Buddy Calhoun.

None of which was the point. That was what Eddie was struggling with. She knew he knew Macquet's story, but he'd sort of half-forgotten it. The businessman had recently lost his wife. Finally, Eddie said, "Now, how'd John Earl's wife die? Refresh my recollection, would ya?"

"The maid found her dead one morning when John Earl was out of town. Pills and alcohol. 'Course everybody knew she was pretty much of a drunk."

"Oh, yeah. It's coming back to me."

"Well, I'm sorry to say there's more. I figured since I'd done such a good job on Nora, why stop now? So I went ahead and did a little more research on John Earl. And guess what?"

"I give up. I don't know." Eddie let go of the wheel and flung his hands into the air. "You tell me. He's got a brother named Stan?"

"Not that I know of. But Mrs. Macquet's untimely demise is not the only tragedy in his life."

"Oh, Christ."

"His company's CFO was shot and killed a few years back—random mugging kind of thing."

"Sort of like the way Donny Troxell died."

"Umm-hmm. Company was in a little trouble at the time. It recovered soon after that. Could have been some crooked accounting, something the guy wouldn't go along with."

"Oh, hell. Could have been anything. Ms. Wallis, this is way too many coincidences."

"Yeah, Eddie. It's real ugly. Do I need to tell you John

Earl's a big Buddy Calhoun supporter?" She knew she should have been scared to death, but actually, she was excited. This was the real deal; she had one hell of a big fish on the line. "I figure what happened, Stan didn't just happen to be in that bar where Carl met him. Somebody got drunk and told Nora about him. She knew where Carl drank and sent Stan there. Carl arranged the hit, thinking he was going to get Nora and all Nora's money as a reward—but that was never in the cards."

Eddie sat quietly. Talba knew from experience that he was thinking. Finally, he said, "Where are you tonight? Anybody staying with Miz Clara?"

"I checked into the Hilton."

"The Hilton! Pretty rich for the firm's blood."

"Yeah, but convenient, and really, really anonymous. The thing's huge, and there's always some convention going on— you can get lost in the crowd if you have to. I feel pretty safe there, but to answer your other question, I'm a little worried about Mama."

"Mmph. Maybe Darryl could babysit."

Hell, no, Talba thought. *That wouldn't work at all.* Miz Clara would probably make a pass at him, she was so crazy about him.

Eddie said, "We need something to tie this stuff together."

"Well, I did get that job tomorrow—at Buddy Calhoun's office. Maybe I'll come up with something."

Eddie grunted. "Worth a try. Don't forget to call in sick. And do something about Miz Clara, will ya?"

She wondered what he was planning to do about Angie and Audrey. He could probably protect Audrey himself, but Talba could just picture Angie's reaction to his well-meant advice.

B ack at the hotel, she called her sister-in-law, Michelle, planning to humble herself.

"How's my little Sophia?" she began.

Michelle sounded slightly frantic. "She's kind of a handful.

Neither one of us has gotten a night's sleep since she was born."

Thank you, God, if you exist, Talba thought. She wouldn't even have to beg. "Hey, I've got a great idea—you know, Mama would give anything to help y'all out. Why don't you just ask her to come over for a few days?"

"We couldn't do that. It's way too big an imposition."

"It would be the thrill of her life, swear to God. Listen, you'd be doing me a big favor—I have to be away for a few days, and I worry about her all alone over there." Miz Clara was about as helpless as a boa constrictor, as Michelle perfectly well knew.

"Oh? Where are you going?"

"I've already gone, actually. I'm in Mississippi on a case. I just got to thinking about her there all alone. I was actually calling to ask if y'all could look in on her, but I know she'd love to come stay with you, and since the baby's keeping you up . . ." She let it hang there, hoping Miz Clara would forgive her for volunteering her sleeping hours, but there was no help for it. Besides, it *would* be the thrill of her life; she doted on that child.

By the time they hung up, Michelle had already dispatched Corey to go plead with his mama to come help out. Talba couldn't have been happier—Miz Clara'd be safe in her brother's gated community.

Darryl presented another set of problems.

He answered on the first ring. "Talba! Where have you been? I've been calling and calling."

"Well, things got a little complicated with the Patterson case and I had to check into a hotel for a few days."

"What are you talking about? You're not telling me you're in danger?" He sounded outraged, as if it were somehow rude of her.

"I think I'm being watched, that's all. I just wanted to let you know I'm okay."

"Well, thanks."

"And also to tell you . . . I mean, I guess there's a chance they might go after you."

"*What?*"

"Is there any place you could go for a few days?"

"Are you kidding? I'm not going to be driven out of my home."

She almost mouthed the words with him. "Darryl, I'm serious. You can't mess with these people. Would you at least . . . you know . . . be vigilant?"

"I'm always vigilant." *Defensive*, she thought. *Like some gander or drake or billy goat.* All males were the same, as far as she could tell.

"Well, be extra vigilant." That was all she could do, and she knew it. The man wasn't going to go out and buy a gun.

She barely slept, worrying about him and Miz Clara; and Audrey and Angie. Even worrying about Eddie. Man wasn't half as tough as he thought.

Hoping Miz Clara hadn't discovered she was missing a wig, Talba got up the next morning and put it on, along with the rest of the outfit she'd brought for temping. The effect was highly satisfying. A perfect Claudia Snipes.

If she could just remember to quote the Bible now and then, she could fool her own mama.

She called in sick again and then consulted her notes. She was to report to one Margaret Neuschneider, to work the firm's computer help desk (the regular person being on vacation, and Philip, the temp Currie'd sent to replace her, being a noted non–people person). If someone had a problem, it was Talba's job to fix it—for instance, ran into a snag with a Power Point presentation, or hit the wall trying to create a database. She could shine at that, and the beauty of it was, there were long periods when no one had a problem, leaving her more or less to herself. The downside was, the make-work in between consisted mostly of helping the secretaries input data. Boring almost beyond comprehension, but who cared? Like every other employee, she lived for the lunch hour—though for a slightly different reason.

She managed to sneak around on her bathroom breaks enough to figure out where Calhoun's office was. The good news was, he wasn't in today. The bad was, there was no way past his assistant, Barbara Jo, who sat in a little ante-room. Talba introduced herself to her; said she was the new temp; talked about the weather. You never knew who might be good to know.

And as Barbara Jo left on her way out to lunch, Talba sang out, "Have a good lunch now. See you later." Barbara Jo made a face. "Actually, I'm going to get a mammogram."

It never hurts to be nice, Talba thought. *Miz Clara would be right proud of her little girl.* She figured it would take at least an hour to get a mammogram.

After a decent interval, she sneaked into Buddy Calhoun's office, intending a thorough search of his private files. She'd done this before, with other people, and always been lucky. There was always the chance she wouldn't be lucky some-time. But mostly, just around the office, people weren't all that careful about their passwords. And Talba was well armed—she had the names of Calhoun's wife and children and dog; his birthday; his wife's birthday; and she could al-ways guess at the year the computer system was installed. If he didn't use the name of some long-dead favorite retriever, she figured she'd get in.

She looked at the pictures on his desk—mostly of his chil-dren, not the wife. And mostly of the daughter, not the sons. Okay, that one first. She typed in "Sarah." And bingo, she was in. Still lucky.

Her fingers started flying. There were letters here and memos—maybe something good. She put a disk in and started making copies. She wasn't about to read through all this stuff.

Follow the money, she thought, and she looked for financial records. Ah—a file called Campaign Expenses. This one she did glance over, and there was one very interesting entry— "Stan Underwood, $10,000."

"For services," the spreadsheet said. *Every campaign needs services*, she thought, and she copied the file immediately.

She reached in her pocket for another disk—one copy for herself and one for Eddie, she thought—and was about to insert the disk when the door opened. She found herself face to face with Hubert Calhoun, AKA Buddy. The candidate himself. Livid.

Talba struggled to maintain her cool. "Oh, you scared me," she said, and closed the file. "Almost finished."

"What the hell do you think you're doing?"

She looked him right in the eye, making her own eyes wide with amazement. "Excuse me?" She paused a moment. "I'm a temp; checking your e-mail program."

He dropped his briefcase, strode toward her, and grabbed her arm, startling her so badly she dropped the second disk. Involuntarily, she screamed, just a loud piercing shriek, and then, thinking about it, a much louder "Help!" Maybe she could put him on the defensive.

It partially worked. He let go of her arm, but he was still between her and the desk, and she was ready to leave, thank you. No point sticking around for more; she wasn't going to get it.

People were starting to crowd in the door, coming to her aid.

Instead of going forward—what she really wanted to do—she shrank back against the wall, covering the lower half of her face with her hands. "He groped me. He came up behind me and . . ."

Calhoun just stood there with his mouth open.

Talba spoke in a small piteous voice. "Could someone call the police? Please?"

Calhoun said, "I didn't . . . I found this woman . . ."

"I've been at a battered women's shelter. I prayed to the Lord to give me a good job. . . . I thought I was so lucky. . . ." She stared at the two people now in the room with her and Calhoun—both women, one black, one white, and neither, thank God, Margaret Neuschneider, who was blessedly at lunch. She didn't have to fake panic; she felt it.

"Omigod, I'm so scared!" Every word of *that* was true. "Oh, Lord, when am I gon' be delivered?"

For a moment, she thought she'd gone too far, but the white woman fingered a little gold cross she wore at her neck. The black woman, sixtyish and stout, wearing a business suit and glasses, opened her arms, giving Calhoun a nervous little glance over her shoulder. She said, "You're all right, baby. Come on now, you're all right."

Talba hugged her, closing her eyes, as if she *had* been delivered.

Calhoun was starting to recover. He said, "Young lady, would you mind answering one question? Just what were you doing in my office?"

Talba, released from the older woman's hug, stepped back once more, putting a hand on her breast. "He's scaring me. He's scaring me again. Call the police! Please—won't somebody call the police?"

Calhoun started backing down. "I don't really see any need . . ."

"I'm sorry." Talba passed a worried hand over her face. "See, I'm on medication. At the shelter we . . . One of the things they teach us . . . is call the police first and let them ask the questions . . . I'm just so . . . I really need to . . . Look how I'm shaking." Talba raised a hand for all to see. "I forgot my medication. . . . It's for the panic." She turned fearfully again to the older woman. "Can you . . . I'm afraid to go near him . . . Can you . . . ?" She cut her eyes at Calhoun long enough to see that his anger was giving way to something else—fear, she hoped. Who knew? Maybe she'd hit a nerve; maybe he had a reputation for this sort of thing.

"All right, darlin'. I got you." The woman inserted her body between Talba and Calhoun, put an arm around her shoulder, and led her past Calhoun, her face half-turned in his direction, giving him a kind of half-dirty look. Talba let the woman lead her back to her workstation, where she picked up her purse. She sat for a moment, rubbing her face, shaking her head, trying to regain her composure. "I think if I just . . . Would you mind showing me the bathroom?"

Talba prayed for two things: that the woman wouldn't come with her; and that Margaret Neuschneider wouldn't come back from lunch. She sure didn't want to have to come up with an explanation for being in Calhoun's office. There was nothing on the disk she'd dropped. If she could just get out of here without getting searched, she was home free.

Chapter Twenty-seven

"What's your name, child?"

"Claudia Snipes. What's yours?"

"Suzeraine Thompson—you want me to call you a doctor or something?"

Talba made a show of indecision. "No. No, I think I'll be fine if I can just wash my face and take my pill. And get back to the shelter." She jerked her head toward Calhoun's office, worried that he might try to call security. *If he does,* she thought, *I can keep begging them to call the police. If worse comes to worst, I can call them myself. I just can't get searched, is all.* She said, "I have to get away from him. I have to go home and pray; and talk to my counselor. And see if I can get the good Lord to help me come to terms with this."

She stood a little shakily, and caught the desk for support. "But I don't really feel so good. Where'd you say the bathroom is?"

"Come on. I'll show you."

A kind-hearted woman, dammit. But she forced a weak

little smile. "Thanks, Suzeraine. I really appreciate it."

Surely the mile they made you walk to Death Row couldn't be as long as the one to the ladies' rest room on Calhoun's floor; when she saw it in view, she mumbled, " 'Scuse me," and started running.

She ran into a stall, locked it, and started coughing and gagging violently, making a big show of throwing up. She heard Suzeraine come in behind her. "You okay in there, baby? Anything I can do to help?"

Deftly, Talba transferred the disks from her pockets to her pantyhose, one in front and two in the back. For good measure, she hid her PI license in her bra.

She came out wiping her face with a piece of toilet paper, went straight to a basin, and rinsed her mouth like anyone who'd just thrown up. Then she took her time splashing her face and drying it.

Suzeraine smiled at her. "Better?"

She did her weak-smile thing again. "A little bit."

They walked out together and when they came to the elevators, Talba pressed the button, and turned to her benefactress. "God bless you, sister," she said, and gave Suzeraine a hug.

The woman looked puzzled. "Where you going?"

"Home. I'm real sorry this job didn't work out. I sure did need it."

"Well, I'm sorry too, darlin'. You take care of yourself."

The elevator doors opened to reveal Margaret Neuschneider. "Hi, Claudia. Going to lunch?"

Talba stepped in. "No, ma'am. I'm going home and I'm never coming back to this place ever again for any reason."

Only when the doors closed did she breathe a sigh of relief. But now came the hard part. In a way, she'd made it easier for Calhoun—removed herself from the spotlight; she wondered if she should have made one of those nice ladies take her back to CompuTemps.

She pressed 3, took off her jacket, removed her wig, and wrapped it in her jacket. Her heavy, sexy extensions fell to the middle of her back. It was taking a chance; she might fool somebody looking for a short-haired woman, but if she were caught, she'd have a hell of a time explaining why she'd come to work in disguise.

No one was waiting for her on three. So far so good. She stepped into the stairwell and clattered down. One floor; silence. Two floors. More silence—and then a second clattering. Someone was coming up from the first floor.

She turned around and started climbing again. From behind, she'd look nothing like the woman Calhoun would have described to security; yet exactly like the woman Stan probably had a picture of. Speaking of Stan, what if it were he? She risked taking a peek.

No. It was a uniformed guard.

She fumbled for her cell phone, which she had programmed to speed-dial 911 if she pressed 1 and Eddie if she pressed 2. The man elbowed past her without so much as an "excuse me," clearly in a hurry.

Talba turned the other way and started running, going down again. She heard a confused noise behind her. And the next thing she knew, a rhino was after her.

At any rate, she ran as if it were. It was probably only the one guard, but there might be reinforcements on the first floor. The basement too? Maybe not, but she was dead if they'd thought of it. They could probably murder her there in perfect privacy. Uh-uh, she'd take her chances with a crowd.

There was another guard waiting when she stepped out of the stairs, and also two women waiting for the elevator. The guard said, "Claudia Snipes?"

She shrank back, but spoke up big. "Don't you come near me. See this phone?" She held it up. "I'm gon' call the police right now, you come anywhere near me. Ma'am? Ma'am? Help me. Could y'all help me, please? Some man tried to attack me up there and they're tryin' to cover it up—could one of y'all find me a po-liceman, please?"

The guard was an old white guy, looked to be in his late sixties. He took a step backward, obviously cowed.

Talba bolted.

About that time the other guard, a young black guy, really

buff, burst out of the stairwell. "What's going on?"

That was the last thing Talba heard of that conversation. She was outside now, streaking down Gravier Street, with people all around. Surely no one would bother her here, out in the beautiful sunshine.

But she heard someone pounding after her.

The question was this: were they going to try to kidnap her, work her over, find out what she knew, or turn her over to the police?

It occurred to her that now, away from the building, they could make her disappear and those nice ladies who'd taken care of her would be none the wiser.

She turned her head ever so slightly. The brother was chasing her, and he was waving something. "Hey, miss! Ya dropped ya wig."

The damn thing had fallen out of her jacket. He was waving it around in front of the whole parish.

Well, hell. There were plenty of people around, she was out of breath, and this guy was in such fantastic shape he was probably going to catch her no matter what she did.

She stopped but kept her distance, letting anyone watching see by her body language that she didn't trust him. "You were chasing me before I dropped it," she said.

"S'posed to detain you. You steal somethin'?"

"That son of a bitch felt me up; scared me half to death."

"Who?"

"Calhoun. Buddy Calhoun, the great white hope for black people. Grabbed my titties like it was okay. He probably *is* gon' accuse me of somethin', stop the story from gettin' out. Shit!" She'd momentarily forgotten the church-lady routine. "You know where I'm livin'? In a shelter for battered women—at home, my husband gets drunk every night and pounds on me. I need to get out of that mess. I need a job so bad—and *this* is what the Lord sends me! I get felt up, scared to death, and now I'm gettin' chased."

"Hold on, now. Hold on. Ain't nobody gon' chase you no more. You seem like a nice lady—I just want to return ya property's all. I'm 'on leave ya alone now. Don't you worry.

Nobody's gon' hurt ya." He held out the wig very gingerly, making it an olive branch. Standing as far away as she could, and still touch it, she reached out and grabbed it by a loose curl. He dropped it instantly. "See?" He gave her a beautiful smile. "That didn't hurt a bit. Good luck to ya now."

He turned and walked briskly away.

Breathing a sigh of relief, she thought, *Well, they can't pay them all off. It's just possible that every employee of every building in New Orleans isn't part of Calhoun's crime empire.*

But she only half believed it. She watched the guard out of sight, went into a building full of people, pulled out her cell phone, and called a taxi.

While she waited, she called L. J. Currie. "Hey, L. J., what kind of job was that? Some bastard in that office attacked me."

"I just hung up with Miss Neuschneider. She said there was a 'misunderstanding.' "

"Yeah, well, that's one thing you could call it. Tell her you'll be sending only men over there in future." She was starting to believe the story herself. "But there is something you should know. I didn't mention I was a Baroness gone slumming."

"No?"

"In case anyone asks, I'm staying at a battered women's shelter. An experience like that's real hard on somebody like me. They'll be lucky if I don't sue."

A throaty chuckle debouched from the phone. "You are some piece of work, Your Grace—you know that?"

"My mama tells me every day of my life. Gotta go, L. J.— here's my cab."

"Don't forget my six hundred dollars," he said. "Payable by Monday."

Talba was actually so close both to her office *and* the Hilton, the cab was superfluous. She was still being super-cautious. She got in and tried to think what to do next. She didn't even want to call Eddie from the cab—drivers could be found and paid off.

Finally, she decided it was okay to go to the office as long as she didn't look like herself. "The casino," she told the driver. "Canal Street entrance."

Inside, it was dark and confusing. She walked through to the Poydras Street side and crossed to the Hilton, where she went to her room and donned the overalls and baseball cap, her copious hair tucked underneath, a pair of shades on her face. She looked in the mirror and frowned. These were no clothes for a baroness.

But they gave her all the confidence in the world. She walked out of the Hilton, barely looking around her, she was so sure no one would make her.

Indeed, when she got to the office, Eileen Fisher asked if she could help her.

Talba took off the shades. "Got any morphine?"

"Talba! Is this your day off or something?"

"Casual Thursday. Eddie here?"

"Oh, yes. He's been swearing all morning—forced to do employment checks, since you weren't here."

She found him hunched over the computer, his fingers gnarled at the keyboard, tension in every cell of his body.

"Miss me?" she said, and hurled her cap onto his extra chair. Her extensions tumbled around her shoulders.

"Ya just love a dramatic entrance, don't ya, Ms. Wallis?" He looked at her over reading glasses she'd never seen him wear. Must be his computer drag.

She removed the cap and sat down. "You'd be proud of me, Eddie. I spent the morning telling lies. Beautiful lies. Do I look like a battered woman to you?"

She ran the story down for him.

"That's it, Ms. Wallis. Now ya catchin' on. Tell me somethin'—any purpose to all this? Ya find anything?"

"Actually, yes." She'd carefully told the story in such a way as to leave a dramatic ending. "Stan's last name, I hope. Underwood ring a bell with you?"

He shook his head.

"The campaign paid a Stanley Underwood $10,000 for services."

"What services?"

"My question exactly."

"Ya backgrounded him yet?"

"I'll do it now."

She grabbed her hat and went to her own office. Eddie hated working two at a computer.

She was back in a few minutes. "Interesting guy."

"What do you mean by that?"

"For openers, he owns a 2001 Lincoln Continental."

"Ya got my attention."

"He's forty-two." She picked up one of the pictures Catherine Mathison had shot. "Brown and brown, six feet, a hundred eighty. What do you think—about right?"

Eddie grunted.

"Lives in Chalmette with three other people—Frank, Margaret, and Rufus Underwood."

"What the hell kind of setup is that? Thug Family Robinson?"

Talba ignored him. "Look, we've got his plate number. All we really have to do is identify the guy with that plate—who we know is Stan Underwood—as the guy who's been tailing us. Because he's the same guy in the police sketch."

"You know police sketches aren't considered very good."

Talba named her police connection. "Langdon's sharp, Eddie. She's not going to discount it."

He nodded. "Yeah, it's our best bet. What's your plan?"

"What's my plan? You're asking *me*?

"I'm axin' ya."

She shrugged, improvising quickly. "Surveil his house, I guess. Much as I hate the idea."

" 'S a lot of effort," Eddie said. "Heck of a lot of effort." He closed his eyes for a moment, and the effect was that of locking a pair of steamer trunks. Finally, he said, "Why don't we just flush him out? We pull a sting, see, like we did to get the pictures."

She could see him getting into it.

"We bring in a third party—could be Catherine again, could be anybody. You call me on the office phone, say ya got something in Buddy Calhoun's office that proves he had Clayton killed, and I gotta meet you at such and such a place. I go there, ya hand me the disk, and when Stan shows up to follow me and get the damn thing back—which he will—Catherine photographs his license plate. Boom! We got him."

"Unless he doesn't show up in the Lincoln—remember, he was driving a gold-colored Ford in Mississippi. Hey, wait a minute! Wonder whose car the Le Sabre was?" Without even saying good-bye, she left, went back to her office, and ran Frank, Margaret, and Rufus Underwood through a motor vehicle database. For once, Eddie followed her.

She looked up when she had it. "Sure enough—Frank and Margaret are proud owners of a Buick Le Sabre."

"If he shows in that one, we've still got him."

"Listen, Eddie, a lot of stuff could go wrong. He could send someone else or steal a car like before. But it sure beats the alternative. You know what Chalmette's like—blue-collar white. I try to work surveillance there, I'm dead meat. Sure, let's try the sting. When do you want to make the switch?"

He looked at his watch. "Right away. Hell. Logic says you'd have called the minute you got chased out of that office. The more time goes by, the more it looks like a setup." He yelled out to the anteroom, "Eileen, can you get Catherine Mathison on the phone?"

They set up what details they needed, then Talba left the building by the back door, hurried back to the Hilton, changed back to her navy skirt and white blouse, and made a phone call. "Hey, Eddie, I got something."

"Ya mean a virus or somethin'? Thought ya had the curse."

"Eddie, listen to me. I *got* something—on the Patterson case."

"What the hell ya talkin' about, Ms. Wallis? Ya been off for two days."

"I was doing some stuff on my own."

He sighed showily. "Start talkin', Ms. Wallis."

"I've got evidence that connects Clayton's killing to—you ready for this?—Buddy Calhoun."

There was a long pause, during which Eddie breathed like he had asthma. "Ms. Wallis, ya losin' me."

"Swear to God, Eddie. I've got a disk."

"A disk."

"You know—a computer disk. A floppy."

"Umm-hmm. And what's on that disk?"

"Eddie, I don't have time for that now. I'm not at home—I'm in a safe house. But they know I've got it."

"How in the hell would they know a thing like that?"

"They caught me. I had to lie my way out of it. But Calhoun himself was the one who caught me. He knows damn well what I've got."

"Now ya scarin' me."

"Tell me about it. The quicker I get this to the police the better. I'm on my way now."

"Are you crazy? Ya can't do that, Ms. Wallis. You forget who ya workin' for? Ya can't go takin' in some huge piece of evidence when I don't even know what it is. Ya want to make me look like an idiot?"

"Eddie, trust me—this thing is a hot potato."

"Miz Wallis, I make the decisions in this firm. Ya forget that?"

She made a show of sighing. "All right. I'm on my way over."

"Not to the office you aren't."

"Why not?"

"You know why. They followed us before. They might be watching the building."

"Oh, come on. Don't you think you're being a little paranoid?"

"That's how ya stay alive, young lady. That's how ya stay alive."

"Okay, Wise Man of the Mountain. Where do you want me to meet you?"

"How about the library? I can go in and use one of the computers there."

"What do you mean, 'I?' "

"I mean, you'll bring it to me, get back to ya safe house, I'll go in and look at it, and decide where to go from there."

Chapter Twenty-eight

It was a good sound plan, meant to lull Stan into a cozy feeling of false security—make him think he had plenty of time to scope Eddie's car out, then wait to head him off when he came back out of the library. Only Eddie wasn't going in. He was just going to take the disk from Talba and drive like a maniac to the Third District police station, where Talba's friend Langdon worked.

Talba would round the block, lose any tail she had, and do the same.

They'd be in city traffic the whole way. Unless Stan was crazy enough to start shooting in front of half the population of New Orleans, they'd make it okay. Catherine Mathison would shoot Polaroids of Stan, his car, and his plates, and meet them at the station. If Stan used the Lincoln, they'd have the whole package, ready to deliver. If he didn't, they'd have to stage a phone call in which Eddie told Talba how badly she'd screwed up, how much of nothing was on that disk, and what an idiot she was. Then they'd have to go to plan B—surveillance in Chalmette.

Eddie got there first and parked. Talba drove by, handed the disk in the window, and that should have been that, except that a large white man—Talba couldn't tell if it was Stan or not—broke Eddie's right front window with something heavy, flipped the lock, and got in the car before Eddie could get out of the parking spot.

Talba caught the action out of the corner of her eye. At the same time, a form the size of a bear appeared at her own right front window, but their timing was off, Stan's and his pal's. She saw what was happening to Eddie and hit the accelerator too fast for the bear to knock out her window.

Eddie was on his own and Talba might as well have been. She had no backup except Catherine, who wasn't armed or particularly well equipped to deal with any of this. However, she did have a cell phone and Talba hoped to God she was on it right now, reporting Eddie's position and plate number, as well as Talba's own.

The thing to do was to go immediately to the Third District, where she'd be safe. She knew that. But by the time the police got to Eddie, he could be dead—and she had an advantage. They'd made a mistake by hijacking his car. A very big mistake. It had the GPS in it. She might lose it in traffic, but all she had to do was turn on her computer, and she could track it exactly, could phone in its position to Langdon, her cop friend.

Technically, she didn't need to follow, and in fact, she didn't have a clue what she could do for Eddie if she got there first, but there was no question of deserting him.

For a few minutes, she just drove, paying little attention to where she was, just making sure she got away from the scene and didn't have a tail. Her phone rang: "Talba, Catherine. I called your buddy Langdon, but she wasn't in, so I talked to someone else." Her voice sounded shaky. "You all right?"

"Fine. Which way did they go?"

"Out Loyola. Towards the aiport."

"They still have Eddie?"

"Yeah. Oh, God, I feel so helpless. I couldn't even get the pictures."

"Well, don't worry about that. Listen, Catherine, Eddie's car has a tracking device."

"A what?"

"I'll explain later." *If there is a later.* "What I'm saying is, I can track his car. I can tell where they're taking him. And I'm following."

"Talba, don't. The police'll take care of it."

"I'm going. Can we stay in phone contact?"

"Listen, Talba. Do you have a gun?"

"No."

"Well, I do. Pick me up."

So much for Catherine not being armed. Talba swallowed hard and thought about crossing a bridge she thought she never would again. Once before, she'd fired a gun—twice, actually; and both times had been disastrous.

She said, "I can't, Catherine. Eddie told me about you. You've got kids." Catherine had kids and a husband, and grandchildren as well, but it was the word *kids* that always struck a nerve.

Catherine didn't answer, evidently thinking it over.

Talba shut her eyes and made herself speak, feeling she had no choice. "Let me have the gun."

"Okay." The answer came fast—no way did Catherine Mathison want to get in a gunfight. "Where are you?"

"I'm at LaSalle and Poydras—right by the Superdome. You?"

"Three minutes away. You want me to come to you?"

"Please." That gave Talba time to boot up her computer and check out Eddie's position. First, though, she put in her own emergency call to Langdon. Then she got out her trusty Toshiba; she went nowhere without it. Stan and Eddie had covered a lot of ground already. They were already on the Interstate, going toward New Orleans East. They could be headed anywhere.

There were woods and swampland there, right in the city itself. She had to get on this—and fast. Her phone rang, making her jump.

"Baroness? What's going on?"

"Skip. Thank God. Listen, this is complicated. But the short version is, Eddie's life is in danger. Someone just kidnapped him and they're headed towards New Orleans East. They're in his car, which has a GPS in it—"

"LoJack?"

"What?"

"We can track LoJack. Is that what it is?"

"Uh . . . no." She hadn't gotten LoJack; she had no interest at all in a police-controlled system. The appeal of the GPS was that it was hands-on. "I have to track this one myself. I've got him on my computer—and I'm on my way. Tell me a few hundred officers are too."

"Talba, listen. Please stay where you are. Pull off the road and wait for an officer."

Like hell she would. But this was no time to mention it.

"He's at . . . almost at Esplanade. His car is a 1999 white Cadillac." She gave them the plate number.

"Okay. And where are you?"

"I'm at LaSalle and Poydras."

"Stay there, would you? An officer will come and monitor the GPS."

"No, I'm going to keep going. Here's my cell number."

"Talba, don't be a fool."

"Look, I'm hanging up—just give my cell number to the first officer who answers the call—I'll keep him or her up to date."

"Wait! Not all our officers have cell phones."

"Well, he can radio you and you can call me."

"That's ridiculous, Talba. I want you to stay put."

"Hell, Skip, even Miz Clara doesn't get to boss me anymore."

Langdon's gasp was the last thing she heard before she hung up. She was working on adrenaline and unable to stop. Adrenaline and anxiety. Damned if she was going to be passive when Eddie was in this kind of a fix—he wouldn't if it were she.

But she also knew her plan was better. It would save time, and it was simpler. The thing Langdon objected to was that

Talba wasn't a police officer, and the hell with that. Cop rules weren't her rules.

Catherine pulled up as Talba was checking out her tools and handed over the gun. Talba did two more things before starting her car again. She put her Tee-ball bat on the seat beside her, along with the gun; and she put Langdon on speed-dial. Then she took Loyola to I-10 and got on it, one eye on the computer on the seat beside her. Eddie's car was almost at "the high rise," the overpass above the Industrial Canal. Still heading east. She couldn't shake the notion that they were taking him into all that swamp. They were going to kill him, there was no other reason for going there. She should have heard sirens. Why the hell didn't she? Where were the cops?

She looked in the mirror, impatient, and that was when she saw the Buick bearing down on her, not even making a show of hiding—the same white Le Sabre that tailed her before. How the hell had they picked her up?

Maybe by accident. Maybe Stan was following his buddy and happened to run into Talba, also following his buddy. And now he was following her. Killing two birds, as it were, with one stone.

Talba reached for the cell phone, but the other car started ramming her. She needed both hands to drive. The man had no respect for his own car, let alone hers.

She assessed her situation. They had to know she'd called the police. Everybody had cell phones. But what they wouldn't know was that she'd told them exactly where Stan was headed. Because they couldn't know about the GPS.

She really, really had to keep them from finding out. And, incidentally, it would be good to keep breathing.

The car rammed her again. And again. It was getting damned bumpy. He was trying to force her onto the shoulder. Once she stopped, Stan could just shoot her and be on his way. She wished to hell she'd told Skip his name.

Well, they didn't know about the gun either. To her chagrin, she happened to know how to shoot a gun. Should she try to shoot out his tires or something?

Negative. Surprise was all she had going for her, on any front whatsoever. She'd just pull over and when he came over to get her, blast him in the face with the gun.

Except that she knew she wouldn't.

Not even to save her life could she do that. The better plan was to hit the ground running. She had now crossed the high-rise herself, and was somewhere near Jazzland. There was plenty of open land. She could draw fire, get him away from the GPS.

It was foolhardy. She knew that. But she was a sitting duck in the car. She stuck the gun in her waistband, pulled over, grabbed her Tee-ball bat, opened the door, and started running, wondering if the guy was going to start shooting at her. Out here, she could shoot him. Just not in the face, at close range. Only out here, she'd probably miss.

He squealed to a stop and a millisecond later was clomping toward her. It seemed to her there hadn't even been time for him to open his door.

Well, hell. She didn't want to get too far off the road. Maybe here, a motorist would see them squaring off and call the cops. It would be an embarrassing place to commit murder, and the least she could do was embarrass him.

Also, she would have the element of surprise once more if she went on the offensive. She'd read something once about self-defense against rape. Prison interviews with rapists had revealed certain very interesting things, the main one being that they didn't pick blondes or prostitutes or cute chicks under thirty—they picked easy targets. For instance, they picked women with ponytails because they could grab them by the hair. They might pick a woman with her keys in her hand—keys meant nothing to them—but they'd avoid one with an umbrella she could use to keep them at bay.

Listen, Talba thought, *if an umbrella can stop a rapist, a Tee-ball bat can stop this bozo.*

She slowed to a crawl, pretending to be tired. When he was almost upon her, she turned, winding up the bat and shouting, "Hyaaaahhhhhh!" like some kid playing at kung fu.

She saw his eyes before the bat connected. Startled. Not

exactly a deer in the headlights—more like a dog when a cat arches its back. And the principle was exactly the same. She had to look a lot bigger and scarier than she was.

The bat got him in the chest, and he was already raising his arm to take it away from her. Good, he was otherwise occupied, not watching her feet. She kicked him in the balls.

Anyway, she aimed for the balls, and she almost hit the target dead on. If she had, she'd have disabled him. As it was, she did hit groin, but evidently not the most sensitive area. He stumbled but didn't fall. The hand going for the bat faltered, and she momentarily withdrew her weapon, stepped back, then cracked the bat full in his face. Still, he didn't fall. He grabbed again, catching the end of the bat, pulling it away from her. She let go, and this time he fell, the victim of his own momentum—sat down on his backside. Ha! Talk about your kung fu—his force working for her—yes! She felt so powerful she yelled again. "HEEEEEyaaaahhh!" If he hadn't had so much blood in his eyes, he might have had that startled look again.

She used the moment the yell bought her to whip the gun from her waistband and point it at him. "Don't move." She was breathing hard, and the adrenaline was starting to wear off. Her hands were shaking.

He started to get up. She was wondering whether she could pull the trigger when she heard a crunching behind her. A male voice said, "Freeze, police!"

Oh, God, was it the police? Turning around just wasn't an option. She looked at Stan. He was just sitting there, staring past her, not getting up after all.

She did what the man said and froze.

"Put the gun down and turn around."

"I can't put the gun down."

"Put the goddamn gun down or I'll blow your fucking head off."

No arguing with that. She bent down and laid the gun gently between her feet, where she could kick it if Stan tried anything.

"Both of you—put your hands up. You in the pigtails—

turn around. Slowly. You on the ground. Stay there."

Talba turned slowly around, and a sob escaped her. She was looking at a sight more gorgeous than a tropical lagoon—not one, but two white, redneck, fat-bellied, entirely dangerous-looking uniformed policemen were holding guns on her. That was beautiful, just beautiful. The problem was, she could only imagine the bureaucratic nightmare that lay between her and Eddie.

Swallowing, she figured she might as well get the farce started. "I'm a PI," she began.

"I don't give a fuck what you are."

"Yessir, I know. I reported a kidnapping to Officer Skip Langdon at the Third District. Can you check with her, please?"

The two guys glanced at each other, then at Stan.

"By the way, I have every reason to believe that man is still armed."

One of them continued to hold a gun on her while the other one shook Stan down—finding a gun and a knife—and cuffed him.

Was she next? Talba wondered. And indeed they frisked her, but gently. "Listen, my partner's been kidnapped."

The thing about cops at work, they didn't answer you; pretended they'd never heard a word you said. So she just kept talking.

"Eddie Valentino—y'all know Eddie? This guy's partner kidnapped him in his own car, but it has a GPS in it, and I have his location in my car."

According to police code (which she gathered from Officer Rouselle's performance strictly forbade minimal politeness to helpful citizens), they remained expressionless and silent, but she noticed one of them went over to her car and peeked in.

She pressed her advantage. "They're going to kill him. Could you call Detective Langdon, please? Use my phone—I've got her on speed-dial. She'll verify what I told you."

Again, no answer.

"At least radio Eddie's location—see, it's right there on that computer screen. Maybe there's an officer . . ."

One of them was talking on his own cell phone. And finally, he said, "Detective Langdon wants to talk to you."

"Sure, but your pal here's still holding a gun on me."

The other cop holstered his weapon, and Talba couldn't help herself. She gave him a flicker of a smug look, but only a flicker.

"Skip, I'm sorry. Listen, I'll make it up to you."

"Give me Eddie's location." Langdon was as poker-voiced and impersonal as either of the other two.

Okay, she'd have to live with it.

"Still on I-10, still heading east. Past Jazzland a couple of exits." It had only been about seven minutes, but with minimal traffic, you could really move on the Interstate. Talba was panicked.

"Talba, the officers told me what just happened. Do you have any idea how much danger you're in?"

"Skip, I've got to go now."

She heard a big sigh on the other end. "Okay. Give me Officer Charvet."

Talba handed the phone to its owner, who talked a minute and got off with a frown. "Langdon's sending backup to pick up the prisoner. That way one of us can stay with him and the other can go to the scene."

The other cop shrugged. "I'll stay with him."

Charvet looked like he was about to pop, as eager to get there as she was. "Mind if I borrow your computer?" he asked, suddenly tame as a puppy.

In a pig's eye, she thought. She tried out a smile on him— might as well practice her people skills. "No problem. But you have to borrow me too."

"Huh?"

"The computer stays with me. Give me a ride, why don't you?" She figured that was about as likely as a sudden snow flurry, but what the hell—a police car was going to be a lot faster than hers.

The two cops looked at each other, evidently trying to marshal arguments against it. The one who wasn't Charvet shrugged again, unable to think of any. Finally, Charvet said, "Get in."

She ran for her computer, and in a moment they were speeding toward Eddie. "He's almost at Michoud Boulevard now. I sure hope you've got somebody close."

Charvet didn't answer.

Talba tried again. "Is anyone there yet? At the scene, I mean—with Eddie?"

Charvet had evidently taken a vow of silence.

Okay, fine. She didn't need any new friends.

The car on the screen was still moving. There were only two people in it—Eddie and his kidnapper. Surely, the guy wouldn't shoot him in a moving car.

She and Officer Charvet were slowing. Traffic was coming to a near stop. Then a full stop.

They were stuck.

Charvet got on the phone. She heard him say, "Traffic just stopped. What's going on?"

And then it started moving again, slowly at first.

Charvet said, "What are you telling me?" And then, "Shit! Goddammit to hell!"

Fingers of fear closed on Talba's throat. She looked at the screen—Eddie's car was still moving. So it wasn't Eddie— he ought to be fine.

"What is it?" she said, pretty sure she wasn't going to get an answer.

The big cop didn't disappoint her.

Enough of this, she thought. *There's no law they've got to act like apes. It's probably discretionary.*

"Look, I haven't done a damn thing to you today. Matter of fact, I'm doing my level best to help. Matter of further fact, I'm no helpless dip. If Eddie and I are right, that man your partner's got is a professional assassin who's killed at least four people that we know of, and he's gotten away with it. He's in the employ of some extremely important and powerful people in this state—he's like an assassin to the stars. And guess what? I took him out with a Tee-ball bat. Little *moi*."

The guy did a double-take in spite of himself. He said, "My *kid's* got a Tee-ball bat."

"Yep. A kid's toy. I used that and a well-placed kick—if you know what I mean." She hoped she wasn't overdoing it. She didn't exactly feel like Superwoman, but she wasn't lying.

"Stow it, Pigtails. What about the gun?"

"Borrowed."

"Who from?"

"Another PI." Talba avoided giving Mathison's name, unsure whether or not she had a permit for it.

Charvet let it pass, opting instead for his famous cop-statue imitation.

She gave him a couple of minutes, then asked, "What'd you say was happening here?"

"Traffic jam." But the flow was getting back to normal.

"Not that. The 'shit, goddammit to hell' thing."

He pointed to the road up ahead. "They took out a police car."

"What?" Talba leaned so far forward, trying to see, trying to make sense of it, that she almost knocked the computer to the floor. And it was coming into view—a police car, now on the side of the road, having just been pushed there. It must have been shot at—which might mean there were two men with Eddie now, one driving and one shooting. The first one could have stopped to pick the gunman up.

Nervously, she glanced at the computer. The car was still traveling.

Officer Charvet rolled up to the district car. "What happened?"

The driver of this one was a black female. She said, "Shot out my radiator." *I wonder*, Talba thought, *if this one's nice.* But, remembering Sergeant Rouselle, she didn't have much hope.

A white male, also in uniform, was looking under the hood. "Who're you?" the black cop said.

"I'm a PI. Talba Wallis." Talba offered to shake hands. "You know Skip Langdon?"

To her amazement, the woman smiled. "Skip? We go way back. I'm Shaquita Radford."

Officer Charvet was infuriated. "Radford, goddammit, ya comin' or not? Call ya partner."

Talba's hands were sweaty. If they didn't quit arguing and get there soon . . .

Radford yelled, "Hey, John, get your butt over here."

Charvet said, "Get in the back, Pigtails."

Talba was all too uncomfortably aware that the back was a cage. "Why?"

" 'Cause we're picking up two officers, that's why."

"But—"

"Look, ya want to go or not? Officers outrank civilians." He jerked an aggressive thumb over his shoulder. "Move your ass."

What the hell. She was just glad to have a ride. Clutching her computer, she got in the back. The cop named John joined her, and then they were burning up the road, Charvet's siren squealing.

"They're stopping," she said.

She was staring at the screen in terror. If they stopped, they must be ready to kill him. But surely they wouldn't, with cops on the way—had they thought Radford's car a coincidence?

"Where are they?" Charvet asked.

"Just up the road." She swallowed. "They got off at Michoud Boulevard."

Radford said, "Pray, honey. If you know how to pray, do it."

Talba was considering the possibility when she heard another siren . . . actually, it sounded like two more. There were other cars in the area.

Radford said, "Step on it, Charvet!"

And Charvet pointed downward. His foot was on the floor.

They were all silent for the next few minutes. The scream of sirens filled the air; the beating of drums filled Talba's chest. They took the Michoud exit, turned left, went over a bridge, and came to a dead end.

And what they saw there made them laugh, a momentary

release of tension. Ten or twelve district cars were ahead of them; had built a semicircle around the parked Cadillac.

Okay, so they weren't that badly needed. But the fat lady still hadn't sung.

An officer was speaking over a megaphone. "Hands on your head and walk towards me."

Talba turned off the computer and collapsed against the seat. "Whew!"

And Radford said, "Wonder if they got here in time?"

Talba's palms started sweating again.

Chapter Twenty-nine

They pulled up, parked, and piled out like kids at the beach, Talba swiveling her head frantically, trying to make sense of things. Of even one thing.

There was a wall of cars and a throng of cops, guns still drawn. The tension was like another wall.

Talba could see two prisoners now, being frisked and cuffed. But no Eddie.

"Eddie," she called, more or less to the passing breeze. "Eddee!"

Radford shouted also, to the officer in charge, whoever he was. "Hey, her partner was in that car."

Two officers moved forward, opened the doors, and shook their heads. "Well, he's not now."

And then Talba became aware of a soft thudding. The two guys looked at each other and turned toward the trunk. One of them shouted, "Hey, Eddie, you in there?"

Three loud, staccato thunks answered.

"Hang on, now. Hang on. We'll get ya out."

His partner went to get the key from the prisoners. And

then they opened the trunk and helped Eddie out. He was in one piece; he was walking.

But he kind of had a hand over his face. When he removed it, Talba saw he'd been hit—with a gun, probably. The left side of his face was swollen and already purple.

With no hesitation, no shyness at all in spite of her audience, she hollered, "Eddie, you all right? You okay, Eddie?" and started toward him.

He looked up at her and grinned. "Ms. Wallis. See—the cops got here first. Told you that damn GPS was worthless."

E ddie dreaded looking at the paper the next day. And the day after that, and the third day as well. Six months into it was the worst.

A lot of men in his position would have killed for the kind of press he was getting, and so would he, except for one thing: his daughter, Angie.

As the days went by, the headlines escalated:

POLICE RESCUE PI IN BIZARRE KIDNAP ATTEMPT

KIDNAPPERS TIED TO GUBERNATORIAL CANDIDATE

CALHOUN WITHDRAWS FROM RACE

And finally, when the whole story had come out, and the reporters had time to tie all the loose ends together:

HOW A SMALL PI FIRM UNCOVERED A CONSPIRACY OF
MURDER-FOR-HIRE AND BROUGHT DOWN A POLITICAL MA-
CHINE

It should have been the proudest day of Eddie's life; in some ways it was. But the idea of listening to Angie congratulate herself one more time on making him hire Talba Wallis made his teeth itch. The minute he saw that paper, even before he read it, he grabbed Audrey and said, "Let's take a little drive over to the Gulf Coast."

That way, at least his daughter couldn't start in till Monday—and it was a sure route to marital bliss. Audrey always got romantic on the coast.

There were a couple of other bitter pills. They got Stan for the kidnapping and the attempted murder of Nora Dwyer's husband, but so far they'd been unsuccessful in getting him to deliver Calhoun. And why *should* he talk? He had a good chance of beating the Dwyer rap (since Dwyer himself was the only witness) and he'd be looking at several centuries of jail time for the other murders—why cop out? But at least Calhoun's career was ruined. There was some satisfaction in that.

Stan and one other person were charged in the Dwyer case—Stan's brother, Rufus. What a pair of aces these two were. Grown men living at home with their parents, Frank and Margaret, who owned a mom-and-pop grocery; both men helped out in the store. And led double lives as assassins.

They were self-taught, it seemed. The police found a few books on drugs and poisons in their house, and a gun—maybe the gun used to shoot at Eddie and later, Tanitha Richard—but that was it. The brothers had evidently had luck the first time and then hung out their shingle. They might get convicted and serve a few years but Eddie personally thought they should fry, though he recognized that he had more reason than most to think so.

One thing, though. Ms. Wallis got what Eddie figured she'd probably call "closure" on her friend, Babalu Clayton Maya Patterson. Calvin Richard was the key to the whole thing, and at least he finally had the decency to come forward.

H e turned up at the office three days after the first newspaper story and asked for Talba Wallis. A wary Eileen Fisher ushered him in: he was in uniform and intimidating.

Talba was so shocked all she could think of to say was his name: "Calvin Richard."

He said, "I owe you an apology. Can I buy you a cup of coffee?"

"I could use some caffeine." And off they went, not to the nearest coffee joint, but all the way over to the PJ's on Frenchmen Street. Richard seemed to want to get far away.

"I've told Langdon the story," he said. "They reopened the Clayton Patterson case in view of all the new information.

Stan and Rufus did it, and we know they did it, but the best we can hope for is Dwyer. We'll never get 'em on Patterson." He observed a private moment of silence. "I wish to hell we could. For Clayton's sake. I helped ruin her life, and I keep thinking about it. About everything—the whole fucked-up mess that ended in her getting killed. All that crap that happened a hundred years ago. I wish to God I could go back and undo what I did. I wish to God I could."

Talba felt as if she were in Clayton again, at that charade of a funeral. "I've got to tell you something, Calvin. You did not ruin her life. And neither did anybody else. She had a good life, no matter what anyone in your hometown thinks. Just because she didn't marry the captain of the football team and become a housewife . . . She was a good person and she was doing good work."

Richard gave her an ironic smile. "Actually, that wasn't an option. The captain of the football team was black. In fact, he was me. That just wasn't in Clayton Patterson's stars." He looked at the ceiling, as if he might actually be studying Clayton's stars. "Look, this isn't easy. Langdon suggested I tell it to you." When he lowered his face, it had a half-smile on it. "My wife too. Fact, she's been nagging at me since you first called, even though she was the one they shot at. So I'm gon' do it, okay? I know you were Clayton's friend. God knows she needed all the friends she could get."

Talba said, "I'm listening," a little coldly. She hated this "poor Clayton" routine.

"I was in love with her in high school—yeah, yeah, I know Marshannon says she just had a thing for brothers, but it wasn't that way, man. No way. Sure, he thinks she flirted with him—and maybe she halfway did. But Clayton was just a real friendly girl, man. If she flirted with Marshannon, she flirted with every white boy in the school too. Wasn't anybody Clayton didn't flirt with—or so they thought. Hell, the male teachers and the principal both probably thought she had the hots for them—and maybe she did, I don't know. I choose to think she was friendly, and flirting was part of the way she connected. But a lot of us were just too self-absorbed to notice we weren't the only one. Every eighteen-year-old boy thinks he's the only kid in the world. I know I sure did. But I also knew better than to have dreams about the banker's daughter." He gave Talba a meaningful look. "The banker's *white* daughter.

"But one day I just couldn't stand it—I don't know, Clayton and I, we were alone in a classroom, I can't remember why—maybe we both came back for something we forgot. Maybe even on purpose. But I do remember what happened in that room. When she was leaving, I touched her on the arm and said, 'Take care,' and all of a sudden we just started talking—but, you know, not really. Just in that kind of moony way embarrassed kids do when they're attracted to somebody. Next thing you know I kissed her. And then I said I was sorry and she ran away. Then she sent me a note asking me to meet her, and that was when it started."

"Wait a minute. What about Donny Troxell?"

Richard nodded. "I'm gettin' to that. Her parents were real racists—maybe you know about that—and they threatened me; wouldn't let us date. Well, hell, we were kids! We thought we were tragic heroes and everything, but we thrived on tragedy. We cried awhile and then we let it go. And that was when she started going out with Donny. The whole thing was over for a year by then—and nobody in that school knew a thing about it. Nobody. I'd stake my life they didn't."

"Well, Marshannon didn't. Or Ebony Frenette."

"Ebony! Well, yeah, I guess I was going with Ebony about then."

"She remembers you too."

He shook his head, as if in disapproval. "Don't pull that woman thing on me. This isn't the usual teenage shit. What happened with Clayton was a life-altering event—you understand?"

It sure was for Clayton, Talba thought.

"Well, here's the part where I got used as a patsy—or maybe not. I just don't know at this point. To say things got complicated's pretty much of an understatement. See, Donny started cheating on her, and there she was, the sweetheart of the rodeo, humiliated in front of everybody."

Talba thought, *His mama didn't know that. But then, who was going to tell her?*

"Maybe Clayton wanted to make him jealous. All I know is, she came back to me. One night when the family was asleep, she let me in the back door. Only somebody wasn't asleep—and the Pattersons had a shed out back where they kept tools. They have a fishing camp that I guess needs clearing now and then—and you can guess what they used to clear it."

"I've got a bad feeling you're talking about a machete."

Richard nodded briefly and then started talking faster. "So, look, I'll just tell it from my point of view. We were making love, you understand?"

Talba thought, *What's to understand?* She nodded politely.

"And I heard something and I turned my head to look. That is, I started to turn my head—at that point I never even saw it coming, but if I hadn't moved, that thing would've split my head wide open. I mean, I probably would have been killed. But when I moved my head, I uncovered Clayton's face, you understand? I saw the thing coming down, and grabbed the guy's arm, but it was too late. I mean, it probably saved her life, but he still got her. Oh, yeah, he got her. He got all of us that night."

"*Who* got her?"

"Her little brother, Trey. I swear to God I still don't know if he thought I was raping her or if he just had some crazy idea of doing what his racist daddy thought was the right thing. God, all hell broke loose. You ever heard three terrified teenagers screaming at once? You should of seen it when Mr. and Mrs. Patterson came in and there was their little darlin' in bed with a black kid, butt-naked, both of us, their son holding a bloody machete and precious princess losing about a gallon of blood a minute—you *know* how much a scalp wound bleeds?"

Talba nodded, trying to envision the scene. "I read about

it in the transcript. The phrase 'hanging by a thread' comes to mind as well."

"I guess that's an exaggeration, but I don't know . . . Anyway, her scalp wasn't flapping in the breeze. It was lying down like yours or mine at the time, just with buckets of blood coming out from under it. But I don't know—maybe when they started to sew it back—I just don't know. Kind of gives you the willies to think about, doesn't it?"

Talba tried not to think about what Clayton's life would have been like if her scalp had actually been sheared off—assuming she'd even survived it.

"So what happens is, Mr. Patterson and Trey grab me and hold me and that makes Clayton so mad she won't even go with her mama to take care of the wound, but she's yelling so loud everybody thinks she isn't gonna die or anything. But, man, that attack left scars! On everybody involved." He stared in the direction of his hometown, time traveling. "Umm. Umm. Umm."

Abruptly, he came back. "I was scared shitless and I still am when I think about it. You know how easily they could have framed me for that? Only reason they didn't was Clayton. But that wasn't what they were threatening then—they were gon' kill me. Cut my balls off at the very least. Shit. I peed all over myself I was so scared."

"You thought they'd really do it?"

"Man, you got no idea how *mad* those whitebreads were. Oh, yeah. They were gonna do it. Would have done it, hadn't been for Clayton. They knew she wasn't going to sit still for it—she was right in their faces tellin' 'em about it. Finally, she got 'em offa me, and they *sent me home*. Just like that—they sent me home. Once they cooled down, they couldn't wait to get rid of me. But first they coached Clayton to say she was asleep and didn't see who did it, and they told her—*holding the machete on me*—they told her they'd hunt me down and kill me if she talked. And she said she'd keep her mouth shut and they let me go."

"Hold it a minute. Okay, so they had enough sense not to kill you—I still don't see why they didn't frame you."

" " 'Cause they couldn't trust her not to tell the truth, little brother be damned. She was gonna come out with it, and they knew it. And they could have got the kid off—no question in my mind, they could have. But you know what they were afraid of? You know what really got 'em? They didn't want the good people of Clayton knowin' their precious daughter was in bed with a nigger. *Tha's* what they wanted to keep quiet."

Talba exhaled loudly. "Whoo."

"But, man, they got her good one more time. Mmm. Mmm. Mmm."

"What do you mean by that?"

"She didn't know they were gonna frame Donny. They flat out threw him to the wolves. And none of us could do a goddamn thing about it."

Talba opened her mouth to speak, but Calvin held up a hand to shut her up.

"Oh, yeah, you think we could, but who we gonna tell the truth to? They already had all that trumped-up evidence."

"You could have told his lawyer. Lawrence Blue."

"I could have. But they had another hold on me—they sent some money to my folks with a little note that pretty much indicated my daddy'd lose his job and never work again if I tried something like that."

"Well, what about Clayton?"

He shook his head, regretful for what had been done to her. "That was a real big machine she would have been buckin'."

Talba remembered the pictures of her in the Clayton paper, in various stages of recovery, particularly the one with her head shaved and stitches showing. She'd been made to pose for those pictures, Talba realized now—she hadn't done it for revenge. They'd made her do it as part of their campaign to convict an innocent boy.

"Besides, there was one other thing," Calvin continued. "Trey was still her little brother. They were close, too—she didn't want to see him in jail." He pressed his lips together and said, "You want to walk for awhile? I'm tired of sitting."

The second they were outside, Richard lit a cigarette, blowing smoke like a dragon.

Talba said, "You think framing Donny was Buddy Calhoun's idea?"

"Hell, no. Had to be Sheriff Ransdell. Diabolical old bastard. Calhoun just went along with it."

"And so did the whole town."

"Not that many people knew about me. They sure couldn't have known Donny was framed. But, yes. There was something they went along with—Clayton as pariah. Because that's what happened to her. The minute that family made their pact with the devil, they turned against Clayton—" For the first time, he seemed at a loss. "I never understood how it happened. Okay, she fucked a black guy. But she was their daughter—" He shook his head. "It just doesn't seem like enough. This wasn't the fifties. It was just a few years ago."

"Calvin, let me tell you something about that kind of people—sex isn't the sin, black, white, or purple. What they worry about is 'disgracing the family.' They'd have only hated her for being with you if it had come out."

"Well, they sure as hell hated her for something. You tell me what."

"She was a witness, for one thing."

He thought about it. "It always seemed to me like they blamed her for what *they* did. But I couldn't make it make sense."

Talba's neck hairs prickled. "Makes sense to me." Made her sick too.

They walked in silence while Talba got up the nerve to bring up a couple of things that bothered her. "Why didn't you come forward before?"

Richard didn't answer for awhile; seemed to be thinking of a way to explain. Finally, he said, "You know about my little boy?"

Talba nodded. "Damian? Yes. I thought it might be something to do with him."

"It started about four years ago. Checks started coming. Made out to Damian Richard from some foundation; signed by somebody we never heard of. They always came with a nice letter with some real good reasons why our son had been chosen. But I'm a cop, right? I checked it out. There ain't no such foundation. It was a bribe, pure and simple. I knew it and I took it."

"I don't blame you for that," Talba said. "I don't think anybody would." She shook her head at the sheer size of the deception. "Buddy sure thought of everything, didn't he?"

"He's a detail man. Always has been." He spoke absently, his mind elsewhere. "Tell me something. Doesn't this bother you at all? You really glad you brought Buddy down? You gonna be happy with Jack Haydel for governor?"

"No, I'm not. Hell, no. But, Calvin, look—Buddy Calhoun's as crooked as he is—and a cheap opportunist and a murderer. Sure, politicians are corrupt; that's a given. But you ever heard of one who's actually a murderer? I mean, Hitler and Stalin, sure, but in this country? This guy's way beyond Nixon and Clinton and everybody else. You ever think about that?"

"I swear to God I might vote for him if he were still running."

"You don't care that he killed all those people? And covered up for Trey—who tried to kill *you*?"

Richard bowed his head. "Yeah, I care. I just think he's better than the other guy. This damn thing's warped me, you know that? I've lived with it all these years."

"What happened with you and Clayton after the attack?"

"Nothing. We were never alone together after that—even for a minute. Never spoke again except to say hi. I never got over her, though. In some ways, I never did."

"I should think not." They had walked back around to his parking spot. "I've got one last thing to ask you," Talba said. "Her fiancé needs to know about this. Would you be willing to tell it again?"

Real distress filled his face. "Talba, I can't. Right now my stomach feels like there's a hive of bees in it. I can't go through this again."

She nodded, as if in sympathy. "Okay, then." She pulled a

tiny tape recorder out of her pocket. "Would you mind if I played this for him?"

"Hey! You should have asked my permission to do that."

Legally, she didn't have to and they both knew it. "I'm asking for your permission to play it. Out of courtesy." He scowled, but she didn't really give a damn. "Eddie wouldn't have been kidnapped if you'd come forward. Your own wife wouldn't have been shot at."

"Oh, fuck it," he said. "Play him the goddamn thing." Like he was the victim. He got in his car and drove away, leaving Talba with a bad taste in her mouth. Sure, the scalping and all its attendant effects had been hard on him—nearly getting killed; seeing Clayton hurt; being threatened. And God knows, so had his son's illness. But one little confession didn't make up for all those years of silence—for all the harm they'd done.

Chapter Thirty

"Closure," Eddie called it. It had a nice, long-*o*'d, settled sound. Serene, almost. She sincerely wished she had it. But, in fact, Talba had hardly felt less serene and settled in her life. Impressions of the past weeks swirled in her brain—feelings, images, but most of all, words. Words, words, words.

Oh, God, the words:

Hanging by a thread.

Rudimentary conscience.

Just a real friendly girl.

Oh, Mama, I'm gonna lose her!

Daddy! It's that girl I hate.

Professor Plum. Whatchathink that means?

At least that one made her smile. She'd been longing lately for Janessa, no longer feeling it her duty or some adventure or learning experience to find a sister, but a real need. Why, she didn't have a clue. It could have had to do with the greater sense of family she'd felt since the birth of Sophia, or the loss she felt for a lot of things, many of them illusions. But it was there, strong and clear.

She went back to Eve's for a manicure, but the girl was gone. No one could say why or where to. One day she hadn't shown up for work; end of story.

Without hesitating, though it was the middle of a workday, Talba drove to the house on Mystery Street (another phrase that wasn't lost on her), raced up the steps and pounded. Either no one was home, or no one chose to answer. She left a note, which she followed up with a letter and phone calls, but it seemed Janessa didn't want to be found.

Talba had unwittingly done her sister an evil turn when they were children—not mischievous, truly evil—and the thought that the girl might know and hate her for it clutched at her.

It was the act of a child—nothing she could even remember in the usual sense, but she had done hideous, irreparable damage to that girl. Perhaps that was why she needed her now—to do something good, something to start to commence to begin (as Miz Clara sometimes said) to make up for it.

She made up a big pot of red beans and rice and took it to Reverend Scruggs. "How's Ella today?"

"She is . . . barely with us, I'm afraid. Her light, her beautiful light, is shining its last."

"I'm so sorry, Reverend."

He patted his belly. "But we have been eating well, thanks to you. Miz Lura Blanchard has been many times to see us, always bringing something fine and nourishing. Of course Ella barely touches anything, but I have benefited greatly. Thank you kindly for remembering us to her."

Another funny phrase: "to remember" one person to another. She thought it meant to say hello by proxy, which she hadn't. She spoke before she thought. "I'm glad *something* worked out."

Reverend Scruggs smiled, eyes twinkling. He seemed to be making his peace with Ella's imminent death. "Are you in need of pastoral counseling, child?"

"You know, I could probably use some."

"Feel at liberty to unburden your soul."

Talba laughed, pretending to check her watch. "Have you got about a week and a half?"

"I have all the time in the world, except when Ella needs me."

"I just dropped by to tell you I found my baby sister."

"Congratulations, Sandra. I'm happy to hear it."

"Finding her was easy. Dealing with it is something else again. I had very weird feelings about her. Snobbish, sort of. She looked like so many girls you see on the street—fat, sloppy . . . aimless, I guess. I didn't think I had anything in common with her. But then I started thinking about it—about what would make a person like that. She has no mother and her aunt more or less hates her. She's living with a family that might be very nice—I met the mother and she certainly seemed to be—but they probably have no time for her, either. Anyway, I thought maybe . . . I don't know, maybe I could do something for her. And then I realized I also wanted to get to know her; I just wanted her in my life."

"What could be wrong with that?"

"She rejected me. Doesn't answer my letters, phone calls, anything."

"Have you tried e-mail?"

Talba was shocked. She hadn't even thought of it. "She wouldn't . . . I don't think . . ."

"Perhaps you underestimate her. I have one thing to say to you, Sandra. Ecclesiastes 3."

"What?"

"Borrow Miz Clara's Bible. Something tells me you don't have one yourself."

She left, promising to come back and knowing it would be soon, when Ella died. On the whole, she felt the worse for the visit.

But out of curiosity, she got Miz Clara's Bible and looked up the verses. The chapter was really a poem, one she'd known a long time ago, and a version of the one she never wrote, the one about the inevitability not only of death but of life, which had hovered in her when Clayton died and Michelle lived and Sophia was born.

It was the passage that began, "To everything there is a season," and it made her feel as settled and serene as anything had lately.

But that wasn't saying a hell of a lot. At the moment it wasn't all that comforting that somone had written hundreds of years ago that there was "a time to kill." Killing seemed to have gone into overtime lately.

Exactly when, she thought, *is it going to be time for Trey Patterson to go to jail?*

The answer was never. In Louisiana, the statute of limitation on aggravated battery was four years, and on attempted murder, six. It had been more than sixteen since the crime and nobody in Clayton wanted to prosecute, anyhow. In Talba's mind, the worst criminals were King and Deborah Patterson, who betrayed their own daughter. When were they going to be punished, or even realize what they'd done?

Never.

And how about John Earl Macquet?

When hell froze over, maybe. Without a confession from the Underwoods, the police had nothing.

Talba sat down and wrote her own damn poem, which she read at Reggie and Chaz the following week, wearing batik pants and matching flowing top printed in gold and black, a combination she happened to know was stunning on her. She accessorized with a turquoise medallion and earrings, along with an African pillbox-style hat, mostly red, heavily embroidered with gold. According to her mama, she looked like "some fool who's been to one too many rummage sales," but Miz Clara was wrong, of course.

She looked every inch a baroness.

It was her second reading since Stan was arrested, and Janessa had missed the first, though Talba followed up on her original, impulsive invitation with a phone message. This time she'd e-mailed her (Reverend Scruggs was right, the girl did have e-mail) and once again, scanning the audience, Talba didn't see her. Darryl was here, though, and three other people she'd specially invited—Skip Langdon, with whom she was trying to make up; Jason Wheelock, who was still struggling with his own "closure"; and Mary Pat Sutherland, with whom she'd had coffee twice and had started liking after all. She was planning to read the "Three Sisters" poem she'd written for Babalu, and she'd asked both Jason and Mary Pat to read some of Babalu's poems. She hoped it would turn into a mini–memorial service.

When it was her turn, she said, "I've got a new poem to read tonight. I was going to call it 'Springtime for Clayton,' but I thought a hundred years from now, when my work is taught in schools and colleges the world over, that might not make a whole lot of sense, so I'm just gonna call it something down-home and unpretentious." And then she said the name of the poem:

Addendum to Ecclesiastes

I been feeling funny in my head—
uneasy in my mind—
and all messed up.
Lost soul ready-made
For some preacher to preach at;
And I did cook the reverend some beans.

Thought I might cop me a sermon—
Least a homily or something.
But the rev catch on I ain't no churchlady,
Give me a poem instead.
He say, "To everything there is a season—
A time to be born and a time to die."
And I think, no shit, Sherlock.
Been seein' a lot of them things lately.
Both of 'em.
But I be open-minded,
Think, tell you what here,
I'm gon' just dance to the rhythms of the universe.

I'm gon' sow and I'm gon' plant
Gon' bust some things and build some things,

Gon' weep and laugh, gon' mourn and dance
See—I'm dancin now.
Miz Ella die, I mourn.
Okay, I can do all that.
But that poem say, "To everything there is a
* season."*
Everything, y'all.
A time for love and a time for hate—
(The Bible really says that)
A time to keep silent, a time to speak
A time to kiss, a time to wait
Well, I can wait—
(Come 'round when you ready, sister girl)
But I ain't done with this time thing.

I want a time for everything,
Like the reverend says.
I want my time to come.
How 'bout a time for all good men
to come to the aid of the party?
(Any party don't think it's crime time)
How 'bout some hard time for somebody deserve it?
Time in for bad behavior
Quittin' time
For some fine elected crooks;
The time of day
For folks never had
They own sweet time.
Summertime—
When the livin' is prime time.
Hurry up, please, it's time!
The time has come, the walrus said,
'Cause time is money, here.

Just wrestlin' with a few things, rev.
I'm gon' go back now, and
Score me some down time,
Go back to dancin' to

The rhythms of the universe.
It's past my bedtime.

Just can't help thinkin'
As time goes by.
Thinkin' maybe
time's a wastin' here.
How 'bout some
Equal *time?*

Chapter One

May is the cruellest month.
September has its moments, being hurricane season, but its meanness is unreliable. May is a sure thing.

On Mother's Day, give or take a week or so, the Formosans swarm, only slightly less consistent than the swallows at Capistrano. They continue their inexorable flight, sometimes in terrifying indoor clouds, well into summer.

Formosan termites, accidentally imported some years ago, are eating the city of New Orleans. They are doing it not in bug-sized nibbles, but in greedy gulps that some people say they can actually hear. They swear that in the dark of night, as they lie awake kissing their investments good-bye, they can hear the buzz of so many tiny saws, mandibles chomping their floor boards.

Perhaps they are merely blessed with good imaginations, but a visitor who arrives in the merry month, strolls a few blocks, and finds himself wearing a vest of termites may be inclined to credit them.

The unsuspecting stay-at-home finds himself in a fifties

sci fi film. It begins with a single bug. It may fall on his clothing or perhaps the desk upon which he's writing. He brushes it off and another falls, like an earwig from the eaves of a porch. He looks up and sees a few winged creatures bouncing off the chandelier. Odd, he thinks, and goes back to his reverie. And soon there are more bugs. And more. And more. The room may fill with them, thick shrouds of them, circling, diving, turning the air into a seething dark mass.

It may seem the sensible thing to run screaming for cover, but in fact there is an easier way—our hero can simply turn off the light and they will leave or die. Or he can just wait, if he can stand it. The winged ones, the alates, or breeders, have about a two-hour lifespan, between seven and nine p.m., usually. Unless, of course, they manage to mate, in which case they will start a nest. The largest nest found to date had a diameter of three hundred feet.

Unlike other termites, these can build aerial nests, right in your walls. Brick or stucco houses are fine with them—they'll eat the doorframes, window sills, picture frames, furniture, and telephone bills, plus your favorite hundred-year-old shade tree. Except for exterminators, who shake their heads and look grim, like oncologists delivering the bad news, they have no natural enemies. The alates, so shocking in their thick, swirling clouds, are only a small percentage of the population, according to entomologists. A mature nest may contain five to ten million termites, though seventy million isn't unheard of.

Formosan termites now infest eleven Southern states, plus California, New Mexico, and Hawaii. Louisiana has the most severe infestation in the world (despite headway being made by state and federal baiting programs), and it is only natural that the bug has become, like the *loup-garou* (or Cajun werewolf), part of the local mythology.

The stories are legion: An alfresco wedding attacked by something resembling a Biblical plague. A window shut just in time, as hundreds of tiny bodies, drawn by the light inside, smash as if on a windshield. An ordinary backyard, covered in minutes by a carpet of termites. Fat garbage bags of wings, as many as ten or twelve, shoveled from the floor of a house.

Indeed, the month of May affords a brush with nature rarely seen by urban-dwellers. Those of a metaphorical bent try not to think about the Mother's Day aspect.

Detective Skip Langdon, a veteran of many Mays in New Orleans, was trying to help her beloved through his first, mostly with diversionary tactics. She had seen Steve Steinman's face when he discovered the termite launching pads on his newly purchased, newly-painted, hundred-and-twenty-year-old ceiling. He looked as if someone had died.

"Am I insured for this?" he said, and she desperately wished there were something she could do. The insurance companies weren't that dumb.

"Why didn't they find them when they inspected?" he asked, outraged.

"You can't know they're there unless you rip out the walls."

"Uh-oh. I've got a bad feeling that means I've got to do that now."

"Maybe you won't. They can probably drill holes for the poison." But she was lying. They might well have to rip out the walls.

No exterminator would be available for weeks, of course, and it's said the Formosans can go through a floor board in a month. The thing to do was keep his mind off it.

JazzFest was over and the heaviness of summer was nearly upon them; Mother's Day brunch at a fine old restaurant sounded like a prison sentence. Yet Skip was a mother of sorts, or at least an aunt to the adopted children of her landlord, Jimmy Dee Scoggin. Dee-Dee was gay, and his partner, Layne Bilderback, had recently joined the household shared by Jimmy Dee and young Kenny and Sheila Ritter, the offspring of his late sister.

Dee-Dee wheedled. "We have to do something to remember their mother—keep the feminine spirit alive. Isn't it the decent thing?"

Steve said, "How about a hike?" and Dee-Dec countered, "Don't you get enough wildlife at home?"

But Skip pounced on it. If Steve wanted it, she wanted it. She wanted him in a good mood about Louisiana. He had moved there recently and restored a house (the one being gnawed), after months and years of thinking about it. A documentary filmmaker and film editor, he'd lived in California the entire time he and Skip had been dating. Their long distance relationship had deepened on proximity. Skip was getting comfortable; liking it a lot. Steve had come to New Orleans for her, and his being there had enriched her life so much more than she'd anticipated that she felt responsible now. And motivated; eager to make him happy. A walk in Jean Lafitte Park, over in Jefferson Parish, ought to be wonderfully therapeutic.

There was almost a no-go when Jimmy Dee said they'd have to leave the dogs behind—Steve's shepherd, Napoleon, and the kids' mutt, Angel—because they couldn't go in the park itself and it was too hot to leave them in the car.

But in the end the three kids—Dee-Dee's two and Steve—rose above it.

They went in two cars, the uncles and Sheila in one, Kenny with Skip and Steve. There was a reason for this—Kenny, being in his early teens, hero-worshipped Steve. The two uncles could have gotten their feelings hurt, but had the sense not to bother. The average fourteen-year-old preferred baseball to opera; metaphorically speaking, it was that simple. And Kenny was such a gentle soul, even as a teenager, that no one could imagine he'd ignore anyone on purpose. Sheila was another matter. She'd probably chosen to ride with the uncles just to snub her younger brother.

Spilling from the cars, they stepped onto the natural levee that ran along Bayou Coquille and instantly heard the silence of the swamp. It was louder than the bullfrog croaks and insect ditties and bird songs and animal slitherings that, in fact, were a concert in themselves. The two conditions were like stereo—you could listen to either or both, and the effect was like being on another planet. As the trail descended to the flooded forest of the swamp, the noises grew louder and so did the silence. The air, though it was nearly ninety in the French Quarter, here seemed fresh and soft with breezes. It was too late for the wild irises, which bloom in great fields of purplish blue, but a few of the pale lavender water hyacinths, to some more beautiful than orchids, still floated on the water, gorgeous to look at it, but in fact choking out the life of the bayou. In its way, the water hyacinth—imported from South America rather than Asia, is as deadly as the termites. A single plant can produce 50,000 others in one growing season, killing the native plants, thus reducing available food for animals.

Yet to Skip, the day was so beautiful, the views so tranquil, the natural mix so seemingly harmonious that it was possible to forget un-harmonious nature—weed-against-weed, man-against-bug, cop-against-thug. People were oddly quiet as they walked the trail; even Sheila, given to complaining about the personalities and intellectual capacities of her companions, was as sunny as the day, which would have been perfect even if they hadn't happened upon a Cajun band on the way home, playing at an outdoor restaurant where people danced under a shed. They stopped and had iced tea, enjoying the dancers, some of whom wore shirts from a Cajun heritage organization, and one of whom wore a masterpiece of taxidermy on his hat—an entire duck, feet and all, intact except for its innards.

Afterward, they went home and barbecued. While Layne cooked, the other grown-ups sat in the courtyard Skip shared with the Ritter-Scoggin family, drinking gin and tonics while the kids watched television, Napoleon snoozed, and Angel tried to wake him up. The air was velvety, with a little breeze, and the mosquitoes weren't yet biting. It was absurdly familial. Skip was completely, deliciously happy, a feeling she sometimes distrusted.

But that night she dreamed, and the dream was like life. In the dream, she had a beautiful house, and then a tiny hole appeared in the wall; out of the hole came swirling hordes of termites, traveling in vortexes like tornadoes. More and more swarmed until the air turned black, and then there was no air, only chaotic, moving, living walls, trapping her and invading her nose, her ears, smothering, strangling . . .

Steve shook her awake and she told the dream, still moaning, shivering though it was late spring, unnerved out of all proportion.

"They aren't that bad," he said. "It'll be okay. But thank you for your empathy."

The dream wasn't about his termites. Someone could have said it was about him, about her fear of their relationship, her dread of becoming engulfed. But she knew it wasn't that. She knew what it *was* about, and she knew why she couldn't stop shaking.

It was about fear of dropping her guard, of looking away for even a second, of forgetting the danger that always lurked.

She had been happy too long and something was happening to wake her up, to alert her to be wary. Yet the task was impossible. She couldn't be wary every second of the day. She couldn't protect even herself, let alone those she loved. No wonder she had dreamed of a pulsating monster, a force of nature that overwhelmed and smothered.

Fear was like that, a shrink might have said. But that wasn't it, not quite. Her enemy was like that.

Nearly two years ago, Errol Jacomine had disappeared, but he would not stay gone. She knew this; she had destroyed two of his careers—twice thwarted his attempts to win control over his fellow human beings, to gain a following and to dominate. He would be back and he would try to kill her sooner rather than later. To forget it for a day in the woods, for an evening in her courtyard, for a moment, for a millisecond, was dangerous and possibly deadly.

Jacomine's son, Daniel, had been arrested, charged with half a dozen crimes, and eventually convicted of murder as the result of one of Jacomine's schemes. He was due to be sentenced in a couple of days.

How that would affect his father Skip couldn't know, but

it had probably precipitated the dream. Jacomine might not even notice, perhaps having written Daniel off. He could do this—he seemed sometimes to have no feelings.

On the other hand, he perceived himself at the center of the universe. He might feel proprietary towards Daniel, no matter how unlikely he was to have true paternal feelings. And if he did, he might . . . what?

Surface. Treat it as an occasion to make himself known. Trade an eye for an eye—kidnap Kenny and demand Daniel. Anything.

That was what the dream was about.

S he left for work feeling hunted, and resentful of her psyche for rubbing her nose in it. She knew all that, and what could she do about it? Exactly *what*? she asked herself angrily. Later, the dream seemed more a premonition than a warning.

That morning as always, she walked the few blocks to the garage where she kept her car, pointed the remote at the automatic door (a process that never failed to give her childlike pleasure), and waited for the door to raise itself high enough to allow her ingress. Instead of the familiar rumble, an explosion ripped through the quiet morning, followed by a loud *ping*, like a beer can hitting a metal drum.

She felt an arm around her waist, another at her back and then she felt herself falling, a great weight upon her. She tried to fight it, but it was too heavy—she was helpless. Her head hit the pavement.

It took a second to put it together. The explosion had been a shot, the *ping* a ricochet.

Another shot blasted the momentary peace, a second bullet thunked into the sidewalk. Closer. She felt her muscles contract, involuntarily seeking shelter.

She heard a woman scream, and she held her breath, but a shocked hush had enveloped the corner.

After a moment, a man said, "Owww." The man on top of her, she realized. Someone was shooting at her, and he had

pushed her down, remained on top of her so that she couldn't
move.

When she had waited long enough to be sure the shooting
had stopped, she said to the lump atop her, "Police. Are you
hit?"

The man rolled off, and she saw that he was a light-skinned
black, well-muscled, wearing jeans and white T-shirt—la-
borer's garb. He said, "You're police?" Her detective status
meant she wore no uniform.

She didn't see any blood. "Are you all right?" She was
frantic.

He was examining himself. "Yeah. Yeah, I'm all right.
That was real close, though."

A crowd was gathering around them. Unless the sniper was
in it, he no longer had a clear shot. Skip scanned the rooftops,
wondering where the shots had come from.

The idea of asking what happened made her fell shamed
somehow. She closed her eyes for a moment, trying to get it
together, and the man said, "Somebody just tried to kill you."

"You saw him?"

"No. I was right behind you when I heard the shot. Didn't
stop to look around—you understand?"

"Thanks. I appreciate what you did. But how did you know
he wasn't shooting at you?"

The man shrugged. "I didn't ax no questions. Just hit the
pavement."

When they paced it off, she could see that the man wasn't
really right behind her—he'd had to run a step or two to
tackle her. She'd been facing the garage door, and the bullet
had hit it immediately to her right. She was between it and
her rescuer.

There was no doubt in her mind it was meant for her. She
grabbed for her radio.

After that, it was chaos. A sniper in the French Quarter was
a big deal, shots fired on a police officer an even bigger deal.
But when it was Skip Langdon, it was nearly enough to de-
clare an state of emergency. Everyone in the department knew

Jacomine was as likely to come for her as get up in the morning and put on his clothes.

He might even come in person, and catching him would be as big a coup as discovering the whereabouts of D.B. Cooper.

Certainly her sergeant knew all this—her good friend and sometime partner, Adam Abasolo. Skip knew he was going to call for the works investigating this one, and the works was what Skip got. In minutes, District cars blocked the whole place off, the streets crawled with cops, and the downside—TV cameras for days.

The poor man who saved Skip's life was treated like a threat to society, taken over to the Eighth District, questioned and bullied until he well and truly understood that no good deed goes unpunished. Skip made a mental note to thank him somehow, but wondered how. What did you do for a perfect stranger who risked his life to save yours, and then found himself in a living nightmare? He'd obviously been on his way to work—maybe he'd even get fired.

She was having an extremely pessimistic day.

It seemed she'd barely picked herself up when Turner Shellmire turned up, a rumpled, pear-shaped figure in the midst of all the glamour of sirens and flashing lights. Shellmire was an FBI agent she'd worked with on the Jacomine case—or cases, actually. Though he came from the agency the New Orleans police liked to call Famous But Incompetent, he wasn't either. Certainly not incompetent. He was one of the best cops she'd ever worked with, and he was a straight shooter. They were as close to being friends as a police officer and an FBI agent possibly could be.

She played it light. "Hey, Turner. Slow day today?"

He didn't return her grin, instead examined the dented door and sidewalk. "He almost got you."

"What about the kids?"

"I've sent people to get them. Also Jimmy Dee, Layne, and Steve."

"Layne? Even Layne?" He'd only married into the family; it didn't seem fair to him.

Shellmire nodded. "Jacomine would go for him."

Skip knew it was true. Jacomine played mind games. If he couldn't get at her through somebody really close, he'd try for someone once removed, knowing that would pile guilt on top of her other emotions—guilt and the rage of the person who was closest.

"What are you going to do with them?"

He opened his arms in exasperation. "That's the problem. We can keep them safe for a day, maybe, but they've got to have a life."

At the end of the day, when all the questions that could possibly be asked had been asked, the lifesaver—a man named Rooster Blanchard—had finally been released, and still the sniper hadn't been found and not a single fact more was known than the kind of gun he'd used and the angle the bullets had come from, Skip went to see her sergeant. "AA, my nerves are shot. I've got to get the sonofabitch."

"You sound like you're asking for a leave of absence."

"Just a transfer. I want to go to Cold Case for awhile. Please. Just let me try it."

"Skip, he's a needle in a haystack. And furthermore, you can't just work on one case."

"At least I could work on it some. That's all I ask."

The sergeant's eyes went shifty on her. "Langdon, you're not the person to work on this. You know that. Anyway, I can't spare you."

She ignored his last sentence. "Oh, come on. I wouldn't be working the shooting—just the cold case."

"Did you hear me? I can't do it. I've got to have you for the cemetery thefts. I want you to head the task force."

Here in the Third District, where Skip had been sent when the department was "decentralized" and the Homicide Division disbanded, things were usually pretty quiet. But the cemetery thefts were big—about as high profile as a case that wasn't a triple murder could get in New Orleans.

Somebody—probably a ring of professional thieves—was removing cemetery statues and selling them through the lucrative antiques market. In a city that took its saints and angels as seriously as it did its pre-Lent festivities, this was big, bad crime. A department that stopped it was going to be a popular department. Heading the task force was a handsome plum.

Still, to Skip's mind, it was trivial compared to getting Jacomine. She said, "AA, I'm flattered, but . . ."

"The Superintendent asked for you. Says it's the mayor's idea. Two City councilmen have also called—at the mayor's request, probably."

"Oh, shit."

He could have made a crack about the price of fame, but Abasolo looked as downcast as she probably did. "Yeah. I'm sorry, Skip. Wrap it up fast and we'll see about the transfer."